SHADOWHUNTER

NEPHILIM QUEST BOOK ONE

LEENA MARIA

Leena Maria

ISBN 978-952-93-6364-3 (paperback)

ISBN 978-952-93-6365-0 (EPUB)

ISBN 978-952-93-6366-7 (MOBI)

www.leenasbooks.com

JOIN LEENA MARIA'S NEWSLETTER

Leena Maria's Newsletter subscribers are always to first to hear about Leena's new books and publications.

You can sign up for the newsletter at www.leenasbooks.com

WHAT IF YOU SLEPT

What if you slept?
  And what if, in your sleep, you dreamed?
  And what if, in your dream, you went to heaven
  and there plucked a strange and beautiful flower?
  And what if, when you awoke, you had the flower in your hand?
Ah, what then ?
  - Samuel Taylor Coleridge

WHISPERS

Whispers.

They were with me already when my mother cradled me as a newborn. They were there when I learned to stand and walk and started exploring the world on my own. They were there when people looked at me and I could see surprise and fear in their eyes.

"Do not mind, my lovely," mother whispered to me when I understood I was different from others."Yours is a gift that has to stay in the shadows."

And so I stayed there, at the edge of the shadow world, the one they called Shuet, the Shadow. I hid from the sunlight and night became my friend. And I learned to talk with the shades and the stars and the whispers of the night and they taught me their deep secrets.

1

IN THE SHADOW OF WAR

She ran for the shelter, clutching the baby in her arms.

"Soon, sweetie, soon! We're on our way to safety, I promise." She was saying it as much for her own benefit as the baby's, as if simply saying the words could make them come true.

The baby did not cry. It listened to the sirens, eyes as round as plates. The Luftwaffe was bombing London, again. People had lost count of how many consecutive days they had been running for the shelters with the rising and falling scream of the siren filling their ears, sweeping them onwards like terrified animals towards a place of refuge.

"Come along, Miss, 'Itler's not going to wait for you, dear!" The ARP warden took her by the elbow to encourage her along with the others. Then he saw the baby in her arms. "Sorry, Madam! But please, hurry up do, missis!"

She was not only escaping the bombs, but also the creatures that were after her baby. Their baby. The only precious thing she had left of him and their love. Her reason for living.

Beautiful. He had called her beautiful. And he had not yet seen his daughter.

She had not been aware of her heritage before she met him. She had only fallen madly in love with the tall young stranger. In the midst of the war they had clung to each other as though they were drowning and the touch of the other would save them both. He had told her what she was, and after the initial shock the knowledge had finally eased her pain of being different.

She no longer cared about her childhood – the way all the others had mocked her, how she kept getting herself into trouble, and that final day, when she had taken all she could stand. After that, all the children avoided her, and even though no one believed their stories, she became an outcast. Before, they had bullied her, now they did not even come near her. She spent the rest of her childhood alone, without a single friend, completely ignored.

When she was old enough, she moved to London and found a position as a servant. No one commented on her tall frame in the kitchen. They hardly spoke to her at all, and she lived for those moments when anyone threw her a word, even if it was just an order to peel potatoes. She remembered with warmth the day the grocery boy took a liking to her.

"Hullo, Beanpole!" he said the moment he saw her. "What's the world like from up there? I bet people are always saying you've got your head in the clouds!"

"Nothing I can't handle! I just duck whenever a bird flies towards me." She quite surprised herself by coming smartly back with a reply that earned a delighted chuckle from the boy.

"Handy for me that you're so tall," he grinned, "now I don't have to knock on the door, 'cause you'll see me coming for miles off, wontcha, eh, Beanpole?" He was cheeky, but so cheerful and kind that she couldn't be offended. She found she was smiling despite herself.

He carried the groceries into the kitchen.

"Where d'you want them then, gel? Over there?" He touched his cap and was on his way with a wink and an appreciative lipsmacking noise. She was still smiling when a voice cut in from behind her.

"Oooh, someone's got an admirer!" It was one of the maids, the pretty one, who had seen the whole thing. She fluttered her lashes mockingly, with her hand on her round hips. "Fancy that, you've got yourself a follower who likes 'is women to look like a boy!"

To emphasize her meaning, the maid threw back her shoulders so that her own rounded bosom made the boot-boy's eyes pop out.

After that they called her the Beanpole, and snide remarks by the other girls about her thin frame made it clear that they thought no man would ever be interested in her. Still, most of the time they weren't too mean, just showing a sort of sly sympathy for an unfortunate young woman who did not look as a woman should.

She kept quiet, and continued timidly to do her job the best that she could, eager to please the others and even smiling at their comments about her boyish figure in order to win acceptance into their ranks.

When she came of age, she began to have a constant fever, but oddly enough she did not feel any weakness. By then the war was underway, and in the midst of all the uncertainty and fear she had met him. She saw him first, and stopped in surprise. There weren't many men who were even taller than she was, so he stood out amongst the others. There was something else about him; something that she seemed to recognise. She was sure she had never met him before, though.

"Good afternoon, Miss!" He lifted his hat to her, taking her by surprise, as she walked towards the pond in the nearby park. She liked to sit and watch the water, and the ducks swimming. Sometimes she took them bread crumbs from the kitchen, not that there was often much left these days, when every scrap of food counted.

"He... Hello," she stammered, instantly captivated by his intense gaze. To her horror she blushed. Her heart thumped loudly in her ears.

He was tall - so tall - just like her. And handsome. He was probably the best looking man she had ever seen. He was just standing there, looking at her in...what was that expression... wonder? As though he couldn't believe what he was seeing. And then his eyes began to smile, and her knees suddenly felt weak, so that she had to take a step to regain her balance.

"There may be a war on, but I've never known a smile knock someone off their feet!" he said. "Well, not anyone as lovely as you, anyway."

It took her mind a few seconds to catch up with what her ears had heard. Lovely? He had called her lovely! She peeked at him to see if he was joking. No, his eyes looked as though he meant what he said. He apologised for his forwardness.

"I'm sorry - I didn't mean to be offensive. Would you - walk with me?" he asked, and, noticing her nervous gaze searching for other people, he added "Just round the park, of course." He held out his arm to her.

After a moment's hesitation she had agreed. They walked together for almost half an hour. He was polite, thanking her when she told him it was time for her to go, and lifting his hat again. They met again the next day. And the next.

And then he stole a kiss from her under an old oak tree and her response was so fierce that her cheeks burned with shame for the entire evening. A week after she had first met him they became lovers.

He had been escaping from something; because he only agreed to meet her as far from crowds as was possible in a big city like London. She did not ask what he was hiding from, too afraid to, for fear of losing him.

They had three wonderful months together, meeting in parks, and in his room, when they could. Her visits to him were as secret as she could make them, though sometimes she wondered if the other servants guessed.

One evening, when she was lying in his arms, nervously knowing that she was late and that she should have already left his little room in his boarding house, hoping that she could avoid his landlady again, that he looked into her eyes so intensely that she was almost scared.

"There is something you need to know about yourself," he said.

"About myself?" She did not understand.

"Yes. You are not who you think you are," he said, gently tucking a lock of her hair behind her ear, and kissing her softly under her jaw, in the place that made her gasp with pleasure.

"I'm not? Who am I then?" She smiled, trying to make a joke of it, but feeling apprehensive.

"We share a secret, you and I," he said and locked eyes with her, but there was none of the usual laughter in them, only tenderness and... fear?

"I know..." she tried to sound light, "if they knew what I have been doing with you..."

"It has nothing to do with this," he said, tracing her shoulder with his finger, "And yet it has everything to do with this. I have put you in great danger."

She looked at him questioningly, waiting for an explanation.

The explanation came in short, hesitant sentences, while he held her tight, as if fearing she would break from his arms and run away. It was not what she had expected. While the words came out, she listened mutely, stiff as a statue, not believing what he said. Not wanting to believe anything he said, because every word confirmed the fear she had been trying to escape all her life. Every pretence of her being normal was shattered forever, there in the shadows of the ordinary little room that had witnessed their deep love for each other.

"I think they have found me. I saw one of them in the park, but none yet near this house," he finally said, "It is not safe for you to be seen with me anymore. After tonight I have to disappear. And you must promise not to try to find me here. If I am right, they will be observing this location soon, and will follow anyone who comes here, to see if that someone could lead them to me. You must believe me - your life is at stake. Please, for the sake of our love, don't come back here. I shall look for you again, when it is safe. And trust me, I will find you." He kissed her again.

That was their last day together. The following day she looked for his tall, unmistakeable figure, but it was not at their usual place in the park. Nor the day after that. She wandered around the park, searching everywhere, but knowing in her heart he would no longer be there. But she could not help herself. It took all the self-control she could muster to stay away from the boarding house.

And soon afterwards she found out she was with child.

She managed to keep her pregnancy a secret for a few months, but because she was so tall and thin, it began to show sooner rather than later. She could not hide in loose dresses much longer, and before too long they would throw her out of the house. She could not let her parents hear of her shame.

But where could she go? No one would take on a maid who was pregnant and unmarried. And she would never return back home, to be mocked by the villagers.

"What's up, Beanpole?" The grocery boy appeared suddenly at the top of the area steps, although she had thought no one was around when she went out to catch some fresh air and fight the nausea that was now her constant companion. "Not enjoying your position in the fancy house with all the toffs?"

She could not help a tear escaping and quickly wiped it away, leaning slightly forward so her dress did not stretch over her belly.

"I guessed it. Them pretty gels are teasing you all the time, aren't they? You mustn't let 'em upset you. You know what - I might have a place for you, Beanpole. One that would suit you better. My sister just got married and moved out and it's her landlady, what now needs a maid to help her. She's blind, you see. You might even be able to live there without paying rent, if you'd agree to look after her. I know my sister did. You wouldn't mind working for a very grumpy old blind lady, would you? The old girl's all right when you get to know her."

This time tears really began to fall. It was the answer to her prayers. An old lady who was blind!

"Tha.. thank you..." she managed to hiccup.

"There, there, gel..." the boy patted her hand, trying to appear older than his years. "And I've got news for you, too. I've got me call-up papers." He seemed proud and excited.

"Your - call-up papers? But - you're far too young to be conscripted!" Her own problems were forgotten for a moment.

"I'm eighteen, Beanpole. Just 'ad me birthday - so there we are."

"They won't send you overseas, though, will they? You're too young."

"Dunno. Have to wait and see. Well, aint you got a hug for a man what's going to serve 'is nation, Beanpole? Lovely scent you always have on, and I don't mean the smell of onions! I'd like to get a bit closer."

"Of course!" She felt a sudden rush of affection for him. He was so young. Absurdly young to fight.

He put his arms around her, not caring that his head only reached her chin - and immediately let her go and looked down at her belly in surprise.

"Put a bit of weight on round the middle, haven't you? Oh Beanpole - you aint in the family way, are yer?"

She nodded, mutely, tears springing into her eyes again.

"Who was it, my girl?" He looked angry, "Who did this to you?"

"I can't tell you," she whispered, trying to wipe the tears that refused to stop running.

The boy stood there quietly for a while, and then nodded his head.

"Good thing the old girl is blind. Just you carry on for another day or two, and my sis will fix things up with the old lady. You try to keep your secret a bit longer, and you'll be out of here in a couple of days, if they'll let you go."

In two days she resigned and moved into the little house of the blind old lady. They made an agreement that she did not need to pay rent for her tiny bedroom, if she ran the household for her landlady.

The old lady had been quarreling with her neighbors for so long that there was no danger of any of them popping in for a visit and seeing that the new maid was pregnant.

So there she stayed, working hard so the landlady would not throw her out. She hid her growing belly in a long thick winter coat whenever she went out, trying to find clues to where he had gone, visiting all the other places where they had met, hoping for a note, a message. The only place she did not go to was the house he had been living in. He would never have left her voluntarily, not with the feeling of deep belonging that they shared, so something must have happened to him. Had he died in the hands of those he feared so much?

She did not find any trace of him, and when her pregnancy became too obvious, she stopped going out. They blocked the windows with cardboard at night and she stayed indoors, hiding in the darkness of the blackout.

Shortly before she was due, there was a knock on the front door late one evening. She tried to keep her huge belly hidden behind the door when she opened it. There was the grocery boy's sister, carrying a big professional-looking bag. The woman smiled up at her.

"Step outside, duck, so the landlady won't hear," she said in a barely audible voice, "She has the ears of a bat, that one."

She reached for her winter coat hanging by the door, leaving the door slightly open. An ARP warden came round the corner, spotted the chink of light and yelled "Oy! Put that bleedin' light out!" Quickly wrapping her coat around her like a cloak, she stepped outside closing the door behind her. The grocery boy's sister opened the coat enough to take a look of her bulging form, measuring it with a pair of knowing eyes.

"Hmph. Yes, not long now. I'm Molly, as I think me brother told you? I've come to stay with you until the baby arrives and I'll help you with the labour. Some swine got you into trouble, eh, dear? "

At that she stepped inside and proceeded to greet the landlady with the pretext of having to stay in the city for a few days and asked if she could stop over for a few nights. The landlady agreed, perhaps convinced by some eggs brought as a gift.

Her labour started two days later, early in the morning. Soon, she was clutching her belly as the spasms began. She needed to get out of the landlady's house as soon as possible, so they hurried off, with Molly calling out that they needed to "get some bits and pieces of shopping." Molly walked with her to an empty house, supporting her when the pain made her lose balance. It was a smart house whose owners had gone to the country for the duration, and Molly had the key to it because her brother delivered goods here when the owners were at home, and she cleaned for them.

There, in the kitchen she gave birth to her daughter, helped by her unofficial midwife, who seemed to know exactly what she was doing.

"Our ma was a midwife and I've helped her plenty of times," Molly explained, "as well as her having seven of her own. And you are doing just fine, despite the pain. Hold my hand tight when you want, sweetheart, and don't you try to hold back - that includes screaming if you need to!"

The baby came out surprisingly fast into Molly's capable hands, though it felt as though she was being torn in two. She tried not to cry out because of the neighbours, but could not stay completely quiet. Luckily no one came knocking on the door.

The grocery boy's sister cleaned the tiny baby and wrapped her in a shawl she had with her, and when the afterbirth had come away, helped the new mother to her feet.

"Here are some pads for you to hide the bleeding. I'm sorry that you can't stay here. I'll help you back to the landlady's house, but you'll have to take it from there."

She looked down at her new daughter, and then at Molly.

"Do you really think she'll believe us, the landlady?"

"Dunno, sweetheart, but we have to try. Do you think you can walk now? That's a good girl. And little 'un's fine. Just fine. So pretty. One of the prettiest I've ever seen. Are you sure you don't want to see if we can find a new home for her, a good one?"

"No! I can't give her up, I can't!" The anguish she felt at the idea was beyond belief.

They carried the baby girl to the old lady's house, pretending they had found her on the street with a note on her saying the mother could not keep the baby.

"What? Someone abandoned a newborn on the street? I can't believe the morals of people in wartime!" the old lady said, clearly cross. "A foundling! What on earth do you intend doing with it?"

"Her," said Molly, "it's a girl. The baby is far too tiny to be taken anywhere else. That's my opinion. She might not make it anyway. Might as well make her few days on this earth happy and comfortable - better than taking her to an orphanage, they're nasty places, them! She'd likely die there. She'll need constant attention, though. I've plenty of sisters and aunties, so I get lots of advice on how to take care of newborns. I'll see if they can help. Perhaps my brother could bring some bottle milk, if needs be?"

"It won't survive without mother's milk!" the old woman shook her head, "But I suppose we can't do much else. I'll give her a few days."

"Not a word though," said Molly. "You know how people talk."

Luckily the new mother had plenty of milk, and despite her tiny size, the baby hung onto life, sucking at her breast hungrily as she fed her in the privacy of her room.

"Well, well, well," marvelled the old lady, "I'd never have thought it possible that a newborn could thrive on anything other than mother's milk. Never thought to be learning something new at my age!"

Once it was clear the child would live, the landlady surprised them all by falling in love with the little baby. If the old lady suspected the truth, she was kind enough not to voice her suspicions. After the grocery boy's sister left, they were allowed to stay. Strange though her circumstances were, she found herself almost content with her baby and the old woman, who was now almost a substitute grandmother.

The connection between the new mother and her baby was so strong that she spent all her free time sitting by the cot, admiring her perfection. That anything so beautiful could have come from their love made her mute with gratitude. Looking at the sleeping baby she either felt such love her heart would surely burst or she fell to the pits of deepest despair, missing him so much that it hurt her, fearing what might have happened to him.

"I will protect her, I promise you," she whispered to the empty room one night when she could not sleep and was sitting guarding their baby. She gently stroked the unbelievably soft skin on her daughter's cheek. The baby did not wake up but a tiny hand wrapped around her finger. She could not take her finger away and sat there with hot tears running down her cheek, mumbling words of protection and love.

And then she began to see the shadows. At first she thought it was some problem with her vision. They seemed to follow her, slipping just out of sight when she turned to look at a movement she thought she had seen from the corner of her eye. Then, one day, the sudden noise of something clattering to the ground behind her in the street made her jump, and when she turned around quickly, she was certain she could see a shadowy figure behind the fallen dustbin, just for a few seconds.

Now she was certain they were real creatures. What her lost love had told her about the ones that were after him made her very scared, but why exactly these shadows should be following her, she did not know. Were they trying to find him through her? Why had they not shown up earlier, if that was the case? How had they found her? What were they looking for?

She had her answer the day one of the shadows materialised inside the old lady's house. She returned from the kitchen with a tea tray for the old lady, and saw her sitting in her armchair, tenderly holding the baby. She was crooning an old nursery rhyme to the child.

"Bye Baby Bunting, Daddy's gone a hunting, to get a little rabbit skin to keep a Baby Bunting in..." The absurd words rang in her brain and would not go away.

It's a trick of the light, she told herself. A trick of the eyes. A trick of - the brain. But that - she did not want to think about that, the possibility that it was only in her mind. It was standing right next to the old lady, who had no idea of the presence of the nightmarish creature, and kept on cooing at the child. The mist - entity - reached out human-like arms towards her baby.

Her rage flared in an instant, and her body responded. She slashed the shadow down and killed it with the fury of a lioness protecting her young. Quickly, without hesitation.

The shadow silently crumbled into a heap of dust. The landlady seemed not to hear the sounds the killing made, and thankfully could not see how the shadow had been destroyed, or her deepest secret would have been out. But that also meant there were no witnesses to the existence of the shadows. Only she had seen them.

She was now horrified. He had told her that there were things in this world people had no idea about, and she had nurtured the thought that he was talking in metaphors. She had not quite believed all he had to say about her heritage, because it had been too strange for her rational mind. Now, after what had just happened, there was no way of denying that he had meant it literally.

She served the old lady her tea with unsteady hands, avoiding the heap of dust on the carpet, and then cleaned the floor. The dust looked just like ordinary dust, and there was much less of it than she had expected.

"It's time for her bottle. I'll take her for her feed." With her hands still shaking she reached for her baby, careful to avoid the spot where she had killed the darkness. She fed her daughter in her room, rocking her body back and forth, mumbling prayers under her breath, calling on heavenly forces to protect her and her child. Looking down at her daughter, she came to a sudden decision.

"I need to go out and try to find something to eat. I heard of a place that has some meat and we've still got coupons." She tried to sound calm. "I'll take the baby with me."

"Be careful she doesn't catch a cold. That can be a serious thing for a baby! Wrap up warm." The old lady seemed to be reluctant to let them go.

She had no clear plan of what to do next, but she couldn't get the hideous image out of her head. If one of her nightmares could make it into the house, surely more of its kind would follow later. For now, she did the only thing that came into her mind - she ran away.

Then the air raid siren started its wailing scream, and she took shelter with the baby until the bombing was over. When she returned, in the place where the old lady's house stood there was nothing but a blackened, smoking ruin. The stench of burning filled her nostrils as she watched the hopeless task of the wardens and the fire services as they picked their way carefully over the debris. She knew that they would find no survivors. She turned away, with a catch in her throat, holding her baby even closer to her, kissing her head. But mingled amongst her sadness for the grumpy old woman who had turned out to be so kind, there was relief. Surely the shadows now thought she and the baby were dead too?

She sought shelter in an old church with her child, but did not dare to sleep for fear of the shadows returning. She sat there, with dark rings around her eyes, holding her baby, trying to look as inconspicuous as possible in the midst of others who had lost their homes. They were avoiding her - or was that her imagination? In the corners of the room, she seemed to see shadows, but they were real shadows - the shadows of people who had lost their homes, and sometimes their loved ones. Only, her eyes darted from one figure to the next, seeking reassurance that they were normal people, and not shades.

And now the air raid siren had started to wail again. She ran towards a shelter, through the darkening streets, holding the baby tightly. Her heart was beating so loudly she couldn't even hear the sirens anymore. The shadows on the streets condensed around her, moving at the same speed as she was running. She sobbed silently, scared out of her wits.

They were waiting for her under the notice with the underground sign and text that read "This way to the air raid shelter". People ran right by them, not paying any attention to the shadowy mist that was darkening and swirling by the gaping entrance to the Underground. It was as though they did not see the creatures at all.

The shadows were not alone. In the midst of them stood a tall, dark man. He was leaning against the wall, with his face half-hidden by the brim of his hat, and the swirling mass of shade responded to his slight movements as he inhaled his cigarette and then exhaled the smoke, slowly.

On the other side of the street was another man, without a hat, whose skin seemed to glow strangely in the gloom. This man had piercing dark eyes and his stillness made her wonder for the moment if he was a mannequin. His whole attention was directed on her and her baby, and his eyes did not blink.

The tall dark man with the hat turned his head in her direction and she saw him clearly for the first time as he looked pleasantly back at her. It was the look of someone who was absolutely certain of his power. There was something about him that did not fit in - he did not seem British, somehow.

She knew what he was the second she saw the golden, piercing eyes measuring the baby in her arms. Her lost love had explained all about the yellow eyes to her. And he had warned her of this man especially, if he was whom she suspected him to be. He was just as he had been described to her.

"Give the baby to me," said the man, from the midst of the shadows. His voice was barely audible, but for some reason she heard him loudly and clearly. She did not recognise his accent.

"No." She was holding her daughter so closely to her that she heard the baby give a little squeak of protest.

The planes were right above them now, the last of the running people had vanished through the underground's entrance. The air raid sirens were still wailing and the shadowy mist seemed to swirl around the dark man to the rhythm of the sound. She thought she saw monstrous forms within the misty darkness, half animal, half human. The screeching of the bombs as they fell and the crump of the first explosions came from not too far away. The ground was shaking under her feet.

"Then we shall take her, if you will not give her up willingly," said the man in a bored manner and with a slight movement of his hand gestured to the shadows to move forward. They began to glide towards her.

"Why?" She squeezed her baby even tighter, feeling the rage rise again up her spine as the shadows formed a dark circle around her. The mist licked around her feet and she looked down to see human-like hands grabbing at her legs.

"She is of our kind. She belongs to us. She should have been born to the wife we chose for him, but he chose you. Still, the blood is pure in you, so the child might fulfill our expectations. She will grow and help our race in our journey back to glory."

She knew now for certain he was the one her lover had warned her about. Still, she had no idea what the glory might be that the man was referring to. He sounded like a religious zealot. One thing she knew for certain, however. She would not give her baby up without a fight. Not to him. Not to anyone.

The world blew apart just as the shadows reached out for the baby. The blast blew the darkness away like smoke in a storm. She flew– up, up, away from the demolished street. She landed on the debris of a building shattered by a previous raid and gasped for air. Blood ran into her eyes, but she felt no pain. She only knew she had managed to hold the baby safe, and was lying on her side like a broken bird, crouched around the tiny creature.

The air in front of her seemed to tear apart like paper. She knew she must be hallucinating, because she had hit her head so hard. What she was seeing could not be real - yet it seemed impossibly clear to her. A woman in strange clothes stepped out of the air towards her. She was wearing trousers like a man, made of some worn-out blue fabric, and a bright red, short leather jacket. She had some kind of sports shoes, with odd thick soles, on her feet. And her hair was very short, like a man's... maybe she had been ill and they had been forced to cut her hair...maybe it was some new uniform... maybe...

"Here, let me take your baby to safety."

She looked into the eyes of the woman with short hair. They were ordinary, kind, concerned human eyes. She trusted her.

The woman took the baby from her arms and tucked her safely in the crook of her left arm. Then she just stood there, looking at her with a curious expression on her face.

She fought through the mist in her mind for the word. Concern. That was the word. That was the look on the short-haired woman's face.

"Come, sweetheart. It is your time to go."

She rose with amazing lightness. She couldn't have hurt herself badly, after all, if moving was this easy. They went through the opening in the air, and the woman, holding the baby safely, turned and raised her hand. The woman made a slashing movement and the opening closed quickly. But not quickly enough. She had seen her own body, in an odd, twisted position, in the midst of the bricks and broken glass.

She understood.

"Your time has come, sweetheart," the woman repeated, "You can go in peace – your baby will be safe with us, and we will do our best to hide her from the shadows and their masters."

The young woman had one last look at her beautiful baby. She tried to touch her child's face, but she couldn't feel her fingers. The words came out in a whisper. "Goodbye, my darling." She smiled, and felt great love flow towards her in return.

"Thank you!" she said and her voice sounded oddly clear to her now, and somehow like a gentle wind blowing.

Then she turned and began her journey into a beautiful landscape, heading towards the light that had come to greet her, leaving her old life behind.

2

KITTY IS GONE

I was sitting on the lounger on the patio, with my hands resting on the warm back of Nugget, my cat, when the phone rang. I heard Mom answer it in the kitchen. Nugget carried on purring contentedly on my lap, and I continued to stare at the garden with unseeing eyes.

"Dana!" Mom was calling me in her perky phone-voice.

The heavy lump in my chest was pulling me down so badly that I did not want to move, let alone speak.

"Dana!" the voice was more demanding, "Dana, it's Kitty's mum. She wants to talk to you."

I forced myself to answer, even though it physically hurt to speak.

"I can't," was all I could say.

"Dana..."

"I'm sorry, Mom. I just... can't." As I spoke, I realised I'd called her "Mom" rather than "Mum". I remembered how hard I'd tried to break the habit; tired of the sniggering that broke out in the classroom each time I'd said it. Now, it no longer seemed to matter.

I heard a sound that told me Mom had put her hand over the phone - her rings clanked against it. Her voice came a bit closer to the patio doors.

"I know this is hard for you, but Kitty's mother is worried about Muffin."

"Muffin?" Despite myself, I became a bit curious. Muffin was Kitty's ugly little mutt who loved Kitty with all his heart.

"He misses Kitty so badly. And she wonders if you'd take him for a walk? So sorry to keep you, Rose," Mom clearly took her hand off the receiver, "Dana is just in the middle of something. She'll come to the phone soon. But do tell me how are you getting along now? Is there anything you need, anything at all? You do know you only have to ask?"

Mom kept on chatting in a compassionate voice, and I still sat there, unable to move. There was an aching hole in my heart.

"I'm putting you on hold for a moment, Rose."

The next words would be for me.

"Kitty's mum says if you don't want to see anyone, you don't have to. They'll put Muffin out in the garden for you. Do you think you can do it now?"

"I don't know, Mom..."

"I know this is hard for you, dear, but think about Kitty's mum and Muffin."

The memory of Muffin's joyful squirms whenever he saw Kitty finally dragged me out of my misery. I was not the only one grieving.

"OK," I gave in, "in about an hour?"

"She'll be over in about an hour," Mom announced, "and do take care of one another now, Rose, won't you? Whenever you want to talk, just give me a call. Any time. Any time at all."

It was still morning when I left, and the sun hadn't yet dried the grass. The spider webs were decorated with dewdrops and the light of the sun glistened on them, as if someone had draped diamond necklaces everywhere. Mist was moving slowly in golden swirls in the shadier parts, and little birds were announcing their presence loudly while they flew and hopped about. They were everywhere, busy finding food for their young. It was a golden day, and life was making itself known. The kind of day that I'd have revelled in, once.

I walked along the familiar back road deep in my thoughts. Fresh hoof prints told me our neighbouring farmer had already been riding here this morning. The big round hoofs had pushed deep half circles in the soft verge. His Welsh cob, Cariad, was the kindest horse you could imagine. Kitty often went to groom her and all the other cobs that belonged to Tony and Jen, who bred them. She loved horses.

Had loved horses, I corrected my thoughts, with a lump in my throat.

Muffin's ugly little goblin face greeted me at the gate of Kitty's house. He was so happy to see me he squirmed as if he was going to wriggle out of his skin, and his little stump of a tail wagged so fast it was a blur. I took his leash that they'd left hanging from the gatepost for me, bent over the low gate to attach it to his collar, receiving several wet dog kisses while doing so, and then opened the gate for him. He jumped against my legs and whined until I lifted him up, and then he concentrated on washing my face thoroughly.

I have to say his pure joy made me feel slightly better.

I put Muffin down and he scooted forward, yanking the leash with such force I almost fell. He was really strong, despite his small size. I started running too, not wanting to stay by the garden gate in case someone from Kitty's family surprised me.

Muffin seemed to know exactly where he was going, and I realised pretty quickly where it was, and why. He was going to our secret place to see if Kitty was there. Perhaps it was no bad thing that I couldn't explain to the little guy that Kitty was gone forever. He'd have to figure that out himself and maybe it would be less painful for him that way. For a moment, I sort of wished I was a dog or a cat, but then I realised that it was no easier for them, either, just different.

I heard a car approaching from behind and moved closer to the edge of the road. It took me all my willpower to force myself not to jump frantically onto the verge and I started to tremble. The driver hit the brakes and the sound of the car sliding on the road was too much for my nerves. I screamed and crouched, covering my head with my arms, waiting for the impact.

"You thought I'd run you over?" I heard a familiar voice ask.

In a second the fear was gone and I jumped up to see Grandma's huge smile.

"Grandma!"

She was still smiling as she stepped out of her spiffy red sports car.

"Come and have a hug!"

I flew into her outstretched arms. I never really hugged my mom, but I loved hugging Grandma. Maybe it was because she loved hugging me. Mom was more reserved. I knew she loved me, but she had never been much of a hugger. If she had to hug, it was one of those awkward, one-armed hugs, and she even patted my back just like men always do. I was sure it was embarrassing to look at, so I let Mom off the hook and did not hug her in public.

No such problems with Grandma. I squeezed her with all my strength, and she did the same back. She had really developed hugging into an art form. Despite her small frame she grabbed you like a bear and laughed with joy as she hugged, making you feel like you were the only important person for her at that moment. And to be honest, that was probably the case. She hugged you as if she was not sure if she would ever see you again.

Suddenly I felt a surge of happiness. Surely things would be better now that Grandma was here.

"And how are you now?" she asked me, pushing me to arm's length and looking me in the eye.

She knew, of course, but she didn't pity me, I could see that. She was simply asking a question, knowing what had happened. She knew exactly how to interact with me. I hated all that mushy pity talk that was going down.

"I'm OK, more or less," I shrugged.

"Well, it gets easier with time. But were you on your way somewhere nice?"

"I was going to our special place. Or in fact, it seems Muffin is headed there. We called it our den. Would you like to come along?"

Having someone with me suddenly felt like a good thing.

"Of course!"

Grandma left the car where it was - no one ever drove along that road really, and it wouldn't have done the neat little car's suspension any good to go offroad - and we jumped over the ditch onto the path that encircled the hay field. Grandma always wore jeans and trainers and never acted her age ("How should I know how to act my age? I've never been this age before!"). She was the wild child of the family. How or when this had happened I never really knew. Her early life as far as I could tell had been quite staid and rural, in a farming community, but at some point she had kicked back and become the glamorous and rather intriguing figure that I knew. She was sure fun to be around.

Our trainers and jeans got all wet from the still dewy grass that brushed against us as we followed the little footpath around the turn towards the forest, across the meadow. It entered the forest through some old oaks, and led, curving gently among the trees, to our secret place, mine and Kitty's.

It was Kitty who had originally found it, a little abandoned hut, big enough for two people to take shelter in. It stood at the edge of what had originally been a cultivated field that was now almost overgrown with small trees, and we had concluded the hut had been meant for agricultural tools. Its roof was still whole, and someone had taken the trouble to cover it with felt. It was overgrown with moss now, but still waterproof. It even had a little gas stove.

We had brought two old plastic garden chairs to the hut, and a little table, from our garden shed – the kind you see all around the world in cafeterias and on beaches. My mother was a bit of a pack-rat, and never wanted to throw away anything that wasn't broken, and these chairs and the table must have been from the early days of my parents' marriage, gone into storage when they travelled around and then brought back into service when we came to live here. The white plastic had darkened into a dirty gray that no cleaning could remove. My parents never noticed they were missing. Not that I had ever expected them to. Dad always tried to chuck old stuff out without my mother noticing, and was quite successful at it too, being careful to throw only those things away that had not met her eye for a while. If he had noticed the furniture gone, he'd never have said a word anyway.

There, in our shed, we had sat and talked and laughed... Watching the forest change from season to season, through the open door. We had tamed some curious squirrels, and they frequently came to see if we had brought any nuts for them. I thought about them now and wondered how they were doing. They probably missed us - we must have seemed to have disappeared from their lives quite suddenly.

"So this is where you and Kitty used to hang out?"

I nodded, lifted the latch, and pulled the door open. Grief hit me in the face with such strength I could not help a little sob from escaping. Grandma's hands were on my shoulders instantly.

"Come here. Sit down. You need to talk about it." She turned me towards the chairs and gently pushed me down on one.

"I miss her so much," I cried.

"Of course you do. You were the best of friends." She squeezed my hand. "Now; you need to get it out of your system. Tell me how it happened."

I drew in a ragged breath.

"We were walking by the road and that... drunk driver just hit her. There was this noise and...She... She bled so much. She hit her head, you see..." I tried to describe my painful memories for her, even though I did not want to. It was agonising, but as they came out, forced out bit by incoherent bit, I could feel a strange kind of release.

Grandma nodded, not letting go of my hand, but giving it an occasional gentle squeeze, waiting for me to continue.

"She... She didn't die immediately. She clung to life for a week. That...that's how they described it. Clinging to life. In and out of consciousness. Then she slipped into a coma and died. It was for the best, they said. The doctors. The huge brain contusion meant she would never have been... normal... again, had she survived. Not the Kitty we knew and loved..."

"That is probably true," Grandma said softly. "It doesn't make it easier, though."

Tears rolled down my cheeks. It was more of a flood of tears than just a trickle. Grandma pulled out a clean tissue from her pocket and gave it to me.

"You know... they told me that when she was still half conscious, she talked to invisible beings... Like she saw someone who wasn't there..." I wiped my tears away, tasting their salt on my lips.

"Yes, that is quite common when people are about to die," Grandma commented in a matter-of-fact voice.

"Is it?"

"Yes, it is. They say the invisible people are our loved ones, coming to fetch us when it is our time to leave."

I couldn't think of anything to say to that.

"Did you see her before she died?"

I shook my head.

"She was in intensive care and they didn't allow visitors, other than her family. But her brother sent me a photo of her with his phone."

"Oh dear..." Grandma shook her head. "That probably wasn't a very good idea. I'm sure he meant well, but... "

She was right. The picture was forever etched into my mind. Her immobile bruised body under the thin hospital sheet, with a machine breathing for her, and her swollen face...I knew then what horror meant. Strange how you use a word all your life, but you don't really understand it until one day it becomes real for you. She was no longer conscious at that point. I didn't want to remember Kitty like that, but could not erase the picture from my mind. Kitty - my friend. My best friend in the world.

"He said it was like looking at a car whose engine is still functioning, though the driver had already left. She was no longer there."

We sat there in the summer morning, Grandma and I, on the old chairs outside the hut. She did not ask anything, and let me wander through the labyrinth of the memories of those painful days.

The night she died, I'd known it from the moment I woke up – I had seen her in my dream, with a winged creature that could only have been an angel. The wings had been odd, though. Not white, not feathery, but like a halo of blue around the angel's body. They were in deep conversation with each other, and walking away from me. My throat had constricted the way it does when you lose something or someone you love in a dream, and you can't call out.

Kitty had given the winged creature an object, which looked like a book. The angel had been male, with light colored hair, and, strangely, dressed in jeans and a T-shirt instead of the kind of flowing robes you'd expect an angel to wear, and he'd looked at me over his shoulder while he led Kitty away. I could still remember his bright blue eyes piercing the distance, and I had felt an odd burning sensation in my chest and back, and felt very much awake. And when the phone rang in the middle of the night, while I lay on my bed with my eyes staring into the darkness, I already knew.

The drunk driver who had killed Kitty would be brought to trial in the future and undoubtedly be convicted, but nothing would ever bring Kitty back.

Suddenly rage hit me. In my mind I saw the scared woman stumbling out of her car to almost collapse into the road because she was so drunk. I screamed out loud and slammed the table with my fist. I wanted to face her, I wanted to hit her, I wanted to kill her...

Muffin backed away from me, whining. I forced myself to stop, so I wouldn't scare him.

"Sorry." My voice shook.

Muffin stood for a while, observing me with his head tilted to one side, and then came back up to me with his rear end wriggling madly back and forth as though he should apologise, not me. I leaned down to pat him, and he licked the salty tears from my cheeks.

"Nothing to apologise for," Grandma said. "If you weren't angry at the driver, I would be worried. Now, do you have a mug here?"

"A mug? Yes, two..."

"Inside? Good."

Grandma rose and I noticed she had a bag in her hands. Not a handbag, she never carried those, but a worn backpack. She went inside the hut, and I heard her put the kettle on our small gas stove. After a while she came back with two mugs of steaming instant coffee, placed these on the small table, and then returned to fetch a cake she had brought from the village store.

"Food helps when you're sad. An age-old fact. All grandmothers know it," she declared. She broke off a big piece of the cake and placed it determinedly on a tissue on the table in front of me.

My mouth was dry, and I wasn't hungry at all, but if Grandma had gone to all this trouble, then I would eat her cake.

"That's better. Low blood sugar makes it worse." She was right. Forcing myself to eat did help, even though I didn't want to admit it.

Suddenly Grandma stiffened and turned her head towards the depths of the forest. She sat there, unmoving, for a few seconds, then noticed me watching her and smiled.

"Just thought I heard something. There are no bears in the woods around here, are there? Distant relatives of Winnie the Pooh sniffing about in search of honey?"

I bit into the dry cake and washed it down with hot coffee. Then I managed a smile at her little joke.

"No bears, as far as I know. I don't think any were stowed away in our bags when we left the States."

"Our cake is safe, then. But I'll go and see if there's anything there. Perhaps it's a deer. I'd love to get a photo of a deer in the forest. Do you mind?" She took her phone from her pocket, and rose from her chair.

"No, not at all."

Grandma walked silently away, leaving me drinking my coffee, with Muffin pressed against my legs. I gave him the last bit of cake. Then I sat, looking down at the tiny ants marching over the wooden steps to reach the crumbs on the ground, tears falling silently down my cheeks and even dripping onto the knee of my jeans.

A little bee landed on the steps too. Bees seemed to like me; they were always flying around me, but I was never stung. I could hold them in my hand and not feel fear – something Mom never understood. Sometimes I even hummed to them and occasionally I imagined they answered me.

Muffin, who had been sitting looking hopefully at me wondering if I had more cake, turned his head and then got up and walked through the open door of the hut. I heard him sniffing and scampering about inside. He did not come out again. After a while I heard him scraping the floor and whining. An urgent, high-pitched whine, interspersed with little impatient growls.

"What is it, Muffin?" I asked with a thick voice. As if a dog could answer...

Well answer he did, in his own way. The scraping sounds were furiously rhythmical now, and he was positively howling.

I looked inside through the open door, and saw Muffin in the process of digging his way through the floor behind the little stove.

"Is there a mouse or something?" I asked, walking over to him.

One of the floorboards looked weird. It seemed to be sawn into sections... and the saw marks looked new, if the sawdust on the floor was anything to go by. Now I noticed that there was an old saw in the corner too. The teeth were all rusty and worn. It had not been there the last time we had been here. Next to it were a crowbar and a hammer - and the new nails at the end of the old board looked as though they'd been recently hammered in. Also... there was something marked on the wood. I bent down and peered at it, narrowing my eyes, which had trouble adjusting to the darkness after the bright sunlight. Yes, someone had drawn, or written, something on the floor right next to the saw marks where a piece of the floorboard had definitely been cut through.

I bent closer. D & K. Dana and Kitty. Our initials, the way Kitty always wrote them: the K pointing to the left from the back of the D. "We have each other's backs," she had explained when I had pointed out the wrong direction of the K.

I got on my knees, grabbed the floorboard and managed to get my fingers under the edge. After that, it was easy to lift the sawn piece away. It had been cleverly sawn at an angle so that the lower part was narrower than the upper one and so it fitted neatly into the space without falling right through.

I was looking down through an opening, which gave directly onto the dry ground underneath the floor. Nothing had grown on that earth for decades. And there, placed on the dusty ground, was a little metal box that I knew very well.

The box was white and had a metal handle that fell flat into an indentation on the lid. The lid and sides were covered in little cat caricature stickers. I had always wondered why Kitty did not have a cat, as it was obvious she was crazy about them. Well, probably because she had found Muffin, whom she loved dearly, at a rescue shelter. Muffin was small and his best friend wouldn't have called him good-looking, with his impressive underbite that would probably have earned him an honorable mention in the world's ugliest dog competition. Muffin also hated cats with the same enthusiasm he loved Kitty.

I knew I was looking down at Kitty's little strong box, where she always hid her secrets from her nosy siblings. She carried the key to the box whenever she left home. The last time I'd seen it, it had been on her desk the evening before she was hit by the car. And now it was here... She must have brought it the evening before the accident, after I had left her house. Perhaps because of this she had slept late and was half asleep when I had come to ask her out. Maybe that was why she had not paid attention on the road...

No. I shook my head, though there was no one to see the gesture. It had not been Kitty's fault. It was that damned drunk driver's fault, may she rot in hell.

But why ever had Kitty come here late in the evening with her precious box?

Still on my knees I put my hand through the opening almost up to my shoulder, managed to grasp the handle, and lifted the box up onto the floor. Muffin was whining and running around me, sniffing the box.

The key was attached to the handle with a wide red silk ribbon with embroidered pink roses. I remembered that one too. It had decorated the waist of Kitty's old porcelain doll, the one that sat permanently on top of her book shelf, out of reach of Ella, Kitty's little sister who was still too young to handle such precious things. Kitty had inherited the doll from her grandmother. It was a real antique, not one of those retro-dolls advertised in magazines.

I opened the white box, and an envelope looked back at me. Literally. Kitty had drawn two eyes on the envelope, looking directly at me. The eyes were smiling. She had always been good at drawing, and the smiling expression had been created with skill, lifting the lower lid slightly. The eyes looked eerily real. They looked familiar, too. Even the little mole on the temple, beside her right eye, was carefully drawn. Kitty must have looked into the mirror and drawn her own eyes.

Underneath the eyes something was written in Kitty's bold handwriting. I recognized the long curving loops and strong rhythmical style of it. Kitty's handwriting was like something from another age, and flowed with beauty, grace and character. Nothing like my scribbling – teachers sometimes commented they had trouble reading my handwriting. No wonder – when I wrote, I always felt as if I was in a hurry to finish the sentence. Probably because I typed extraordinarily fast, and writing with a pen was too slow a method to write down my thoughts. They always ran with such speed my handwriting simply could not keep up with them.

"To Dana: to be opened after I am dead," the envelope said.

Muffin glanced through the open door. I thought I heard Grandma returning, and, without thinking, slid the envelope under the waist of my jeans, pulling my shirt over it. Then I replaced the box under the floorboards, got up and kicked the board back in place, just in time before she appeared in the doorway.

"Maybe we should be heading home - what do you think?" Grandma asked.

"Yes, I think so too. Let's drop Muffin off at his house first, though."

We put the coffee mugs back on the window sill, closed the door and began to walk back to the car, with my arm linked through Grandma's, and Muffin leading the way.

3

SHADOW ON THE TRAIL

Fear was haunting the trees in the shape of a shadow looking for prey.

The prey was unknown, but the shadow continued to circle the forest in search of it because the ancient mind that controlled it told it to do so.

Scent was the shadow's text book, telling it whole stories of the forest. The smell of life, death, the old and the new mixed with the fresh smell of trees and plants.

The shadow felt uncomfortable here. This was not its natural domain and it usually visited this world only in the hours of darkness. All this fresh growing forest energy that created new things on its own was a mystery to it. Where all the energy came from, the shadow could not understand. No one had moulded it or created it, at least not in ways that the shadow could ever have comprehended. The energy simply seemed to seep on its own from the ground, or out of the very air around it.

Then its nose picked up the scent of a wounded animal and its spirits lifted. It sped on for a few minutes, following the smell of dried blood on the ground, and found the carcass of an almost completely eaten deer.

The shadow tasted what was left of the animal, though it wasn't hungry. It was good. The energy of the dead body felt familiar to it. It gave the shadow some strength. Invigorated, it continued its silent, aimless circling around the old trees. Like the wind, no-one would ever have seen it if they hadn't paid attention to the sudden silence of birds and little animals wherever the shadow went.

Then it heard something moving, hidden by the foliage. A snuffling type of breathing. The wind brought the scent to its nostrils.

A dog - and not just any dog. It had smelled this one before, by the road before the girl had been killed. There had been an accident, and the shadow had been there. Had - participated in the accident.

The shadow sniffed one more time, letting its nose drink in the scent of the dog. Yes, this was the dog that had tried to wake up the girl bleeding by the roadside. He remembered the smell, and the sound of the little dog's whimpers. And there were other scents too, a young woman's... And of someone else as well... This familiarity of this scent made the shadow uneasy, though it did not know why.

Still, finally, there was a trail.

Soundlessly the shadow turned and followed the scent and heavy breathing of the small animal, and the occasional spoken word between the two people, careful not to make a noise and to stay downwind. It soon came to a forest path that led to a weather-beaten old hut, and waited behind it, deep in the shadows of the forest until the humans and the dog had settled. Then it drew closer, without making a sound. It moved only as far as it took to see the girl sitting in front of the shed.

A slight breeze blew from the direction of the hut directly to the nostrils of the shadow. The smell of roses - perhaps it was the scent of the girl's soap or shampoo. And underneath it all the unmistakable scent of jasmine, with a touch of cinnamon. They had their individual scent, but usually the cinnamon undertone was there. That is how they spotted the maturing young of her kind.

If she was the one sought by the ancient mind, she could not escape the shadow after this, not once it knew her scent.

The girl was crying. The sound made the shadow feel powerful, and it was tempting to grasp the energy and grow on it. Suddenly the girl shivered, as if she sensed something. She glanced back towards the shadow but could not see it from the darkness of the forest. Impatient, the shadow crouched, ready to move closer.

Then it felt a familiar tuck at the back of its neck, which almost made it fall backwards, as if on a leash.

No. Not this one. Need to be sure. Need to be sure.

The shadow reeled back and forth like a fish on a line, finally obeying the voice in its mind, the voice that controlled the leash. She was so close. Just two short strides away.

The shadow breathed deeply, enjoying the smell of the pulsing blood, and warm skin, the sensation of young energy and the feeling of grief.

Then the other woman, who had been sitting behind the girl, stood up and walked into the hut. The shadow was still downwind, and now it caught the scent of the older woman.

The scent brought a memory. The shadow shrank deeper into the shade beneath the bush. Ancient mind spoke.

"You know this one?"

"I know this one."

Chaos. Shadows split apart at the memory. Darkness, explosion and smoke.

"It's *her*?"

Ancient mind knew. It never forgot anyone it had smelled. Now they both knew for certain that the girl was the right target.

"Follow. Do not show yourself."

The shadow knew the girl had no hope from this moment onwards. She was the one they had been seeking all this time. Eventually they would get her. And maybe, if she refused to cooperate, she would be killed. They did not kill their own kind often, but there was always the chance, if she offended him. The shadow laughed soundlessly at the thought.

With new eagerness and anticipation, the shadow flattened itself against the ground, becoming almost invisible. A twig snapped, and the older woman, who had been drinking coffee with the girl, turned her head and looked in its direction.

Then she rose and walked casually straight towards the shadow, frozen on the ground. She would see any movement immediately, and the shadow knew what would happen.

The hunter was now the hunted. Retreat, retreat, said the ancient voice in his mind. The shadow was reeled in as if on a line and the world changed back to formless mist.

4

GRANDMA'S GIFT

We drove Muffin home. There was still no one from Kitty's family around, so I did not have to talk to them.

"'Bye, Muffin." I patted him on the head, feeling a bit sad again at the sight of his little face at the gate.

I got back into Grandma's car and she started the engine and began to drive along the back road towards our house.

Grandma sometimes remarked that in another life she might have been a rally driver. She refused to act her age, a thing my conservative mother could not accept. I often thought that Mom was born old, and to be honest, she didn't have much of a sense of humour. She felt most at ease in her kitchen, away from the turmoil of the world. Grandma, on the other hand, wasn't the kind of person who would spend her days in the kitchen baking pies for church events. She wanted to see life. And she loved her sports car.

"There's not much chance of meeting people on your roads, not in the back of beyond where you live," she had once explained to my mother, who considered her behaviour childish. "I'm always careful when we meet with horse riders and only put my foot down on long clear stretches. And why buy a car like this, if you never have any fun with it?"

"Why indeed..." Mom had muttered through gritted teeth, her fingers gripping the side of the seat, and her butt pressed down hard in it as usual. Fast driving was on top of her list of reckless behavior.

Mom was not a very spontaneous person, I mused as we drove along.

"Have you visited her grave yet?" Grandma asked. Her tone sounded as though she was inquiring if I had been to the beach recently.

"No."

"Would you like to? I can take you there right now. We could pick her some flowers from these fields," her hand drew an arch in the air, covering the blooming fields around us. Early summer really was at its most beautiful.

With Grandma the thing that had seemed so difficult, impossible even, was much easier, and I heard myself saying "OK."

I hadn't admitted it to myself, but the thought of going to Kitty's grave on my own had been too much. And going there with my parents and then breaking down in tears in front of them, was even more of an impossible thing to consider. But Grandma was such a no-nonsense type of a person, and so easy to be with. She was just about the only person with whom I could go to Kitty's grave.

So she killed the engine, and we got out of the car again. The sun had dried the last of the dew, and it did not take us long to gather a big bouquet of wild flowers. Grandma fished a string out of her pocket - it never ceased to amaze me, the stuff that she carried around in them - and tied it around the stems.

"There. Now we have a nice bouquet. Let's go!"

And so I found myself sitting in the sports car (why were they always built so low?), holding a big bouquet of fresh flowers. Grandma knew the way to the churchyard well – after all she had lived in our house for a long time before moving to the city permanently. ("I wanted some excitement in my life after all those years in a rural backwater!")

I knew where the grave was, of course, and walked along the gravel path towards it with dread in my heart.

Much to my surprise Kitty already had a tombstone. It was light grey in color, and her name was written on it in golden letters. Beloved daughter. And the dates of her birth and death, a pitifully short period of time marked by the slash between the dates.

Suddenly I felt clumsy and heavy, and stopped. I didn't know what to do with the flowers, just stood there holding them awkwardly in front of me, staring at the tombstone.

"Well don't just stand there – give Kitty her flowers." Grandma gave me a little nudge.

I stepped forward and stiffly bent to put the flowers on the grave. There was no grass growing on the earth yet. The thought of Kitty buried there made me nauseous.

There were other bouquets as well, all fresh, so either others had only visited her grave in the last two days, or someone had been tending to the grave and taken any withered flowers away. Little angel statues and teddy bears and candles were strewn everywhere. Names of my classmates under "Miss You" notes and poems. A Christmas tree ornament even - a stylized bird made of some glittery red material. Our flowers complemented the little display beautifully. A robin flew to the stone and observed us for a while before flying off to feed its young.

"How lovely," Grandma said tilting her head slightly to one side, her hands on her hips. She sounded as though she was commenting on a painting or a piece of decoration. There was a pause while we looked at everything, and suddenly it was real for me. Kitty was dead. But strangely, I didn't feel like crying any more. It was so peaceful here, and the little - gifts - everyone had brought her were so kind and loving. It was as though in death, we suddenly really knew her as she truly was.

Grandma was speaking, and I tuned out my thoughts so that I could hear what she was saying. She repeated it for me, because it was obvious I hadn't heard the first time.

"I said," she repeated in a matter-of-fact tone, "has she tried to contact you yet?"

I looked at Grandma, not quite believing my ears.

"What did you say?"

Grandma sighed. "I asked if Kitty has tried to contact you yet," she repeated yet again, in the same matter-of-fact tone as she had used to pose the question. "They do, you know."

"Who?" I did not understand.

"The dearly departed, if you will," she looked slightly amused. "It is quite common. If you know what to look for. And aren't afraid of the contact, of course."

It's OK, I thought to myself. Just Grandma having a temporary fit of weirdness. Or perhaps she's trying to cheer me up. My Grandma, the medium. Next she'll be donning a turban and calling herself Velma the Mystic or something.

Her cell phone rang and she took it out of her pocket, checking who was calling. That was just as good as answering, as I could not resist touching the letter tucked under the waist of my jeans. The message from Kitty.

"It's your dad... Hello, Mike! Yes, not long now. In fact, I met Dana on the road on the way to your house. OK, yes, we'll be right there."

She slid the phone back in her pocket. She never had a handbag, just sometimes her ratty old back pack, but mostly she carried all the necessary stuff in her pockets. ("What doesn't fit in my pockets, I can do without. I've always thought handbags get in the way of action." She never specified what she meant by "action".)

"Well, the chef is about to make his famous pasta, and would like us to be there when he bears it to the table. Let's get going."

I sat quietly next to Grandma while she drove us home. She did not say anything more on the subject of Kitty contacting me. She was like that, never pushing her opinions on others, or continuing a discussion if she noticed the subject made someone feel uncomfortable. My puzzled expression must have convinced her to drop it.

The pasta was delicious, as always. Dad really knew his way around a kitchen. He had been a professional in the hospitality business for many years before we'd come to live in this peaceful rural idyll on the border between England and Wales, where he now focussed on consultancy and teaching. When he was young, he'd worked his way through university in many different kitchens, happy to start at the lowest level every time, because as he always said, you learned more that way. It was a great opportunity to study different cultures - European, Asian, African - he immersed himself in it all. He did most of the cooking at home, leaving only baking to my mother, who happened to love it. I helped them both, and hoped I would learn both their skills - it was like having a private restaurant, living with them.

When I was very small and Dad was building his career, we'd lived in different places - Italy, Greece, Korea and America. I had been so young I didn't really remember very much about any of them other than the States. Dad, who was American, had met Mom in England years earlier while he was a student travelling around - she and Grandma were originally from a Kentish farming family and now that we were back in a rural area she felt really at home there with her church activities and so on. I loved it too. Apart from anything else, there was a real sense of antiquity and mystery about where we lived and I had become fascinated by history and archaeology. Grandma, though, had kicked back at living the rural life at some point and gone off for adventures.

Mom had made a delicious strawberry cake for coffee, and we discussed ordinary things while we ate. Kitty's death was not one of the subjects. After the pasta and cake everyone was so full, we practically rolled to the living room and almost dozed off on chairs and sofas. For a while Dad pretended to be reading a magazine, but his eyelids kept on drooping lower and lower, until his head bobbed to the side and he began to snore lightly, all cosy in his favorite armchair.

It was tempting to join my slumbering family, but I did not want to sleep, so I forced myself out of the depths of the comfortable armchair, and went to my room. Exercise, I thought. Work off this meal. My thought was to get the binoculars and go observe nature in the forest so that I could get some quiet time after what had turned out to be a demanding day. I reached for the binocular case on top of my bookshelf. The strap must have been jammed between two books and when I pulled a bit harder than I'd intended, one of them fell on my toes. That was the only explanation for it.

"Shit! Shit shitshit!" I hissed to myself and jumped on one leg holding the toes of the other. "Damn book!" Surprising how much something as relatively light as a book could hurt when it fell that far.

I heard a chuckle from the doorway. Grandma was standing there, leaning against the doorframe, laughing quietly.

"Well, excuse me if I don't share the joke. My toe feels as if it's broken!" I managed to get out.

"Sorry, dear. I wasn't laughing at your pain. I was laughing at Kitty."

"You... what?" I forgot my throbbing toes and stared at Grandma. I was still standing on one leg like a flamingo.

"You just met one of the ways they communicate with us."

"They?"

"The dead." She leaned on the doorframe. "The dearly departed, deceased, passed away, perished. You know."

I just started to say "Look, Grandma - " but didn't get any further.

"What are you talking about?" Mom shouted from the living room. She had the most acute hearing, if someone was talking about "suspect things". Much like me. It's like being in a room full of people, everyone talking at the same time. You can't tell what each individual says, but if they mention your name, you hear it immediately.

"Angels!" Grandma shouted over her shoulder. "Books about angels!"

There was no answer to that. Mom could not really object to angels, even though they were a metaphysical subject, therefore "suspect." Metaphysics was something she could not tolerate. But angels were mentioned at church, which she frequented. So even though she did not quite believe in angels, they were acceptable in her social circles.

"Well, maybe it's best we don't talk about these things in front of your mother. She feels very uncomfortable when anyone talks about death. She is so scared of it. No point in trying to change her opinion, until she is ready for it." Grandma's voice was low, as if we were conspiring together.

I wasn't sure what Grandma meant with the "until she is ready for it" part, and did not ask.

Yes, my grandmother had always been a bit strange, that was true. That was one of the reasons I found her so interesting. But we had never discussed dead people contacting us before. That was stranger that the average strangeness of Grandma.

"What do you mean I met with one of the ways 'they' communicate with us?" I couldn't help but add a sceptical edge to my voice. Grandma ignored it.

"Books are quite popular message deliverers. They drop them off shelves."

I shook my head.

"No, that's just coincidence... Has to be."

"Maybe, maybe not. But keep your eyes open. The world is full of stories about communication from the other side. Surely not all of those stories can be just imagination. Ever considered there might actually BE something on the other side? And that our loved ones might want to let us know they still exist? But we won't talk about this any more, if it makes you feel uncomfortable. Actually there's something I want to show you. How about going for a walk in the garden? I need to stretch myself a bit after that big meal."

She turned with the grace of a dancer and I followed her out of the house.

We walked past Mom's beautiful flowers, towards a little brook that ran behind the low hedge defining our garden.

"I have something for you." Grandma put her hand in her jeans pocket. She took something out that glistened pale green in the sunlight, and handed it to me.

A pendant of something that looked like jade.

"It is not jade, if that's what you are thinking," Grandma read my thoughts. "It's glass. But not just any glass - it's meteorite glass from the Western Desert of Egypt. Millions of years old."

The piece of glass was in the shape of a teardrop, but not cut or polished, it just seemed to be naturally teardrop-shaped. It was mounted in a golden fitting of the same shape. I saw indentations in the gold. Something was carved on the back of the necklace. I turned it in the light in order to see better.

A female figure, depicted from the side, the hand closest to me pointing down, the other hand straight forward, with wings attached to the underside of the arms. She had something on the top of her head that vaguely resembled a chair. In front of her were two fan-like objects, Her hair and her pose were...

"Egyptian," Grandma completed the sentence I was thinking. "It is very old. It has been passed down the female family line for at least centuries, always passing to the eldest daughter. It belongs to you."

"But why doesn't mother have it then?" I had to ask, as mother was Grandma's only child.

"Well, I thought that it's better to give it to someone who appreciates ancient Egypt. Your Mum would probably never wear it. After all it depicts the goddess Isis. Or Aset, as they called her in ancient times. And your Mum is rather strict about matters of faith."

Well, that was true. I just couldn't imagine Mom ever wearing an ancient goddess around her neck. She might even have thrown a necklace like that away, or had the gold melted down for a new ring.

"How old is this?" I wondered, turning the pendant so that the sun's rays hit it from different angles.

"Ancient, I think it may even be thousands of years old... If you look at the work it doesn't seem modern. And so - well, perhaps you'd better keep it hidden, since we don't know its full history. And even if you told someone with an interest in it that it had been passed down for generations in your family, it might be difficult to explain to officialdom that it hadn't been stolen from some ancient tomb or something."

"Why are you giving this to me now?"

"I thought it might cheer you up after Kitty's death."

The sun reflected softly from inside the green glass. I looked at the carving in the gold again.

"What do these two fans mean?" I pointed to the fans with long handles in the space between the outstretched arms of the winged goddess. "I mean, they are fans, aren't they?"

"Yes, they are. They read shuet. It means shadow. It does not make much sense. The placement in front of Isis would suggest you read it 'the shadow of Isis'. It may be this came originally from a priestess who called herself that. We will probably never know. Shuet certainly was not a real name as far as we... I know. The ancient Egyptians believed the soul consisted of many parts, and shuet was the 'shadow self' if you will. No parent would have named their child Shuet."

For a fleeting moment I wondered who the "we" were, but did not ask. Probably some of Grandma's Bohemian friends.

The pendant felt surprisingly heavy in my hand, and it was as if it made me feel the pulse in my wrist beat much more strongly than before. I felt a slight tingling sensation, or so I thought. Perhaps it was just Grandma's story.

Suddenly I thought I saw some shadowy movement at the edge of the forest not far off. Grandma must have seen it too, because she turned to stare intently in the direction of the movement.

Nothing was moving there now, and after a while we walked back towards the house. When we came closer to the porch, we could hear my parents discussing something. Or rather, someone.

"Why has she turned up now?" I heard Mom ask Dad in the living room. She was trying to keep her voice down.

"Why not?" Dad laughed so loudly that Mom shushed him.

Dad had always liked Grandma, just like I had. No talk about any difficult mother-in-law relationship there. It was as if they were chips off the same block. They understood each other's jokes and spent a long time chatting and laughing on the phone as well. Mom, on the other hand, almost never called her mother, and if Dad gave her the phone after talking to Grandma, she usually took it with a long sigh (which I am sure Grandma always heard), and her words always sounded awkward.

"She is so strange!" Mom complained. "We're just not on the same wavelength, never have been..."

"It's a good thing that she doesn't hold your differences against you then, eh? She's always cheerful, always the same," Dad chuckled. "Come on, Hun, you'll get along fine. If not, I'll keep her busy so she won't make you lose your cool. Besides, it will do Dana good. She needs cheering up. She has no close friends now that Kitty is gone.

Maybe she'll get new friends in the fall, when school begins again, but right now she is pretty lonely."

Mom mumbled something under her breath.

I glanced at Grandma, wondering if she was upset by what was being said. She just grinned back at me and gave me a wink.

"You wouldn't believe we are from the same family, would you?" she whispered. "To tell you the truth, I sometimes find it hard to believe as well."

I couldn't help but grin back.

I had always wondered what my Mom really held against Grandma. She didn't hate her, but there always seemed to be something unspoken bubbling under the surface, as if Mom was somehow indebted to Grandma. I wondered if she had lent my parents some money in the past, to help them over a rough patch. That would explain it. Mom did not want to be indebted to anyone, about anything.

"Well, let's get inside before they wonder if we've disappeared," Grandma smiled, now digging in her jacket pockets - the contents of which never ceased to amaze me. "Anyone for a game of cards?" she asked with a loud voice and stepped on the porch, waving a worn packet of playing cards in the air.

5

KITTY'S LETTER

That night I finally had the chance to read Kitty's letter. I took it from under my mattress where I had hidden it. Glancing at the door to make sure it was closed, I opened the envelope with a little knife, as quietly as possible. Then, taking a deep breath, still standing in the middle of my room, I began to read.

"Dana, If you read this, I am dead," the letter began. *"Sheesh what a cliché of a sentence! Like something from an Agatha Christie novel, isn't it?"*

After this, she had drawn a smile. I was horrified to read on, somehow. But I could not turn my eyes away from the paper.

"Look, I know this is going to sound crazy... In fact I cannot quite believe I am writing this. If I am wrong, you'll never know, and we'll see each other soon, and I'll know it was just my imagination. I'll collect the box, or maybe leave it and this letter where it is for us to find sometime in the future. We can then have a good laugh about it when we are old and grey... Oh, I don't know. Maybe I just better stop rambling and write what I sat down to write."

Curious, I turned the first page of the letter to see what was written on the reverse of it.

"You remember when we talked about ghosts and what will happen

when we die? Well of course you do, and have probably been wondering about it now that I am... gone. Gone to wherever it is we go when we die. I need to tell you that I somehow know this is going to happen. I have had such vivid dreams lately where Darryl has come to meet me."

Darryl was her brother who had died of a brain tumour. Four children in Kitty's family, now two of them dead...

The memory of Kitty's parent's at the funeral flashed vividly into my mind's eye: ashen faces, humped shoulders, unable to speak when they lowered their flowers on her casket - I couldn't bear the word coffin... Little Ella standing behind them with round eyes, not understanding where her big sister had gone. And Andy, Kitty's big brother, holding Ella's hand with an expression somewhere between grief and rage.

I felt like choking, cleared my throat and continued reading.

"Darryl was so real, and I felt so totally happy that I began to wonder whether I was getting closer to the veil between our life and... well, whatever you want to call the afterlife. I have read about such things happening. People who are about to die, feeling very happy and unafraid before it actually happens. And that someone from the other side comes to fetch them, someone they know and love. Darryl certainly fits that description."

Kitty had been interested in NDEs or near death experiences, and had read a lot about the subject on the net. But it was something she could discuss with no one but me. It was not a topic most teenagers at school would talk about - death was somewhere too far in the future for them, and older people seemed too scared. Kitty's loss had awakened her deep interest in the subject. She had tried discussing it with her parents, but they were churchgoers like my mother and thought it was dangerous for Kitty to investigate anything of that kind. That did not stop her, of course, and we had been talking about NDEs. I had also felt a bit queasy about it, and changed the subject as soon as it didn't feel impolite. Death wasn't my favorite subject either. Now I wish I had listened more to what she had to say.

I read on.

"And then, in my dreams, I began to see glimpses of what was likely going to happen to me. I had these dreams often, and they became more real, dream by dream. I saw a car, and I was looking at myself on the ground, floating above the scene, and I felt totally calm and happy. Yes, calm and happy, as if nothing was wrong in those dreams. I observed myself there on the roadside, probably dead, or at least dying, and there was nothing to it. Can you believe it? To see your own death and not feel fear?

In some ways it was scary, I admit, but I could not feel afraid. It just felt the way things were meant to be. And you may call me crazy, but I felt like my... mission in life, for lack of a better word, would begin there. And Dana - it was all about you, whatever it was I was supposed to do with my life. Yes, I know. It sounds strange. I wonder about these dreams, and whether they are a warning to try to prevent this from happening. But how can I avoid all the cars in the world? Well, I can't. So I decided to live on, come what may. And, as you are reading this now, we know that death came.

I want you to know I am not afraid of death. When I think of it, it feels like a bright light in my mind, and I feel Darryl there. How could I fear my own brother? If he is there, then all my other loved ones will be too. Grandma. Grandpa. Misty."

Misty had been her Shetland pony. Too small to ride, but she had been in the family for thirty years and her death had been a difficult thing for Kitty.

I reread her words about her mission in life, and that it involved me. A horrible thought came to my mind - had her strange dreams caused her to step in front of the car so it would not hit me - had they given her the illusion she was meant to protect me? But no, something did not match here... The car had swerved from the curve directly towards me, and Kitty had stepped sideways... but not in front of me - she had stepped away from me and the car, a basic reaction to avoid being hit.

To my eyes it had looked like the driver tried to hit Kitty on purpose, which I did not understand. She should have been able to avoid hitting Kitty, but did not. Instead she had swerved towards Kitty again, when Kitty tried to jump away. If the car had continued on its original course, it would not have hit her... nor me, having made the first evasive move.

For a second I had been staring straight at the driver, but for the life of me I don't remember seeing her face. It was as if there had been a shadow behind the wheel... A psychologist said that was caused by the shock, and I might remember it later. She had asked me to call when it did, if I needed help when I remembered her. But I doubted I'd ever call - why would I?

If the shrink was worried about my reaction to remembering the driver, she need not be. I remembered the drunken lady very well from the moment she stumbled clumsily from the driver's seat, and wobbled out on her high heels, supporting herself against the car. And I hated her already. I did not need any shrink to tell me I should let my emotions out.

I could still see the dent in the hood and the shattered windscreen in my mind's eye, and hear the sickening thump in my ears. The memory made me gasp for air, and I had to sit on my bed and bend down with my head between my knees for a while. Slowly I relaxed, my lungs began to breathe normally again, and I managed to go on reading.

"Those dream discussions with Darryl felt very real. One night he showed me a big orange butterfly and said he would send it to me. It was wintertime, so I did not take this promise seriously. Do you know what happened the next day? You should. Remember that biology class, when Eva fell over backwards on her chair?"

I did. Eva had been tilting the back legs of her chair, something she often did. That day she rocked further and further back until eventually she managed to tip it right over, and she lay flat on her back, shrieking, much to the joy of the whole class. And during that same lesson, suddenly a big orange butterfly had flown into the classroom. Where it came from, no one knew, but in an instant it was there, and it flew right down onto Kitty's desk.

"Quiet everyone!" The teacher had calmed the class, which was in an uproar by then, because like all students we relished any unusual happening that gave us the chance to rock out a bit, and two such in

one class was almost too much to hope for. Then she explained that some butterflies wake early in the spring, when the sun gets warm enough. Yes, even with snow outside. Ours was an old school, and probably the butterfly had hibernated in some crack in the wall, now warmed by the early spring sun.

"So you remember the butterfly now? I was certain Darryl sent it, and that little creature was proof to me that we don't cease to exist when we die.

I would like you to believe that too.

Obviously I am now on the Other Side, in the Unseen Worlds. I will try to contact you by sending you signs I still exist. What you need to do is to keep your eyes and ears open, and try to sense when I am near. I have read it is not easy to approach sad people – I mean approach from 'the Spirit Side'. It has to do with heavy energies. So you need to be calm, and try to remember the fun we had, and I will try to reach you then.

Maybe I'll drop a book for you to read – that would get your attention, bookworm that you are!"

The hairs on the back of my neck rose. I mean literally, I could feel them bristling.

"Yes, I just might contact you through a book. I cannot tell you what it is, because I have to keep its secret, and someone other than you might find this letter. Still, it has to do with dreams. You will understand what I mean when the time comes."

I didn't know what to think. Part of me shrank from the idea of the 'Unseen Worlds' and the 'Other Side'. But now the book falling on my toes seemed like something Kitty had... planned? Why else would she talk about contacting me through a book? And what was the secret that the book from my shelf held? I would have to read it through carefully again.

"Oh, and do take Muffin back home. I am certain he is there with you. He is probably the one who found this letter, isn't he? I used to train him to find things I hid. I always used a little rose perfume on the things I wanted him to find, and that's what I did here too."

True. The silk sash that had held the key to the box smelled of tea rose. Kitty had probably used a drop of her treasure - a small bottle of Body Shop's genuine tea rose oil her mother had bought when she was young. They did not sell it any longer and one drop of it smelled like a bouquet of roses for hours. Just roses, no other perfume. Kitty loved roses.

Used to love roses.

There was a P.S. at the end of the letter.

"P.S. And Dana – even if I don't succeed in reaching you, I want you to remember that you will always be my best friend. I am sure we are soul twins. We just happened to be born in different families, but there was a reason we met. I will love you always. And our separation is not for all eternity - eventually we will meet again."

She had drawn one more smiling face and a heart and signed her letter with a big, bold "Kitty".

I sat there for a long while. Finally, I folded the letter back into its envelope and sat quietly for a long time, surrounded by the voices of nature falling asleep that came through my open window.

I went to bed, and on a whim took the pendant Grandma had given me into my hand. It felt heavy, and warm. Familiar, and reassuring, as if I had owned it all my life.

That night I dreamt of a woman sitting in a dark tent, writing on paper that looked like papyrus. I could only see her pale fingers holding a reed pen, and the flickering light of an ancient looking oil lamp – a shallow pottery container filled with oil. The tip of a wick protruded from a little hole at the end of a neck reaching out horizontally from the container of the lamp. The lamp was burning with a warm flame. I knew the writer was a woman from her delicate pale fingers. I could not see what she wrote, but I knew with the certainty of a dreamer that she was telling someone about the death of another that was dear to her.

She had no tears left, but I cried for her loss as well as mine in my sleep.

6

GOING FORTH BY DAY

Oh my heart which I had from my mother!
Oh my heart which I had from my mother!
Oh my heart of my different ages!
Do not stand up as a witness against me, do not be opposed to me in the tribunal,
do not be hostile to me in the presence of the Keeper of the Balance,
for you are my ka which was in my body, the protector who made my members hale.
Go forth to the happy place whereto we speed;
do not make my name stink to the Entourage who make men.
Do not tell lies about me in the presence of the god;
It is indeed well that you should hear!
-Book of the Dead

I am now sitting in a tent that has been raised for me right next to wabt net wet, the place of embalming, where mother, true of voice, shall have her body prepared to be the home for her ka and ba so that her light soul, akh, can become a child of Nut and spend eternity with the northern stars.

There is no question in my mind that mother was murdered, and I know exactly who did this - I recognised the signs in her body. I curse my sister. People speak in whispers of a new monster, Ammit, that will eat the hearts that are not pure, when people reach the last judgment. I know my sister's heart is heavy with the thoughts of evil deeds, and I know my curse will reach her. May Ammit devour her heart, and may her soul be restless forever more, never finding peace again. May it die a second death and be forgotten for all eternity.

I am writing this to you, my father, because I promised mother I would let you know of her death. I also write this to tell you how you can find the Place of the Neteru - the place where mother shall be buried in secrecy. It is a place of deep secrets, and there she can be found with the secrets she guarded with her life, if you, my father, wish to search for her.

Mother warned me that whenever words are written down, secrets can be revealed, and no written secret lasts forever. And so I shall hide the clues along the Path of the Dead, for you to find if you understand. And you are the only one who could ever understand the path, mother told me.

I have taken good care that mother will be embalmed in the best way possible. I am not poor, and Mother of the King, Tiye - life, prosperity, health - has made offerings too, items that are of great wealth and value to her, to show her affection. She and mother were close, closer than many know. But Tiye - may she live - is not here to see the burial. She is now in Akhetaten, preparing for the great jubilation of all nations. There also is my sister now - stuck with her duties, dancing under the Aten's blessed rays, to celebrate his glory for all eternity. She cannot leave because she is in the retinue of Neferneferuaten, and does not wish her to know what she knows, as all would be taken from her. Also her accomplices cannot reach her now because of her duties under the sun. And it is good. Because of this we can leave in secrecy.

I know who are the spies she has sent to observe all I do, being prevented from coming here herself. They are to find where the Abode of the First Gods is, the place where mother will be buried. But rest assured, my father, she will not know this from me because not even I know. There is another who will lead us there. I have been there before but I do not know where it is.

I was with mother when her soul left her body, and I will take care it can unite with her body again and live forever more in the Field of Reeds, in the kingdom of Osiris, until it is time for you to meet again.

I had her taken to the place of washing, the she-netjer, which serves the blessed dead of the keneret of Mi-Wer. Her body was washed and she was then taken here, the place of embalming with great respect shown to it all the way. The women of the keneret wailed and threw dust on their hair, ululating their grief for all to hear.

I have witnessed the process of embalming myself, though no other outsider has been allowed to see this before. But they feared me, and they feared the Mother of the King, and so on her orders I was given permission, after careful purification. And so all hairs of my body were shaved, my mouth was purified with salt, and I sat, in a corner, out of the way, and observed the violent ways used to prepare us for eternity, so that we can keep on living.

This is why I know that today the Slitter has done his job, and has made the incision on my mother's lower belly, next to the left thigh. I know this because while sitting in my dark tent I heard the other embalmers chasing him, and I heard the shouts of the people who loved my mother and who are guarding us even now. They attacked the Slitter as is proper, hitting him, and throwing stones at him for violating her beautiful body. I have taken care he will be rewarded later with a golden arm ring to thank him for his service, and he will give me the blade used on my mother so no one else can use it - it shall be buried with her. I know the Slitter well, for he has often talked with me in the darkness and I know his attitude towards the dead is respectful. He is not the kind to steal the amulets, to insult beautiful bodies or do his job poorly or demand things from the dead.

So my mother's viscera have now been removed for embalming, and they will now continue, with her body on the embalming bed, the men squatting around it to perform their sacred duties. Mother of the

King, Tiye - life, prosperity, health - has given part of the necessary ingredients so that mother can raise from the dead in seventy days as Osiris was resurrected by Isis. Her ka and ba will be united and she will become an akh, a living soul . She shall never roam the earth searching for peace. The right words will be spoken for her, the Opening of the Mouth performed by me as the law dictates of the heir of the dead and offerings shall be made for her for all eternity.

There is palm wine to wash my mother from the inside and the outside. There is fine linen thread to sew the incision together and a golden plate to cover the wound. There is divine salt, netjry, for the preservation of her body. There are onions to fill mother's eyes and legs. There is lichen to fill her body cavities and sacred bees wax for her mouth and nostrils. There are sweet spices and Mother of the King, Tiye - life, prosperity, health - has even sent sacred incense of Punt and juniper oil of Byblos to make mother's body smell sweet eternally. There is resin to make sure she will be preserved forever.

Bandages of fine linen are waiting - mother made them herself while still alive, and gave orders how they are to be used - exactly as she says. They are covered with sacred writings in her own language, in a language no one understands, except me, and you, my father, nearest her body. I shall be observing the wrapping to see it is properly done. All the secrets of the times to come are written in the outer bandages, in a language the guardians of her body understand. And what I know of the times to come fills me with great sadness and fear. I see kingdoms fall into pieces, I see great wars, illnesses and famine - but I also see great hope for mankind.

And so I have seventy days to finish the scroll of the Going Forth by Day for her - exactly the way she told me to do it. I will not let anyone else do it for I, a woman, have learned to write like the scribes - they paid for my knowledge with their own secrets. It is my duty as her daughter to prepare for my mother the path through the shadows and dangers of death. I have the papyrus, I have the reed pen and red and black ink. I have plenty of oil for my oil lamps. The pictures have already been painted according to my mother's advice, by a scribe in the House of Life of Amun before Aten's people attacked to destroy every memory of the great god, when people still had an afterlife, and were not made to suffer all eternity in their dark tombs at Akhetaten at night and flock to the offering altars of the great temple of the Aten by day.

My mother will not be advised to flock with them. She will go forth to the day of the Field of Reeds the way people of Kemet have always done. She will have her heart weighed at the final judgement against Maat's feather of truth, and her heart shall be found light and pure. Her voice shall sound true in front of the gods when she denies having done the forty two evils and they will believe her, my beautiful mother, true of voice. I will see to that by writing the texts myself, above these beautiful pictures, and I shall place her scroll into her hands, inside her coffin at the end of these days.

And I shall make a copy of her scroll to you, my father, and send it to you by messengers my mother chose, even if it means I will not have time to rest for seventy days. She wanted it, my mother, true of voice. She wanted you to follow her path to eternity, so that you too would know your steps in the land of eternal life, and meet her there when the time is right. You will see the pictures in her scroll give the advice you need to walk the Path of the Dead to her. She said you will understand what you see in the pictures.

I am to leave this letter for you in the trustworthy hands of the ones mother chose for the task. Mother told me how to send you a message so you will find its hiding place. I shall do as she told me. I shall walk into the mist, following the path she advised me to take, even though I have never had the courage to step there before. I shall speak the words she told me to say, to the ones who shall write it down. My message will be safe, because when I say it, the old ways will have been forgotten, and no one will understand it until the time is right again. But you, my father, will understand the words when you hear them, and find this letter, and the first clue to the secret path to the place where mother has been prepared for eternal life, and where the secrets of creation are hidden.

Others, chosen by mother, will try to reach you through different paths, to ensure somehow her message will reach you, following the advice she gave to them. And we pray the gods some message will reach you, and you will find this letter, even though the journey is long and dangerous. We know we shall be hunted for the secrets we carry, mother warned us of this.

So please, my good father, walk the path to find my mother's scroll and go forth by day with her.

7

AMONGST THE BOOKS

The next day Grandma wanted to take me shopping. I accepted gratefully, welcoming the normality of going to our town, which was small, more like a village, but it had a few decent shops to mooch around. And a bookshop, which happened to have a sale on at that time.

I loved books. My room was practically lined with them, and my favorite birthday or Christmas gift was always a bookstore gift card from the day I learned to read. I also spent a lot of time in the local library, reading books. Because I had to watch my funds, I obviously could not afford all the books I wanted, so I often went to the library to check out if a title I'd heard about was worth buying.

I had put in my Christmas order early by telling my parents that I wanted an e-reading device, whether Kindle, iPad, or Nook. I had already seen how cheap books were in electronic form, and looking at my book shelves groaning under the weight of the volumes I had purchased, I knew I would either have to start moving my books to the guest bedroom or get that e-book reader. Seriously, I sometimes imagined that my bedroom floor was going to collapse under the weight and used to joke that it would be the first ever "death by books", though since losing Kitty I didn't really make jokes about death any longer.

Anyway, my books were already in double rows on each shelf and the thought of having one device with all the reading material I could ever want in it was almost too good to be true.

But I still loved printed books. They felt like old friends in my hands. I guess I would always have "old fashioned" printed books as well, just like my dad collected old vinyl records. There was that special something in old-fashioned books...

So, of course I wanted to go to the book shop, and Grandma parked her sports car right in front of it in one graceful curve, steering the wheel easily with just one hand. The car got appreciative glances from the members of the male population who happened to be passing by. As did Grandma herself. I hoped I had inherited her genes and would age as beautifully as she had - she looked thirty years younger than she was. Really, not kidding.

The only strange thing gene-wise was that both my parents were quite short, yet I was considerably taller than they were. When I was a child, Dad used to joke that there must have been a giraffe in our family tree somewhere. And I, being in the first grade then, had asked about this possibility at school. After my teacher stopped laughing, I did not speak to Dad for two days.

I smiled at the giraffe-memory now, and followed Grandma through the open door into the book store.

I loved the smell of books and the sight of all those racks, relishing the moment. What should I look at first? Books about cats, I decided and walked over the worn wooden floor towards the books about nature and pets. Grandma vanished somewhere amongst the taller shelves.

I more or less just drifted down the corridors of the book store after that, reading the book titles, picking up some of them to find out more from their back covers, and then moving on. I noticed Grandma at the metaphysical section, in front of a slew of books about angels. Well, where else, I thought. I wanted to tell her what had just happened, and was starting to move towards her when out of nowhere someone almost ran me over. I fell against a bookshelf and hit my knee, hard, right on the bone.

"Owwwww!" I grabbed my knee. I knew there would be a gorgeous bruise later on. For a moment the pain overtook me and it was a few seconds before I could think of anything else.

"Oh, sorry! I do hope I haven't hurt you seriously?"

At a glance, he was maybe a few years older than I was, but it was somehow hard to pinpoint his actual age. He was very tall - a rare exception to the young guys I knew. Looking down on them tended to have a bit of a cooling effect on any romantic intentions they had, to put it mildly. Sure I had been on a few dates, and had my experiences of awkward kisses, but nothing serious. I was certain that me being so tall was the cause. I figured that men, for whatever reason, mostly feel insecure if their girlfriend is taller than they are. Standing on tiptoe while kissing a girl seemed to be too much for the male ego - that was my experience, anyhow.

His T-shirt revealed muscular arms. It wasn't a body builder's physique, though, just the well-proportioned muscles of someone who had clearly done some physical work. Two very blue eyes stared down at me. I almost forgot to be angry with him - he was so handsome. And oddly familiar... I just couldn't place him. I had the weirdest feeling he looked at me as if I was someone he knew. Maybe he was the big brother of one of my friends or classmates? But no, I dismissed that... I knew I would not have forgotten someone like him, even if I'd only met him once before.

"Watch where you're going!" I snapped anyway, a bit taken aback by his ice blue, honest gaze.

"I am sorry," he repeated, looking embarrassed. Oh, and did I mention handsome? Blond hair, blue eyes and a pale skin to match it.

Rather too pale for the midst of summer. His skin was nearly... translucent? It certainly had a glow that looked almost airbrushed. Maybe he was a fashion model I had seen on a magazine cover? Or the net?

He calmly observed me observing him. In fact he seemed to be looking at me with such intense curiosity I began to think there was something wrong with my face. Had my mascara run? The pain had momentarily brought tears to my eyes, and I did that thing that you do, where you're trying to see a smudge on your face without letting on that you're doing anything apart from concentrate on the other person in the conversation. He certainly deserved my full attention. Wow, he was pale though.

"No, I am not an albino, if that's what you're thinking. Nor a vampire. I'd be in fashion though, if these books are anything to judge by, don't you think?" He had clearly noticed me looking at his skin, and smiled and waved his hand at the young adult books on the shelves. "I've been traveling for a while and only just came back to the sunny side of the world."

He sounded very educated for his age. Also his smile was.... captivating. I found myself staring at his beautiful lips. He seemed amused, and that of course made his smile widen. His face was heart-stoppingly gorgeous when he did that. Then it occurred to me I was ogling him, and that he had realized it too. I blushed.

Bending down to hide my embarrassment, I began to dust the knees of my jeans even though the bookshelves I'd crashed into - had been knocked into - were clean and completely dust-free. When I looked up again, he had vanished. I glanced around, and quickly even stood on my toes to see over the taller shelving, but he was nowhere to be seen. Surely he couldn't have ducked behind one of the shelves and be hiding there? He was real enough - I had the pain in my knee to prove it.

I picked up my old duffel bag. I'd brought the one I used at school, because I usually ended up buying soooo many books. I had also put a light jacket in the bag in case it became chilly ("Chilly this time of the year? We do get summer in England, you know. Well, some years anyway." I could almost hear Kitty laughing. "You are just like your mother - prepared for every conceivable catastrophe.").

"So, did you find anything you'd like?" Grandma's voice asked me.

I jumped. She had marched right next to me without my noticing. She moved as silently as a hunter in the movies.

"Nnn...no, not yet!" I stammered.

"Want to look some more?" Grandma was already carrying a few books herself. "There are some books I could still go over for a while."

"Sure, maybe a while longer."

I did not admit even to myself, that the reason I wanted to stay was to see if the young man was somewhere in the store. He really was a sight for sore eyes...Kitty's laughter seemed to sound again in my head. "A sight for sore eyes? You sound middle-aged sometimes. Eye candy, Dana, eye candy!"

But I did not see him again, which I found a bit strange, considering that I had a direct view to the store door over the shelves, and I was absolutely certain he had not gone out. Surely no one would use the back exit to a store. Unless he was staff?

In the end, I did buy two books - one about cat breeds, as I'd planned, and another about the pyramids of Egypt. It was one of my dreams to travel to Egypt. My father had promised he would take me there, when I graduated. But the turmoil of late, after the unrest of the Arab spring, was making my father reconsider his agreement.

Carrying her heavy bag of books with considerable ease Grandma then dragged me across the street to a clothes store, to "supplement your wardrobe" as she put it.

"You look as though you're wearing someone's grandmother's hand-me-downs, my girl!" She shook her head. "And I am not talking about myself!"

Obviously not. She was always so casually elegant. One of those ladies who looked good in everything she wore - though it was mostly jeans and some exciting blouse or jacket. Her trimmed body of course played a big role in that. I had long had the suspicion that she lived in a combined gym and beauty parlor. No one should be so fit at her age. She looked like a long distance runner.

After buying me a new pair of jeans ("Oh forget the baggy ones!") and three shirts ("Don't even think cowboy-style!") she yanked me off to a shoe store.

Eventually I looked like a born again shopper with all the bags I was carrying, and I got approving and slightly envious glances from my classmates who happened to walk past us when we headed for a cafe.

"Hi, Dana!" Elaine waved a tanned hand so that the gold bracelets on her slender wrist clinked together. "Nice jeans!"

I managed what I hoped was a laid-back smile, while I tried to stay erect in my high-heels and make out I wore them every day. ("Don't you ever be ashamed of being tall! And keep your knees locked - nothing looks worse than someone in high heels with their knees bent," I remembered Grandma's advice). High-heels, for heaven's sake! What was Grandma thinking! But obviously I had done something to get the approval of the Blonde Section - Elaine and her giggling court. All in different shades of blond hair color: ash blonde, strawberry blonde, bombshell blonde and golden blonde.

We weren't exactly on the same page, even though superficially I looked the part that day. I was a bookworm, for one thing. They called me "a nerd" and also English terms that I hadn't understood at first, because I never knew the latest singers or make-up trends, and wasn't interested in movie stars or the latest sighting of whoever happened to be Hot in their books. They mimicked my American accent and made fun of me, but they avidly tried to dress and act like the American High School teenagers that they saw in TV programs. Knowledge of history didn't rate very highly on their list of "what's hot". When I'd once told them that I wanted to study Egyptology, they had looked back at me with blank eyes. Finally one of them had said "Egyptology? What the hell's that?" emphasising her words in a way that indicated I was a freak, in their own terms. Still, I wasn't considered an enemy, because I posed no obvious threat to them on the dating scene, being so tall and not wearing much makeup, and with my mind being off on other things a lot of the time.

I managed a relaxed wave and walked past the Blond Section, feeling their eyes on my back. Their combined perfumes hit us like a wall as we passed.

"You do need some nice high heel shoes, now that you are turning into a gorgeous young woman, Dana," Grandma commented, as though she'd been reading my thoughts on the Blonde Section and dating. "At home you can loll around in whatever you want, but when you go out on a date..." she made some appropriate noises in imitation of a man's approval. I was waiting for her to give one of her loud, shrill wolf-whistles - that was another one of Grandma's skills - but thankfully on this occasion, she didn't burst my eardrums.

I sighed and rolled my eyes.

"Not you too! Mom is always trying to find out if I've got a guy hidden away somewhere!"

Grandma laughed out loud and voiced her doubts as to what my mother would do if she actually found a boyfriend hidden in my room. While the scene of such an event played vividly in my mind, Grandma opened the door to a little coffee shop. She rushed to meet and greet her old friend, who ran the shop, and as that would likely take a few moments, I went ahead and sat down to a table next to the window. I reached for my cell phone in my bag and felt something that should not have been there.

A book. Well, of course there were the two books Grandma had bought for me, but this one was definitely neither of those By the feel of it, it was an old book. I took it out of the bag.

"What's in a Dream – a Scientific and Practical Interpretation of Dreams" the cover said.

I had always been interested in dream interpretation so I opened the cover to have a better look.

The book was old – it said it had been printed by the G.W.Dillingham company, NY in 1901. There was something written inside the cover – in old fashioned handwriting, the words written with real ink. It seemed to be someone's dream, written down in the book because the dreamer had thought it important.

"I dreamt of angels and ghosts in the sky, fighting for the throne hidden in the mists. There was a war going on in the mountains, in the seas, over the lakes, rivers, fields, cities and villages. Castles and towers fell into the fire. Waves of the ocean threw ships on dry land. Lightning struck from thunder clouds and death was walking the streets. I took shelter in a house in the hills, deep in the forest, where I was safe. I traveled through a gate to a land of sleep, and suddenly I awoke, surrounded by friends and there was great joy and light and laughing and hugging. But we knew we would have to draw our

swords, take the key, open the door to the garden of Adam and Eve, and of the apple tree of wisdom, the seed of which was sown by the guardians of the orchard. But the snake, the dangerous adder was spying on us with its soldiers, under their flag and black banner and flames were devouring their hearts. We escaped them to our strongholds of stone where their jaws could not bite, but they stole our children and turned them into monsters who attacked their parents, their brothers, and their family. And tears rained in the midst of ruins where once beauty resided. So we went running to a library of books and ancient letters, to gain victory over our enemy and end this battle. And in the library there grew a beautiful flower, a lovely rose which I took. And when I woke up, I still held it in my hand."

A strange dream to be sure...

There was something more scribbled under the dream. 1-1, 2-2, 3-3, 1-1...

"What's that you are reading?" Grandma had managed to sneak right up behind me without making a noise. How did she do that?

"Oh, this? It seems to be an old dream book. I found it in my bag but I have no idea how it got in there."

"Hmm... maybe it had been there for a while and you'd just forgotten you had it. That's happened to me in the past. Here, I bought us cappuccinos. Don't let yours get cold."

She placed the tray on the table and bent closer to have a look at the handwritten dream.

"What a strange dream!" she echoed my sentiments. "Maybe you should try to interpret that!"

"That might be fun," I admitted, closing the book and putting it back in my bag, managing to get my finger caught in the bag's zipper in the process. When I sucked the blood from my finger, something bumped against the window next to my face. I almost screamed.

A little girl without front teeth was smiling back at me, her ice-creamy hands leaving palm prints on the glass. She had a Hello Kitty balloon tied to her shirt button and the wind was bouncing it against the window right at my eye level.

On the other side of the street I saw the blonde young man. He just stood there, looked at me directly, his eyes piercing the space between us. I felt a sudden shortness of breath - the beauty of his ice blue eyes was out of this world, even at this distance.

For a fleeting moment I almost remembered him. Then a truck drove between us, and when it had gone, so was he. Vanished into thin air.

After the initial shock of his sudden disappearance, I felt a surprising surge of disappointment.

8

THE HIDDEN MESSAGE

When I look back, I wish I could have had the option of just throwing the book away, so that nothing would have changed. But how could I not be curious? Also, throwing the book away would not have stopped the change. What was going to happen would have happened nevertheless, and I would have been in much greater danger, unprepared.

I really thought at first that it was a book about dream interpretation.

I had no idea how the book had ended up in my duffel bag. It could have dropped into the open bag from the shelf when I fell against it, I supposed. The only flaw in this scenario was that the bookstore only sold new books. There was no second hand stock at all. Anything this old wasn't available there.

But somewhere, someone had placed it in my bag. I had a bad habit of not closing my bag securely, because where I lived felt safe. Our little town was so old fashioned that anyone caught pick-pocketing would have been dragged off to the local church, where he (or she) would have been put on the gallows, or made to write a thousand times "Thou shalt not steal" on a blackboard in front of the whole congregation. Or possibly both. Something along those lines, anyway. It was hard to tell, because it was the kind of thing that never, ever happened. If you dropped a penny in the street, someone would be sure to point it out to you and hand it back.

I suspected the young man at the bookstore had a hand in it. Of course he might have dropped the book in my bag by accident. Or even deliberately. If I ever saw him again, I would ask straight out, I decided, not admitting I was hoping I might actually see him again. Whatever it was in this case, I had no way of knowing to whom the book belonged, and as it was, I could not return it to its rightful owner.

So, when the evening came and everyone went to bed, I propped my pillows comfortably against the headboard, put on the reading light, took my notebook and pencil, and started interpreting the dream written inside the cover, all snug under my lightweight summer blanket. I thought I'd probably fall asleep pretty soon.

I didn't. I had no idea that this dream book would change my whole life, and nothing in my world was going to be normal ever again.

I took a chocolate (yes, I confess that I'd actually placed a box of strawberry chocolates on the bed to truly enjoy the book, which I still thought was about dreams).

"Now let's see what the book says about angels..." I took the first word from the hand-written dream and started leafing through the pages. "Amputation... anchor...andirons... anecdote... angels!"

I expected to read something about divine intervention or some such thing, considering when the book had been printed. But what I read was all gibberish, at least the first part.

"To You dream of hold in angels is prophetic your hands a of book disturbing influences about the in the soul gates between our It human brings a world and changed condition of the Unseen Worlds the person's lot. If the dream is unusually pleasing, you will hear of the health of friends, and receive a legacy from unknown relatives.

If the dream comes as a token of warning, the dreamer may expect threats of scandal about love or money matters. To wicked people, it is a demand to repent; to good people it should be a consolation."

"What on earth are they trying to say?" I said out loud, making Nugget lift his sleepy head and glance at me.

I decided to try a random word. Nugget. Cats. I would see what the book said about cats.

"To dream of a cat, denotes ill luck, if you do not succeed in killing it or driving it from your sight. If the cat attacks you, you will have enemies who will go to any extreme to blacken your reputation and to cause you loss of property. But if you succeed in banishing it, you will overcome great obstacles and rise in fortune and fame..." I read to Nugget. "Hmm, someone did not like cats, it seems... but at least that is coherent. Something must have gone wrong at the printing company when it came to angels... Oh well, maybe I should just go to sleep and see if I have a dream I could try and interpret with this book."

I placed the book on my bedside table and switched the light off. Instead of sleeping, my mind started nagging about something. One two three, one two three... I was repeating the numbers in my mind over and over again. And then I realized, why. 1-1, 2-2, 3-3, 1-1... The numbers written in the cover of the book. They had to be meaningful. What if...

I reached for the bedside lamp and put the light back on. Then I took the book, opened its worn pages and searched for the *angel* again.

"Ok, now what is this 1-1... Probably it means words. So the first word is 'To'," I reached for my notebook and wrote the word on top of a page, "but why the second number one..."

I stared at the interpretation of angel but did not get it.

"Could it mean the word is a pair with some other word...?" I asked Nugget who instead of looking at me tucked his nose under his paw in a silent protest at being disturbed by the light again.

"OK, let's give that a try then. If it is a pair of words, then logically the next word is the other half of the pair," I announced and wrote the word "You" on the right side of the word ""To". I noticed both words were written with a capital letter. Another mistake by the printing press, it seemed.

Or was it...?

"2-2..."

I wrote the next two words on the left side of the notebook page, and the two words after that on their right side. Now I had three words on the left *"To dream of"* and three on the right: *"You hold in"*. Both beginning with capital letters, both... the beginnings of a sentence!

Quickly I wrote the words 3-3, to the left came *"angels is prophetic"* and to the right *"your hands a"*.

"To dream of angels is prophetic' and *'You hold in your hands a'*," I mumbled out loud, excited I had cracked the code, "and now it seems it is back to 1-1 again... '*of*' goes to the left and '*book*' to the right... Then 2-2..."

When I had finished, on the left it said, *"To dream of angels is prophetic of disturbing influences in the soul. It brings a changed condition of the person's lot."* And on the right I had written *"You hold in your hands a book about the gates between our human world and the Unseen Worlds"*.

Before Kitty's death I would have stopped reading right there, following Mom's advice that such subjects were not safe to study. But did I? Have a guess. Instead of closing the book, I searched for the next word in the dream on the cover.

"*Ghosts,"* I whispered to Nugget whose whiskers twitched in his sleep and whispered the words of explanation to ghosts the dream book: *"To The dream of legends have the ghost of always told of either another one of level of your parents, denotes existence, or parallel that worlds. you are exposed to danger, and you should be careful in forming partnerships with strangers."*

I wrote fast now, and to the left of my notebook page appeared a sentence telling me that *"The dream of the ghost of either one of your parents, denotes that you are exposed to danger, and you should be careful in forming partnerships with strangers."* And to its right I had written *"The legends have always told of another level of existence, or parallel worlds"*.

"Sky is the next word..."

This time I did not bother writing the dream interpretation anymore, but just wrote down the other words. "*Sky*" revealed the sentence *"These are not merely stories – these worlds really exist"*.

I felt goose bumps rising on my arms. There was a hidden message in the book, and the handwritten dream was the key to it. You had to read the words in the right order to get the message.

I could not stop now. Mechanically I reached for a chocolate and wrote down what the word *"fighting"* would add to the story. *"There are many who have found their way to the other realities and many who would want to find the way."*

I did not notice the time passing, Sentence by sentence the odd story appeared in my notebook.

"So keep this book hidden, and do not speak of it to others else you put yourself in danger. These Unseen Worlds are all around us. We can live there in our physical bodies, and we travel through them when it is our time to leave our earthly existence. Sometimes it is possible to make contact with those who have already died, though this is not easy for our lack of the finer senses needed for such contact.

There have always been people who can contact the other side, usually through years of study. Some are naturals. And frequently these people are labelled mad, swindlers, or servants of the devil. And there have certainly been plenty of swindlers taking advantage of the grief of others, pretending to be mediums. But there are also those who can see and hear the souls of those who have passed."

My eyes were glued to the dream book and my notes.

"The afterlife exists, and there is a buffer zone between our physical world, and the afterlife. People can reach this buffer zone in their sleep. Some people learn to wake themselves up when they are in this buffer zone. This is called lucid dreaming. It is a skill that can be learned, but usually it only lasts a few seconds.

And this is also the level to which those that have gone before can return with relative ease. Here they try to communicate with their sleeping loved ones, and this results in vivid dreams where we meet with our departed ones. Our finer senses are awake when our earthly senses are asleep, and can make it possible for us to remember those dreams, usually a few moments after we wake up, and before our analytical mind explains the dreams away as wishful thinking."

I threw the blanket aside, got up and took Kitty's letter from between the pages of the dictionary where I had hidden it, and read what she had written about Darryl. And the other thing she had written about... where was it... there: *"Maybe I'll drop a book for you to read - that would get your attention, bookworm that you are. Yes, I just might contact you through a book. I cannot tell you what it is, because I have to keep its secret, and someone other than you might find this letter. Still, it has to do with dreams. You will understand what I mean when the time comes."*

When I read these words, my skin turned to goose bumps. Had Kitty got this very book too? If so, from whom? Would that explain her great interest in what happened after death? Suddenly I remembered my dream from the night Kitty died, the one where she was fetched by an angel... and how she had given him what looked like a book... Now it was not only my skin that was all over goose pimples - I felt my hair standing up on end, too.

"What is not known is that there are openings into this buffer zone from the physical world. If someone manages to train their mind to keep awake, they can come and go to and from this zone freely, using these gates. They can only reach their own level, which is dictated by their energies. This means there are very dark and heavy places there, created by dark minds, as well as lighter ones. The deeper a person goes into the buffer zone, the less time has an effect on them. Whoever stays there doesn't grow any older, even when time is passing in the physical world. "

I was beginning to wonder about the modern terms used in this book. Exactly how old were the expressions "buffer zone", "analytical mind" or "lucid dreaming"? Much more modern than this little book's appearance. The next sentence answered this question.

"This book was written in the beginning of the twentieth century, so that it could travel through time to pass on the word of the gates to those people throughout history who might help. So we have continued to look for them from the future, studying history to find them, and giving them this book to read. We have other methods to reach those who lived before this book was printed. We need people of different times to work with us. "

To work with whom? To help in what? Help whom? And what did

the writer mean by "visiting them in the past?" Time travel? It had to be time travel... but time travel was not possible. My eyes were now glued to the old, brown pages. Their condition at least revealed this book had travelled a long way in time.

"Unfortunately the knowledge of the gates has spread. Now these gates are being sought by those who should not be allowed to find them. And unfortunately there are ways to enter the buffer zone without the gates, though humans cannot do it on their own. Still, with some help, many have found their way there. They use the buffer zone for evil purposes - and they stay practically immortal within it, building their own kingdom there, deep inside the zone. They call this place the City of Immortals. The inhabitants of this place cause havoc in the human world when they visit it in their shadow form. We have learned they have other aspirations as well, much worse than simply finding riches and power in the past. To find them and to stop them, we need a group of helpers. These people are carefully chosen."

I was beginning not to like what I read. What was it that the *"humans cannot do.... on their own"* and what did *"when they visit it in their shadow form"* mean? What the heck was this book trying to say? It felt more and more like the ramblings of a madman.

"Also you should know that not all who die go into the lighter levels of the afterlife. They are the ones who have done horrible deeds to others, and as a result their energies are so low they would have difficulties in moving any higher even if they wanted to.

Some of these dark souls like to stay near the physical world, and feed on people's fears. These would be the ghosts. Being in contact with human fears helps them stay in their own, lower energy worlds, because human thoughts are energy. Negative and positive thoughts are real things in the buffer zone; physical, mouldable material. And those who live in the buffer zone, on the lowest levels of the Unseen Worlds, have built their worlds from these energies. If their world begins to thin out, they go to the human world, and cause fear, and take that energy and rebuild their domain."

OK, this was officially beyond strange. Whoever wrote this need not fear I would ever quote any of this to an outsider. I'd end up in a padded cell in no time. But I realized I could no longer stop reading, either. Mechanically, I took another chocolate, but I couldn't really taste it any more.

"These souls, together with the living people of the City of Immortals and their shadows, are the source of the ghost-, vampire-, werewolf and evil spirit-stories. The shadows can go anywhere they want to, with no need to use the gates; they can come into the human world, and then vanish back before they are caught. Humans cannot do this unaided. No one is safe from these shadows, not as long as they can freely walk through the borderline between the human world and the buffer zone."

Oh great - I had been a very scared young girl, believing in ghosts and vampires, and it had been a huge job for Mom to make me unbelieve in them. It wasn't that long ago that I'd stopped using a night-light. And now this... odd book told me I had been right all along? That those horrible creatures actually existed?? And to make it even worse - there was no way I could be safe from them?

"And now to the reason you are holding this book: It contains information on how you can find a gate to the Unseen Worlds. You need to find it on your own, following a trail of clues, to gain permanent right and skills to walk through the gates. And you have been considered able to do this by someone who has travelled that path. Someone, who trusts you have the qualities to do the work.

"You are invited to join us, if you know how to follow the clues, and find your way to us. It is essential that you don't reveal this knowledge to anyone, as that could lead the "Immortals" directly to us. So far, because of the differences in our energies, we have managed to stay hidden from them in the buffer zone. But they do know we exist. Our fight against their shadow world has made us their enemy. Nothing would be more important to them than to find the gates we use in the physical world we all share, so they could walk freely between our world and the buffer zone.

"The name of the person who told us about you is written on the back pages of this book. Check that before deciding if you want to continue."

I sighed. I knew. And when I saw Kitty's signature as the last one in a long list of names on the empty pages at the end of the book, I was not surprised.

"If you accept the invitation, follow the next advice to see what happens."

It was night already, and just as when I was a child and had read a book that was too exciting, I just wanted to feel secure, and sleep without nightmares. So I decided I'd return to the book again when it was daylight.

For a brief moment I considered finding my old night light from the cupboard, but then decided against it. I folded back the bedside lamp, drew the blanket up to my ears, and closed my eyes, hoping I could fall asleep.

9

SHADOW IN THE GARDEN

That night I had a vivid dream. So vivid, it was almost as though I was awake.

I was standing in a beautiful garden. When I looked around I realized it was the garden around our house, but it was as if all the flowers that had ever grown there were blooming at the same time. There were thousands of flowers in the most glowing colors – much more vibrant than I ever remembered seeing them. The house had almost vanished in their midst. It was like something out of a Disney film.

I felt someone approaching and turned around.

It was Kitty. She was visible only from the waist up, but it was her. When she moved it seemed as though she was wearing the garden as her dress – the flowers followed her movement, flowing with her like an evening gown. As she moved through the scenery, the garden became a supernatural fabric that fitted to her and revealed her form. If you have ever seen photographs or videos where scenery is projected onto a living person, you'll get the idea.

She was almost exactly the Kitty I had known, only somehow... clearer. Her colors were bright, but translucent.

"Kitty!" I shouted with joy, "you are alive!"

She said something but there was no sound. I concentrated,

bending closer so that I could listen better. Her lips moved but I heard nothing. Also it seemed as though she was constantly falling backwards away from me. The only way I can describe it was that it was like having vertigo, I can't explain it better than that.

"I can't hear you!" I said, frustrated.

She stopped talking. She was not looking happy, nor was she smiling like she always did. She looked at me and closed her eyes. She stood there, and then opened her eyes. She pointed at her eyes, then closed them again, and I understood. I closed my eyes too. I felt drowsiness take me and I began to fall, but in a strange way, I heard her. I didn't hear her words with my normal hearing – instead I got them, if you can imagine it, like a ball of thoughts straight into my mind, and when I concentrated on the "ball" it opened and I simply knew the words, without hearing them. Again I just can't convey this in any other way.

"Beware of the shadow." I felt roses falling down around me and somehow they were important. They were like the white roses that grew under my window.

I woke up with a jolt.

It was still night.

I knew I had really met Kitty. If the old book was right, I had been there, in the buffer zone, in my dream state. And Kitty had come to meet me. To warn me of a shadow. What shadow? And what were those roses about?

I thought I heard something outside. The slightest of sounds. I would not have paid attention to it, but then I saw Nugget. He was sitting on my bed and all the hairs on his coat were standing up. He was growling very quietly, every muscle tensed.

I felt a spasm of panic, as all my childhood fears reared their ugly heads. The shadows hiding, trying to catch me... It took all my courage to get out of bed. I moved very quietly and took my bathrobe from the back of my chair. I had socks on, so I could move quietly. I knew all the creaking floorboards – the house and I had grown up together. Instead of stepping I slid my feet forward like walking on thin ice.

I slid across the floor avoiding the creaky boards, and got to the door without a noise. The door handle was another thing – if you just pushed it down swiftly, the lock made clicking noises.

I must have spent an eternity pushing the door handle down ever so slowly. But I did make it out of my room without making a sound. Then I had to stand there in the darkness and let the handle rise just as slowly as I had pushed it down. It took forever.

I went past Grandma's room and into the living room. I made myself slide into the shadows next to the window, though the darkness there set my nerves tingling and pulse racing, and very slowly inched myself so that I could see into the garden.

And there it was. The shadow. I did not notice it at first, because everything was so peaceful and quiet. There was no wind, and that is what revealed it to me – the rosebush under my window was shivering. It was not a very dense bush – it hadn't been pruned properly, and as a result it had grown veritable trunks that did not have too many leaves near the ground. Because of this, you could usually see the white wall through it, but now you could not. Something was blocking the wall from being seen.

Nugget had followed me with stiff legs, his back arched, and his tail thick. Now he stood on the arm rest of the couch right next to the window, hissing. He licked his lips nervously, and started to growl.

"Shut up!" I said to Nugget quietly, but if you have ever tried to control an infuriated cat, you'll know they don't take orders. The electricity coming off his coat was almost visible. I know that if I'd touched him, there'd have been a snap of static.

And of course the shadow reacted to the image of the cat clearly visible through the window. I saw the shadow move and pressed myself against the living room wall, hoping I could not be seen from outside. I stood on tiptoe so my feet would not be visible.

From the corner of my eye I glimpsed something very dark glide past the window. I could not see anything clearly, but I thought that it moved like an animal, on all fours. I did not see any glowing eyes or anything fit for a horror movie, but this something was certainly not like any animal I had ever seen. It stood up on its hind legs, and that's when it almost looked half human. I felt terror rising up my spine.

Nugget's voice was turning into a wail, and soon he would give that horrible scream cats do, when they chase something out of their territory. He'd wake the entire household.

"What is it?" I heard Grandma's whisper.

"Something in the garden..." I whispered back.

Suddenly Nugget calmed down. He stood for a while and stared into the garden. His bushy tail slowly returned to normal. Then he jumped down from the sofa and ran to the kitchen. Obviously the shadowy animal was gone. I saw the wall behind the rosebush again.

"Did you see what it was?" Grandma asked.

She appeared surprisingly elegant considering she had just woken up. Her hair should have been a mess, but no. She looked like she'd just returned from a hairdresser's appointment. Did she sleep standing up? Or use a neck-rest like the ancient Egyptians so that her head never touched the bed?

"No. Some shadowy figure."

Much to my surprise Grandma froze. I could see her figure against the light of the summer night showing through the kitchen window across the hall, and her slight movement stopped as abruptly as though she'd walked into a wall.

"Shadow?" Her voice revealed no emotion, which was in odd contrast to her stiff posture.

"Yes. It was funny, really. I had a dream about Kitty and she warned me about shadows. Or a shadow, to be exact. I could not sleep after that and came to get some water from the kitchen," I lied, "and then I saw Nugget hissing at something."

Grandma remained quiet for a while.

"Oh well, it was probably a stray dog or something like that. Better go back to bed now that it has gone," she shrugged eventually and turned to walk back to her bedroom.

I was absolutely certain she was lying. You know when someone you know well is playing a role. Grandma was too careful to appear as though she was no longer interested in the subject. She knew something about that shadow. She knew about Kitty as well – it was she who had said Kitty would try to contact me, without knowing about

Kitty's letter. The strange book warned about... horrible creatures. Kitty had then warned me about a shadow, and suddenly a shadow was lurking under my window. Too many events were falling into place as parts of the same puzzle.

But I couldn't ask Grandma now. Our conversation would wake up my parents.

I walked back to my bedroom and closed the door. I would ask her when we were alone.

I could not sleep anymore, so after tossing and turning a while, I put the bedside lamp on, picked up the small book and continued reading.

10

THE BOOK'S SECRET

It took some courage to start reading the book again. I mean seriously: imagine exactly how you would feel if someone threw you a book and said "Here! Read this and learn how to go to the realm of the dead". Dead as in deceased. Dearly departed. Who - or rather what - would you expect to meet?

And I could never even watch horror movies, because my imagination was way too active. My idea of the dead was pretty close to the creatures in Michael Jackson's Thriller video. Did I even want to reach that realm? Before Kitty's death, no, definitely not. But now... I missed her so much that I knew my curiosity was growing to see if I could contact her again, for real, not just through some mysterious hints. Especially after that night's dream, and seeing the shadowy creature. Yes, it had scared me out of my wits, but it also confirmed for me that the message of the book and the dream were real.

So I took a deep breath and opened the book to read how to find the gate that took me, literally, to the Other Side. The Unseen Worlds.

"We cannot give the location of the gate in writing – this book may fall into the wrong hands. It may have done so already, physically, or by word of mouth. So we need to reach you in a place where it is safer, and where we can guard you against any shadows.

In short: you need to learn lucid dreaming and wake up in the buffer zone. We will be waiting for you there. We are already observing you and your dreams, so we shall be ready for you."

Someone was watching me dreaming? They would know all my deepest secrets in that case. I blushed out of sheer embarrassment.

"Do the following: firstly, during the daytime, look at your hand frequently. Every time you see your hand, count the fingers and say to yourself 'Is this a dream or am I awake?' Secondly, look at books and anything with writing on it, read the words, concentrate hard on the letters. And thirdly, if you see a clock – look at it quickly, twice, to check the time. Ask yourself again, 'Am I awake or is this a dream?' And teach yourself to stay very calm, almost emotionless when you are doing this.

It may take you days, even weeks, but your mind will learn to look for these things, and it will happen that one night, when you sleep and dream, you will notice a book or some writing, a clock, or your hand, in your sleep and your mind will remember what you taught it while you were awake. Your mind will pay attention to these things.

When this happens, do the same thing you did when you were awake. Count the fingers – you notice they are not normal. They may be stumps, you may lack a finger or have too many. You notice you cannot read text. You will see the time has changed between your glances at the clock.

When you have taught your mind to always question if you are dreaming or are awake, it will do so in your dream too, when you see any of these signs. And this is when you wake up in your dream. If you don't get excited, you will remain there, in your dream, fully awake. If you get excited, the dream reality will fade away from around you, because your strong emotions draw you back to your waking reality.

This is why it is important to teach yourself to remain calm. It will give us time to pass our message to you. Trust us, we are here all the time, seeing you when you dream, waiting for you to wake up in the buffer zone."

And that's it. There was no more text in the book. Frustrated, I threw my blanket aside and got out of bed. I had expected a map at least. Or some magical object that would transfer me to another realm. But lucid dreaming? Sheesh...

Still, to be on the safe side, I had to hide the book, if only so that Mom would not find it... But where? If these shadows could come and go as they pleased, surely they might lurk anywhere, and see where I hid the book. But if the book said it should be hidden, then hide it I would.

It was too thick to put behind a painting. Anyone would turn the paintings around if they were looking for hidden stuff.

If I put it in my bookshelf, it would be enough to pull all the books out of the shelf and find it.

Then I saw Nugget. He was curled up in his very hairy cat-bed under my desk. Mom never touched the bed ("Too much of a big, hairy deal - pun intended!"). There was no point in cleaning it, because Nugget shed a fair amount of hair, and the black, round pillow he slept on had turned red with time.

The pillow had lots of padding, and a zipper at the side - the idea was that you could toss the outer pillow case into a washing machine. Mom announced that all that cat hair would just choke the machine and that it would be my responsibility to clean the pillow using some other method.

Well, I had never done that, which did not seem to bother Nugget in the least. The pillow looked a mess, to be honest. Not something you would want to touch voluntarily. But Nugget loved it, and the more "Nuggety" it became, the more he adored it and the deeper his purring grew as he rolled about on it.

It was the best I could come up with, anyway. I lifted Nugget out of his bed and opened the zipper on the side of the pillow. I separated the layers of padding inside and slid the book in there, closed the zipper, and put the pillow back. Nugget had already hopped on my bed to continue his dreams.

I stopped to look at my hands, when I pressed the hairy pillow back into its basket. I counted my fingers and asked myself quietly:

"Am I awake, or is this a dream?"

11

THE STORY OF THE WAX CROCODILE

The odd thing about her was that she was a beekeeper. A woman who should have been the mistress of a house, taking care of her family. She could have grown old among her loved ones, content in the certainty that one day her children would perform burial rites for her, to guarantee her soul a happy afterlife. But instead she had chosen the lonely life of a beekeeper and spent her life among her "children" as she called them. If anyone thought of it as odd, they did not say so to her face. After someone talked with her for a while they understood her deep wisdom, and chose not to mock her.

My earliest memories were of watching her tending to her bees. Mother never seemed to mind leaving me together with Mut-Bity. That was not her real name, she never revealed it to anyone. Not even us. But I called her that because I thought she was the Mother of Bees.

I sat in the shadow, under a small tree, wrapped in a big linen cloth, and paid attention to Mut-Bity's work.

"These creatures should always be revered," she said to me solemnly, staring at me under her eyebrows as if she needed to be angry with me.

"Yes, Mut-Bity," I replied as was expected of me.

"Do you know why?" she kept on looking at me with solemn eyes.

"Yes, I do," I said and pulled my toes under my wrap so the sun would not touch them. "They give us honey!"

That was an easy one, as Mut-Bity was just kneeling in front of the beehives, smoking the bees with a burning piece of dried cow dung. She did that when she wanted to check how they were doing, how much honey her children had gathered. The smoke calmed them down.

There were nine hives in all that she carried with her. They were of burnt clay, so they were much finer than many other hives I had seen elsewhere. Those were usually made of dried mud of the River. Mut-Bity's were stronger and better than most, and she took great care of them. She had put them so that there were four on the bottom row, three on the next and two at the top. The tubes tapered slightly towards the other end.

"Now that was easy," Mut-Bity repeated my thoughts, "But there is more, tell me."

I looked at the bees buzzing around her, mesmerized by their hum in the heat. They seemed to gather around her whenever she approached the hives, and I had never witnessed any of them stinging her. I was lost in the hum of the bees for a while and my thoughts wandered.

"Shuet?"

I almost jumped back to reality.

"Women can demand honey jars in their marriage contract," Mut-Bity said, "And believe me - a woman's lot is not enviable, so any sweetening to it is much recommended! That is why I preferred just the sweet part and did not get married."

We shared a companiable laugh. Her cheeks were baked dark in the sunlight and laughter created long thin lines that curved over her cheekbones. Still she did not look old. Just sun-baked. So different from the delicate skinned fine ladies of the nobility, who spent their days indoors, weaving and supervising servants. And also very different from the servants and slaves who were aged by their hard work. I never really wondered about Mut-Bity's age. She was old like all adults were and that was it.

"Tell me about beeswax," she asked me.

I looked down the field towards the River. Little boats were sailing there. I saw a burial boat with mourners on the way to Abdju. Someone who had not made the trip to the burial place of Osiris in their lifetime, probably. So the family took them now on that trip after they had been prepared for death, before burial.

I recognized one other boat - it was another beekeeper with whom we often travelled. The bee-season was almost over here, and soon we would move downriver towards the north, to new fields that needed the bees. It was time to ask for the local peasants for donkeys to get the hives to the riverbank and into the boat.

"The priests and magicians need beeswax," I said, but not being in the mood to concentrate too much, I added, "Tell me the story of the wax crocodile!"

Mut-Bity rose and wiped her hands on her dress.

"Now why would you like to hear that story? It is scary, no?"

She snapped her fingers in front of my face, holding the fingers tight together and opening and closing them against her thumbs, as if her fingers were crocodile jaws. I giggled.

"No it is not! The bad man got punished!"

"How do you know he was a bad man? What if he loved her? What if her husband was mean to her? You never know, so do not judge!"

I looked at Mut-Bity questioningly, trying to see if she was angry with me. The sun made my eyes water. Mut-Bity smiled and wiped the tears from my cheeks, knowing they were caused not by sorrow but by the sun. She pulled my covering over my face so that she disappeared from sight and I could only see her feet. Strong feet, with surprisingly delicate ankles. And thick soles. I looked at her toe nails, wondering how she kept them so neat and clean, walking in the dust and mud barefoot like the rest of us. My own toes, peeking out again from under my covering, were very dusty and dirty. I think I had stepped on donkey dung on our way to the field.

"Very well. I shall tell you the story of the wax crocodile," I heard the smile in her voice.

She sat down next to me and pulled me closer with her strong, thin, wiry arm. I loved being held by Mut-Bity. Her touch was so soothing.

"Aba-Aner was a great magician who lived a long long time ago, during the times of the great king Nebka. Aba-Aner was a priest and knew of the hidden powers of magic. He found out his wife had a lover, a young man from the king's retinue, but did not tell her he knew how she had ordered their country house by the pool to be made ready. She then met this young man there, and they ate, drank and enjoyed each other's company - and bathed in the water.

No, Aba-Aner did not tell her, or anyone else, that he knew. Instead he created a crocodile of beeswax, seven fingers long. He recited certain magical spells over it and gave it to his steward. He knew his wife's lover would come and bathe at the pool the next time they met. And so he did, and the steward threw the wax crocodile into the water.

The crocodile turned into a real crocodile, seven cubits long, which attacked the youth and pulled him under water."

I held my breath. I knew the youth had done the same for he was still alive in the next part of the story.

"Aba-Aner was with the king for seven days, and after those days he was summoned before the king. He said: 'Your Majesty would like to see a prodigy which has happened in the time of your Majesty.' And so they went to the pond. Aba-Aner summoned the crocodile to bring up the youth, and the crocodile obeyed. It had to, because Aba-Aner was its creator and knew its magical name. And he then told the king what the youth had been doing with Aba-Aner's wife."

Under my cloth, I covered my eyes with my hands. This was a bit too scary, really, but it was daylight and so I could hear the rest as well.

"The king said to the crocodile: 'Take what is yours and go down.' And the crocodile once more took the youth and pulled him into the depths of the pond, and he was never seen again. The young wife of Aba-Aner was taken and burned and her ashes were scattered in the pond... "

I couldn't help but let out a little squeal.

"And so they both died and were no more," Mut-Bity said in a deep storyteller's voice. "And they had no bodies their souls could return to after that... They were doomed."

"But they could have lived on..." said a strange voice behind me.

12

EYES OF BLUE AT THE BOOKSTORE

Days passed and still Grandma showed no signs of leaving. I heard Mom grumbling to Dad: "Has she moved in permanently?"

It seemed to me that Grandma had suddenly changed her plans after the night of the shadow in the garden. Previously she had told us she was intending to stay only for three days. Now she told me that she was enjoying her little holiday so much she would be with us for longer. Somehow I was convinced it was because of the garden episode, even though she never mentioned it again. To be honest, she seemed to be purposely avoiding the subject.

"And you, Dana... is there something wrong with your hands?" Mom asked me one morning after having a complaint session with Dad.

"No. Why?"

"You keep looking at them all the time as if you had a rash or something."

"Oh, maybe my skin is a bit dry." I came up with an explanation quickly. "I should buy some hand cream, I think. Too much digging in the garden..."

That much was true - I had been working in the garden. I had very carefully checked the rosebush under my window the morning after the shadow. I'd found some black and grey hairs there, but when I came to pick them up to put them into a little plastic bag, they deteriorated straight away. They broke at my touch into tiny bits and dust that basically just vanished into thin air. I had never seen anything like it before.

I wanted to see if the shadow had been to any other parts of the garden, and so I tended to the flowers and bushes as the pretext whilst I was really searching for clumps of hair similar to the one under the rose bush. I found nothing. On the dusty road there were some slight imprints, but it was impossible to say what or who had caused them.

"Good. I need to go to town, you can come with me to buy your hand cream," mother decided, clearly pleased that I was finally showing an interest in skin creams and all that stuff.

"Should we ask if Grandma..."

"No, let's just go, right away," she insisted. Her voice told me in no uncertain terms that Grandma's presence was not wanted.

So we did not wait for Grandma, who was out on some errand, and had promised to be back in time for dinner.

Mom drove our old hatchback slowly to town – she had always been a nervous driver and chose to drive slowly. Sometimes too slowly. But if someone passed us by and swerved back right in front of us in protest for us blocking the road, she never said a word. Instead she just squeezed the wheel, her knuckles white, and looked straight ahead. For some reason I held my breath when Mom drove at her regular snail-pace, but I never did when Grandma's little red sports car flew along these small back roads.

The little bell of the beauty parlor's door rang cheerfully when Mom opened it. Mom loved to have any opportunity to visit here, and spent some time choosing a face cream for her and a hand cream for me.

"Hand cream for the young lady?" the lady behind the counter grabbed my hands and pulled me towards her before I could say cat. "Tut tut! You have been digging in the garden without gloves on, haven't you?"

"I do try to tell her... but she has always been a bit of a tomboy," my mother sighed and the two women shook their heads in agreement, making me feel like I had broken some unwritten female rule.

We left, with our shopping swinging in a stylish small paper bag Mom held. Mom looked happy, as she always did after the opportunity to buy some of life's little luxuries.

"I could go to the hairdresser's..." Mom pondered and looked at me, "if they have time for me, that is. Could you find something to do in the meantime?"

"Sure, of course!" I was more than happy to head to the bookstore again.

It was a bright, sunny day, and I felt as though I had nothing to fear. A week had already passed since the night I saw the shadow, and I had almost convinced myself that it had just been a homeless dog. That would have explained Nugget's reaction to it. He was not the kind of cat you see on YouTube snuggling up to a dog. He did not like dogs. Period. A video of Nugget and a dog would not be something that would get any "awwww" or "squee" comments on social media.

Sunshine made everything beautiful and my spirits lifted after the beauty parlor episode. I cheerfully greeted Mrs. Brown who was reading a ladies' magazine behind her counter, and made my way slowly down the aisles, checking out what was new. Mrs. Brown was something of a marvel in her small-town bookstore – she always had the latest bestsellers, but also books from special fields as well – like Egyptology.

I found an interesting book about Amenhotep III and was leafing through its pages when a slight movement caught my eye. I turned my head to see better, and there was nothing where the movement had been. I was certain I had seen something to my right, and yet in that direction this particular isle of shelves ended at the wall – and the movement had been between me and the wall. There was no place for anyone to hide.

My heart thumped in my throat and I could feel that my palms began to sweat. The shadows... They could be anywhere they wanted or so the book had said. I glanced at my hand. One, two, three, four fingers and a thumb. All perfectly in order. Definitely not a dream.

Everything was dead still. I tried to look normal and turned back to my book, my scalp tingling with fear. There was a mirror on the wall in front of me, a few shelves away, and I glanced at it.

There. Something moved again – it was as if there was an invisible form that somehow warped everything around it into its shape, a bit like Kitty in the dream. You could barely see its outline, but it was there. And it seemed to be human. If you imagine how an invisible man would have been shown in a movie, you'll get the general idea.

I snapped the book shut and almost ran to the counter. Even though I was starting to panic something in me noted that I could still read the title and the author clearly. Not a dream!

"Aha, you found your book, then," Mrs. Brown smiled and I realized I was still squeezing the book. "It came into the shop only two days ago. I thought you would like it! If someone had asked for it, I would have told them it was reserved for you."

"Oh, well, yes..." I dug out my wallet from my handbag and realized I did not have enough money to buy it. "Oh dear, it seems I didn't bring enough..."

"Hi, Dana!"

I swirled around. It was *him* – though this time he looked even more handsome because his skin had tanned a bit. He smiled. The kind of smile you would expect to see in a movie magazine. Or a fashion magazine.

"How fortunate that we bumped into one another again - well, not literally this time! Here's what I owe you. Thanks for lending it to me!" He put the money into my hand so fast I had no time to react.

There was just enough for me to buy the book. Mrs. Brown smiled and her pudgy hand took the money from my still open palm in one elegant swoop. She put the book in a bag and handed it to me. I thanked her like a robot, and walked out, not quite certain of what had just happened.

He followed me out into the street, very closely; I could feel the heat of his body when his tall frame almost touched me. I did not like anyone standing so near to me. I turned around, with the intention of telling him that, and in the process managed to get the toe of my shoe stuck in some crack in the pavement. The resulting pirouette made me fall right against him.

His arms were around me immediately. I could feel his heat – he was so hot he felt feverish. For a second I was glad I had put on one of the shirts Grandma had bought me, instead of the worn and washed-out old T-shirts that I preferred to wear, which were way past their colorful days. Then I realized what I was thinking and that I was there, not moving, leaning against his chest. Suddenly I became very aware of his arms around me. My brain went into overdrive, telling me that his mysterious appearance had had once again coincided with something weird happening. First the book, now the... something in the bookstore.

"Let me go!" I breathed. My voice sounded feeble, even to me.

He did, immediately, and for a short while I looked him straight in the eyes. I had never seen eyes that blue. And of course I blushed. Damn! I hated that I blushed so easily. I could feel the red patches rising on my neck and cheeks. Oh great. I bet I was covered in blotches. His gaze slid to my necklace – the one Grandma had given me. Then his eyes were back on my eyes, with a slightly amused twinkle. The draw of his gaze was strong and insistent. I had never felt such... presence in anyone's eyes.

I shook myself awake, and counted one plus one. I felt half paralyzed, and forced myself to move and step back from him.

"Who are you? Are you one of the shadows? Why did you give me that book? How do you know my name?" My questions blurted out one after another, not giving him the chance to answer them.

Suddenly I was furious, maybe because I was embarrassed at being drawn into those blue, insistent eyes. I was certain now that this young man was not ordinary. He had been there when I got the book. He had appeared right after I saw the invisible... something... in the bookstore. He knew my name. How could he know my name? I had never met him... Or had I? I wasn't sure. He certainly had a feeling of familiarity about him. And damn he was hot. And I don't mean just his body temperature.

"Shadow?" his smile widened even more. Good grief, he actually had a dimple. "No, I don't consider myself a shadow. Indeed not," he chuckled to himself. A low purring chuckle that made me swallow.

"But in there..." I pointed at the bookstore, "there was something - or someone - who is not... human. I saw it. Or didn't. It was like movement... Invisible..."

I shut up and realized that his eyes had grown serious as they stared into mine, as though he was searching for something. Of course. My sanity. That was the thing he was missing. If he was not one of those shadows Kitty had warned me against, then he probably thought I was nuts. Not only did I stumble against people for no reason, but I also mumbled about shadows and invisibility.

"Dana!" Mom's voice saved me.

I turned hastily and walked away from him, still feeling the warmth of his body through my thin shirt, sure that I had made a total fool of myself.

13

THE DREAM

That night I finally made it. I had been staring at my (now beautifully soft) hands and counting my fingers for a week. I had looked at clocks twice every time I needed to know the time. I had stopped in the middle of any text I was reading, and asked myself quietly whether I was awake or dreaming.

The first few days, nothing special had happened. I had ordinary dreams, not even nightmares. I did, though, have the feeling I was being observed. Still, I explained to myself, that this might have been because I had read someone was observing my dreams, not a sign that someone actually was doing it. I suppose I needed to assure myself that I was still sane, and not quite believing what I had read.

And then it happened. I was fast asleep with Nugget lying by my side. I dreamt of the bookstore, and reached for a book. I saw my hand and suddenly I thought "Is this a dream or am I awake?" I counted my fingers and two of them were stumps! My mind popped right open and suddenly I was aware I was dreaming, watching the dream book I had just taken from the shelf.

I had taught myself to stay calm, so I concentrated on trying to read the name of the book. There was nothing on the spine. I opened the book; there was nothing on the pages.

"Dana!" someone said softly, "look at the fifth name on the list."

I turned around and saw a woman - her wheat-colored hair was in a loose bundle on her neck, she had no makeup, and she wore a bright blue shirt.

She spoke one more time, keeping my eyes in her hypnotizing gaze, which had me mesmerized.

"He lives in..."

She said a name of a city.

"Go, you are expected," the woman said.

And then I suddenly felt the enormity of what I was experiencing. I was actually awake in my dream! I had made it!

And this is when the dreamscape started melting away from around me. I tried to grab it with my mind, but it was too late. The bookstore faded away, though I felt desperate to get back there.

Instead I fell back into my dreaming state, and now I really felt I was being chased. Something was waiting for me there, and it wanted to catch me. I tried to run but my legs would not move. I turned around to see a shadow bounce at me like a big animal. Its hands shot through the air, trying to grab me. They were human-like hands. I saw its face, it was almost human, but had a muzzle...

I screamed. Immediately a flash of heat and electric blue color enveloped me. And then I woke up. Nugget was sitting right next to me, hissing softly. Oddly it was not an angry hiss, it was more like the cat was puzzled at something. It was staring at the wall behind me, but when I turned to look, there was nothing there. Only a faint bluish glow, which was probably my eyes playing tricks on me. It dissolved in a few seconds.

Had I screamed? I listened with my heart pounding. No one moved in the house and after a while Nugget also calmed down.

I did not want to read the book now, not when I was this scared. I had been given my clue, and when I returned, a shadow had been waiting for me, trying to get to me, to make me tell the secret, I was sure.

I lay down under my blanket and spent the rest of the night staring into the shadows of my room until I could not take it anymore, and put on all the lights.

14

THE LIBRARIAN

Mr. Donnelly's finger traced the backs of the books in the library. The peace and quiet was enjoyable, not a shadow in sight. The constant light seeped through the windows, and the shelf was close enough to it so that Mr. Donnelly did not need any other light.

He had a flat-bottomed basket on the floor next to his feet, filled with old books that would have made the heart of many a librarian beat faster.

He pulled out a dusty volume and tenderly opened the cover. He read a few words, shook his head slightly and placed the book in his basket. Then something he saw made him narrow his eyes and lean forward.

"Not again! I do wish people wouldn't do that!" Mr. Donnelly complained quietly, under his breath.

There was a book behind the other volumes in this forgotten shelf. Someone must have pushed it behind the others when they replaced a book sometime in the past. He'd guess it was one of the assistants – some of them simply did not share his passion for order. They returned books to the wrong places, making them effectively vanish. Mr. Donnelly had catalogued much of this library, and created a shelf numbering system, but if a book was not returned to its right place, you had no idea where to find it any more, unless you came across it by accident. The library was so big it had spread out into many adjacent buildings around the original one. Whoever had occupied the other buildings had been forced to move out.

Mr. Donnelly suspected there were several important volumes missing from the shelves. Sometimes it was glaringly obvious, for instance if he spotted a long-term gap, or if he knew the book well and he had not seen it in its correct place for some time. That was why he spent hours going through the shelves methodically, in search of those missing books. These he put in his basket and then took to their rightful places.

And now, it seemed, there was another misplaced book hiding behind the others. Mr. Donnelly sighed and moved a few books out of the way so that he could put his hand through the gap and lift it out.

He pulled it out and turned it so that the light from the window reached it better. His eyesight was not what it used to be – he would need to have new reading glasses soon.

"What's this then? Never seen the like of this one before..."

Mr. Donnelly knew his library well. He could not remember all the books, obviously, but he was sure he would have remembered if he had come across anything as unusual as this.

This book looked out of place, considering it was on a shelf that contained books from the 18th century. It had thick leather covers, but these were in poor condition, as if the book was centuries older than its cover indicated. As far as Mr. Donnelly knew, the Eiffel Tower did not exist until 1889. And even though the leather cover was much torn and damaged, he could clearly make out the outline of the Eiffel Tower on it. This meant the book was in the wrong part of the library completely. Those library assistants... he would have got rid of a lot of them, if possible, but if he had told the Masters about their poor work... No, he knew what would happen to them, and did not want to be responsible for such a thing. And so he continued his lonely tours around the library, replacing books in their proper places, and scolding the assistants privately, if he caught them doing poor work.

He took the book to a reading table by the window and leaned over it. Yes, the Eiffel tower it certainly was... He turned the cover gingerly. He could tell that it was made of real wood, and covered with thick leather. His experienced eyes enjoyed the richness of the paper, which had survived despite some very rough travels, it seemed. Clearly this book had been kept in a very dry place to have survived so well.

He turned the book slightly and as if confirming his analysis some very fine sand fell at his feet from under the leather cover

He looked at the text written in beautiful old-fashioned handwriting on the first page. It was an odd language, but he could make out two names. Elijah and Merit. Merit's name came first, and the text was signed by Elijah.

"To Merit, from Elijah, it seems..." Mr. Donnelly nodded to himself.

Interesting. As far as Mr. Donnelly knew anything, Merit was an ancient Egyptian name. But of course in modern times parents found it fashionable to give their offspring ancient names again. Elijah was a man's name, so Mr. Donnelly suspected Merit was a woman.

He turned to the next page and saw a drawing. Of course. The book was a sketchbook, which explained why its pages were made of good, thick rag paper.

Mr. Donnelly leaned closer to have a better look at the drawing - yes, indeed he needed new glasses. It was a circle of stones, it seemed. It looked somewhat familiar...

"Six central stones in a row... a ring of stones around..." Mr. Donnelly turned his head from side to side like a bird, as if that would reveal more of the drawing. "Yes, of course!"

Now he recognized it. These were the standing stones from the Nabta circle in the Nubian Desert, one of the ancient astronomical calendars built of stone that were found around the world. He had read about it in the past in his research for the Masters... He had considered that perhaps ancient stone circles would provide a clue to their search, but so far had not managed to find anything specific along that line of discovery. There were intriguing hints in the old stories, yes, but nothing he could put his finger on...

The drawing of the Nabta circle was itself encircled with writing in a language he did not understand. Interestingly it seemed that the writer – and logically it would be Merit to whom the book was given - had written first normally, under the drawing... And indeed the word Nabta was written there. Pleased at being right Mr. Donnelly lifted his glasses from his nose and spent a few moments cleaning them to his handkerchief – a habit of his whenever he had made a correct academic assumption.

Now the odd part was that at some point she had turned the book around and written new lines between the ones already written.

Mr. Donnelly leafed through a few pages. Yes – all the pages were like that. The handwriting very soon turned from normal size to very small, as if the writer knew she was running out of paper. Still she had made drawings, amazing drawings of what looked like ancient Egyptian monuments and landscapes.

Intrigued, Mr. Donnelly placed the sketchbook in his basket for further study, and continued his round in search of misplaced books.

15

THE PROFESSOR

"Why on earth do you want to go there?"

Mom looked at me over the rim of her coffee mug, displeased at the idea of me leaving unsupervised to visit a strange city.

This time I was prepared.

"We have to do a big history essay next year and there's a museum where I can get some background info for it."

"That sounds like a great idea to me," Grandma beamed over her breakfast – immaculately dressed and coiffured as ever. "And as a matter of fact I have an old friend there that I could go and meet, while I drop Dana off at the museum."

"Perfect!" I said before Mom had any more time to think of objections. She somehow always managed to come up with reasons not to do anything Grandma wanted to do. Sometimes I felt the teenager in our family was not me, but Mom. And Mom's behavior seemed to worsen every time Mom and Grandma were together. I often wondered if it was something to do with me.

"That sounds like a good idea!" Dad commented cheerily in between big bites of toast laden with bitter orange marmalade, his favorite. "You can't start too early when it comes to preparing for big essays!"

He winked at me as a sign he was on my side, as if to say he was in on a conspiracy. The real conspirator, however, was Grandma.

I had finally fallen asleep, with the lights on, and slept like a log. Grandma came to wake me up for breakfast, noticing the dream book on my bedside table.

"Been reading all night, sleepy head?"

"Umm, yes..."

Grandma took the book into her hands and flicked through the pages, ending up at the list of names at the end. I did not tell her about the message I'd discovered in the book.

"How interesting, all these names - just think of the many hands through which a book as old as this must have passed." She looked across at me with a curious, penetrating gaze. "And this is quite an unusual name, too, wouldn't you say?"

She tapped her finger on the fifth name in the list. I hoped my face did not reveal anything when I pretended to be seeing it for the first time. Then Grandma surprised me by digging her phone from her pocket.

"Shall we look him up in the phone book?"

"Huh?"

"Yes, just for fun. Let's see if we can find someone with that name, shall we?"

She spent a few moments wiping her phone screen - I noticed how short her fingernails were.

"Ha! Thought as much... Reginald Rowan, professor. And by coincidence, he works at a university in a nearby city... and this particular Reginald Rowan is an old acquaintance of mine, in fact. We - er - go back a long way together. He's quite a character. Tell you what - let's pay him a visit. It would do you a world of good to get out of this neck of the woods for a while and see some city life. You can say it has something to do with your studies, if your mother doesn't like our impulsive decision. I know what she's like."

I couldn't believe it all sorted out itself so easily. Literally. It was a bit too convenient... Grandma being there when the book appeared in my bag out of nowhere, and knowing the very person I was told to meet in the lucid dream. I decided I would get to the bottom of this, but with my parents within earshot I could wait until later.

I was still puzzling over all this when we set off within the hour, Grandma and I.

I had chosen to carry the dream book with me. It fit into my handbag well. I had selected this bag because I could wear it over the shoulder, and its zipper was hidden under a flap. I also kept it in front of me, and held the strap with my hand. Safer than to leave the book inside Nugget's pillow. I never knew when Mom would get it into her head to attack my room and clean it. She did that occasionally, and I had learned to keep my most private things with me. Like now, Kitty's letter and the book.

I'm not saying Mom is nosier than an average mother, but the temptation might be too much if she saw either of these things. I had written fairy stories when I was younger, and could never forgive my Mom when I heard her talking about them to someone on the phone – she had read them without telling me. So it had happened before. Once bitten, twice shy, as the saying goes. Mom was not the only one in our family who wanted others to respect her privacy.

For some reason Grandma wanted to join the motorway as soon as she could, when she could have chosen pretty back roads with barely any traffic where she might have had fun with her small car. She also seemed disinclined to talk. I didn't comment, though, as we drove along in the midst of other traffic, following the speed limits, heading towards an attractive campus university on the edge of the urban sprawl of the midlands.

That is also why we were at the museum's door a few minutes before the museum even opened.

"I have some things to attend to," she said, "so you might as well have a look round the museum, if you like. We could meet the professor in an hour or so. I'm not sure where his office is located on the campus now, but you can ask from the info desk. It's close by, in the building at the back of the museum. I'll meet you at his office in an hour, OK?"

Grandma zoomed away before I had even time to answer.

This whole thing seemed so irrational I looked at my hands. Four fingers and a thumb. Everything as it should be. I sighed. Sometimes it would be good if reality turned out to be a dream and you could wake up from a particularly scary or sad bit.

Once Grandma had disappeared, I considered whether to take a look round the museum, which did look interesting, but then turned on my heel and hurried past the building to the gates of the campus. I went straight to the university information desk, which was in the building right next to the gates just as Grandma had said.

"Yes, can I help you?" a young woman was sitting behind the counter. I had expected older people and was a bit surprised – this one did not look much older than I was. Then I got it. Summer job, of course.

I told her who I was looking for, and she gave me a printed map of the campus area. She circled the right building for me. I thanked her and went on my way. There was no point looking around the museum - my mind was worrying over the message hidden in the dream book to such an extent that none of the objects in the collection would have registered. I would go and wait by the professor's office until Grandma came.

I don't quite know what I expected, but his office didn't look too impressive to me from the outside – an ordinary door with his name-plate on it. I stopped in front of it, and for the first time felt nervous. So far the momentum had just carried me along, but now I had to decide what exactly I was going to say to him about the dream book - if anything. "Hello, have you heard of the buffer zone? I was given this interesting book that tells me that you do - I have no idea where it came from - but I was told to meet you in a dream?"

Yeah, right... If the whole book was a hoax, the professor would most likely consider I had bats in the belfry.

Thinking that I probably had half an hour or so till Grandma appeared, I was musing on the book and its curious message when the door suddenly opened and an elderly, tall man hurried out, almost knocking me over.

"I am so sorry, miss!" he exclaimed, "a bad habit of mine, reading while I walk!"

He was standing there with his glasses perilously near the tip of his nose and a thick book pressed against his chest.

"That's quite all right," I said. "Are you... Professor Reginald Rowan?"

"Indeed I am - ah - sorry, I don't seem to recall your name? Do we have an appointment? I am sure my secretary has forgotten to inform me... or I have forgotten to check my appointments. Probably the latter one... can't blame the secretary, dear heart, a very efficient lady as she is, and probably rather desperate to be stuck with me."

"Well, yes, we have a meeting, sort of. Or rather my Grandma has, and she brought me along. She isn't here yet, though..." I interrupted when he had to stop talking for a second and catch his breath. Then, deciding this was as good a time as any, I inhaled deeply and asked: "But if I said yours was the fifth name on a list, would that mean anything to you?"

He looked at me straight in the eye (he was quite tall), and suddenly his somewhat scatterbrained demeanor changed. There was a very sharp intellect there staring at me over his glasses.

"Fifth, you say... Where is this list, if I may ask?"

"In an old book..." I said.

"Now this wouldn't be a book about... gates?" he whispered.

I stared at him for a few seconds before answering, as if his looks would reveal whether he was trustworthy or not. The knowing look in his eyes convinced me to answer honestly.

"It would..."

"Are you sure you were not followed?"

"I don't know. Probably not..."

"You haven't seen odd...shadows?" his voice was so low I almost did not hear it.

He clearly knew.

"No, I haven't seen any here. At home I did, once. And then there is this odd young man who pops up out of nowhere and..."

He straightened and suddenly I wasn't sure anymore that he was old at all.

"In here, quick."

He opened the door and practically pushed me inside, while already talking on his cell phone, canceling some appointment. Then he closed the door and took off his glasses. I noticed there were no wrinkles around his eyes.

"Now. You and I need to have a serious talk. But first, show me the book so I know you are the real thing. And to convince you, here is my signature, so you may compare it to the fifth name."

He scribbled his name on a piece of paper. I could immediately see the signature was similar. He used quite extensive loops for his R's. My dream had led me to the right person.

16

TIMELESS REALMS

Professor Rowan gave me a look that revealed he had a keen intelligence behind the slightly nutty-professor-like appearance.

Then he navigated his computer with a few clicks, and strange music filled the room. It was loud and sonorous and seemed to resonate in my spine in an unpleasant way. I squirmed involuntarily with discomfort for a few seconds, wondering how any music could have had this effect on me. I felt as though I was developing a high fever and had to force myself to sit still.

The professor saw me frown and smiled reassuringly.

"Don't worry; the room is sound-proofed. The other staff know my hobby is primitive singing and bells and bowls, and they kindly allowed me to sound-proof this room. At my own expense of course, and after I gave permission for the little faculty choir to have their weekly practise here - there's plenty of room for them as you can see. What they don't know is why I want to play this kind of music - it prevents the shadows and their masters from hearing us."

I was not sure that knowing we were sitting in a sound-proofed room improved things at all. Nor the knowledge that there were shadows around us. Not to mention the "shadow masters", who must be way scarier than the shadows. I glanced quickly at the clock in the room, away again, and back. Nothing had changed. Fingers - one, two, three, four, thumb. Normal. Dammit, normal!

I didn't know for sure whether I could trust the professor or not. Still, I had come too far to shrink away now. I took the book out of my bag and showed it to him. To my surprise he did not reach for it, but instead just leaned back on his chair, nodded, and sighed.

"Yes, that's the book. Now, I need to know who told you about it. How did you get it?"

"I was in a bookstore and this young man almost knocked me over. He came out of nowhere. I fell down, and it was only later that I noticed this book was in my bag. I believe he put it there."

"What did he look like?" Suddenly I realized of whom the professor reminded me. He was just like the professor from the film "Back to the future", only his hair showed evidence of being combed earlier that day, and it was chestnut colored, streaked with grey. I got the feeling that somehow he was not as old as he tried to look, though as I could not stare at him openly, I couldn't pin down his age with certainty.

"He was blonde. Very blue eyes. Very tall. And hot."

"Hot as in body heat?"

"Er, yes," I felt myself blushing again at the memory of the young man.

"Quite, quite..." the professor nodded to himself as is he was pleased with something. "Good, very good..."

He continued to mumble to himself and I waited.

Finally I coughed and the professor almost jumped. Even though the small voice I managed to make was almost buried in the strange metallic music, the professor obviously had very good hearing.

"I do beg your pardon... I suppose you need explanations now. But first: who told you to find me, and how did they tell you who, and where, I was?"

"To cut a long story short - I had a dream. A lucid dream. In it, a lady told me to find the fifth name on the list at the back of this book, someone that lived in this city. And by chance... " I didn't get any further because as soon as I said the word "chance" Professor Rowan interrupted me.

"No such things as chance, my dear, no such thing... I shall explain this to you now. The story will seem incredible, but I suppose you have already crossed the line of incredulity, having read what is in the book, and having seen one of the shadows. Not to mention having had the experience of a lucid dream."

He said "the book" in almost reverent tones, as though it was a personality that he knew and admired. Then he lifted his eyebrows, which made his forehead crease, and looked at me as if asking my permission. I nodded, and he continued.

"Very well then. So the book tells us that there is a buffer zone between our physical world and the Unseen Worlds, where time does not exist for anyone who gets there. Does this sound believable to you?"

"Well... not really. I mean I suppose we would know about it."

"And indeed we have known about it, always," the professor beamed as if I had been a good student and given the right answer. "There are so many stories in which someone falls asleep and wakes up years later – time has passed and they enter a changed world when they awaken. You must have heard some of them. These narratives have their roots in reality. One of the oldest is the story of HoniM'agel. He was a Jewish scholar, who according to the tale, fell asleep one day..." The professor switched to the historic present, as though he was seeing the story unfold in front of him. "Prior to falling asleep, he sees a man planting a carob tree, and asks him why he would do such a thing, when it was of no benefit to him. It would take 70 years for the tree to mature and carry fruit, and the man who planted it would be dead. When HoniM'agel awakens, he realizes he is under the very same carob tree, which has now fully matured. Big branches are reaching for the sky above him. Time has passed, and he discovers that he even has a grandson now."

"I have never heard of HoniM'agel..." I admitted

The music made an especially loud howling noise. I cringed. I would describe it as just like toothache in my back. Was I getting ill? Sounds didn't have this effect on me normally...

"Bronze singing bowls," the professor explained, "but moving on: have you ever heard of the seven wise men who fell asleep for two hundred years?"

I vaguely remembered hearing something of the sort, and nodded.

"The seven sleepers of Ephesus, as they were called. Early Christians, who hid in a cave and fell asleep for 200 years. This supposedly happened around the year 250 CE. Another old story is the legend of Ranka – a young Chinese man who ventured deep into a forest and met two old men playing a board game. He accepted some food from them and munched away on it while he watched their game. He dozed off and when he came to, he was alone. The axe handle he was holding had rotted, the axe head had fallen to the ground, and he had a long beard. He returned home and his family had disappeared and no one remembered him anymore."

"Reminds me of Rip van Winkle," I said.

"His story was fiction, but it was based on these folk legends," the professor dismissed Rip van Winkle with a wave of his hand, "and there are many more... Take for example the eighth-century Japanese story of Urashima Taro. As a young man he saved a tiny turtle that was tortured by children. He took it back to sea and would probably have forgotten all about the episode, if a huge turtle had not approached him the next day.

The big turtle told him that the little turtle had actually been Otohime, the daughter of the Emperor of the Sea. The Emperor wished to thank Urashima Taro, and the big turtle used his magical powers to give him gills. Then they swam to the bottom of the sea." Professor Rowan made a turtle swimming gesture with his hands. Once again he was there in his mind, you could tell. "He spends a few days there, but then wishes to return to his own village. The princess lets him go, but gives him a box as a departing gift, asking him not to open it.

When he gets back to the surface, everything in his village has changed, and when he asks if anyone remembers a man with his name, they do. They tell him a man with his name vanished at sea long ago. Three hundred years had passed since then.

He opens the box and - this is a fascinating bit - there are many variations as to what is in it. One version reveals that white smoke coming from the box turns him into an old man, and Otohime's voice comes from the sea, telling him his old age was in the box. In another version he turns into a crane, in yet another he is given a magic pill that makes it possible for him to breathe underwater. "

"Nice story..." I was trying hard to be polite, when in fact all these legends one after another were making my head spin.

"Did you know they actually have a shrine in Japan, UrashimaJinja, where an old text tells of a man, Urashimako, who left in the year 478 to visit a land where people never die? He returned in the year 825, and he too carried a box with him. He opened this one, and again a cloud of white smoke came out and turned him into an old man."

I opened my mouth to say something, but by now the professor was well into his lecture.

"In Ireland a story of Oisin tells how he falls in love with beautiful Niamh, and together they ride to the land of the ever-young. After a while he begins to miss his family. Niamh lends him her horse, and warns him not to dismount. When he gets back home, three hundred years have passed, and everyone he knew is dead. Oisin falls from his horse and turns immediately into an old man."

The professor, in his enthusiasm, began to pace the floor.

"In the story of Muchukunda, in the Bhagavatam," he nodded over his glasses in my direction as if he expected me to know what the Bhagavatam was, "the king Muchukunda helps the gods to fight demons. In the divine realm almost no time passed, and he was told that one year in heaven equaled three hundred and sixty years."

He stopped and turned towards me.

"So you see – there are plenty of stories of people visiting a place where time does not pass. In many cases, after returning, they turn old in a matter of moments or days, often as a result of some magic falling apart. And here's what's true about these stories and how they relate to the Book of Gates..."

A red light lit up by the door, warning that someone had pressed the silent doorbell. The professor clicked on his computer and looked at the security image provided by the hallway camera.

"Ah, my old friend!" he exclaimed, looking at the screen.

Just as things were beginning to get interesting... I sighed and waited patiently while the professor walked to the door and opened it. A voice came from the corridor.

"Quickly – shadows are gathering around the university. We need to leave now!"

It was Grandma.

17

A SAFE PLACE

"I knew you were involved in all of this," I yelled at Grandma. Not because I was angry, but because there was no other way to make her hear what I said. "And could you please turn that horrible noise down?"

We were speeding in her sports car on the motorway, once again weaving our way in and out of the slower traffic. This time she did not stick to the speed limits but drove like someone possessed, despite the speed cameras staring down at us from nearly every bridge. I sat in the middle, and Professor Rowan was on my other side, looking like a big spider with his long legs folded into the small space available. He was holding a small loudspeaker in his hands and from it the brass bowls music was howling at full volume. It really resonated in my whole body in a horrible way and my spine especially, which was something I did not understand. Toothache of the spine I kept telling myself, wincing at the sensation.

"Sorry, no!" Professor Rowan yelled back, "the vibrations keep the shadows at a distance, if they are following us!"

I rolled my eyes. Grandma was going to have some explaining to do once we finally stopped.

The fact that no police car was around was a miracle. Grandma really stepped on the gas and the little red car responded instantly. I tried to see what was written on the road signs flashing by, and it did not take long for me to realise we were not heading homewards.

"Where are we going?" I yelled.

"To a safe place!" Grandma yelled back, and after that said nothing. Probably because saying anything required just that - yelling.

The professor opened the window for a while.

To my surprise, Grandma shouted angrily "Close that, now!"

The professor mumbled something (I did not hear it, but saw his lips move), looked embarrassed, and closed the window.

It took us two hours to reach our destination. Two hours that almost drove me crazy, listening to the singing bronze bowls, their howling sound resonating in my bones. We did not talk during the drive, for obvious reasons. Covering my ears did not help either. The last part of the route headed off into the hills along minor roads. I guessed from the journey time that we were probably somewhere in Yorkshire.

The safe place turned out to be an old manor of some kind – the year on the wrought iron gate announced it was established two hundred years ago, and everything about it and the surroundings spoke of old money. A discreet metal plate announced the place was called the Magellan Spa. Some people were walking around the grounds - most seemed to be middle aged or older. A few who were sitting on elegant wooden loungers outside the building wore very luxurious-looking bathrobes.

"Ahh... safe at last," Professor Rowan said and the music stopped the second we were inside the gates.

My ears continued to ring and my back ached from the sound.

"What is this place?" I asked. A few curious glances were directed towards us from the passers-by, but nothing more. It seemed we were not that interesting, we were probably seen as just more new guests.

"Officially a high-society spa," Grandma said, as we got out of the car, "and it looks as though you will be staying here for a while. Follow me!"

She headed for the mellow stone building and we followed, trying to match a pace that was so fast that even the professor with his spider-legs had a hard time keeping up. I had to take a few running steps every now and then.

Grandma sped in through the front doors and we followed. To my surprise we did not enter the big reception hall in front of us behind a glass wall. Grandma turned to the left and we followed her into a corridor that ran along the inside of the front wall of the building. We walked all the way to the furthest wing of the great house before pressing the button of a bell next to a solid, heavy, carved wooden door. A small plaque announced the area was private. I wondered if this was the wing where the owners of the building lived, having turned most of the building into a spa.

A surveillance camera stared down at us from above the door. Whoever was observing us seemed to be happy about what they saw, and there was a soft click from the door in front of us. Grandma pulled the door open.

We entered a hall, the size of which one would expect to see in a two hundred year old massive building. Other than the size, the hall's appearance did not fit with the interior of an old building at all.

The walls were the only thing that were old about this space. It had modern furniture, a reception desk, computer booths and a big, framed screen on the wall. On the screen was a film of a beautiful mountain landscape.

"Layla!" A woman ran to meet Grandma with outstretched arms.

"Lilith!" Grandma hugged the woman, who then turned to me.

She was the same woman I had seen in my lucid dream. The shirt was different, but the hair was in a similar bundle on her neck, she had a few freckles on her cheeks, and reddish blonde eyebrows.

She stared at me, clearly surprised.

"You *brought* her here?"

"There was no time to let her go through the test and find her way on her own," Grandma explained. "The shadows found her."

The woman, Lilith, looked at me in alarm. Then she collected herself, smiled and extended her hand.

"Well, now that you are here, you are very welcome. Usually anyone who comes through our doors has to find us on their own, following the clues we give to them in their dreams. If they cannot find us, they are not ready."

"Ready for what?"

"To walk through the gates. And it may be that you are not really ready either, not yet. Nor ever, perhaps. But we shall see. Tell me now the sequence of events that forced you to break the rules." She had turned her head away from me to talk to Grandma and Professor Rowan.

"She found the book as was arranged," Grandma said, "but then a shadow appeared, where none should have been. The shadows did not follow me, of that I am certain. They must have been there already for some other reason. But - strictly speaking we are not breaking any rules here anyway. Dana passed the lucid dreaming test, heard your message, and found Professor Rowan as a result – with very little help from me - so the first stages went exactly as they should have done. The problem arose when the shadows followed her when we went to meet our professor here - this made me certain they really were after her. I don't know how they managed to follow us, because I drove at a speed they usually can't keep up with, but they did, and they did so in far greater numbers than I had ever seen. Usually they move alone, but this time there was a group of shadows. And at least one of them must have been especially fast."

"They are after the book?" the professor suggested.

Grandma shook her head.

"No, I don't think so. There is more to this. I don't doubt they have managed to get their hands on the book somewhere along the way anyway. Nothing new there. And not really dangerous to us, even if they managed to find the message hidden in the book, as the way to the gates is not in any way revealed in words. They know about us too. Me and the professor, I mean. I am their old acquaintance already, and they have seen the two of us talking in the past. Also if they have read the book since Professor Rowan wrote his name there, they've certainly done their research and found him on their own. Maybe they guessed where we were headed from the general direction we took." Grandma had turned back to explain to Lilith.

"So you mean they were after the girl? How could they have found that she was..."

Lilith shut up mid-sentence. I looked at her curiously. Found about that I was... what?

"Has to be," Grandma nodded, "that has to be it. But the main thing is we are now safely here, and this time there was no shadow following us."

I have to admit the whole thing felt unreal. Kitty's death, the book, the lucid dream, the shadow, the stories of people living unchanged while hundreds of years of physical life passed elsewhere. Not to mention the strange young man, whom I seemed to recognize from somewhere, but couldn't remember where. And who obviously knew who I was. Not forgetting that the professor seemed to know who the young man was as well.

And this speeding to a "safe place" because shadows wanted to get to me - what was that about? I had not seen any shadows while we drove here. Had I ended up in the middle of a bunch of weirdos? Some cult, perhaps? What they were talking about did not make any sense to me, but seemed to be normal discussion for them, like the weather or something.

Looking around me it was obvious that if they were part of some weird cult, it was a very rich one. Everything was brand new and glistening.

I stole a glance at the nature film playing on a big screen - its upper frame was twice my height, and the lower frame was at floor level. Someone was walking across the meadow, approaching the viewer. He looked familiar... There wasn't exactly sunshine coming from anywhere, maybe the sun was hidden behind clouds, but still his hair was glistening golden, as if illuminated. He was very tall and well proportioned. Wide shoulders, muscular arms, narrow hips, long legs.

He walked closer, and suddenly I recognized him. My jaw dropped. The blonde young man from the bookstore! It was definitely him. So he was an actor? That didn't surprise me, not with his looks. And that would explain why he looked so familiar, though it did not explain how he seemed to know me...

While I pondered on this, he walked even closer, until he was facing the camera. I was expecting something to happen that would move the plot forward, waiting for him to start speaking as the camera moved in for a close-up on his face, or that another scene would start.

Instead he stepped through the screen, straight into the hall.

18

DIANA

I felt myself swaying slightly with shock. That saying - you could have knocked me down with a feather - that's how it was. He saw me, smiled and bowed his head slightly in recognition. I could only stare at him. He did not come to talk to us, though–people hurried to meet him, and he walked off, talking with them. Before he vanished through a door leading away from the hall, he glanced over his shoulder. His eyes locked on mine for a second and then he was gone.

I realized I had been staring at him with my mouth open like an idiot.

"That is one of the gates." Grandma pointed to the screen. "This place was built around it to protect it. The gate used to be invisible, and moved around the area before it was stabilized – in the past it could be found only by walking through it. If you read the history of this area, you'll find several references to missing people. The most likely explanation is that they happened to walk through this gate - a local road passed close to it, and people stopped just about here, by the roadside, to rest."

"Missing... you mean that once they got in there, they did not come back?" I asked and almost unconsciously moved backwards away from the gate.

This time Professor Rowan answered.

"Not all found their way back. And the fact that there are several gates around the world, explains all the stories of people who thought a day had passed, when in fact it had been decades, even hundreds of years. Some never did find their way back, and you could say they died eventually. But they probably did not even notice it, as they were on the Other Side already. They just moved on and probably wondered why everything suddenly seemed more magnificent and their bodies felt lighter. Obviously at some stage they realized the truth - either on their own or when someone told them that they had died. Their physical body sank back to our physical world while their lighter spirit body continued moving on. This may provide an explanation for the fact that sometimes dead bodies cannot be identified. How could they be? They may have been born hundreds of years earlier."

"So how is it possible for anyone to go through the gate from here and manage to return to their own time?"

"That is what we learn here," Lilith said. "Well - some people learn it, some don't. But we never leave anyone wandering about – experienced travelers take care any of new ones, and bring them back safely. We have good trackers who usually quickly find those who are lost in the buffer zone. Daniel, whom I believe you have already met, is one of them."

She nodded in the direction that he had disappeared. Daniel. So that was his name.

"What happens to them then? The ones who don't learn whatever it is they are supposed to do there?" I asked.

"They remain here in their normal physical life and help the best they can—through research, for example. We gather vast quantities of data about major events as well as daily life in history. Our researchers are storehouses of knowledge," Lilith continued with pride.

She seemed to be ready to give me a straight answer to all the questions that were bubbling up in me directly. My intense curiosity meant that I wasn't too shy to carry on asking, even though my next question was undoubtedly one of the oddest I had ever asked anyone.

"Why? You... time travel?"

Lilith nodded matter-of-factly.

"We do. The timeless buffer zone is connected to every time that ever existed. That means we can move through time there - with certain limitations. It is not easy, and there is a high risk of getting lost, if you don't know exactly how to do it. Another problem is that if you are not careful, you can mess up the past, which may cause havoc in the future. We avoid it at all costs, but the Immortals, the shadows and their... Masters...don't, and it can take a lot of work to put right whatever they have changed. They need to be stopped. If we hear of a major disturbance that they have caused, we travel to the time before it, to try to prevent it from happening in the first place. That may result in physical aggression, when we wait for them at their point of exit from the buffer zone."

"How do you know it has happened, then? I mean if they have changed the past, how do you know it has even happened? And how do you know the changes they have caused are bad?"

The whole concept of changing the past - and altering the future as a consequence - was mind-boggling, but I was trying to keep up. I had glanced round for a clock without finding one, but a surreptitious look at my hand showed that all was as it should be.

"Good questions... usually they kill people, or rob them of their belongings, and we consider that these are crimes that should be stopped. So in the name of humanity we try to do this whenever we can. As for finding out where they have done their deeds, we follow the trails they leave behind. They leave veritable paths in the buffer zone, because they use the same routes year after year. We have our scouts near these paths, and we see them moving there, we follow them, and intervene where we can," Lilith explained. "Also our history researchers know their specific eras so well that they notice right away if a text in a history book suddenly changes. That is how we know something has happened there, and we send a team to investigate. These changes in the past don't erase everyone's memory. What I'm going to say next will probably be no surprise to you. I am sure that you've experienced this - you hear about an event in the news, and then, suddenly, you hear another piece of news that completely negates what you know, for a certainty, that you heard before."

"What exactly... any examples?" I wasn't quite sure that I understood.

"Well, let's say that you knew London had lost the vote for the Olympic games. And suddenly you hear in the news that construction work has started on the Olympic stadium in London. You know there is a glitch. But if you talk to other people, most of them have no recollection of things ever being different. The kind of people we want to work with us are those who can remember and note such things happening. They usually have the skills to move in the buffer zone as well, we have found."

"And so you - gather troops, as the book says."

"So we do gather troops, yes," Lilith nodded, "to stop the crimes done by the Immortals, their shadows and their... Masters."

I made a mental note of her hesitance about naming the Masters of the Immortals.

"But how did these gates come about? Were they always there or did someone make them?"

"Now that's where it gets interesting," Professor Rowan positively beamed in his eagerness to explain. "You see... Have you ever heard of..."

"Whoa - stop. It's best that we talk about these things after everyone gets settled in. Also, I need to call Dana's parents and come up with a believable explanation of why we are not coming back," Grandma interrupted.

I did not like the sound of that.

"What do you mean—we are not coming back?"

"As long as the shadows are after you, it is not safe for you to leave this building," Grandma said, "but leave this to me."

Lilith left Grandma to her phone call, and led me up the stairs to the second floor. Our steps echoed slightly from the closed doors lining the long corridor, none of which had any nameplates. I noticed how fit

Lilith seemed to be - she took long steps and moved with the grace of a dancer. Exactly like Grandma.

Lilith knocked on the last door on the right.

"Diana? May we come in?"

The door swung open, and a young woman stood in the doorway, holding a book. She appeared to be about my own age, maybe slightly older. Her dark brown eyes were smiling, and I liked her the instant our eyes met.

"Always, Lilith! And whom do we have here? A newcomer?" she smiled broadly.

"Yes, a newcomer. She is here before her time, because the shadows are showing some extra interest in her. She was brought straight in here by Layla, her grandmother."

"So you are Layla's granddaughter! Pleased to meet you!"

I could not help smiling back at her.

"Everything will be explained to you when the time is right," Lilith assured me, "but there's so much to take in and the priority is to find you a room, so here we are."

"Welcome, welcome! Glad to have company!" Diana gestured for us to step into the room. I noticed there were two beds there, on opposite walls.

"Dana has brought nothing with her, so maybe you could help her out with some clothes and other things while she's getting settled?"

"Of course! Leave that to me!"

Diana seemed to be one of those types who burst with energy. She practically danced back into the room when Lilith turned and left.

"Who is Lilith, anyway?" I took the opportunity to start digging out more information right away.

"She is one of the leaders here. They make the decisions regarding which team goes where. And when. Also she is our expert in waking up sleeping people."

"I suppose you mean lucid dreaming?"

Diana made a little pirouette. Very elegantly, I might add.

"Yes, you suppose right. She found you too, didn't she? After you read the book, obviously."

"Yes... yes, she did. Have you read the book too?"

"But of course. Quite a few of us here have, I think. Though in my case I only saw it after I arrived here. Do you still have it?"

I took the book out of the bag and Diana seized it.

"Just the same as the last time I saw it - there are a few more names at the back..." she leafed through the name list, "but none from my times, as the book did not exist then. Nor could I read then."

"You said 'your time'... When was that exactly?"

"The middle of the nineteenth century," Diana had a look in her eyes that was hard to fathom. "I was the daughter of a slave and a plantation master, sold to my family when I was a child. I worked in the house, because of that. And because I was pretty and had lovely, coffee-colored skin."

I sat down heavily on the bed.

"So how old are you, exactly?"

"Well, I was sixteen the day I escaped. The date was May seventeenth, 1849. I and the daughter of the house, whose maid I was, were shopping in St Louis. I suspect madam - we had to call our owners 'master' and 'mistress' - sent us there, because the master of the house had begun to pay attention to my looks and visit my room."

I looked at her, shocked.

"You mean... are you saying he..." I could not finish the sentence.

"Yes. It was considered his right at the time. But the mistress of the house would not put up with it and decided to send me away. I think she intended to sell me, but as it was, the daughter of the house was very fond of me, and I was allowed to stay," Diana shrugged and I did not know what to say.

"And that is why we were at the family's town house when the fire alarm was sounded. Bells started to ring out madly and I was sent to see what it was about. I saw that the steamboat White Cloud was on fire on the river. It floated down the Mississippi, setting twenty-two other boats on fire. The flames leaped onto the buildings on the shore and soon there was an enormous fire. Massive! It all happened so quickly. I was too curious and suddenly the flames were close by, and there was no way I could turn to escape. That's when Lilith appeared, out of nowhere. She grabbed me by the arm and pulled me away. I fell asleep – now I know I could not stay conscious in the buffer zone – and when I woke up, I was in another part of the country. In Boston, in a house with an elderly lady. She would look after me while I practiced."

Diana started scooping her stuff off the other bed.

"You mean practiced lucid dreaming?"

"Yes, what else? She taught me, and I would have done even stranger things to please her. If she wanted me to learn to awake in my dreams, then I would do my best to learn. Not a big price to pay for freedom."

She took the bundle of her clothes and books she had gathered from the bed given to me, dropped them on the floor next to her bed and continued talking.

"Took me three months to finally get there. Lilith was waiting for me. It was enough that I managed to wake up in my dream. She did not put me through any tests or set me searching after any clues – the times were not safe for any young girl to go alone anywhere, slave or free. Lilith simply appeared in our friend's living room one evening after meeting me in my dream. Stepped through the slit, and took me with her, and brought me here."

"Slit? What slit?"

"Hmm... it'll be better if I let Lilith explain some things to you. Your head is probably spinning as it is."

She was right about that.

"OK. Let's go and get you some clothes, if you are to stay."

Diana opened the door and motioned me to go to the corridor.

"How can you live in another time?" I had to ask this young woman who was 160 years old, strictly speaking.

"No problem there. I leave one time-space reality and disappear from there. And I enter another one, where time keeps on ticking just as it would have done in my old life. It really isn't all that complicated. So I am exactly my physical age, despite the fact I skipped a few decades. Or centuries."

I snorted.

"Sorry. At the moment all of this feels quite complicated..."

"It won't, after a while. You'll get used to the idea. But the rest of it quite boggles the mind, I can assure you."

She was right.

19

THE STRANGE LANGUAGE

Mr. Donnelly spent several days trying to work out what the language in the notebook was. It had to belong to some small language group... It was not related to Latin that was certain. Also the names Elijah and Merit didn't really give anything away about their possible origins.

Then finally Mr. Donnelly's attention turned to a small sketch that stood out from all the drawings of the Egyptian monuments that surrounded it. The tall tower with the clock faces on it looked European and possibly medieval, if it were not for the modern appearance of the roof of the tower.

"A cathedral, perhaps?" mused Mr. Donnelly.

In the library, book after book on church architecture revealed nothing quite like it. Mr. Donnelly knew with the certainty of the dedicated researcher that it was simply a matter of time as he methodically turned the pages of each volume in turn. The next book was a thick and quite heavy one.

"Aha!"

There it was, finally! The image on the cover nearly matched the one in the drawing.

"The Cathedral of Turku in Finland...so the language is probably Finnish! No wonder I couldn't read the text in the notebook – it's not related to any other language in Europe. Except Estonian - and possibly Hungarian? I seem to remember there's a connection."

Mr. Donnelly sat back, his thoughts running on ahead. He needed to learn Finnish - but how? He couldn't show the notebook to anyone. The intensity of his sense of protection towards it surprised him. It was so fragile. He didn't want anyone else touching it, damaging it perhaps.

"Of course!"

He remembered a restaurant in the city the Scandinavians frequented, and that evening he dressed in presentable clothes. In the library he usually wore slippers and an oriental-looking dressing gown for its comfort. But now he put on a proper suit and his better shoes, and headed out to dinner.

Just as he had suspected, he found a few Finns in the restaurant in question, mingling with a bunch of Swedes - they did not seem to have any trouble in speaking Swedish, which sounded hilarious to Mr. Donnelly's ears.

"Mr. Donnelly, how nice to see you here." One of the Finns was a researcher he had often seen in the library, but they always spoke English with each other, and Mr. Donnelly had never actually asked whereabouts in the human world the other man had come from.

Once he had made the initial contact, Mr. Donnelly started to eat there regularly to chat with the Finnish scholar informally. They also met in the library. It was easy for Mr. Donnelly to raise the matter of learning the difficult language and the other man seemed happy enough to teach him. One day he even produced a little book "Finnish for Foreigners" and gave it to Mr. Donnelly.

"But this book is quite new!" Mr. Donnelly exclaimed upon seeing the price tag.

"Yes, I stole it for you," the Finn said, looking slightly baffled at his surprise. "There are new books in the world, you know."

"Yes, yes, thank you..." Mr. Donnelly mumbled, embarrassed, "I suppose I have been spending too much time inside the old library..."

The other man laughed.

"Yes, well, maybe you should go visit the world sometimes."

Mr. Donnelly managed a frozen smile, and hurried off mumbling about an urgent matter. How could he have expected the other man to know he wasn't allowed to leave the city?

20

SHADOW COUNCIL

"You lost her."

The voice was chilling and imperious. Sitting completely still on her throne-like chair with her back to the night, she might have been a beautiful statue. Her moonshadow stretched across the floor to the deeper pool of darkness in the midst of the councillors. The deep shade seemed to shift and shrink as her glance fell on it.

"She must be found," said the seated woman. "She is our key to the Path."

Around her she felt, rather than saw, the others nodding slowly and respectfully. Her words were never challenged.

"Do - they - know about her?" one of the council asked. He was a handsome, tall man, whose age was difficult to pinpoint.

"They know what she is, but they do not know what she will be, if everything has gone according to plan; and I do not doubt that it has. My father has done his work well. If they had known about her earlier, she would have been taken to safety sooner. But they will find out, given time. When they start her training, it will come out, eventually. Such skill must be ours! She is our Key."

Only the tight voice revealed how angry she was. Her pale face, lit by the rays of the moon reflecting from cold and gleaming walls, revealed nothing. She showed no emotion. Her beautiful yellow eyes observed the others calmly. They stopped at the darker shadow at the foot of the circle of figures for a while and narrowed, but then moved on round the others again.

"What can we do to seize her before - her change?"

"We must find out where she is. Hack her parents' phone and computer. We will find out her location eventually, even if the shadows have failed."

There was a murmur of agreement from the circle of councillors.

"Firstly, though," the woman looked into the dark mass of shade. "This is the reason that we lost her. It has failed - as the Hunter has told us."

The shade seemed to be drawing into itself, an ever disintegrating ball of darkness. This was the end. Its existence was dissolving in front of the burning yellow eyes. Nothing could be said in its defence. Everyone waited for the order of destruction. Eventually, the woman spoke

"This - " - she gestured at the dark shape - "Should be annihilated. But - we will not do that."

The amorphous shape began to take form again. A lowered head with flattened ears started to emerge from the mass. Limbs began to appear and reappear as if struggling for life.

"The reason is that this is the only shadow knowing her scent. Its Hunter cannot be there in daylight, so we must use it again. Next time, though," - there was a pause - "there will be no next time."

The shadow was taking form, growing more and more distinct. The ears began to prick forward, the nose to scent the air. The shape, not quite human, not quite animal, emerged from the darkness, shaking it off as animal shakes off water. It was now standing upright. The man who was its Hunter stepped forward and summoned it with a gesture of the head, as to a dog. It shadowed the hunter at his heels as they left the room.

"That was - unusual. I have never known her be merciful before."

The shadow crouched at his feet, seeming to want to touch them. The Hunter stepped away from it as if it were a fawning dog.

"Leave that! And get to work. Follow all the main roads from the university, one by one, until you catch her scent. And then – do not lose her again! Send a thought, and I will come."

The shadow sprang eagerly to its feet and darted out of the room and building so fast its Hunter could barely follow it with his eyes. His shadow was known for its extraordinary speed. The Hunter turned around to return to the council chamber. However, just in case, he would start molding another shadow, so it would be ready if the first one had to be obliterated.

The clouds parted and suddenly the bright moonlight poured onto the terrace. The Hunter gave himself a few moments, his eyes locked on the celestial orb. For a short while a vision of her filled his mind. Her limp body in his arms in the moonlight, the only time he had ever been allowed to touch her, to do what was needful. And the feeling of her life inside his body now, wordlessly flowed into his very being. So close, yet forever lost to his physical touch

Something stirred in the Hunter's heart. It was as delicate as the brush of a butterfly's wing, a whisper, a caress, as though she were awake in him, holding his cold heart in her warm hands.

Then his cold body shivered and his heart thumped, once, before settling back into its silence.

He tilted his head back, and from his open mouth came a blood chilling howl that spoke of pain and longing. The voices from the council room hushed.

The moon slipped back behind the clouds, and the moment was over. He stood still for a while, and then walked back to the shadows of the night where he belonged.

21

PALE STRANGER

"What are you doing here?"

I had never heard Mut-Bity's voice so strong, so... threatening before. She rose to her feet and positioned herself behind me, between me and the stranger, a man. All her movements were calm and steady. So steady and deliberate that I knew she was prepared for anything.

"I heard one of my kind might be here and came to claim her. Is this she?"

"Your kind do not walk in the open, under the sun," Mut-Bity said and only a slight tremor in her voice told me she was shocked. And that she hated and feared him, whoever this man was.

"But we do, when the necessity arises," the man said pleasantly, and inhaled deeply, "now, let me see..."

I felt an odd sensation. All the hairs on my skin seemed to be standing up, as though my body was readying itself for escape. A strong tingling sensation ran up my spine. The sizzling numbness felt similar to the feeling of knocking an elbow against something sharp.

"Mmmm..." he breathed in again as if savoring an appetizing fragrance. I heard a slap. I knew that sound. The last time I had heard

it was when my sister dipped her finger into a honey jar when Mut-Bity had turned her back for a moment.

Then it suddenly went very quiet. I felt as though the linen cloth over my head was rising into the air where my hair was standing up on end.

"You of all people should have more wisdom than to touch our kind..." the man murmured, but oddly enough he sounded amused at being hit by Mut-Bity.

"I know exactly who you are, and what your kind do," Mut-Bity hissed. "This girl does not belong to you. And I warn you, if you ever come to the same village as I, I shall be ready..."

"And what, exactly, do you think you could do to me? Are you not afraid, woman?" The man's voice sounded suddenly threatening. This, I thought, was how the demons that haunted the desert sounded - it was like the desert winds howling, blowing sand clouds towards the River. "We could kill you whenever we wish. Or worse... make you our servant whenever we wish."

A strong pair of male legs appeared from behind me and stopped in front. Before I could even think what was so odd about them, the linen that was wrapped around my head had been swept from my face and I looked into the most extraordinary eyes imaginable, staring into mine from under the shadow of a hood.

They were golden. Not brown but golden like the sun. Shining, and surrounded by bluish shadows. And the man himself had the oddest skin... pure white, like alabaster, but with a golden tint... I could see bluish veins in his neck, as though his skin was transparent. I could not tear my eyes away from his pale golden complexion.

He looked just like me. Except that I had sky blue eyes.

"I wonder... Where do you come from, my child?" he murmured with a voice that seemed to draw my mind out through my chest. I opened my mouth to answer, not able to resist. And suddenly they were all there.

The whispers. They were usually quiet during the day, or in the bright light, but now they suddenly filled my mind, as though they were whispering in my heart. I could not hear the words, they made a constant, heavy, loud buzzing sound that cut off the voice of the man, as a knife cuts through fruit, so its soft echo did not touch me anymore. And then the whispers reached outwards from inside me, pushing him off my chest, and out of my mind, forming a wall of buzzing protection around my heart.

The man jerked backwards. His mouth opened and a loud hiss escaped his surprisingly wide lips. He sounded like a furious snake. I, hidden somewhere inside the buzzing voices, calmly wondered why he reacted like that. Then I realized the whispers of my mind had taken the form of bees... all the bees from Mut-Bity's beehives had suddenly appeared from somewhere, and were swarming in the air around me. More appeared as I observed their dance in the air. I was sitting inside a bubble of bees. My eyes were still on the blue, dark vein on the man's neck, and I watched as a bee, a strange bee, lighter in color and bigger than the others, followed my gaze and landed on his neck.

"No!" Mut-Bity said with a sharp voice, and I knew she spoke to the bee. But the bee had already stung. Right into that vein.

The man yelled and slapped his neck. He stood back and pressed his neck with agony in his eyes. They had lost all interest in me and seemed to turn darker. His whole skin was growing ashen, grey. It started from the spot where the bee had stung him and slowly spread across his skin. Like a rotting fruit...The sweet smell of overripe fruit that enveloped him grew even stronger when he moved, trying to wipe away the pain.

Mut-Bity quickly positioned herself between me and the pale stranger, pushing me backwards.

"You witch!" he groaned and bent forward, grabbing his throat with both hands, sliding his fingers across the bee sting, over and over again, as if he was trying to stroke the pain away. His mouth opened and I found myself admiring his perfect long white teeth. Saliva started to drip from the wide open mouth and fell at Mut-Bity's feet. She quickly moved away from it, pushing me even further back, so that none of it came anywhere near her toes.

And then he was gone. I did not see him take any steps. There was only something shadow-like moving very fast, like a fading swirl of dust, or as though he was sinking underwater, and then he disappeared. Mut-Bity reached for my hand, to stop me, but I had already reached forward and scooped the small bee from the ground by my side, where it had fallen.

It had broken into two, I could still see its feelers moving slightly, but it was as good as dead. Its sting was missing together with a piece of its body.

"No..." I felt sudden sadness.

The voices in my mind hummed in unison, grieving, and I could feel a small spot in the midst of them that was fading. I had never paid attention to it before, but now that it was going, I realized I had felt it all along and would miss it when it was gone. I suddenly realized I had felt this happening before. Tiny bits of my mind closing, fading, disappearing. And new ones appearing in their place. Had I felt the death of Mut-Bity's bees?

Another hand reached out and placed itself over my palm. The dark brown hand of Mut-Bity.

"Go in peace, beautiful soul," Mut-Bity mumbled in a half-singing tone that broke with sadness. "You did well, you saved her soul, and you shall now live as a spirit for ever more."

I felt that small part of the hum in my mind disappear, and it was as if a speck of light disappeared with it. The light only lasted for a short moment, and with it a sensation of ... joy, and then it was gone. When Mut-Bity raised her hand, the bee was dead.

I bent to look closer. I had never seen the like of this bee before. It was white. And it had oddly purplish wings. The bees I had seen had two pairs of wings, but this one had three. They glistened in the sunlight.

I had seen two creatures that were like me, creatures without color. Creatures that I never knew existed - I had believed I was the only one.

22

A GIFT FOR MR. DONNELLY

With the help of the book and his Finnish friend, Mr. Donnelly was progressing slowly with the Finnish language. It was not the easiest to learn, with all its inflected forms, but Mr. Donnelly was a scholar and he was in no hurry.

"Yes, but we have all the time in the world, don't we?" the Finn chuckled when Mr. Donnelly pointed out how long it took him to learn the language.

"Indeed we do," Mr. Donnelly smiled somewhat sadly.

"Oh come on, lighten up, will you? We are privileged to be able to live here, untouched by time," the Finn said, "Here, look what I got from the world this time! I brought these for you!"

A bagful of wonderful Moleskine notebooks. Mr. Donnelly took one into his hands. He enjoyed the feel of the sleek black covers, and the rubber band that held the covers shut. His eyes filled up at the kindness of the other man. This was the closest to a friend he had ever had, really.

"And here's more! Have you ever even used one of these?"

Mr. Donnelly turned the mechanical pencil around in his fingers.

"No, I haven't. How does it work?"

"Here, let me show you..."

"Surely this is one of the most wonderful inventions!" Mr. Donnelly exclaimed after a brief explanation. "No need to sharpen the pencil!" he continued, marveling.

"You really have been buried here in the library for decades, haven't you?" the Finn shook his head. "And there's one more thing... Look in the bottom of the bag."

A Finnish - English dictionary. Mr. Donnelly was speechless. No one had given him presents since he was a child. The Finn coughed, slightly embarrassed at the emotion showing clearly on Mr. Donnelly's face.

"Well, have fun with them! I need to get going now."

He turned and walked away. A shadowy figure that had been waiting for him at the end of the corridor turned and followed him like a dog. Mr. Donnelly squeezed the tote bag happily against his chest and hurried towards his office. He would start translating the sketch book into these notebooks right away.

23

BREAKFAST WITH DANIEL

I have no idea how Grandma did it, but her call to my parents resulted in a week's stay with her. She told them that she had met an old friend who was just leaving on vacation to her holiday home on the west coast of Scotland, and that we were invited.

"It'll be a wonderful opportunity for Dana and who knows when she may get the chance again?" Grandma had reasoned. "Soon she'll be immersed in her studies."

This was a good enough story, but how she managed to make my mother accept my leaving without visiting home first to pick up clothes was nothing short of a miracle.

Mom always wanted to know where everyone was going and created a strict timetable for it in advance. She had folders for every trip, and lists of things to take, and she carefully ticked these off while she packed - and unpacked - bags. Her folders included timetables for trains and buses, maps of the travel destination and every conceivable emergency phone number. She felt insecure if people just went off impulsively and wanted to know the exact minute someone was expected back home, or was intending to visit.

"So you'd better be ready with some convincing tales about how wonderful it was up there," Grandma said. "I have enough photos of the area. I can send them to you, to make your story more believable. Let's just hope they don't begin to wonder why you aren't in any of the images."

So there I was, a few hours later, wearing my borrowed clothes at the private cafeteria for the center's personnel, where Diana had taken me for dinner. The clothes were more or less the right size - it seemed there were other tall people there too.

Now I was getting more openly curious glances from the people than I had when we arrived. I tried not to stare at them, but it was hard. I had never known any time travelers and just had to look at them to see if they appeared strange in any way. Well, they didn't.

There were people of all ages. Many were young, like us, but about half were older, and a few quite old. They were sitting with their trays, dressed in ordinary, casual clothes, the kind that were familiar to me. Jeans, T-shirts, hoodies, trainers. Comfortable seemed to be the main theme.

"Diana!" Someone was greeting her.

Diana waved her hand in the general direction of the caller. I stole a casual, sideward glance, because I recognized the voice.

Daniel was sitting there with four other people. He was by far the tallest of them. I quickly looked away and concentrated on choosing my dinner so I would not embarrass myself by blushing. Why did he have such an effect on me? And from whom had I inherited the tendency to blush anyway...

"I was told Daniel is one of the most experienced of the... what do you call yourselves, really?" I asked Diana.

"Travellers. Or Walkers. It wouldn't be great if we accidentally called each other Time Walkers and an outsider heard. Traveller is neutral enough not to make anyone too curious," Diana answered, selecting chicken for dinner. I noticed something that looked like vegetarian Thai food and piled my plate full.

"No meat?" Diana observed.

"No, I prefer vegetarian food," I replied.

I half expected her to ask next why did I not eat meat. For some reason people often asked that and then continued by either telling me I could not get all the necessary nutrients, or started defending their own consumption of meat, but instead Diana just shrugged.

"Here you can be vegetarian, but in the past - well, it can create difficulties if you don't eat meat."

"You mean I might get the chance to travel into the past, too?"

"Possibly, if you can manage it. It is not easy."

We carried our trays towards an empty table, past Daniel. I had another quick look at him and nodded, when I saw him looking straight at me.

"Hello there!" he flashed a beautiful smile at me. "Glad you made it!"

I couldn't come up with anything intelligent to say in response, so I just nodded again and headed towards our chosen table, focussing on where I was going and praying I wouldn't stumble against something this time. Thankfully my legs cooperated and my tray didn't end up anywhere it shouldn't have done.

Diana was already sitting down. She hid a smile as I approached.

"He's quite something, isn't he?" She winked at me.

"Hmm? Who?" I pretended I didn't have a clue what she was talking about. "Oh, I don't know..."

"Oh, I do. He has that effect on everyone. If he wanted, he could twist anyone around his little finger. But that's because of what he is..."

"What do you mean? He is what?"

"Sorry, I shouldn't have said anything. Lilith and the others will explain when the time is right," Diana's lips snapped shut.

Yeah, great... Like dangling a carrot on a stick in front of a donkey. I tried to look nonchalant and shrugged my shoulders.

"Whatever."

The food was delicious and as I was ravenous, it wasn't difficult to concentrate fully on eating. And when I finished, Daniel and the others had gone.

"So can you tell me about what was behind the gate? I saw Daniel walking there. What was that place?"

"Well... I'm sure you will learn all about it soon enough," Diana was clearly being careful with her words.

It looked as though I wasn't going to get any decent answers out of her. Best to wait for the official explanation about the gate, then.

I didn't have to wait long. I slept restlessly through the night and never deeply enough to have dreams. It was always like that when I slept in strange places. It was as though the child within me raised her head again and all the childhood nighttime fears and nightmares came rushing back. Diana slept like a log in the other bed, but her peaceful slumbers did not make me feel any more relaxed. I opened my eyes to check the time at the digital alarm clock at least once every hour.

And then the morning came and someone knocked on the door.

Diana was nowhere to be seen. I thought I had not slept at all, but obviously I had dozed off for a while and she had left quietly, not wanting to wake me up.

I got out of bed in my checkered pajamas and, quickly combing my unruly hair with my fingers, opened the door. I expected Grandma, or Lilith, or perhaps Diana would be standing in the hallway.

It was Daniel. He was leaning to the opposite wall in his jeans and T-shirt looking like a film star, arms folded across his chest. He appeared to be quite amused by my undisciplined appearance.

"Hey, sleepy head!" he smiled down from his heights. "Nice hair-do you've got there!"

I blushed like a ripe tomato, my fingers still smoothing my hair.

"I'm here to tell you more about the gates and what we do here," he told me. "I'll wait for you in the lobby. We'll go and have some breakfast first."

I wanted to slam the door shut, but managed to close it in a dignified manner. Only then did I swear like a sailor. Then I ran to the mirror, which confirmed that I looked like something out of a horror story. My hair was sticking out like the antennae of a satellite, and I had no makeup on, obviously. I looked horrible.

I went into the small bathroom and cleaned my teeth (the Centre had given me a bag of basic bathroom items). Then I realized I had no makeup with me, except for the pink lipstick I'd been carrying in my handbag. As a rule I didn't wear much makeup, but right now I would have given just about anything for a little mascara. Or a concealer - I had deep dark circles around my eyes.

I did all I could - splashed cold water onto my face and combed my hair (there was no brush in the necessities bag and of course no hair-spray so I had to tame the sputnik-look with plain water. I decided against the lipstick - it would have looked strange on its own without any other makeup. Then I put on my borrowed jeans and shirt and trainers. I was as ready as I could be, so I opened the door and faced the world for the last time as I currently knew it. I had the feeling that the way I saw it was about to change forever.

Daniel was standing in the lobby, as promised, talking seriously to an older lady. When he saw me, he left the woman and walked over to me.

Yes, I admit it: he was so gorgeously handsome; I felt my heart melt in my chest. It felt awkward, and rather than feeling elated, I hated myself for it. I was sure I looked just like one of the Blonde Crew at school, drooling over some handsome hunk - with the exception of the lack of makeup. However hard I tried not to, I was sure I was ogling him like a spaniel by the dinner table.

"Good morning," I greeted him stiffly, trying to be as matter-of-fact as I could.

He looked a bit surprised at my formal words, but did not respond in kind. He just gestured towards the cafeteria. I turned and started walking. He was not walking quite as closely to me as when we had left the bookstore, but I could still feel his body heat.

"Are you all right? Or do you have a fever?" I hadn't intended to ask him, but to my horror I just heard the words come motoring out of my mouth. It was as if I lost all my self-control when he was around.

"I am fine, thanks for asking," he smiled, which brought out the dimple.

Hell, did he have to smile all the time?

We quietly took our trays and started choosing breakfast.

After a sizeable omelet, a big mug of coffee, some toast with bitter orange marmalade (my father had taught me to like it too), and lots of orange juice I felt sure enough of myself to lean back and look at him directly.

As before, he looked right back at me. I saw golden dots swimming in the brilliant blue of his eyes. I gazed into them again. Yes - golden dots that were so bright they appeared to be moving.

"What...?" I almost asked, but didn't.

"What what?" he looked slightly amused (he seemed to find me permanently amusing), leaning back in his chair, measuring me openly with his gaze.

It felt like a caress on my cheek.

I managed to form an ordinary sounding question.

"So, what am I supposed to learn today?"

"You are supposed to learn what the gates are, and what the buffer zone is."

"I already know that. The gates are doorways to the Unseen Worlds, or afterworld... and the buffer zone is between those other worlds and ours. Oh, and it is also a pathway to different times. The book and Lilith already told me that much." I needed to sound smart; I was so off balance in his presence.

Daniel nodded.

"That's the easiest explanation. But you need to learn more. Such as how they are used, and for you to have better understanding, you need to experience the whole thing yourself. That is why I'll be taking you through our gate in the lobby."

My breakfast suddenly wanted to get out again. The scared little girl fearful of the dark was howling somewhere inside me.

"Is it safe?" I heard a mousy voice blurt out the question, and realized it belonged to me.

"It will be, with me." Daniel put down his coffee mug. "So, are you ready? Shall we go?"

"Just the two of us?"

"Yes, just the two of us."

"Right now?"

"No better time than right now. Let's go."

I really had no other choice but to follow him, with my knees wobbling, towards the lobby. Now that I was going to face the other side for real, I was not so sure I wanted to. Dreams were one thing, but to physically enter the place where the dead go... I began to feel nauseous as the fear crept into my mind, dragging itself to the front of my consciousness with sharp claws. Zombie faces swam up from the dark depths of my brain. Fangs, blood, curses... creatures half human, half beast. Every bad horror film I had ever seen, or book I had ever read, was suddenly playing out in full colour in my head. I had forgotten how terrified of the unknown I had been as a child.

Daniel seemed to sense my emotions, even though he had his back to me. He stopped and looked at me over his broad shoulder. What he saw on my face made him turn around. I must have looked like a doomed deer in car headlights. His expression became concerned.

"Hey..." he cupped my face between his hands and leaned down to look into my eyes, "there's nothing to be afraid of, I swear."

"What about the shadows...?" I squealed, panic squeezing my voice higher.

His hands were burning hot on my cheeks; his blue eyes were swirling with strength.

"They cannot enter where we go. Trust me."

I was drawn deep into his eyes, and for a while was really afraid my knees would melt and I would turn into a puddle on the carpet. The warmth in his eyes was radiating a comfort that I'd never experienced before and it finally convinced my fearful mind that he could be trusted. I was sure he could clearly see all the fear of the dark and shadows that was lurking in my head. All I saw in his eyes was sympathy, and self-assurance. He wasn't the least bit scared.

I breathed deeply, slowly gaining my composure. He had to know what he was doing.

"Thank you. You're an angel... I have always been so afraid of the dark and the unknown. About what happens when we die..."

He blinked with a look of surprise. Then he smiled, took my hand, and led me to the hall and the gate. I concentrated on looking at the solid frames around it. It was the weirdest sight. Here were these old fashioned gilded frames, and between them was an opening to... somewhere outside our physical world. The odd thing was it looked perfectly normal and physical to me. I felt a twinge of embarrassment for feeling so afraid.

Daniel put his arm around my shoulder, and pulled me tight to his side. I swallowed, feeling his body against me, warm, safe and strong.

"Ready now?"

I took one deep breath and nodded.

"Ready," I managed a whisper.

He gave me one tight squeeze, and led me through the gate.

24

THE WORLD BEHIND THE GATE

We flew. Everything was so strange that I didn't even pay attention as to how exactly we were gliding over the landscape. We were just gliding. Maybe I should have focussed on it more, but it was as though my normal awareness had entered a frozen state at the thought of being in some other reality. I simply concentrated on Daniel's physical touch and the strength of his arm holding me securely against his side.

We were floating through the most beautiful scenery, almost touching the ground, but not quite. I looked at my feet dangling in the air, and the sensation was similar to that of lucid dreaming. There seemed to be a bluish halo surrounding my legs.

There was a glorious meadow, and a forest. And after a while, high mountains appeared on the horizon, crisp and sharp in the clear atmosphere. The sky was a luminous blue color. And to my surprise the air was filled with scents - somehow I had imagined it would be like being in a dream, where I could not smell anything. The aroma of flowers and pine trees was very clear. That convinced me I was definitely not dreaming.

We landed by a river. A crystal clear river. I could see big fish swimming in the glassy water. Huge ferns grew on the banks of the river and ancient trees towered above us. The colors were so vibrant, so amazing. I had never seen anything like this in my other life. It was as though the very essence of nature was here, and our world was only a faint reflection of it. Just - the sounds of this world were a bit strange - it was as though there was no echo here.

"Where are we...?" I whispered the question. The place was so beautiful it made me fear that the act of speaking aloud would shatter it.

"We are now in one of the upper layers of the Unseen Worlds, the highest we can get in the buffer zone," Daniel said. "This part of the zone is a mixture of the lower vibrations of the afterlife and the higher energies of the human world."

"What forms these... higher energies in the human world?" I asked, wonderingly.

"Emotions created by thoughts and experiences. Emotions create energy. Just as it said in the book - everything is energy. It goes to its own level. Beautiful thoughts and positive emotions and energies keep this level alive, lower energies feed the reality of the lower levels. You can actually create things by deliberately feeling emotions, but that is something not many people know about. It's very logical here, though."

Logical wasn't exactly the word I would have used about any of this. But I was clearly out of my league here and there seemed to be no reason why Daniel would need to be untruthful about something like this. There was no reason to confuse or tease me about this reality.

I looked at Daniel. If possible, he was even more breathtaking here. Tall, relaxed, handsome. This was his element.

"Can you see how these... thoughts, as you say, arrive here?"

"Yes, you can observe that too, but it is not safe for you at this stage. As human beings we all relate to thought at every level. Strong emotions, positive or negative, can sweep you off your feet and carry you away before you become properly aware of them. Only more advanced humans can observe dispassionately the thoughts and emotions that conflict with them in their free-floating state, and so keep their footing, so to speak. You can do that if you know how to remain focussed with intent on a certain emotional level."

"Can you tell me where you can observe these thoughts? Emotions... energies, I mean."

"This side of reality is layered. Like the storeys of a house, to put it very basically. There is space above and under each 'floor', and in the space between the floors is the place where you can see the energies rising to their own level. They rise like smoke and the layer just absorbs the energies and they melt into the reality of that level."

"To do what?"

"They take whatever form is necessary to make the level more solid."

"Can you make unicorns with your thoughts?"

Daniel laughed and I wondered what on earth I was thinking to have asked something as stupid as that. Again the purring sound of his laughter made my head swim.

"Well, some thoughts are more - fashionable than others. Unicorns have been popular for a long time in Western history and belief. They might not be real in the human world, but when enough people think they are, the thoughts about unicorns can take shape here - as unicorns. And here - well, they could appear to be quite vivid as long as people believed in them."

Well, at least he had the good manners to answer a stupid question politely.

"So you say everything here is created by human mind?"

"By human mind, and human imagination. Thoughts are real energy. But do not forget the rest of creation. Animals have feelings and emotions too. As do plants, only in a different form. Some say even our planet has emotions, but I do not know about that. Still, there seems to be a strong unknown source of energy in addition to the ones I've already mentioned."

"Can the creatures created here go back to the human world?"

"Some can, if they are conscious enough."

"Such as?"

"Such as the shadows. They too are created by human mind - the difference between them and, for example, unicorns, is that they are created on purpose."

"Why...?"

"We'd better not continue this discussion, or your energies will sink and we will end up at a lower level. I would not want to put you in possible danger. If you want to stay here, you need to keep your thoughts at the level of these energies. Remember, this is not your normal world. The energies can be molded - and are molded - with your own thoughts. This is what you need to learn to be able to move here safely. You need to separate the awareness of lower energies from your emotions. The second you react to negative matters with your emotions, is the second you start descending to their level."

This was clearly something I would need to think about later.

I looked at the beautiful river, the fish, and the trees. I had noticed that the luminous light was everywhere, but I saw no sun.

"Where does the light come from?"

"It emanates from everything here. At lower levels it is darker. There is no physical sun here."

Beautiful bird song surrounded us.

"Are those birds also created by human mind?"

"No, they are real birds. Dead birds. They don't usually stay very long, though. Usually they are all eager to go back down again - they know they can come back up again very fast. They seem to find this to-and-fro movement rather exhilarating. It's fun for them. They aren't afraid to die in the physical - they well remember the place they will be coming back to."

I stood there, open-mouthed. Then I noticed something behind a big spruce. A little opening with a tiny building... I knew that building. It was the hut. Kitty's and mine, our secret place! It was here! Our thoughts must have created it here!

My feet began to walk before I even told them to. I was going as fast as I could. The ground was solid under my feet.

The door of the hut was open. I stopped.

Kitty came to the doorway with a broad smile on her face.

"Kitty! Oh, Kitty!"

I flew the short distance between us and hugged her with tears in my eyes. I felt her for a moment, semi-solid, and then she slipped out of my arms like a drift of smoke.

I felt Daniel's hands around me just as the forest began to melt away from around us. I had begun to cry uncontrollably. All the sadness, all the longing for my best friend burst out.

Slowly the forest, and the fields formed around us again, and I noticed a doorway at the edge of the woods. We had arrived back at the gate. We landed on the meadow in front of it, right at the edge of the forest. With Daniel's burning hot arm around my shoulders we stepped through the gate and back into the lobby. Well, stepping wasn't the right word - Daniel half carried me.

"What ha-happened?" I wiped tears.

"You felt sad, and were no longer able to stay at the higher energy levels. I brought you back. It was good your friend showed herself to you. It taught you more about the energies than my words could ever explain," Daniel said gently.

I sniffed. He created a handkerchief out of nowhere and extended it to me.

"You can meet her again, once you are ready to rise to those levels."

"You mean I can't now, not yet?"

"Probably no, but we will teach you how it is done. The work is your responsibility."

Daniel patted me on the shoulder and took a step back. I was so disappointed. I would have felt better for a hug.

"Hello there!"

Diana's cheerful voice came from behind me. I turned around.

"Oh dear. You've been to the upper levels, haven't you? And now it feels bad to be back in this heavy world again?"

"You could say that..." I concentrated on not bawling my eyes out and drew a ragged breath.

"She saw her dead friend for a few seconds," Daniel explained.

"Oh, I see. And started to cry and lost the friend?" Diana nodded sympathetically. "That has happened to so many of us. I collapsed when I saw my sister there for the first time and it hit me that she must have died. Well, of course I knew logically that she had died, considering the number of years that separated us, but actually seeing her there in her spirit form made it real for me."

I managed to gain my composure before I started to hiccup. I pushed the handkerchief into my jeans pocket.

"Here's another," Diana reached out her arm. It was a clean paper napkin this time, and I realized I had blown my nose quite vigorously on the cloth one Daniel had given me. I would have to wash it before returning it.

"And after this we'll go and have a hot chocolate with lots of whipped cream in it. There is nothing better to ease sadness than yummy calories," Diana announced.

I blew my nose on this new paper napkin also, in a very un-ladylike manner.

"Well, I have other things to attend to. You go and get your calorie hit." Daniel smiled, turned and walked away across the hall with long, relaxed steps.

Diana put an arm round my shoulders and gave me a reassuring squeeze before leading me to the cafeteria.

"Quite an experience, eh?" Diana commented when our hot chocolates arrived. "The first time is always the best. As you progress, you get used to it, which is the point. You need to control yourself, so you don't just forget yourself there. Daniel takes everyone there for their first visit, because he knows how to keep the energies high even when the other one starts to fall. And everyone does, mind you, it wasn't just you. From then on, it's a matter of hard learning on your own."

"Oh..." I was disappointed, "you mean he won't be taking me... I mean anyone there but once?"

For some reason Diana seemed to find this very funny. She took another sip before speaking again.

"Oh come on... Just join the club. Everyone here is in love with Daniel. Like I said, he has that effect on us all. But you'll see a lot of him around, so you can give him the Bambi-eyes and do your best to work your wiles on him! Which I doubt will succeed. The guy just doesn't date..."

She started to laugh again as I turned red.

"I'm not in love with him!" I retorted.

"Sure, sure, hon..."

While the hot drink lasted I made considerable effort to talk about something other than Daniel.

25

THE OPENING OF THE WAY

"We have five kinds of group here; anyone coming in is tested and then assigned to study the area in which they show the most aptitude. The groups are Gatekeepers, Weavers, Hunters, Guardians, and Researchers. You will learn more about them later," Lilith explained to me as she led me along the corridor of one of the wings.

"Sounds like Hogwarts," I couldn't resist saying.

Lilith laughed.

"Sort of, yes. But this place is firmly built in physical reality, even if you could say much of the buffer zone or the levels of the Unseen Worlds are figments of our imagination. Because that's what they are. They have always been there, but whatever physical form they take is dependent on the thoughts, emotions and imagination of people. It is a forever changing world."

The Centre was quite big – three wings reached backwards from the main building, into a large old garden with huge trees. In one wing was the staff dormitory, Lilith's office, and the private cafeteria, and the two others were in spa use. The Magellan Spa visitors could not enter the corridor leading to the private wing, which was the westernmost one. The gate was in the lobby on the westernmost wing, which you could not enter freely, even from the private wing. Every door leading to the great hall was locked, including the cafeteria's, and only opened when someone looking through a surveillance camera pressed a button to open the door. I had not noticed them at first, but there were four guards in the lobby, each sitting in their own glass cubicle.

"Let's talk about the gates in more detail."

Lilith opened the heavy door to her office, which was situated on the front side of the building. She could see everyone approaching the Centre and spa from her desk by the window– no wonder she was out to meet us as soon as we arrived.

Daniel was in the office, sitting in an armchair with his long legs stretching in front of him. He was reading a book. A very big, old book. Despite its size, he balanced it in his hands in a way that made it look weightless.

"Ah, good, you're here. Shall we go?"

He rose out of his chair in one fluid, catlike motion. The movement was balletic. There was so much strength in the movements of his muscular athletic body.

"Yes, let's go." Without saying anything more, Lilith raised her hand and with one quick movement slashed the air in front of her.

When I say she slashed it, I mean that literally. An opening appeared in the air, as if she had cut paper with scissors.

"Woooo...!" I stepped back, breathless with surprise.

"Maybe you should have warned her..." the corner of Daniel's mouth lifted into a half smile, "looks as though someone is about to run for the exit screaming as she goes..."

"I do apologize," Lilith said. "Everyone here is so used to seeing this that I forgot it might scare you."

Right... as if I wouldn't have been scared to see all the laws of physics broken in front of me? But, not wanting to show weakness in front of Daniel again, I tried to appear unafraid, and even took a step forward to see better. I walked around the slit, understanding now what Diana had been talking about before. The slit disappeared from sight, when I went behind it, and nothing out of the ordinary happened. When I came back to the "front" of it (for lack of a better term), it was clearly visible again. Impossible. Yet...it was similar to the big gate in the lobby. My head whirled at the concept that time and space were physical things that you could cut through.

"Did you just create a gate of your own?" I asked.

Lilith smiled and nodded.

"Yes. There are only three of these in the world..."

She extended her hand and I saw something that looked like a finger cover from a mummy. It was of some transparent, slightly rose-colored material that I did not recognize.

"This isn't real..." I shook my head, "I have gone crazy. Things like this just do not happen!"

"Oh but they do. They always have. Remember the old stories of sleepers...? Professor Rowan told me that he'd told you about them - probably gave you quite a lecture, knowing him.... Some of the details in those stories are not factual, but a basic truth is there. People go to a realm with no time, return unchanged, and time has passed in the human world."

"Time has passed...? But you just said it won't pass."

"It doesn't, not in the buffer zone, unless you are at the very edge of it, almost touching our world - that is a zone where time has some effect. Time does move on in the human world, though. If you go to the buffer zone, it is all about finding your way back to the moment where you left the time-space reality you came from. If you don't know how to do that, you can come out haphazardly, and find yourself anywhere in time. Future. Past. Any time. You disappear from the time that you left, and continue to live in the time in which you've arrived. You cannot be in two places at the same time. And it seems you cannot go to the past and re-enter a time where you have already lived. One of the reasons we have to keep good records about who has traveled and to which time is so we don't try sending them there again. Trying to enter a time where you already are can hurl you unexpectedly into a completely different era to the one intended."

Daniel stepped through the slit in the air, and vanished from the room. Lilith beckoned me to follow, and I braced myself and followed Daniel. Lilith was the last to walk through, after which she repeated the slashing motion with her hand. One moment I saw her office, the next it was gone and we were in another space that looked like an old library. And a huge library at that.

Bookshelves were towering towards the high, high ceiling. Worn sets of stairs led to the upper galleries. Tall ladders were needed to reach the uppermost books on all the galleries whilst the medium height shelves could be reached with the help of the step stools that were scattered all around. And everywhere you looked there were books, thousands of books, sitting in neat rows, stacked up on tables, crammed onto the hundreds and hundreds of shelves. The corridor where we were standing seemed to continue so far into the distance I swear it disappeared into a haze.

I saw two people nearby, sitting at reading desks, concentrating fully on what they were reading. I recognised one of them, a boy who looked like he might be Indian, as a member of the group who'd been sitting at Daniel's table in the cafeteria. I was sure any researcher would give their right arm for an opportunity to investigate a place where time stood still.

"These," Lilith showed me the strange finger shaped cover that she used to make the opening, "are ancient. We do not know the nature of the material, but it seems to be even harder than diamonds. They tear openings between this physical world and the semi-physical world of the buffer zone. And despite their antiquity and the fact they've been in use for thousands of years, they show no signs of wear."

"Where did they come from, then? Who made them? Aliens?"

Daniel shook his head, amused.

"No. Ever heard of the Nephilim?"

"The... what? No... I don't think so... Who were they? Or what?"

"That depends... " Daniel's expression was unreadable.

"The Nephilim were the offspring of what we are used to calling angels and mortal humans. Their story is referenced in the Bible, for instance, as well as other sources," Lilith said. "The angels - or rather Watchers, which is the original word for them - were male in these stories, and they should not have had relations with human women, but they did so nevertheless. Their offspring were the Nephilim. They were taller, lived longer, and learned a lot of ancient wisdom from their parents because the Watchers taught their human women knowledge that humankind was not ready for yet, or so the story goes."

Lilith sat on a little couch in the library and patted it for me to sit too. I did. It was quite a relief to sit down on something surprisingly solid and real.

"When the two species mixed, human and angel, the results were sometimes unexpected. For example, some of the children craved human blood, and it extended their lives, which were already unnaturally long."

She waited for the information to sink in.

"You mean... They were... vampires?"

"Indeed. That seems to be the word that has come into general use to describe them," Lilith nodded. "There were the Chinese jianshi - they were evil spirits that drained people of their energy. Just like shadows do. The Tibetan Book of the Dead called the blood-drinking spirits "Wrathful Deities". Ancient Greek had its bloodthirsty goddess-es...then there are the classic vampire tales of the mysterious mountains of the Carpathians and the Balkan regions. And legends abound in human cultures in which people try to find an explanation for creatures that want to drink human blood."

She patted my hand. I must have looked shocked.

"So the stories of vampires are actually based on truth, even if they have the later decorations of fangs and bat wings and all the rest of it. Of course there are shadows; and people who resemble vampires, once they are infected, and these feed on humans, one way or the other. But the Nephilim who turned dark, and the vampires they created, were the real thing. And I can tell you there is nothing romantic about them, so forget about all those novels describing love affairs between people and vampires. You would not want any kind of relationship with them... If you survived being bitten and infected by a dark Nephilim, or by a vampire of their creation, you would turn into a kind of shadow yourself, craving blood, and infecting others when you took it. That is how the stories of vampires creating their own kind were born."

Lilith paused and Daniel took up the story.

"Not all of the Nephilim were bad, but the ones that were, seemed to be unable to feel any loving emotions. They were almost emotionless, and their only interest was in furthering their own ends - achieving riches and power over weaker humans. This became their only driving passion and for this they were ready to kill, to enslave, and to do any horrible thing. Eventually this led to war, when people could no longer tolerate them. The myths tell us that God threw the angels responsible for fathering the Nephilim into a fiery pit for all eternity. And that at the same time their offspring, the Nephilim, were hunted down and killed."

Lilith nodded.

"Indeed. We do not know what the actual reason was for it. We don't know whether these were real happenings, later written down in religious form, or if there really was a higher power that punished the angels, but the fact is that the Watchers disappeared from human stories. But not all of the Nephilim died. Many went into hiding and once the war was over, they re-emerged and continued their lives, hiding their true nature, apparently forgotten by whatever higher force it was that punished the Watchers. These surviving Nephilim were the ones who had managed to keep the three devices we can use to enter the buffer zone," Lilith showed me her strange cover again. "We call these simply 'Keys'."

Daniel opened the book he had carried with him from Lilith's office and placed it on my lap. It showed stone wall panels of winged Assyrian gods.

"You can see the winged Nephilim in many ancient paintings and reliefs," Daniel pointed at the pictures, "just look in history books, or visit museums. God-like figures with wings. They are there for anyone to see. Throughout history most the remaining Nephilim kept mostly to themselves, in some kind of attempt to keep their blood pure, but others found human wives or husbands. They conceived children. And so now some diluted Nephilim blood can be found in the majority of humans."

I leafed through the pictures in the book. Angel statues, winged gods and goddesses. I noticed Isis there and almost as a reflex my hand rose to touch the pendant hanging under my shirt.

"OK... But what about the gates? Who created those? The Nephilim? And if so, why was there a need for these gates, if they already had the Keys?" I pointed at the rosy colored finger cover Lilith held very carefully on the palm of her hand.

"We believe the gates might have been created using these Keys, but we can't be sure. Perhaps they were opened and never closed again when the Watchers disappeared. But this is just a theory, that perhaps once they were opened and left open, it became impossible to close them after a while. Like an old wound that cannot heal itself again. Maybe the gates were used in the War of Angels. We do not know. There are so many secrets that have vanished with time. The locations of the anchored gates in the physical world have miraculously remained a secret to the Immortals and bad Nephilim. Still, the Immortals have a way of moving between the buffer zone and our world. We know for sure the dark Nephilim take them between the physical world and the buffer zone. Their shadows are involved in this movement too. Coming back to the physical world is not, on the whole, difficult, but humans cannot reach the buffer zone on their own unaided."

"And this is why you have created this place?" I said, gesturing around me in a circle to indicate the whole Centre. "To stop the Immortals and Nephilim?"

"Partly, yes. And partly because we've learned about something very dangerous and ancient that wasn't destroyed, even though it should have been."

I looked around in the library. I realised that there were many more people than I had first noticed. They were leaning on the bookcases, or sitting at little desks scattered everywhere, wherever there was a big enough space. And everyone was reading silently or writing notes.

"So, what is it?"

Lilith and Daniel glanced at each other. They were clearly trying to reach a decision.

"Once we have told you, you are not safe in the outside world anymore. Not until you have learned to protect yourself from the shadows. Are you ready for this? To stay for a long time, if necessary? Can we trust you?"

"I don't know why you have trusted me with this much information already, to be honest," I confessed, "but if you tell me more, I promise I will keep your secret."

"We have reasons to believe that you will keep your word," Daniel said and I got the oddest feeling there was a hidden meaning in what he said that had nothing to do with simply deciding to trust someone. "Also Layla vouches for you. That is why you were given the book. We suspect you have hidden talents. You should, considering your genealogy. And so you will find you life's work here, in one of our groups."

For a moment I wondered what was so extraordinary about my very ordinary parents. I saw Lilith quickly glance sideways at Daniel.

"OK. Shoot. Tell me what this dangerous, ancient thing is. Some sort of weapon?" I asked.

"No, it is knowledge. A book," Lilith patted the book on my lap.

"A book. Is that what all these people are searching for? Is it somewhere here in the library?"

"In an indirect way, yes. They are looking for clues in our books about where the book sought by the Nephilim might be. It is called the Book of Watchers – we believe this contains the ancient writings that the angels used to teach their children. It must contain skills that are absolutely terrifying in their power. We fear that at its worst, after reading this book one could literally tear apart the veil between the worlds of the living and the dead. And the Immortals want to find it too, as they believe it would give them free mobility between the physical world and buffer zone. It might surprise you, but we did not know such a book existed until we caught a shadow that revealed information about the book before the shadow's creator withdrew his consciousness, destroying his creation. Ever since then the shadows have been created to be mute. We take this as proof that such a book really exists. The huntress who caught the shadow and forced the information out of it was Layla."

"My grandmother? A Huntress?"

"A Huntress of shadows, yes."

That was something to muse over... For a short, hysterically amused moment, I wondered what mother would say if she knew. But her knowing anything about this was an impossible thought in itself, so I discarded it.

"But how can you know for sure that such a race as these angels actually existed? Aren't they also imaginary creatures?" I realised even as I spoke that I was going to have to revise my interpretation of "imaginary." I stared at a picture of the "Mystic nativity" painted by Sandro Botticelli. A ring of angels was flying over the stable, three angels sitting on the roof, and angels hugging people and pointing at the manger. The angels had wings of different colors.

"They might not be what you'd expect them to be. Much of they way they look in the pictures and reliefs is a human invention, of course. But they did exist here once. The Nephilim are a living proof of this. They inherited a lot of their physique from their ancestors," Lilith explained.

"Living proof? I've never seen any such a thing as a Nephilim!" I said. "Nor has anyone else I know."

I wasn't exactly in a place to deny everything they'd said, having stepped through the gate. And having seen my dead friend with my own eyes, and touched her with my own hands, even if it only was for a fleeting moment. Still there was too much to assimilate in one sitting. I had never been religious, and considered angels to be like fairies – pretty, and not real. Like the angels in Botticelli's painting.

"But you've almost certainly been seeing Nephilim in your life, even if you didn't realise it at the time. You will recognize them if you know what to look for," Lilith told me. "First of all, they are tall. Secondly, their eye color is brilliant – it can be golden, which is often the sign of a dangerous Nephilim. Or they can be brilliant blue, which usually tells you are dealing with a good one. That's a very general rule, not a fixed one. Nephilim skin can be any color. Human genetics dictate the appearance of that somewhat."

"And they have wings?"

"Well, yes, in a way. Not the feathery things people have been depicting in art, but energy whirls of magnificent colors, which spread out, resembling wings. They are transparent, see-through," Lilith continued. "Of course they keep them hidden unless they are certain it is safe to open them. And they can function in angelic ways without opening them fully. Flying for example."

"Tall, bright eyes, wings they don't show... Anything else? I know quite a few tall, bright-eyed people, without wings, who don't fly. Come to think of it - I never knew anyone who could fly."

"The people you know don't share the last physical characteristic that separates the Nephilim from ordinary people. Heat. Body heat. They have a much higher temperature than we do."

I froze.

"Heat... They are... hot?"

"We are," Daniel said and spread his wings.

26

WINGS

"You really are a show-off, aren't you!"

Diana's voice floated into my consciousness. I must have been asleep. The bed felt quite hard, though. I opened my eyes and much to my astonishment I was looking up at towering bookshelves. I was lying on the floor... Why would I be lying on the floor?

Diana's face hovered over me.

"Good, you are awake. I've been telling our angel-boy here what's what. To scare someone like that without warning..."

I remembered. I jumped to my feet so fast that I bumped against Diana, who lost her balance and ended up sitting on the floor. Daniel was standing nearby, and to his credit it has to be said he did look embarrassed. At the moment he looked like an ordinary, tall young man.

"Did you just have wings??" my voice was rasping with shock, but it did not stop it from rising hysterically towards the end of the question.

"Yes..." He looked at me under his brows – that breathtakingly blue gaze.

"You'd better let her see them again, Daniel. It doesn't exactly look as though her mind is taking in what she saw," Lilith commented dryly. Her tone revealed she was not very happy with Daniel either.

This time he did not pop them open like an umbrella, but instead turned his back on me and opened them very slowly so I could see them better.

How to describe the wings? They were definitely not like the traditional giant swan wings of angel statues and paintings. No bird feathers of any kind. No – they were somehow quite immaterial.

The wings appeared from under his shirt as if the fabric was no obstacle at all – two little colorful points of light, blue in shade, which first grew upwards like someone had drawn a glowing line with a brush. And then they grew outwards. It was a bit like watching ferns unfurl in a high-speed movie... They rolled open by spreading up and out, high above his head, tips touching. When they were fully open, they melted together, and formed a perfect half circle behind Daniel's upper torso. The lower ends of these wings were separate and curled slightly forward past his legs, enveloping his lower body. Suddenly I remembered the bluish halo around my legs when we flew over the fields.

And they were shimmering with blue and gold – slowly pulsating in transparent color, which emanated light. A bit like blood pulsing in veins, only like the veins were transparent and the blood – or color – was visible. I could see how the link to them in the human mind would be the wings of a bird – or maybe a butterfly. Or perhaps just a very bright aura. They seemed to bend air around them a bit like the edges of a leaf floating on the surface of water.

"Wow," I breathed out in utter astonishment. Two of the closest people reading books glanced at the wings and returned to their books. Business as usual here, it seemed.

All I could do was stare at the wings in awe, with my mouth open. Daniel turned back to face us. I snapped my mouth shut, and hoped in vain I did not look like a total idiot.

"So you are one of the Nephilim?" I asked him the obvious.

"Yes. From one of the least diluted bloodlines. That's why the wings are so big."

Daniel looked almost relieved, and suddenly I understood. He would have to hide his true identity from everyone in the outside world. If he showed his wings, he'd probably end up in some laboratory and would have lost his freedom for good. Or, maybe not... with the Keys in use I am sure he would be able to escape from anywhere. If he did not have a Key, then Lilith did and...

My imagination was beginning to create scenarios again. I firmly told it to stop.

"And the bloodlines with more human blood result in smaller wings?" I analyzed.

"In time, yes, usually. Sometimes there are no wings at all, and sometimes the more human bloodlines surprise with huge wings. So it isn't a straight-forward downhill shift for the Nephilim race, if there is more human blood in it. It seems the angels and humans were originally somehow related – this is logical when you think about it, as they could produce offspring - and there is the potential of finding... angelic skills... in human blood as well. Some kind of genetic mutation may bring it out, I think," Daniel answered.

"So are the fairies of the stories then actually Nephilim with much diluted blood and thus smaller wings?" I pondered.

Diana snorted and Daniel rolled his eyes at her.

"That was quite a legitimate question, Di," he said.

"Sorry, for a second there I saw you as a little fairy sitting on a flower... or perhaps on a mushroom with a caterpillar smoking a hookah. Three inches tall, a very good height indeed!"

Daniel glared at Diana, who was clearly having great difficulties in taking control of her slightly hysterical giggling.

"Are the Nephilim babies born with wings, then?" I was full of questions.

Daniel's eyebrows rose at the question, and Diana, who had just got herself under control, burst into another fit of laughter.

"No, the wings develop later," Daniel shot Diana another glare. "The Nephilim come of age when the wings begin to grow. The age may vary, but it's not usually before we are in our late teens, often after we have turned twenty. It's an occasion of great celebration among the

Nephilim. But it may be a shock to the new Nephilim, especially if they are not aware of what they are."

"It's a good thing they don't grow sooner," said Diana, mock seriously. "Imagine the trouble of babysitting them! Tiny Nephilim scooting around in the air - like pilots with the common sense of a toddler..."

I had to admit the idea of flying babies was somewhat hilarious, but I was too new to all of this, and very curious, so I did not waste my time in laughing but turned back to Daniel.

"Can I touch your wings?" I asked.

Daniel withdrew half a step, his facial muscles suddenly tightening, but he nodded.

"Nephilim don't like people touching the wings – it can be rather painful because of the differing vibrations. But I suppose I owe it, having scared you like that."

He turned sideways to me and I touched the blue and golden wings of light as gently as I possibly could, instinctively stroking in the direction the colors pulsed. The sensation was odd – as if I was touching warm, running water that ran upwards, with the exception that my hand did not get wet.

There was the slightest feeling of material against my palm, and my hand could not go through the wing - it was more like a feeling of pressure against my skin, not anything solid. Like two magnets rejecting each other; the harder you press, the stronger the feeling of an opposing force.

I raised my other hand as well and stroked the wings with both hands. I felt a clear resonance, an electric feeling in my fingers.

Daniel gasped.

"I'm sorry!" I snatched my hand back, certain I had hurt him unintentionally.

"It's... It's all right," he said tightly, I could see the muscles on his jaw moving when he gritted his teeth together. "I told you it is not easy for us."

Lilith frowned.

"Are you sure everything is all right, Daniel?" she looked at him with an expression I could not analyze.

"Yes, quite all right," Daniel managed a smile and looked like his charming self again.

"Are there any more of your kind here?" I looked around the people in the library with my hands carefully behind my back.

"Some, but they are not here at this moment. And most of the Nephilim are of the other kind... and should never be allowed to enter the Centre."

I looked at his wings, now more relaxed. It looked as though they were gently swaying in some unseen breeze. Towards his torso, and out again. A bit like a butterfly slowly fluttering its wings. In and out... in and out... just like... was he...? I looked at his chest, which stayed flat and immobile.

"Daniel... Are you breathing with your wings?"

Diana gave a low whistle.

"Impressive... You have only just arrived, seen angel wings like for two minutes, and you have already discovered one of the best kept secrets of the Nephilim!" she said.

"I am. Breathing with my wings, yes," Daniel admitted.

"Even when they are withdrawn?"

"Even then, yes. They are then inside our bodies, but function just the same."

"So they are your lungs?"

Daniel shrugged and raised his arms in a gesture that seemed almost Latin.

"Nephilim do have ordinary human lungs as well," Lilith explained, "but also another breathing system, which is connected to the wings. They can extract much more oxygen into their blood stream through their wings, and remain functional in situations where ordinary people would have lost consciousness for lack of oxygen. Such as under water."

A whole new series of questions developed in my mind, regarding mermaids, but there were too many to put into words right there and then.

Daniel was standing next to me, and I think my arm twitched a little – I could not help it, I so wanted to touch those beautiful wings again. In a snap his wings disappeared and his chest began to move with the rhythm of normal breathing again.

"OK, that's that. Wouldn't it be time to show Dana what we do here?" he asked lightly.

Somehow I was certain that he closed his wings so hastily, so that I could not touch them again. He turned to face Lilith, careful not to meet my eye.

Oddly, I felt insulted.

27

SHADOW ON THE SCENT

The shadow ran tirelessly, casting back and forth. It had been seeking for clues along the four other major roads without stopping, but still hadn't found the scent of its prey. It was now heading for the fifth. It was patient. It knew eventually it would find the trail.

"Bring her unharmed," the Hunter had said, "she is important."

The shadow did not question its Hunter – but because of their connection, for a while it caught a glimpse of a memory in his mind. Buildings fell down, the sky filled with flame, shadows flew through the air, and there was a baby the Master wanted badly. Finally, the body of a young woman, twisted in an unnatural position on top of debris. Then the pictures disappeared, leaving only huge disappointment that something that should have been theirs had disappeared. It was a scene the shadow knew well, because it had been there too.

Probably the most terrifying thing about the shadows was that they lacked awareness of their own true nature. Their consciousness extended so far and no further, as if they were creatures that had been deliberately stopped at a particular stage of development. Their belief in their own existence meant they would do anything, just like any other living thing, if they needed to fight for survival. They existed and ceased to exist in an illusion of individuality.

The shadow would please the Masters. It would find the one it was sent to fetch. That way it would live. Life was the goal - its own life.

28

GRANDMA AND THE BOOK OF WATCHERS

"This library is in the upper levels of the buffer zone, and we work constantly to keep it located there too. If you see people just sitting here with their eyes closed, they aren't sleeping! They're doing energy work to keep the library afloat in the higher levels of the buffer zone. It in a way floats in the mist, and it is not likely the creatures of lower levels could find it, as long as we manage to keep it up. Its existence has seeped into legends, though, and some call it the Akashic library," Grandma explained to me when I tried to take in the vastness of the library, swirling around like a dervish almost. "These books come from every age of history. We have saved many irreplaceable books from destruction. When we know there was a major fire in history, for example, that could destroy valuable texts, our teams travel back to try to reach the books before their destruction and bring them here. They do not belong in the physical world anymore, but they are kept safe here in the buffer zone."

We were walking through the library. Each apparently endless corridor was lined with bookshelves from the ceiling to the floor.

"Don't you ever run out of space here?" I asked

"No. We create more space whenever necessary."

"How?"

"That's something we teach to all our groups. How to master the material of the buffer zone with your thoughts. It is moldable energy after all. You just need to learn to use your mind as the tool to shape what you need."

"Really?"

"Yes. What you create, remains solid, as long as you keep on paying attention to it. That's it in a nutshell, but of course there is lot more to it, which you will learn with time, I am sure."

That sounded so sci-fi I thought I'd better not probe any further. Not now. To me thoughts weren't material. They were just... thoughts. How could they have substance? How could they create anything solid?

"Can you show me?" I asked Grandma.

"Of course - that's the best way..." She stopped and bent down so her palms touched the floor. She remained there, concentrating with her eyes closed. I noticed a slight smile on the corners of her mouth and at the same time the solid floor under her hands changed - it looked like plastic putty almost. She scooped it into her hand and straightened up. Then she put her other hand over the putty-like material and smiled, at her inner joke it seemed. The little hole on the floor slowly disappeared and soon the floor looked like it had never been touched.

I could see the material moving between the palms of Grandma's hands, changing color too. Then she opened her hands and there was an ornament - a little red cat sitting on her hand. It looked just like Nugget. I took it in my hand - it was perfect.

"You concentrate on what you want to create, take enough material to make it, and then think about your chosen object. It may not turn out what you want it to be, though. Depends on your emotions at that moment," Grandma wiped her hands on her jeans.

"Amazing... you even managed to create the exact look in Nugget's eyes!" I lifted the little ornament up to my eye level. Did I even see whiskers?

"Oh well, it's nothing much..." Grandma belittled her creation but I could see she was pleased at my reaction, "Now, let me show you something interesting."

She led me further into the library.

"Here is a part of the library we are especially proud of," Grandma pointed as we proceeded deeper into the library. "See all these scrolls?"

Indeed there were rows upon rows of scrolls on the shelves. Ancient looking in their shape, but not worn or crumbled with age as truly ancient manuscripts would be.

"These are from the library of Alexandria in Egypt."

I stopped in my tracks.

"Really?"

"Yes. The library demanded that every scroll that entered Alexandria was to be copied and put into the library collections. Every ship that came to the harbor had to comply. Scribes copied the texts and created one of the most fabulous libraries in the world, filled with knowledge from all the surrounding ancient kingdoms. The library burned down, and there is a saying circulating that you know you are a historian if the thought of the burning of the library in Alexandria still makes you cry."

I could relate to that.

"And you managed to save the scrolls?"

"Not all the scrolls, but these ones, yes. It was very dangerous - that was the farthest we have ever gone in history, and that's when you discover that the phrase 'the mists of time' is not just a meaningless one. Reaching back so far is full of issues, but we sent one of our most experienced Time Walker teams to the scene and managed to get there. Local people were trying to save the scrolls, and they joined in the effort, dressed in the clothing of the time. They took as many scrolls as they possibly could, and brought them here."

"But shouldn't these scrolls be given back to the world?" I bent closer to see the scrolls nearest to us, not daring to touch them.

"That could change history. Besides, they look too new to convince anyone they are ancient, for the obvious reason they were brought to the buffer zone when still relatively new. No radiocarbon dating would show they are old. We only take books when they are about to be destroyed, and bring them here. And we bring many of them here because in some book or scroll, somewhere, there has to be something written about the location of the Book of Watchers. We need to find it."

"Lilith said that you were the one who found out about the Book of Watchers. That you hunted down a shadow and..."

"Yes... You see, Dana, I have been a Huntress since I was a teenager. I was invited to join the Time Walkers just like you - given the same dream book as you. It appeared one night on my desk and I thought it was my mother's - she was very interested in dream interpretation. So I read it and passed the lucid dreaming test. My skills were obviously in the hunting of shadows, and that is what I have been doing ever since. I suppose I have somewhat of a reputation in the world of shadows, and that is why I was so surprised a shadow had crept into your garden... they fear the Time Walker Hunters so much, and me especially, that I would have expected them to wait until I was somewhere else before approaching you."

"Approaching me? Why would they want to approach me?"

"All in good time, Dana..." Grandma said. "You'll hear it when the time is right. We'll see."

"Won't you just tell me what it is? Why all this cryptic we-shall-see-stuff?"

"I know I am right in certain things, but I may be wrong in others... I prefer not to talk about something until I am sure. But whatever the case, you need to stay here in safety for a while. We have actually come up with a plan with Reggie about how to get you away from your little town without drawing too much attention to the matter."

"Reggie?"

"That would be our history professor. Reginald Rowan. The same one who keeps on pulling out his hair after reading all the wonderful books and scripts in the library and not being able to use them as source material in his research. Can you imagine what it is like to a history researcher to hold the actual ancient proof that something happened in history, and because it is in this library and nowhere else, not being able to ever use it in the scientific circles of our ordinary world? Reading the theories of others, seeing their errors and knowing the actual truth, but never being able to say so?"

I had a feeling Grandma was trying to divert my thoughts away from why the shadows found me interesting. I let her. I would find out.

"Fill me in on the shadow and the Book of Watchers," I asked instead.

Her face grew serious.

"I was hunting shadows in the human world with my trustworthy red steed," she began. "My car," she specified with a twinkle when my face obviously showed I had no idea who or what the steed in question was.

"Oh, OK. Right. You chase them in your car?"

"Of course. The shadows are very, very fast, but they cannot outrun a decent sports car. After all they are semi-physical forms and subject to the laws of gravity like the rest of us. So they run using the surface under their feet, bouncing forward with their legs, just like us. This gives us an advantage here. Our form is more solid, and thus we have more power in our movements and deeds. Imagine someone jumping on the moon - they move like that, and can't quite use gravity to their advantage, even if they are still very fast."

We kept on walking along the corridors of the library. There were no lamps here, but light seemed to seep in from somewhere anyway. Everywhere, really.

"So, I had just bought my red sports car, and was on my patrol duty where we knew the shadows liked to appear, when I spotted this particular one. He was lurking in an alleyway, near a bar. That's one of their favourite locations – the energies of intoxicated people draw them like a magnet. When drunk people leave the bar, they follow them so they can steal the person's energies, and if possible, reveal themselves - a downright terrifying sight for the drunk. They come in different shapes and forms, but they are all like something out of a horror movie. You were able to see them, when you were a child, do you remember?" she asked suddenly.

I stopped short. It was one thing thinking of drunks seeing demonic shadows and being convinced it was down to the drink, but this was now touching me personally. All the old night horrors sneered at me from the darker regions of my mind. I remembered the twisted forms, and the half-human, half-animal faces, the evil grins. Wherever there was a deep shadow, I'd been able to see them there as a child.

"You mean... they were not nightmares like mother said?"

"Oh they were nightmares, all right, only real ones. You refused to sleep in a dark room, because you had the ability to sense the shadows. And if they came close, you saw them too. Luckily for you, you were strongly protected, and they did not realize who you were. They were only drawn to you because of your ability to see them. Of course they thought they could scare you easily because of that, and that would make your energy easy to steal. They like stealing the energy of children, because it's so strong. They don't usually kill them, but they can come to drink their energy again and again, because children create new strong energy so quickly. Eventually, though, they cause the child to become ill, and maybe even die, if they feed on them too often."

"Ok, that's it. What do you mean by that? Who you were... and who protected me? I want an explanation right now." I put my foot down.

"No, I won't do that. Not yet. We shall see in a short while. I need to tell you about the shadow, the Book of Watchers, and our plans with Reggie for you first. All in good time."

Grandma was so frustrating! I actually stomped my foot against the floor, like an angry child, but she just smiled.

"So, I noticed this shadow, waiting in the alleyway near a bar. It wanted to scare someone, maybe even kill them, to feed on their energy. If you encounter a shadow doing this, you can actually watch the energy transferring from one to the other. It just leaks out. The scared person almost shoots out energy and the shadows roll that energy into a shape like a ball."

Revulsion probably showed on my face, because she continued, "Yes, the best way to describe it, strange though it sounds, is that it looks like a dirty snowball. And then they just eat the energy, leaving the person depleted of it and ill. If they manage to scare someone to death, they get an enormous amount of energy - they can survive on it for weeks."

Grandma's description was so vivid that the feeling of fear in my chest and stomach when I had seen the shadows as a child came flooding back.

"So, I drove past, and the shadow did not recognize me – I was downwind, as it were, a favorable direction from my point of view, and it had not spotted my car yet, so it couldn't smell me. I parked my car on the other side of the block and got up on the roof using the fire escape ladder."

As Grandma described how she'd caught the shadow, I could see her in my mind's eye walking down a darkened street with her determined, lithe gait, like something in a movie. And climbing up the fire escape onto a roof? Surely what she was telling me couldn't be true?

"I still can't believe that you do this!" The words burst out of me before I had time to stop them. "All on your own?"

"Believe it!" said Grandma and her voice had a steely ring that was new to me.

"But - aren't you scared?"

"I was in the early days. It's a skill like anything else. It's all about instinct - and one's instinct develops with time and experience. Anyway, on this occasion I had been following the shadow for some time before an opportunity presented itself..."

My Grandma the Shadow Hunter. For a while I thought about her climbing onto a roof using a ladder. But then again, she was very fit for her age. And looked a lot younger than her advanced years. She would manage it easily.

Grandma noticed me looking at her body. She smiled.

"I know. I don't exactly look as though I was in my seventies, do I?"

"No. You don't. What's the secret?"

"The buffer zone. It sort of helps, the absence of time. If you spend a lot of time in the buffer zone, you age much slower in the real world too. And also, it can be in the genes. I suppose my body is somewhere in its forties "

"I hope I have inherited your genes."

"I wouldn't be too sure of that..."

I wasn't sure I had heard right. Why would I not have inherited my grandmother's genes? At least some of them, the youthfulness being one of them, hopefully.

"But, back to the shadow. I jumped down on it from the roof and..."

"You what?" Now it was my Grandma the superhero?

"Quite, you don't know everything...you'll learn all about it soon enough. Let's just say I know how to jump from heights without hurting myself, using the buffer zone – it has to do with using Lilith's Key. Which I did. I landed behind the shadow, and managed to lasso it before it could flee."

"You lassoed it. All righty... and no one paid any attention to a grandmother throwing a lasso in an empty alleyway?"

"Not in that part of the town... no, no one saw. First of all no-one does see the shadows, when they are in their hiding mode, and secondly I was away from the alley with the shadow before you could say "Get out of there!" I took the shadow to the rooftop to destroy it."

"Sheesh! Are you sure you are my grandmother? I'm beginning to think someone's kidnapped the original and replaced her with an android. You sound like a killer out of a police series!" I eyed her in shock.

"Well, I am. Sort of. What makes it possible is the shadows aren't really real."

"This one sounds real enough!"

"They have been created from the substance of the lowest buffer zone – from the very same kind of negative, fearful thoughts that they hunt for in people. They need to feed on negativity to keep their solid form. And the core, which keeps them functioning and conscious, is an extension of the Hunter."

I didn't understand one bit.

"I'll try to explain this for you... their Hunters – well, they are like our Hunters, only they belong to the Immortals. Their job is to hunt down the people we find valuable, the ones who can learn how to move in the buffer zone, and through time. When they find them, they kill them. They don't want us to get any new Time Walkers for our team. It is a war."

I shivered.

"In the buffer zone, while the Immortals were learning to work with the energies, and molding their world, they also learned to concentrate a part of their consciousness away from themselves. It stays connected to them through an energy cord. They feed some of their energy out, into a shadow formed out of the buffer zone material, and send them away. You could say the shadows have a consciousness of their own because their material is made of human consciousness, but it is not concentrated consciousness. It cannot function on its own. The Hunter's energy is the thing that makes it truly functional. It is the Hunter, who is inside the shadow form, using it as an extension of themselves."

I tried to keep up with Grandma's explanations.

"When the Hunter withdraws their consciousness away from a shadow, the solid form they have created simply disintegrates. The shadow just crumbles away. Nothing remains. So when I say we kill the shadows, we disconnect the energy cord that leads back to their Hunter or Immortal."

I must have still looked confused, because Grandma, clearly trying hard to put this into words that I could understand, said: "The closest analogy that I can give you is that of the puppet. It has no life of its own, yet it moves, talks and can create the illusion of existence. A puppet master can even come to believe in the reality of his creation and the creation take on an apparent life of its own."

This was really starting to make me shudder, since who hasn't been frightened by the idea of a demonic doll at some point? It's not just the stuff of nightmares; it's a key component of horror movies.

"Would you like to see a shadow?" Grandma suddenly asked.

"See? Here?" Panic made me almost squeal and Grandma patted my hand.

"No, sweetheart, they cannot rise this high up in the buffer zone. I mean show you in another way. Here, follow me."

She led the way along criss-crossing corridors to a little room squeezed in between the towering book cases. It almost felt like standing in a chimney, looking up. The room was just big enough to house one small television - and a rather old one at that. Attached to it was a VHS player, and the shelves next to it were full of old VHS tapes.

Grandma searched for a while, and then found what she was looking for. She put the TV on (it seemed to be attached to some sort of car battery for power) and pressed the buttons of the player.

"This is a very rare glimpse of a shadow that one of our hunters managed to video in the eighties. It only lasts a few seconds, so look carefully to the left of the screen. The shadow follows the man walking there."

The street was badly lit, but I made out a man walking towards whoever had videotaped this. The darkness seemed to intensify behind the walking figure and I bent forward automatically to see better.

A shadowy... something was there, following the silhouette of the walking man. Half human in shape, with odd hands that seemed to float in the air, it tried to grasp its victim. Then it froze, and suddenly disappeared.

I had no words. It had looked very much like the shadow in our garden.

Grandma put the VHS cassette back to the shelf and continued explaining while she led me back along the corridors.

"The most effective way to destroy the shadows is to use the same Keys that we use to create our own gates to this buffer zone. But as there are only three of these Keys in the world, we can't risk losing them, and normally we use more traditional ways of physical force. This isn't very pleasant to look at, as they can plead for life. Now they are mute, but they can still make gestures. If, however, they did have a soul, we would see it leaving the body in the buffer zone. But that never happens. We simply see the cord snap back to the Hunter that was giving energy to the shadow. And the substance of the shadow simply merges back into the pool of energy it came from. So strictly speaking the conscious energy goes back to the one who gave it to the shadow, and the shadow's basic energy remains, only sucked back into the energy mass of the buffer zone. It doesn't cease to exist; it simply melts back into the energy pool from which it was created. So in our view no one is really killing anyone or anything."

I hoped I had brought my notebook with me. I should have written all of this down.

"And this particular shadow in the alley was not pleading for its life. It was cursing me, and spat out something it shouldn't have. It hissed that when the Immortals found the Book of Watchers, I would be very, very sorry for the day I was born. This is when the shadow's Hunter connected to the shadow, probably feeling its anger, and killed the shadow himself, realizing what the shadow was revealing to me. So you cannot really say it was me who killed it. The Immortals killed it themselves. And ever since then, all of the shadows have been created differently so that they are always silent. That's what convinced us this Book of Watchers was worth investigating."

"Ever since then we have been searching for clues about it," Lilith's voice came from behind us. "We have found enough information to be extremely concerned. The dark Nephilim, and the Immortals, are planning something major, and it threatens the whole world."

I turned around.

"Aren't there any higher entities that could stop them? Like those who have died and reached higher levels of existence?"

"Why would they want to come back to these denser energies, when they have reached the higher levels and have a new, more pleasant life there? On this earth we all have free will. We can do what we want to, and there is no one else to blame for the bad things happening here. Wars, murders, cheating... all of these are our own doing. There's no creator we could put the blame on but ourselves. We made this bed, we must lie in it." Lilith's voice was calm. "So whatever happens here is our own doing. If the Immortals and bad Nephilim try to gain power, it is up to us to stop them."

"Ok, don't know about you, but I am hungry," Diana appeared from behind a shelf – no doubt she had been listening to our discussion. "Is anyone else ready for a bite to eat?"

"Now that you mention it..." Grandma patted her flat stomach, "food sounds like a good idea. Let's go."

29

SCENT

At last, something. Not much, but enough. The shadow had caught a scent. Perhaps they had rolled down the car window for a time, because it could follow her unmistakeable essence in a straight line for some distance. Then it disappeared again. It did not matter. Once a shadow had picked up the scent of its prey, it was only a matter of time - and this shadow knew it was on the right road. All it needed to do was to search all the junctions and the smaller roads ahead. At some point she would have left the car, and the shadow would find her.

30

GATEKEEPERS

Daniel was avoiding me, or so it seemed, after displaying his wings in the library. He no longer greeted me at the cafeteria. He turned the other way when he caught sight of me across the main hall, pretending he was occupied with something on a computer, or that he was deep in discussion with someone else. And once, when I said hi to him when we passed each other in the corridor, he didn't even answer. Instead he hurried past me with a quick nod, and I felt that he had even stepped aside to avoid coming into contact with me.

"What did I do?" I asked Diana, "I must have hurt his wings very badly for him to be so mad at me."

Diana shrugged.

"I don't know. I have never seen him like that, he is usually so in control of his emotions. But then again - I don't know of anyone else ever touching his wings before. He might behave like that towards anyone who did the same. Touchy subject for the Nephilim, the wings. Pun intended. His brother Elijah always avoids opening his wings if anyone is within touching distance."

"So he has a brother?" A statement of the obvious, but too late, I'd said it.

"Yes, as handsome as they come, but much more solemn than

Daniel. He hardly ever smiles. There is some tragedy there but we don't talk about it."

I tried not to pay attention to Daniel's behaviour, but it was hard. I was suddenly left feeling like a worthless piece of garbage, not deserving the attention of a mighty Nephilim. This, of course, made me angry, and I decided I would not give him the satisfaction of showing I cared.

Because why should I have cared? We didn't know each other. He had no obligations towards me.

Instead I decided to concentrate on learning about the different groups in the Centre.

I had already met some members of the first group - the researchers with their noses in books in the library.

"They have frequent meetings where they share and cross-reference their findings. Hints in texts about the Book of Watchers, as well as probable happenings in history that seem to involve Nephilim intervention - that kind of thing. Decisions to send Time Walker groups to historical events are made according to their meetings," Diana told me when we were lying in bed waiting for sleep to take over. "They are the ones who didn't excel in the other skills needed in the buffer zone, or they aren't sufficiently advanced in their training, so they can't physically join the Time Walker groups. They make themselves useful while they learn. "

I had a feeling I'd be joining them soon.

Diana was my unofficial guide to the Center, and one morning she yanked me away from my breakfast so suddenly that I splashed coffee on my jeans.

"It's time for you to meet the teachers. We're starting with Mrs. Olanda. She should be available at the moment - and she hates anyone to be late."

Diana's explanation was flung over her shoulder as she hurried me along to one of the classrooms. Mrs Olanda was a round, short lady with deep dimples in her cheeks when she smiled.

"Olanda is my first name but everyone uses it. And you should too, young lady," she beamed at me, "if not for any other reason than the sheer difficulty of my last name... it's a tongue-twister!"

We were standing in her classroom. No one else was around, and I knew I was going to face some sort of a test.

"Now, I am the teacher of the Gatekeepers, as Diana here must have told you."

Diana nodded.

"Do you know what Gatekeepers do?"

"No idea... other than that they probably guard the gates?"

"Yes, it's as simple as that. When we create a gate with the Keys, the Key holder can't sit waiting until the Time Walkers come back. They can be gone for days, because once they enter their appointed place in history, time continues there at the same pace as it does here. So if they stay for two days in another time, the Gatekeeper needs to stay in front of the gate for two days. The Key holders are important people, who have to be ready to go and handle emergencies. So, once they open the gate they can't sit and do the Gatekeeper's job. We only have one Key holder here and that is Lilith."

I waited, and Mrs. Olanda continued her explanation.

"Once the gate has been opened, it needs to be guarded. It's a highly responsible task. We need to make sure that no-one tries to use it - from either side - without permission. The Gatekeeper is the one who ensures that only the right people get through and that means the same group that left through the temporary gate in the first place. This may sound overprotective, but if you consider how much the Immortals would like to find an open gate in the lower levels, so that they could keep it open in order to move freely between our world and the buffer zone... "

She left the words hanging in the air for a while for maximum effect, and then continued.

"There's a difference between the permanent and temporary gates. The permanent gates are connected to the higher frequencies of the buffer zone, so it is not very likely the Immortals could find their way to them from there. If they were "high" enough to reach that level in the first place, they would have achieved a state of existence that meant they most likely wouldn't want to go back to their lower energies any more. So to reach the permanent gates on their own level they would need to find them in our ordinary world, in our denser frequencies. Having achieved that they could try locking the gates to the lower frequencies on the other side as well, and that would mean to the City of Immortals. There is a way to do that, but it requires Nephilim skills. Daniel knows how this is done, but does not share the knowledge, so it won't leak out."

I pondered, visualising the permanent gate that I knew about here in the Centre.

"Ok, I think I've got the general idea..."

"Good. These temporary gates made with the Keys, on the other hand, open to the lower levels of the buffer zone and that means the very level that the Immortals live in. And the dark Nephilim, who are not like our Daniel."

I swallowed nervously. Whether it was the reference to the bad Nephilim or Daniel that made me nervous, I wasn't altogether sure.

"But how could anyone stop them from using the temporary gate made with the Keys? If the Nephilim are strong, can't they just force their way through...?"

"They could," Mrs Olanda agreed. "First of all, the gate needs to stay open at our end, because the Time Walkers will have to use it when they return. If they don't, they may land in the wrong place - and the wrong time, even when they have experienced Weavers with them."

I was going to ask about the Weavers, but decided not to. I would learn the whole thing in time.

"You saw how Lilith opened and closed the gate?"

"Yes, I did."

"Very well then. She uses the Key to both open and close the gate she creates. But it can be closed in another way too. You simply need to draw the edges of the slit together and press them until they merge together. The more recent the cut is, the easier this is. After a week it requires real strength. I will show you."

Mrs. Olanda gestured for me to approach the slit Lilith had made for us before leaving the classroom.

"Peek in, if you want to," Mrs. Olanda said good-humoredly. "I know you are curious."

Her smile was catching, and I grinned back at her and put my head through the slit. I only saw grey mist, and a vague impression of a path, solid in the midst of the swirling mist.

"That is the path that starts from this classroom. We have entered on our journeys so often from here that our steps have begun to mold the buffer zone's material into something more solid that looks like a real path. That is also why this classroom has outrun its purpose. We don't want the path to reveal our whereabouts, so we'll move to another classroom from this one after this group has returned. The path will dissolve pretty soon, when no one walks on it anymore," Mrs. Olanda's voice came from behind me. "Now, come back."

I stepped backwards. Mrs. Olanda raised her arms theatrically, and took hold of the sides of the gap. She gently pressed the ends together, squeezing the edges between her fingers, and then stepped back. The slit was still there, but the spot where her hands had touched, was shimmering slightly. After a while it lost brightness and dissolved into nothing. The opening was slightly shorter as a result.

"Now you try."

I raised my hands and touched the edges. It was the oddest feeling. It was not of real physical matter, but I could feel static prickling my palms, and a somewhat similar feeling to the one that Daniel's wings had caused in my hands. I grabbed the nothingness and almost reluctantly it followed my hand. I felt like a mime, pretending to do something imaginary. I pulled the sides together, having the slightest impression of a silky fabric in my fingers, and squeezed. Little blue sparks shot from under my fingers.

"Not so hard," Mrs. Olanda smiled.

I let go and looked at what I had done. The same scar-like shimmering line appeared in the air as had done with Mrs. Olanda's hands, and after a while it dissolved.

"So that's the closing part. Now to the guarding of the gate... may I introduce Jason?"

"Hello!" said a deep voice from behind me. I whirled around with my heart in my throat. I had not noticed anyone entering the room.

Jason obviously spent a lot of time at the gym - he was not very tall, but looked as though he could bend steel bars. His hair was carefully gelled into fashionable spikes. He was a little over twenty years of age, I estimated. He shook my hand, but did not crush my fingers to show his strength, as I was expecting.

"Hello!" I smiled back at him and he grabbed his heart theatrically and pretended to faint.

"Ooo... we are in the presence of beauty! Be still, my heart!"

Mrs. Olanda chuckled.

"Behave, Jason! We need to tell Dana here how the Gatekeepers use their skills to fight the Nephilim when required."

"It's all in the technique. They are very strong, and very fast," Jason switched to seriousness in an instant. "If they are in their human form, we use ordinary fighting skills. That means just about anything under the sun. We learn as many fighting techniques as possible, both Oriental and Western - boxing, kick-boxing, sword-fighting..."

"And if they are in their angel form?" I wanted to know.

"Then we attack the wings. Daniel taught us how," Jason explained. "You can kill a Nephilim by attacking their wings. It has to do with their breathing process. If they don't have time to withdraw their wings, and you cut to the base of them - right where the wings come out of their shoulders and backs - it's like cutting their windpipe. They suffocate, or at least they are badly crippled and will have to withdraw. It seems it is difficult for them to switch back quickly to their human lungs, if the wings are outstretched."

I suddenly understood there must be a lot more to the wings than I had imagined. I really must have made some unforgivable blunder when I stroked Daniel's wings. I had no right to feel hurt because he was avoiding me.

"Where did Daniel come from? And his brother? I understand there are not many good Nephilim out there...?"

Mrs. Olanda placed her hands firmly on her round hips.

"Now that is not something you can go asking anyone else about but Daniel. It is a rule of this place that we only hear about someone else's previous life from that person themselves - that includes the Nephilim. They tell you their story if they choose to tell you. Many of us here are from another time, and have often had traumatic experiences before reaching this place where we feel at home."

"I'm sorry..." I knew I was blushing.

"Oh come on, no need to feel embarrassed, Dana!" The wide smile that Jason aimed at me was comforting somehow. "You'd never heard of this rule before, and now you have, and know how to behave in the future."

"Quite so," Mrs. Olanda also smiled kindly at me. "If you are interested in hearing Daniel's story, you can go and ask him yourself."

"Let's get back to the Gatekeepers, shall we?" Jason reminded us. "As you can imagine, we need a lot of Gatekeepers here. If the Immortals get a whiff of the location of a temporary gate, they respond as quickly as they can and they come in force, not alone. Force is their first and foremost tactic and so they gather together into a group before they attack. And first they always send out shadow scouts. This usually gives us time to act."

"We use scouts too," Mrs. Olanda clarified. "For every group that goes time walking, we have one Gatekeeper here by the gate, and two or three others near the gateway on the other side - depends on how many groups we have out at any given moment, and how many Gatekeepers we can spare. They spread out in their positions and stay absolutely still. Sound travels for great distances in the buffer zone, and a keen listener will hear anyone coming from a long way off. If they hear noises, they go check out who is coming. Usually it is our own group of Time Walkers, but there have been occasions when they have been shadows or Immortals. Sometimes even a Nephilim. They are the worst - they have very keen senses, and scouts have to retreat very very silently to avoid being detected."

"Also the Nephilim sense of smell is too good..." Jason sighed, "so no spicy food or smoking for the Gatekeepers."

"Indeed not! And no aftershave or deodorants that smell like an oriental spice market," Mrs. Olanda wagged an index finger at Jason as if he had been guilty of such behavior. "Also no one is allowed to enter the buffer zone if they have a cold. One sneeze could bring a horde of shadows to the spot."

"What do you do if you notice the shadows approaching?"

"We retreat and close the gate from our side."

"Leaving the Time Walkers in a trap?" I didn't get this. "Won't they walk straight into danger?"

"We send a message to the Weaver of the group, and they will weave their way back to another temporary gate - or the permanent gate here. That is why we can never have all the Weavers away at the same time. The number of Weavers that are out there with a group must always tally with the number of Weavers that are here on duty. The Weavers here know where the group has gone and know how to find the Weaver in the past, so they can connect with them from this side, creating a new path for them to follow, and showing them the spot where the gate will be opened."

"Sounds interesting... What exactly do they weave?" I wanted to know.

"You'll learn that soon," Mrs. Olanda assured me.

"Well, I don't think I would be much of a Gatekeeper..." I bent my arm in a mock attempt to show my biceps. It wasn't a very impressive muscle, I can tell you.

Jason chortled.

"You might be good at Oriental fighting, if you gave it a try. I wouldn't be sorry to see you at the gym! And you will be there sooner or later to learn the basics of self-defense and Nephilim-killing. It is compulsory."

He gave me a wink and laughed when I blushed.

"Jason, behave!" Mrs. Olanda shook her head. "Close that for us, will you."

We walked out of the room. I looked over my shoulder and saw Jason press the gate shut using his whole arms. It was done in a few seconds.

31

TRANSLATING THE NOTEBOOK

Translating the notes in the sketchbook wasn't easy, because the Finnish text had been written by hand, and sometimes the handwriting wasn't altogether tidy. It became ever more cramped and crammed into odd spaces as the writer had filled up the book. But slowly, with the help of his language book and a dictionary, Mr. Donnelly made progress. He translated the first few sentences, and after that he was so exhausted from his intellectual work he knew he would have to take a break and put down his mechanical pencil. It was quite enjoyable, really, to let his brain work on something new, but demanding.

He quietly read through his translation again.

"Elijah, where are you? I remember how we were watching the stars at night, next to the Nabta stones, and next morning when I woke up, you were gone. I tried to go back into the mists on my own, but I couldn't. It's as though you were never here. I know you would never leave me. So what has happened? Have they caught you? Have they... killed you? I don't know where to go. Nothing but desert everywhere and all I have left now is one bottle of water. I cannot wait for you any longer. I have to leave to survive."

"Interesting," Mr. Donnelly mumbled to himself, "Elijah left Merit in the middle of the desert? Whatever for?"

Suddenly the air seemed to turn electric. Familiar prickling lifted the hairs in his arms. Quickly he closed the notebook, attached the mechanical pencil to the rubber strap on the cover and put both the sketchbook and the Moleskin in the lowest drawer on his desk, under a pile of loose papers.

When the Masters stepped through the door, he was seemingly deep in his studies on angelology, scribbling notes with an old fashioned ink pen.

32

LEAVING THE VILLAGE

I dug a little hole for the bee and dropped it there, patting the loose dirt carefully over it. I felt sad. The other bees buzzed around us still, and their voices... their buzz did not sound angry anymore. After a while they dispersed.

Only then did Mut-Bity lift me up onto my feet. She pulled the cloth over my head again, and looked me inquiringly in the eyes. She seemed to be content with what she saw and nodded slightly. She pulled the fabric deeper over my face, covering it from the sun. She then made sure that my hands were covered right down to the fingertips, and after making sure I was completely hidden from the sun, she gave me a little tense hug. Then she took my hand, squeezing my fingers tightly through the linen sleeve and started walking towards the nearby village, across the cultivated land which our bees were helping to fertilise. Her hands were both sweaty and cold. This was strange, because her hands had always been dry and warm in the past.

Mut-Bity did not speak, and her steps were so determined that even though I was full of questions, I did not dare to open my mouth. I just bent my head down, away from the blinding sunlight and watched my white dusty toes appear and disappear from under the hem, letting her lead the way.

She saw a wealthy old man who was sitting in the shade. You could tell he was wealthy, because he had a small donkey by his side, dozing half asleep with its head down, keeping to the quickly diminishing shadow of the house. Its lower lip was hanging loosely, which meant that it felt content and safe. The man probably had servants and slaves to do the work of his fields and he could afford to sit and do nothing. Also his mud-house was well plastered and had a real stone doorway. Mut-Bity marched directly up to the man.

"We must leave right away. I need your donkey to carry the beehives to the River."

"What can you give me in return?" the old man asked, suddenly alert.

I looked at the half-asleep donkey and wondered if such a small animal could ever carry the clay beehives on its back to the river. Or would it react to the bees by bolting away? It had been known to happen when a donkey had swished its tail to get rid of the insects and bees had stung. It did not happen often - unlike wasps bees died after they had stung. They were not malicious, they only stung when threatened.

Mut-Bity had a little sack on her back, hanging from her shoulder, and she pulled a small pot out of it – it contained a hin of honey. I could see how the old man's mouth watered when he realized what was in the pot. He did not reach out for the jar immediately, however, even though I could see the greed in his eyes - there were three bees flying around Mut-Bity's hands. She always had some bees around her.

"You shall have this jar of honey, once all the hives are safely by the river."

Even I knew how valuable such a jar of honey was, bees had worked for weeks to make it, and that alarmed me. Mut-Bity was clearly scared and wanted to leave the village and the fields as soon as possible. And there was no other reason than that odd golden-eyed man.

"Has anyone been here to ask about us?" she asked casually while the man yanked at the rope that hung from the neck of his donkey. I

wondered why he needed such a rope – the animal in question showed no great eagerness to escape anywhere.

"I don't know... I'm not sure, but I did see someone who was strange-looking."

The man's eyes shifted just for a second and spotted my face as I peeped out from the shade of my head cover. I was looking directly at him so he saw my pale face and eyes, and I could see recognition in his face.

"Like her, but eyes were yellow. Very odd looking. No color."

"Oh? Where did he come from?" Mut-Bity started walking towards the field where our beehives were kept at a safe distance from the village. Her voice betrayed nothing; you could only hear mild curiosity.

"I really have no idea..." The old man's feet patted on the path next to mine and the donkey trailed lazily behind us as we walked out of the village. We carried on down the slight slope of a hill that formed an island during inundation, when the River valley became a vast lake. I observed the contrast between his dirty, dusty brown feet and my own white toes. "One minute I was sitting by the wall and at a blink of my eye he just appeared out of nowhere. I must have dozed off."

I heard Mut-Bity let out a hissing sound. It sounded like a sigh but it was her anger-hiss. I understood even less. Or rather – I did understand there that there was a lot more here than met the eye. She knew the pale stranger, and she hated him.

Mut-Bity started walking even faster. The old man had trouble keeping up with her and had to yank his reluctant donkey by the rope to make it get a move on in the heat.

"He did not speak to me, but I heard him talking to someone. Then he strode off towards the fields," the old man kept on talking.

"Did you hear what he said?" Mut-Bity asked.

"Something about a pale child... So he must have been coming to find you. He must have been one of your family, child."

I took a few quicker steps to grab Mut-Bity's hand and did not look at the man.

"Her family is not here, and I know this man is not of her kin,

despite their similar skin." Mut-Bity said, "And a word of warning to you – if you ever see him again, try not to draw his attention to you in any way. You very life may depend on you staying unnoticed. He is dangerous."

The man stopped in his tracks.

"He is no longer here. He's gone," Mut-Bity said, before the man asked, "and I very much doubt he will come back anymore. But still, keep away from the pale ones, especially if they have golden eyes."

The man was obviously very nervous after this. He led the donkey to the side of the field and clearly wanted the deal to be done with as soon as possible.

"You only have nine hives?" he asked. "That doesn't give much honey."

"Here I have only these nine, yes," Mut-Bity said.

Her little fire was still alive and she took a piece of dung that was smoking well. Then she stood and started humming with a low voice. The sound always turned my skin to goose bumps. While she hummed, she bound a special leather- and fabric saddle on the small donkey. It had two great pouches made of the coarsest linen, one on each side of the donkey, and thin ropes threaded over the top of the saddle, so that they hung freely on either side.

And the bees came. They flew in a swarm through the air, and into the hives. All went in, none came out. Mut-Bity kept on humming until no bees were flying anymore, and then gently wafted the smoke around the hives and placed stops made of tightly wrapped linen in the openings. It kept the bees inside but let air through.

Then she just lifted the hives, one by one, and put them in the pouches which kept them parallel to the little donkey's sides. She tied each hive to its place inside the pouch with one of the ropes hanging from top of the saddle so they stayed on top of each other - carefully twisting the loose ends around the hives and back up again. The ropes were long enough so that she could tie them back up to a special wooden knob at the top. I knew the frame of the saddle was made of wood, and the knob was attached to this frame.

Four hives on one side, five on the other. The pouches themselves were carefully made to wrap tightly around the hives and so limited their movement, especially after Mut-Bity tied the pouches together with yet another rope, under the donkey's belly, which made the animal look at her with such a hilarious disbelief I started to giggle.

"I have never seen such a thing..." the old man said admiringly. "You invented this yourself?"

Mut-Bity nodded, but did not speak. Instead she kept on humming – and the bees answered. You could hear them buzzing to her. She raised her voice - they buzzed higher, she lowered her hum - theirs soothed to a sleepy hum too.

The man did not know if he should believe his ears or not.

"You... talk their language?" he finally asked.

Mut-Bity only smiled.

"You are a powerful magician!" the man almost bowed to Mut-Bity.

He kept silent until the donkey reached the River, listening to Mut-Bity and the bees humming to each other. Once the hives had been lifted off his donkey and into the waiting boat - how Mut-Bity had known our boat would be there waiting I had no idea - and he received his precious pot of honey, he turned and began almost running back towards the village, turning once to glance at us with a scared look. His donkey trotted happily behind him, eager to get back to the village from the hot fields.

I was certain that by the time the evening came, all of this would turn into a good story where he would be the hero who chased away a dangerous stranger and met a magician who spoke the language of the bees.

33

NEW AGE SHOP

She walked along the street as though she was on a catwalk, apparently oblivious to the admiring looks of the men. Then she saw the sign she was looking for.

It was a little shop in a run-down part of the city, in a row of retail businesses that had all seen better days. The dusty window display included tarot decks and hanging crystals. The dark blue velvet on which the cards were displayed appeared to have been simply tossed down, with silver colored glitter sprinkled on it in an effort to be artistic and a crystal ball had been placed in the middle. Little angel statues peeked out from the folds of the velvet.

"Fortune telling. Messages from the other side," the plaque above the crystal ball announced. It was decorated with the signs of the zodiac.

Her expression showed the same pleasure as a cat viewing a cornered mouse. She opened the door and stepped in.

The little shop sold anything new-agey. A violet pearl curtain hid the back room.

She smiled. Perfect.

"Can I help you, my dear?" an elderly lady came out from the back room. She wore heavy golden earrings; the bright colored scarf that covered her hair was tied into a knotty bundle at the nape of her neck. Her makeup was too dark - she was trying too hard to give the appearance of a gypsy fortuneteller.

"I do believe that you can," said her visitor. Her seductively beautiful voice rang like silver bells, and she smiled down at the shopkeeper with half-closed eyes. "It is - about messages from the dead. I need your help for someone who has lost her dear friend tragically in a car accident. I would like her to be convinced that life continues after death, so that she can let go of her grief."

Her smile vanished and a suitably sad expression replaced it.

The lady tilted her head sideways and sighed.

"If only people would be as understanding about these matters as you are, dear. You are a real angel to care so much for your friend."

Her visitor smiled, and the shopkeeper thought her eyes were playing tricks for a second, because the young woman seemed to appear amused at what she had heard. But when she looked again, those same, beautifully light brown... almost golden... eyes were full of sadness and concern again.

"Now, tell me what can I do to help?" asked the shopkeeper.

"To begin with, maybe you could give me your card, so that I can pass it to my friend."

"But of course!" the lady hurried behind the counter and picked up a visiting card, which she handed to the lovely young woman. "Now, might I offer you some spiritual help as well? I'm known for my messages from angels. Maybe you could get some advice from them regarding your grieving friend?"

This time the girl laughed, clearly amused. The shopkeeper smiled politely. Then the young woman coughed and said:

"Sure, why not. I've always believed in the existence of angels."

Slightly baffled by her reaction the lady gestured to the room behind the bead curtain.

"This way, dear."

34

HUNTERS AND GUARDIANS

"And now for the Guardians." Diana dragged me out of Mrs Olanda's classroom and into the corridor. "Let's go meet one. I just saw Aemilius walk past. I am sure we can catch him if we hurry."

I saw a sturdy back disappearing through a door and we followed. This door did not lead to any classroom though - this was a fully equipped gym.

"Aemilius!" Diana called to the man who was about to disappear into the men's locker room.

When he turned I saw that he was middle aged, had an impressive scar on his cheek and a profile that could only be described as Roman. He looked like a gladiator in a T-shirt.

"Diana," he bowed, "how can I be of assistance?"

"May I introduce Dana to you - she is new. She is Layla's grand-daughter."

Aemilius bowed to me too.

"Pleased to meet you," he said. "You should be proud of your grandmother. She is our best Hunter."

"Yes, quite... Thank you..." I did not know how to reply.

"Would you tell Dana what Guardians do?" Diana asked and Aemilius nodded.

"We keep the Weavers alive," he said matter-of-factly and then fell silent.

"Perhaps a little more in the way of description...?" Diana smiled.

"We go to past with Weavers and protect their lives with our own. If the Weaver dies, the Time Walkers cannot return," Aemilius was not much of a talker and Diana took over.

"Or rather - they can, but first another Weaver needs to find them, travel to them, connect to a Weaver here, and then lead them home. It has happened, you know."

"Yes. Once we were stuck in England in the summer 1665, when the great plague was raging in city," Aemilius said.

"I was there too. We had been vaccinated and had antibiotics with us, but it was horrible to witness how people died like flies..." Diana's cheerfulness vanished at the memory.

It began to dawn on me that travelling to the past was not just one big adventure for the people here. They really put their lives at risk.

"Can I ask... Where are you from, Aemilius? Rome?" I asked.

"Yes."

"Yes, we stole Aemilius away from the battlefield," I heard Grandma's voice from behind me.

"Sheesh! How do you walk so quietly?" I swirled around with my heart in my throat.

Grandma grinned back at me as she wiped sweat from her neck with a towel. "You can't exactly stamp around shouting "Coming to get you!" if you are a Hunter."

Aemilius smiled too and continued in his broken English: "I should have died in Actium battle, but I had visited an oracle before and was told to observe my dreams. With this advice I was able to ah, dream lucidly. Before battle, someone who knew of my impending death approached me. He convinced me he was telling the truth and asked me to follow him in the midst of the battle. He appeared out of nowhere in the middle of the fighting, and I disappeared from the battle scene, and ended up here."

"The oracle in question was of course one of our Time Walker members," Grandma ruffled her hair with the towel, "there wasn't much literacy around in those days. We got many good fighters that way. But not all chose to follow. Some had had what we call near death experiences and did not fear death anymore. Their experiences had been so positive."

"But the Immortals follow us too when they can, and try to kill them or find another option for those we find valuable to our cause," Diana commented.

"Find another option? What option?" I did not understand.

"People have always dreamt of immortality. They fear death. This fear drives them to extreme actions, when they try to stay truly physically immortal. Some even choose the most extreme measures and volunteer to be infected in order to become vampires." Grandma sighed and sat down on a bench by the wall.

"As in real blood sucking genuine vampires? Human ones? Are you serious?" I could not believe what I had heard. "You mean someone would actually volunteer to become a creature like that?"

"Yes. A human who is infected by a Nephilim, and becomes a vampire - if they survive the infection - can go on infecting other people. Some of them survive, and a strange genetic change happens in their bodies. There is barely a pulse, and their life is extended greatly - if they feed often enough," Grandma said. "Blood is the best nourishment - it invigorates their system. And human blood is the best of all. They can drink animal blood as well, but few do so nowadays. In the past it was different - they only took animal lives, but something changed that around 500 BC, or thereabouts. The first vampires to drink human blood appeared around that time in what is today's Turkey."

"Eww..." I shivered, "are there many of these vampires in the world?"

"Yes, there are, but not as many as one might think. The reason is that when the human body is infected by the Nephilim virus - for we think it is a virus - by the Nephilim themselves, it causes such a severe illness that not many survive the transformation process. Those that do, however, live long lives. Very long indeed. If a human vampire infects another human, the odds of initial survival are better, but their lives are much shorter, although they can still far exceed those of the ordinary human life span. The vampires have kept their numbers low on purpose, so they won't draw too much attention to their kind and they can hunt in peace. If there was an influx of bloodless bodies in a small area, let alone a lot of humans changed into vampires, then that would certainly draw unwanted attention to their kind. They have strict rules about who is allowed to become a vampire. If a vampire makes another person into a vampire without the permission of their leaders, they don't hesitate - they just destroy the new one," Grandma explained.

"The ones infected directly by Nephilim are much stronger vampires, and can live on almost forever, if they take care to avoid the things that are dangerous to them. Their bodies also heal themselves amazingly well, so there isn't much they need to avoid in order to stay safe. The human-inflicted vampires are weaker. Despite their extended life span, they eventually grow old and die, if they stay in our physical world. Of course they can also avoid that happening by living in the buffer zone, and that is what most of them do, and only come to our world to feed," Diana said.

Aemilius bowed slightly to get our attention.

"I may leave?" he asked.

"Yes, yes, thank you for explaining what Guardians do," Diana nodded in Aemilius's direction and without further ado he disappeared into the men's locker room.

"This is unreal... I though vampires were invented creatures." I looked at Diana and Grandma. "How do I recognize a vampire, then?"

"Many of the clichés do apply. They are cold. They are pale. If they haven't fed in a while, they look sick, and have dark circles around the eyes. And they have an odd smell... Their skin smells sweet. Like fruit about to rot. Just like the skin of the Nephilim. The smell is weaker in those vampires who were infected by a human vampire, rather than one of the Nephilim. Still, if you are close enough to smell the scent, you are probably way too close," Grandma said. "Unfortunately female vampires in particular choose to hide their scent by using heavy perfumes. And to make their skin look healthy by using makeup," she added.

"And the teeth? They have fangs?" I wanted to know.

"The ones infected directly by the Nephilim are considered to be some kind of vampire elite... they can prove their origin by their teeth. Like the Nephilim they don't have fangs, but when they attack, their mouths open much wider than those of an ordinary human vampire, and their teeth push out... it is as if the teeth were half inside their skull until they attack and the opening of the jaw forces them out. It's hard to explain, it's almost a mechanical process - you would need to see it happening. Which I hope you never will!" Diana shivered at the memory.

"And the ones infected by humans? What are their teeth like?" I could hardly believe that I was having this conversation in a gym, with two ordinary looking people, one of whom was my Grandma, for goodness' sake.

"They're not much different from our own teeth at first glance. But they are sharper, much sharper. They can slice a very deep cut with just the smallest of movements of their teeth against the skin," Grandma clarified.

"Have you actually seen vampires?" I asked her.

"Yes, lots of times," she said, "in our travels through time. The vampires also use shadows as their scouts, because they are photosensitive, and prefer moving in the hours of darkness. The shadows don't like sunlight, but they can move in it without being affected by the light as much. So, in my hunt for the shadows, I have occasionally met with their vampire masters too. "

"Didn't they try to bite you?"

"If I recognize the shadow belonging to a vampire, I retreat. You learn to recognise them through experience. They are stronger, bigger, and faster than the shadows created by ordinary humans in the buffer zone. Also they feed on animals occasionally, physically eating their flesh. Ordinary shadows created by ordinary people never do that."

Grandma rose from the bench again and headed for the treadmill.

"I'm only human, and no match for their speed, so that's why I retreat if I meet a vampire shadow. The best thing to do then is try to warn possible victims from walking alone. Vampires don't want to be seen, and so they prefer lonely prey. Also they prefer young people, whose blood they consider provides better nutrition, so they are not so likely to attack me if there are any young people around. One time was pretty close, though..." Grandma's face revealed the memory was not something she wanted to dwell on, "but someone came to the rescue."

"Who?" I wanted to know.

Grandma did not answer. The whole subject was so creepy, I wanted to talk about something else anyway. So I decided to ask about the dream world.

"What does it look like in the dream world? Lilith was there to meet me when I had my lucid dream."

"What do dreams look like?" Grandma started walking slowly on the treadmill. "It's a quickly moving environment. Flashes of happenings, sleeping consciousnesses popping to the surface and disappearing again when people wake up. If someone has a very bright consciousness, we follow it to its source, see who it is, and make plans as to whether we should approach them or not."

"Can the Immortals and vampires and shadows reach that place? And the Nephilim?"

"Yes. Shadows do. That is how nightmares come about. Running away from some horror that almost catches you is probably the most common sign you have met a shadow in your sleep. Nephilim hardly ever come to the dream zone, though. It seems they have difficulties in moving in the dream world for some reason - also it seems the dark Nephilim don't experience dreams, because you never find their dreams there. Shadows, on the other hand, move freely in the dream world and may find their victims by observing their dreams, to see who are more vulnerable to their attacks. They don't want to attack strong people either, but prefer those that are easier to catch. The things we dream about speak volumes to them." Grandma started jogging, but did not seem out of breath.

"So they follow the sleepers to see who they are?" I wanted clarification.

"Indeed they do. And not only to find prey for themselves. If they find out we have an interest in someone, they try to stop us from reaching those people, and we sometimes have to send guardians to be around our chosen ones, until they make their way here. You had one too, just in case. You did not see him often, though. Only during the last few days was he visible to you." Grandma increased speed.

"Daniel."

It wasn't really a question, but an observation.

"Yes, Daniel. He is one of our best Guardians. He guarded you for months, when you started showing up in the dreamscape. Your light was extraordinary. Knowing who you were, we did not wonder... There was only one occasion, when his attention was taken by other events, and you were almost killed," Grandma frowned at the thought.

I froze and looked at her.

Yes. We think the drunk driver was trying to get to you. Kitty got into her way, and you were saved."

"Why did they want to kill me?"

"Now that is something we don't understand. We thought they would rather want you alive..." Grandma muttered so I could barely hear her words over the thumping sounds of her jogging.

"Why? What use would I be to them? Would someone please explain?"

I suddenly felt a surprising rage rising up my spine. A strong, tingling sensation that spread to my shoulder blades and made my scalp almost itch with energy. It felt the same as sitting on your legs for too long so that they fall asleep. I tried to control the emotion, but it just wouldn't go away. I wondered what was wrong with me these days - usually I could control myself easily, but now I was meeting with strong emotions inside me every day. It had to be all this unbelievable reality I was exposed to.

Grandma had one look at my face and stopped the treadmill and stepped down.

"We will explain this all to you, Dana, but not just yet. Trust me, this is for the best now. But you will hear everything in time." She placed her hand over mine, then felt my forehead. "Goodness, you're burning. Are you sure you don't have a fever? Maybe a little hot," she concluded. "Could be all the excitement." She sounded almost uninterested, but I noticed how she carefully avoided looking me in the eye.

If they thought I did not notice she was hiding something, she was wrong.

"But Daniel did look after you the best that he could. He was needed elsewhere on many occasions, and when he was away for an extended period, I came to look after you instead. That's why I have popped in for a visit unexpectedly in the past, and also why I came to visit you now, much to your mother's anxiety. We had not seen the shadows around you for ages, despite your light in the dreamscape and did not expect you to be in danger, so I was very surprised at the shadow that crept into your garden. Especially when it must have known I was there," Grandma said. "This shadow must have been an ancient one and very clever, to avoid being detected. And if someone sent a shadow of that kind to hunt you, it means you were in serious danger."

"Wait, there's something I don't understand... The drunk driver - was she an Immortal, then? You said she was actively trying to kill me!"

"She was an ordinary woman under shadow influence. Remember how I told you about the shadow that revealed to us the existence of the Book of Watchers? That shadow was waiting for drunken people outside a bar. Desperate, depressed drunken people. These are very close in energies to the energy from which the shadows are made, so there is not much resistance. The woman driving the car was all of that. Badly depressed and drunk. Shadows can control such people. It's like piggy-back riding. They glue themselves to the person who is in that state, and find a way to connect to the lower levels of their mind. Once the connection is made, they can basically just think what they want the person to do, and they are directed to do it. And that was the case here, too. The shadow told the woman to get in her car and drive, despite her intoxication, and she obeyed."

For the first time I felt sorry for the lady who had killed Kitty. I had had no idea that shadows could do that... well, I had not known of shadows at all.

"Still, I find it strange that they wanted to kill you..." Grandma was almost talking to herself. Then she suddenly changed the subject. "But that's enough of that for now. Let's tell you about the Hunters. To be a Hunter you need to have second sight. That means you need to be able to see the shadows with your physical eyes. It is a skill not everyone can learn. It is an ability many children have, but they actively want to leave that skill when they grow up. Some still see them as grown-ups, and usually doubt their own sanity because of it. The ones who do, and whom we approach, are usually relieved to hear the shadows are real, and not imaginary creatures. These people are given proper training to kill shadows. To say they are enthusiastic about their jobs, after years of fear and misery, would be something of an understatement to be honest."

"They cut the cord..."

"Yes. It can be cut with ordinary weapons too, if the shadow's master isn't paying much attention to its activities and we can take it by surprise. But when the connection is strong, the Shadowmaster can put up quite a fight. They push more energy into their creature - it's a two-way process, they can also take some of the power that these energy-vampires suck into themselves. When the Shadowmaster is fully aware of what's happening, they turn their creature into a veritable killing machine. I just wonder why the teenage preference is to make them look like something out of a bad horror movie..."

"Do - do the Shadowmasters ever appear themselves?"

"Only as a last resort. They don't want to risk their immortality, and prefer to let the shadow go, and create a new one. After all, if the shadow is destroyed, the energy they have given it just reels back in to them. It can be hurled back with quite a snap, and it's not pleasant, but they survive it, I have been told."

"I could see that shadow in the garden," I said, "so do you think I will be a Hunter, then?"

"Maybe. We need to test your skills in seeing them some more. That means we need to go to the city one evening, to a place where they like to lurk, and see if you can see them for real, or whether the shadow in the garden had simply been made more solid. A Hunter sees them in their 'stealth mode' too." Grandma was chatting almost casually.

For a brief moment I wondered what other people of my age were talking about with their grandmothers. Certainly not other levels of existence, vampires and shadows... fleetingly, the thought of discussing flower arrangements and theatre and recipes seemed rather alluring compared to the facts of the hidden reality I was being exposed to.

"Was that invisible person in the bookstore a shadow, then?" I asked.

Grandma started laughing.

"No, that would have been Daniel, who came too close to the veil between the lowest buffer zone and our physical world. At the very edge of the buffer zone it can happen that a person standing there appears as a form that seems to be molded out of thin air. One step closer and he would have shown as a more solid form, if still a rather shadowy one. A bit of a creepy sight, isn't it? An invisible man..." she grinned, before continuing, "We need to take Daniel with us on that trip to the city, though. It is potentially very dangerous and things can turn ugly."

"When are we going?" I turned to Grandma.

"There's no better moment than the present!" Grandma slapped her hand over mine gently but encouragingly. "We'll leave after we have eaten dinner. You'll be in safe hands with me and Daniel."

I could only hope Daniel would agree to come with us, after my breaching of the wing-etiquette...

35

MERIT'S NOTEBOOK

The sketchbook became Mr. Donnelly's obsession when he had time to painstakingly translate the next lines. He even sent his servant on errands in order to be able to read and translate in total secrecy.

"I lay there, dying, when she found me. She walked from the desert as if the sun had no effect on her. She had some kind of an animal skin bottle with her, and she gave me water from it. She carried a piece of cloth on her back, with wooden sticks, and she erected a little tent over me to give me shade. By that time I had already burned my skin. I lost consciousness for a long time. I only remember her giving me water, and humming in a strange way. She must have hunted something, because she began to feed me pieces of dry meat as soon as I could swallow. My burned skin peeled off. When I was strong enough to walk, she forced me to my feet and so we walked. I had no idea how far I had reached from Nabta until I saw the skeletons in the sand. The huge skeletons of ancient whales, lying where they had died in the ancient sea. I realized I had to be in the Valley of the Whales, the WadiHitan, in Egypt."

"Imagine that!" Mr. Donnelly exclaimed aloud, "whales in the desert sand? Never heard of such a thing!"

"I feel so relieved - we are bound to meet some tourists sooner or later!" the writing continued.

After that there was a hole in the page. Another page had been torn out, or eaten.

"Ants!" Mr. Donnelly cursed, recognizing what had caused the hole. So this book had been in Egypt, where ants often destroyed any organic material left lying about.

The text continued.

"...and we reached the lake. A beautiful, big lake, with crocodiles in it, and a fisher village on its shore. And it was a shock. Elijah - all these people were... ancient. There was nothing modern anywhere. No cars, no TV aerials or dishes , no wrist watches, no brightly colored clothing. No shoes. I fear what this means. I sit here in one of the small mud brick houses, surrounded by women and children who gawk at me, trying to touch my hair all the time. As if they had never seen blonde hair. They speak a language I do not understand at all. I don't even understand the language of the woman who brought me here. I am certain it is not Arabic, though."

"No!" Mr. Donnelly banged his fist on his table, looked up, scared that someone had heard. The next page was missing - clearly torn away.

The text continued from mid-sentence.

"...and this is what I saw from the boat. Elijah - it is a pyramid, and it is whole, not eroded at all. I saw a temple in front of it - and it too was whole. I have no idea how to get back to you! I have no other option but to stay here at Mi-Wer, which is the name of this place of women. How could I send a message to you? Could you come back in time and fetch me? How would you find me now that I have left the stones of Nabta? How could you know how to come to this exact time and place? My heart weeps - I have lost you for good!"

Mr. Donnelly had to check and double check that he had translated the text correctly. Finally he had to admit that he was right. And that meant Merit had somehow travelled back in time to ancient Egypt.

"Mi-Wer... I know that name from somewhere..."

Mr. Donnelly considered a moment, repeating what she had written.

"A lake, she said... And a pyramid nearby, it seems. Crocodiles... Mi-Wer..."

He put the sketchbook and the Moleskine with its pen into the pocket of his loose dressing gown. He went out of his office, locking the door behind him, and into the library. With determined steps he walked to the ancient Egyptian section.

It did not take him long to find what he was looking for. In a book about the ancient palaces and abodes of Egypt, he read that Mi-Wer was located in a time that was one of the grandest and richest of the Pharaonic period. Now he knew where and when Merit was trapped. The modern date at the beginning of the sketch book was a few years back in the time of the ordinary world. Mr. Donnelly wondered whether she was already dead. Or... perhaps she was still there, living in mortal time exactly the same way she would have been living it with Elijah, in modern times?

The idea was mind-boggling. Mr. Donnelly had never thought about time travel, because it should not be possible. Yet his own experience in the City of Immortals told him time was not as linear as was generally thought.

"Poor girl," he whispered, "you are still there, aren't you? Living in those distant years, unable to reach Elijah. Do you hope that Elijah can travel across time to reach you, then?"

He had to translate more, as soon as possible. He had to know. With hurried steps he scuttled back to his office, his worn slippers threatening to drop from his feet, carrying the book about Egyptian architecture under his arm.

36

TRACKED DOWN

The message had been passed to the Hunter. The shadow waited, hidden away, out of sight of the big building. It had recognized the smell of not just one, but three Time Walker Hunters that it had encountered during its long life.

This time the shadow knew that it had done well. It had been responsible for the discovery of the meeting place of the Hunters, or at least these three Hunters, a place the Masters had been trying to locate for a long time. It had followed the smell of the car, which was easier after it had left the main road, and its nostrils were not blocked by pollution and dust. And even though the car was out of sight, the smell of Hunters brought on the wind warned it in time and it withdrew before it came within sight of the big house.

Then suddenly she was there, appearing next to the shadow without warning, along with the shadow's own Hunter. The shadow retreated a few steps, and bowed its head respectfully. Both figures were hooded.

Clearly she was pleased, because the next words she spoke were unexpected, both to the shadow and its Hunter.

"Well done," she said to the shadow, "you have earned the right to live. Finally we know where their Hunters are gathering."

The shadow made obeisance, with a curious sense that amounted to achievement. She ignored it, as she and the Hunter were observing the building closely.

"She will be there, no doubt," she said to the Hunter. "What better place to keep her safe than nested in a lair of their Hunters."

"Indeed, my lady," the Hunter nodded from within the folds of his cloak. He never exposed his skin to daylight, if it could be avoided. His skin looked too different from ordinary human skin in bright daylight.

"Now, the question is how to get her out of there."

"A direct attack..."

"No, for the present it is vital they have no idea we have found them," she snapped. "There will be no attacks, or else they may quickly hide her from us again."

"No, my Lady. We shall follow your orders."

"It is well that you do..." she said, but her tone was almost absent-minded rather than intimidating. "Thankfully, this was easy to predict. It was most likely that they would hide her, if they sensed us observing her, but I made plans long ago to lure her out, if needed. Once we removed her friend it became even easier."

The Hunter considered her words, knowing that ultimately the girl would have no chance.

"You," a nod towards the shadow, "will watch this place closely. If the Huntress leaves, follow her. We will send more shadows to assist. You must not fail. You will not fail."

The shadow bowed almost to the ground in front of the beautiful and imperious woman. It would have answered respectfully, but the Masters had taken away its ability to speak. That was all because of the old Huntress. How the shadow would have loved to make her pay, for that loss alone.

She and the shadow's Hunter vanished, as though they had slipped below the surface of a lake. For a while their shadowy figures could be seen, and then they were gone. The shadow lay flat on the hill, behind the bushes, in a depression on the side of the hill, sheltered from any wind that might spread its scent. Its gaze did not shift from the great building. Its patience was endless whilst stalking its prey.

37

HUNTING SHADOW

We set out in Grandma's car that evening.

"We're not going to use the buffer zone, because you are not used to it yet and you'd probably fall asleep. Not that it matters, but it's better to stay awake and alert all the time, if there is the slightest chance of encountering any shadows," Grandma said. "We're driving to the nearest city where we'll meet Daniel. There's been no sign of any shadow following us from the university, so it looks as though we've shaken them off our tail."

It was a bit of a relief to know that I would not be travelling in Grandma's tiny sports car squashed in between Grandma and Daniel.

It took us half an hour to reach our destination. Grandma drove to a rundown area, where there were lots of pubs and a few nightclubs. Some revellers were already stumbling about in the streets and there was cheering and drunken shouting going on.

"There's no point in going to the more upmarket areas – people there use taxis to go home, but here there are plenty of people who are so drunk they often walk when they leave - or get thrown out," Grandma commented. "Many of them don't have cars anyway, or they don't have them with them."

She parked by the side of the road where her vehicle was clearly visible and vehicles came and went all the time. There was a police car parked up further down the street. "If I left this car in a side alley, someone would break into it right away. Also I can't drive near the bar we are going to keep an eye on, because the shadows know my car," she added tartly. "The price of vanity... I can't stay incognito near this car."

We walked along the road. It was well-lit, but I was starting to feel slightly uncomfortable.

"Now, we're going to the alley on the other side of the street from that bar..." she pointed at a light sign that was flashing nearby. It wasn't working properly. "I know that shadows use that one as a rich hunting spot, but they don't know I know, because I have not hunted them here yet. It's let them be lulled into a false sense of security. They get careless then."

We crossed the street. I did not like the looks some of the men threw my way, nor the noises that they made at me. But they didn't say anything, once Grandma had looked at them directly. She had such authority they thought better of it and decided to shut up. I didn't wonder. She walked as though she was in her twenties, and her posture revealed she knew how to defend herself. Her eyes showed no fear. I'm sure no one would have been surprised, if she had suddenly taken an oriental defense position in the middle of the street or done a few back-flips and cartwheels. My Grandma the martial arts movie star...?

The alley itself was like something out of the set of a detective series. Trash cans - or rubbish bins, as they called them here - soggy cardboard boxes, filth. Stuff that had been dumped by nearby shops, take-aways and pubs. If my mother had known where Grandma had taken me, she would have severed their relationship for good.

"We're going to the very back, there." Grandma pointed to the dark end of the alley. "Any shadow that appears will position itself right behind those rubbish bins, where it has a better view of the bar door."

Daniel appeared out of thin air in front of us. I nearly jumped out of my skin.

"How did you do that? Do you have one of the Keys?"

"One can always step down from the buffer zone to one's real living environment, without the use of Keys. That's how the disappeared ones in the stories just suddenly appeared back in their own world, and into a different time without knowing how they returned," Grandma explained. "It's the going back to the buffer zone that requires the Keys or an existing gate. But the Nephilim can go both ways without Keys. The wings seem to create a vibration that opens a portal away from the physical world."

I remembered how Daniel's wings had appeared and the slight bending of the air on their outer edges. It resembled something floating on water - too light to sink into it, but solid enough to bend the surface of the water.

We moved silently into the shadows of the alley, behind some boxes that had been stacked untidily on top of each other.

"Now we need to be totally quiet. I'll touch your hand when a shadow appears – if it appears. Look then on this side of the rubbish bins and see if you can spot it," whispered Grandma.

We stood there, without moving. I tried not to pay attention to the bad smell around us. It seemed that someone had dumped garbage bags down the alley and it stank as though something had been rotting there for a considerable time. I did not want to know what it was. The little noises that I heard suggested we were probably accompanied by rats. Delightful.

As time ticked by, I had to move my body weight slightly from one leg to the other every once in a while, but Daniel stood like a tall statue by my side seemingly without any discomfort. I could not ignore his presence – I could feel his body heat on the right side of my body, while my left side was cold. He was totally quiet, but somehow I sensed he felt awkward standing next to me. If I could have done, I would have apologized for hurting his wings, but we had to stay quiet.

If anyone had told me some weeks earlier that I would find myself in a back alley next to an angel (well, half an angel, I suppose), chasing shadows that were created by individuals who called themselves Immortals, and who lived in a strange buffer zone around our world... where you could meet the dearly departed... or if I had been told earlier that vampires were real... I think I would have voluntarily committed myself for treatment. Now, however, I had visited the buffer zone, seen gateways to it, met my dead friend for an all too brief moment, talked with someone who descended from angels, discovered my grandmother was a Huntress of shadows...

I decided I'd better accept it all, and not think too much about it, or I would really go crazy. The evidence of it all being true was overwhelming so there was no point in fighting it. Maybe my brain would find a way to make it all feel natural to me, given time. How much time though?

We must have stood there for an hour. I found a balanced posture - feet slightly apart, with knees ever so slightly bent. Still, my feet were getting really tired in my light tennis shoes, when suddenly there was movement by the trash bin. The darkness seemed to concentrate more, and suddenly there was a form there.

Grandma was standing close to me and only needed to move her little finger to touch my hand, but I could not nod, because the shadow might see the movement. I could see it very clearly now. To me it looked like some sort of werewolf, only more fluid, and not so angled as you would expect a wolf to look. Its profile showed a canine muzzle, but human forehead and the ears...they were sort of human and animal at once. If you've never considered ears to be frightening, believe me, these were. I had to close my eyes when panic hit me again. White flashes exploded in the darkness of my eyes, like fireworks on the closed lids. Was I going to pass out? I remembered seeing this kind of a monster as a child. I had to control myself. I told myself that if I moved, the shadow would turn and see me. Bile rose into my mouth from sheer horror.

Right then the door to the bar across the street opened and a drunken man tottered out onto the sidewalk. He was trying to light a cigarette and migrated hand over hand, picket-fence-style towards the alley, clicking on his lighter, which refused to cooperate. An angry driver blew his horn as he drove past, but the man was so drunk he just waved his hand dismissively, barely noticing the vehicle.

The shadow rose from its hiding place and stepped in front of the man. He sensed something there and tried to focus in front of him with narrowed, bleary eyes. Suddenly the shadow turned darker and more solid. The cigarette fell from the man's lips and his mouth opened. He was too shocked to speak.

I had never expected to be able see the energy-stealing thing with my own eyes, because I had never witnessed energy as such, not in the way people talked about auras and stuff, but now I could see the man's energy quite clearly. It just shot out from his stomach area, like a fountain. The shadow grabbed it with its... hands. They were more like paws, but they moved as though there were no bones in them, more like...like... tentacles. The creature's hands started rolling the energy into a ball just as if it was preparing a ball of yarn for knitting. The horrified man fell onto his knees because of the strength of the pulling. It was hideous - this strange effect of an almost recognizably domestic movement of yarn rolling, along with something that was akin to evisceration.

Daniel shot into motion in the blink of an eye and arrived at the scene like an arrow from a bow. He raised his hand. The shadow was concentrating so hard on reeling in the man's energy that it did not have time to react. Daniel's hand rose and fell like a whip at the back of the shadow's neck. I saw a greyish flash, and the shadow fell on its face on the street. The energy it was holding in its arms rolled onto the ground and started slowly withdrawing back towards the pancreatic area of the drunken man who was kneeling and moaning on the sidewalk.

The shadow began to lose its form. For a while it crawled about on the ground aimlessly, shaking, with its movements growing ever more feeble. Then finally all movement ceased and it began to decrease in size. It crumpled in on itself like a piece of cloth.

Grandma walked to the man and helped him to get up onto his feet.

"You should not drink so much, young man!" She managed a proper grandma-voice, which contradicted her youthful appearance. "Your body can only take so much abuse!"

"N...no... Thank you.. Did - did - you see it...?" the man's face was grey with shock and he looked wildly around him.

"See what?" Grandma asked kindly.

"The monster..." he whispered.

"There are no monsters here." Grandma's tone allowed no objections. "If you have begun to see pink elephants, I suggest you stop drinking. Or else you might end up with hallucinations for the rest of your life!"

The man breathed a few deep breaths, still looking ill.

"Do you need a taxi?" Grandma asked.

"No, thank you, I think I'd be better walking to clear my head," the man said weakly and turned his back on us. He took a few feeble steps, and began to walk away as fast as his drunken state would allow. He seemed to be sobering up quickly.

"Follow him, just in case," Grandma nudged Daniel, "there may be other shadows around."

The man disappeared round the corner of the block, Daniel walking after him at a discreet distance. I noticed a little card on the ground where the man had fallen, and lifted it up.

"Fortune telling. Messages from the other side. Angel consultation," the card said.

I turned it around. "Kitty's Divinations" was printed under a picture of a cat staring at a crystal ball.

I slid it into my pocket.

Wind took the remains of the shadow and scattered them in a fine dust along the street.

38

LETTERS TO THE MOON

The Hunter did not socialise much with anyone. He felt the weight of centuries on his shoulders, and intellectually the younger Hunters seemed to be like children. Well, they were, compared to him. Some were children he had made himself, to keep the bloodline alive, so that she would never be forgotten and would live on in her children of the night, until he could find a way to get her back.

Sometimes he left the shadow world and traveled back to where he had met her so very long ago, especially when he needed to be alone. He was allowed to do so, because of his long years of service to the Masters. His shadow servant kept up surveillance while the Hunter was gone and alerted him if he was needed.

Tonight the Masters had set the trap successfully. His shadow had observed the whole thing from the rooftop above the alley. It had sent a message to ask if it should try to get the girl once the trap was sprung, but the Hunter said no. He did not want to lose his faithful servant, even though he was prepared to make a new shadow, if this one was killed. Their Huntress, the woman, was too dangerous. He had seen her fight. And the Nephilim they had with them was so powerful the shadow would not have had a chance. No, they must wait for the girl to come to them, alone, and be ready when she did.

After the night's work, he had withdrawn into the buffer zone and travelled along its paths to his own private place in the human world. It was a high cliff in the middle of a wilderness, where it was not likely he would meet humans and be tempted by them. Here he sat like a statue, free of his enveloping cloak and hood. His pale golden skin was colder than the night air. His shiny black hair fell onto his shoulders as he sat motionless under the vast black sky and watched the moon in its orbit. He knew its movements by heart and was keenly aware of the time and place of its rising and setting.

With him he had pieces of paper, and blood that he had taken from a bird he had killed. When he finally moved, it was to write to her with the blood, using a quill from his kill just as he used to do. He dipped the tip of the quill into the little glass bottle containing the blood. The blood did not shimmer with life as it had in the distant past, when she was there to read his notes. It was not the right kind, of course...

But he wrote to her nevertheless, careful not to tear the delicate paper, telling her through his writing how much he still loved her. The whole ritual was a pitiful imitation of the days he had written to keep her to himself. He knew this, but he could not stop. No one knew of his letters, so no one could ridicule him. And even if they knew, they would be too afraid of him to say anything.

He only hoped that she, somewhere in the unseen worlds and everywhere in his body, would hear the words he whispered while he wrote with the blood that quickly died on the paper.

He had been a merchant's son, living in the southern part of Italy, in an area the Greeks had settled. He had learned their language as a child, and had accompanied his father in some of his business negotiations. It was expected of him. He was to be his father's successor.

The merchants had visited wondrous places and he had listened to their tales with an eager beating heart. There were stories of pirates, and horrible sea monsters, distant lands and gods and treasures beyond anyone's wildest dreams. The stories that most raised his interest were the ones about gods and oracles.

One evening a wealthy Greek merchant was dining with them. When he sipped his wine from a fine ceramic cup, he told them about a wonderful oracle, Pythia, at the great temple of Delphi. This temple was dedicated to the god Paean, who in later times would be better known as Apollo.

The oracle was a woman who went into a trance over a chasm whence the fumes of the great rotting snake Pythos rose. She told the future to the ones who approached her.

But she did not see the future for everyone. A goat had to be sacrificed and its entrails examined before it was decided whether Pythia would take her place seated on a tripod ready to go into trance. If the liver of the sacrificial goat revealed that it was favorable for the Pythia to answer a supplicant's questions, the supplicant was allowed to approach her.

The priests never allowed anyone to approach Pythia if the omens were ill. Once, it had occurred, and the Pythia had gone into a hysterical trance. She was never able to awaken from it, and died a few days later. A new Pythia had to be chosen from among the priestesses of the temple.

The Hunter, whose name was Ambrogio in that faraway life, could not forget the words of the merchant. He just knew inside himself that he was destined for great deeds, much greater than simply trading goods. He wanted to see the oracle, to hear directly from her what his great purpose in life was to be. His would be a life of adventure and wonder and riches, he knew that for certain.

His father was a very down-to-earth kind of a man, and Ambrogio knew he would never consent to his son's request to go to consult an oracle. Father did respect the gods, but his unwavering opinion was that it was not wise for a man to believe the ravings of oracles. Better to make one's own luck through hard work and giving offering to the gods at temples, rather than trusting in words which could be misinterpreted.

So Ambrogio made a plan. Instead of ever mentioning his wish to meet the oracle of Delphi, he began to talk about seeing the world and getting to know the places from which they sourced the goods for their trading business. Creating contacts with good merchants across the sea, that was important to its success. After a few months his father consented, agreeing finally that it was a good idea. And so, a trip was arranged for Ambrogio on a merchant boat on its way to the western coast of Greece. If the trip was successful, he would be allowed more opportunities to travel.

Ambrogio found it hard to hide his joy. For months he had been secretly asking everyone coming from Greece about the location of Delphi. He even had a small map drawn by one merchant. This he hid carefully from his father.

He waited for the spring to come, because Pythia did not give oracles during the winter months. And then spring arrived at last and joyfully he stepped on board the small merchant vessel that was heading for the east. He was certain wonderful things awaited him there.

And so it was. The most wonderful, and most horrible things imaginable were waiting for him.

Would he have stayed at home and become a merchant like his father, if he had known the future? Grown a belly and grey hair, and died respected by his community, surrounded by his children?

The Hunter Ambrogio, sitting on the cliff, wrote the last word of the love poem in ancient Greek and gave it to the wind. It was Japanese silk paper, and flew like a little feather in the slightest of breezes, up in the sky, towards the moon.

He watched it without words, engulfed by his emotions. Love, remorse. The memory of her.

No, he would not have chosen otherwise. All the horrors that came later were worth the love in the beginning. The chance to let her live forever in him, in their children. He listened for her in his own being, but she was silent now. Sometimes, when he wrote with passion, and concentrated on the words, he could feel her light touch in his mind. Like the slightest of caresses, an effort to communicate.

But the words did not hold the same power they had held when he had written them with the blood of the winged creatures, the ones that no longer existed. Ordinary ink would not do, it had to be the right kind of blood. Swans they had called them. Swans with silver wings.

He rubbed at the amulet hanging from a leather string on his neck. It was ancient, from the land of Kemet, called Egypt in later times.

He knew the hieroglyphs by heart.

"*In iuwahtuheru en ahau, in iuhebatuimeferpu*," he whispered to the silent moon.

Can one add a day to a lifetime, can one subtract from it either?

The flying paper vanished into the darkness. He rose, gathered his cloak, and quietly stepped back into the buffer zone, into his never-ending service of the Masters.

39

A LILY FOR REMEMBRANCE

It was amazing how quiet everything could be in a small city. Elijah was used to big cities like London or New York or Cairo - where humanity's never-ending noise was always invading the inner space of his mind. The only place where he had found real comfort and silence had been the Egyptian desert. The relief he felt there was almost physical, being one with the earth and its past, as though modern times never existed and he was in a timeless place. Until...

He took a deep breath, drinking in the cool morning air. He was walking along the river, towards the old cathedral where they had given their promises to one another for what he had thought would be forever. He stopped in front of the old building and looked up. This was the national shrine, consecrated in the year 1300 as the Cathedral Church of the Blessed Virgin Mary and St Henry. What had then been a small stone church built to replace a previous wooden one, had grown into a big and impressive stone fortress of faith, where bishops and mighty people were buried. Even a queen of Sweden had found her final resting place here.

Merit had always disliked Christianity because of the way it had treated women, but she had liked this old Cathedral of her hometown nevertheless.

"They had 12 altars here, dedicated to female saints in the Middle Ages," she had explained as if she needed an excuse for liking the building.

There was a small museum in the Cathedral, in the south gallery. Statues of saints and sacred vessels were displayed there - and Merit's favorite piece: a bronze door ring in the shape of a lion.

He had time. He rose the steps to the main entrance, and stopped for a while again to have a look at the steeple, towering 85 meters above. He then pulled at the door handle, and the heavy door opened slowly.

"This church is a house of God and a place of prayer. Let us act with reverence in this holy place and let us respect the right of others to come and pray in silence," said a plaque at the entrance hall.

Then there was another door, lighter to handle. He pulled it open and stepped into the music.

He stepped further and approached the counter in the hall, while the music vibrated in the high vaults as if the stones themselves were singing the glory of God. A young lady was sitting behind the counter, ready to give advice for the asking. There were postcards under the glass counter, and some books. Some more cards were put on sale on top of the counter. He looked into the church hall, let his eyes follow the lines of white pillars and saw the source of the music - a large choir singing without words near the altar, their voices creating a sacred landscape of the mind.

The conductor stopped them and when the music died it felt almost like physical pain - like hearing a car in the desert just when inner peace had set in. Only this time he would not have wanted for the sound to end. For a few torturous moments the silence took over. And then the choir began to sing again and he sighed in relief. It was as though his nerves were open wounds and the music was medicine that softened the pain.

"They are practicing Beethoven's Missa Solemnis," the young woman behind the counter told him in perfect English. "First time performed in Finland."

She looked just right for the job. No makeup, blond hair, a silver cross as a necklace. He noticed how her eyes stopped for a second on the pendant round his neck, the Egyptian Scarab. But she did not show what she thought of it, or of the flowers he was carrying in see-through cellophane wrapping. She just smiled politely. Finns respected other people's space.

Well, he did not look Finnish, so he should not have been surprised at being spoken to in English. The Finns seemed to know their English very well - and they also spotted foreigners very quickly. Not once had anyone started to speak to him in Finnish yet. They might have been surprised to know he knew the language well enough to speak it.

"I would like to buy a ticket to the museum, if possible," he said.

"Certainly. That would be two Euros."

He paid, got his ticket and then turned to the steep steps on the opposite side of the hall. He walked up the flight of stairs, and behind him the young woman pressed the button on the counter that opened the electric lock for him.

There was no one else in the museum. Not even a guard. These people were so trusting... There was a counter on the right, but no one was sitting behind it.

He passed the miniature model of the Cathedral as it was today, the first thing greeting the visitors. On the left of it was another miniature of the older version of the church. He peeked in through the small windows and saw a short yellow pencil someone had dropped inside it.

The bronze lion door ring was to the right, in a glass cabinet against the wall, in line with the miniature churches. He stopped to look at it. The lion's mane was divided into what looked like the rays of the sun, supporting vines with bunch of grapes in a circle around the animal's face. The animal was biting the ring. There was a duplicate of it in the medieval town of Tallinn, he remembered Merit telling him.

"Looks almost like a sun-symbol," Merit had said when they had been here.

So it did. He did not smile at the memory though, but proceeded further into the small museum. Wooden saints in their glass cabinets observed him silently as he passed. A bishop's crosier with an ice-cube-like rhinestone on top caught his attention for a while - in its day it must have looked amazing to the laypeople, reflecting the light, but in this day and age it probably did not catch the attention of young people any more. Not with all the glitter of today's world.

The choir kept singing, and the divine music felt like soothing balm to his heart. He looked over the railing at the musicians and the choir and briefly admired how human voices could create anything so beautiful. He had always loved music, but this sounded exceptionally beautiful. Otherworldly, almost.

At the very end of the museum hall was a large glass cabinet with priestly cassocks. He walked to the left of the cabinet. There was an opening that allowed him to get to a narrow walkway behind the cabinet and look down at a chapel below - the white marble statues of the major general Åke Tott and his wife from the 17th century stood solemnly there. On the high wall reaching up from the chapel, opposite to the back of the cassock-cabinet, red flowers had been painted. They almost looked like something a child would paint - red petals, green stem and leaves. A small wooden door was half open at the opposite end of the little balcony.

He stopped here, and took the white lily out of its wrappings. He had several lilies, but he took only one, snapping the flower off its stem, trying to move so that his back was towards the surveillance cameras, yet trying not to raise suspicions. He then turned his back to the railing, and looked at the pillar on his left, holding the lily flower in his hand. The pillar was made of red brick but it did not meet seamlessly with the vault it was supporting. It extended slightly out of the base of the vault, leaving a small triangular ledge just over his head. He kissed the petals of the while lily and raised his arm to put the lily flower on the ledge.

"I loved you, Merit," he whispered hoarsely, "And now I have come to say my goodbyes, as we agreed. I have finally found the strength to go on."

His voice trailed off.

This was where he had asked her to marry him. She had wanted him to see the lion door ring and they had been standing just here when he proposed. She had looked at the ring he had given her, and then at him, with those surprisingly deep, solemn blue eyes. She had been so solemn always, despite her youth and strong emotions. There was deep humour in her eyes, but she never giggled. You could see the smile deep in her eyes, and hear the fun in her dry remarks, which many understood only later. She was not trying to please anyone.

"We shall make our vows to each other both in life and death." Her eyes had been serious. "If one dies, the one of us who remains shall come here on the anniversary of our promises, when ready to move on, and bring a lily. The lily goes here..." Merit had shown the ledge to him - she had clearly been here before.

"Why there?" he had asked, not wanting to discuss death when they had a whole life together ahead of them.

"Well... because this is my favorite spot in this church." She spread her arms and swirled slowly around, and a rare flash of a smile made his knees melt. "It's a hiding place, where you can be alone. And no one is likely to look at what is here on the ledge, so the lily can remain there as a secret, for a while at least."

He could understand this, looking at the romantic balcony, the painted red flowers on the walls, the vaults, the small wooden door... Hardly anyone entered here, he was certain. The museum was probably not very popular anyway, not in today's secular world, and if the only way to get here was through the museum... a quiet place indeed.

"All right... But what is this about the lily? Why bring a lily?"

"Because it is a symbol of rebirth. You know the water lilies of ancient Egypt?"

He did. They rose together with the sun, from the dark depths of the waters, bloomed for a day, and then receded under water at sunset, back into the inky embrace of the night. The god Nefertem, the "Lord of Perfume" was the god associated with the blue lily. In ancient Egyptian mythology he was thought to be the rising blue lotus out of which the sun rose. The receding lily symbolized the setting of the sun. Even Tutankhamun was depicted as Nefertem in a statue where his head was shown in the middle of a lotus flower. During the dangerous days of the Egyptian New Year the pharaoh used lotus oil as the symbol of renewal. In sacred bouquets a lotus flower represented the symbol ankh, life.

So yes, the lily was indeed a symbol of rebirth. And it was also a symbol of love and sexuality.

He had looked into Merit's deep blue eyes and spoken the words of the Egyptian nineteenth Dynasty love poem, almost choking in the feeling of love humming in his body:

And I will say to Ptah, Lord of Truth:
"Give me my fair one tonight."
The river is like wine.
The god Ptah is its tuft of reeds,
The goddess Sekhmet is its bouquet of flowers,
The goddess Yadyt is its water lily bud,
The god Nefertem is its opened water lily.
My love will be happy!
The dawn illuminates her beauty.

"Love and rebirth," Merit had nodded, "then you understand that bringing the lily means that the other one still lives, and has moved on to the spiritual realms. And to the one left behind the lily will represent being reborn into a new physical life, a message of moving on. I do not believe in mourning for the rest of your life... that you would be irrevocably injured, and unable to leave the past. That is a waste of the precious gift of living. There must be a way of letting go, and moving on, and still feel the connection between the souls."

They had invited the necessary witnesses and made their solemn promises to each other according to law.

He remembered her words so well. And right now he could not believe he would ever stop mourning. The pain was just as strong as it had been, when they had searched for her.

She had disappeared in Egypt. Not a trace of her had been found. No one knew how she died, but eventually everyone had believed she was dead. His beautiful wife, Merit. Even her name meant "loved one" in ancient Egyptian language. How her adoptive parents had chosen this name for her in a Lutheran country, he never knew.

But here he was now, keeping his word for her, saying his goodbyes. He realized he had to let go. His other half was gone for good, and because of Merit's wish, it was his duty to live on, even if carrying the deep sorrow for the rest of his life.

Elijah raised his hand and reached upwards, to place the flower on Merit's secret hiding place, as a promise to move on with his life. He was tall so it was easy for him to reach to the ledge.

His hand touched something. He froze on the spot, and then withdrew his hand, dropping his own lily on the floor. He reached back, hastily grabbed what he had felt and took it out.

A fresh lily with a blue ribbon. There was something tied to the ribbon. He stared at it and his hands began to shake. A ring. A smooth golden ring with one deep blue sapphire in it. He raised in to the light and looked inside, already knowing what he would find.

Their names were clearly written. First Merit, then Elijah. And between the names there were three hieroglyphs. There was a snake, a cobra, on top with its tail hanging down forming a frame on one side of the other two signs. Underneath the snake was first half a sphere - like sun rising from the horizon - and under that a slightly rounded flat rectangle, like a thick underlining. He knew what they spelled. D.t - eternity. Merit and Elijah forever.

The ring had been on her finger when she disappeared, smooth and shiny, new. And now it had appeared, clearly worn and scratched - here, to the very place where Merit knew he would come to say his goodbyes to her. Her wedding ring attached to the flower of rebirth. No one else would have known of this day, of the lily... no one but Merit.

His hands shook and a deep rumble rose from his hidden wings. He reached back to the ledge and felt even deeper. There was something more. A small, flat box.

He pulled it out and opened the lid. He was looking into what he knew was a very old metal mirror. The Egyptian goddess of love and music, Het-Hert, "House of Horus", better known as Hathor, gazed back at him from the top of a handle in the form of a papyrus plant. The formal wig framing her face, and the bovine ears on either side were unmistakeable attributes of the goddess. The mirror was made of... gold. Hathor, also called "the Golden One". He turned it over in his hands, not believing what he saw. On the other side was a lioness's face. Sekhmet, the destroyer and protector of the old sun-god Ra, the fierce side of Hathor. And the disk above Sekhmet was made of reddish colored metal, copper or bronze, representing the blood of humankind she killed.

The round disks fitted together beautifully. He knew he was looking at an 18th dynasty object that was immeasurably valuable, because of the instantly recognisable face that had been used as the model for the goddess.

Queen Tiye, the Great Royal wife of the richest Pharaoh in the history of Egypt - Neb-Maat-Re, also known as Amenhotep III. The mother of Akhenaten.

He saw small markings on the handle and lifted the mirror higher into the light to see better. For a while he stared at the writing, completely still as though he had turned to stone.

There was a piece of paper under the mirror with hand written notes on it. He lifted that out of the box as well, beginning to shake as he recognised the handwriting.

"Elijah – how I wish I could tell you I am alive, and let you know where I am? I am not dead. We sit here by these great skeletons, resting, preparing to leave tomorrow morning. I have taught my rescuer some words in English, and she has taught me a few words of her own language. Soon we shall come out of the desert, I am certain. Then I can find a way to contact you again. I cannot wait, I would like to start walking already, but even with the light of the bright stars I know it is not wise. We shall wait until the sun begins to rise. We are headed straight towards it, to the East and..."

The rest of the page had crumbled away. Then he noticed a little card, note card size, at the bottom of the box.

"She wrote a notebook to you while she was still alive. The rest of her notebook is now hidden in a library in the City of Immortals. It was stolen from us when we tried to bring it back to you, and this page alone was found in the hand of the one they killed. But there was no way for them to understand the language at the time. We finally managed to get one of our own inside the City. We found the notebook and hid it inside the library. 18.England.Enquiry."

That was all it said. No signature. There was only a picture of a stylized bee printed on the note card in such a light color it was barely visible.

He stood there for a while, anger rising up his spine while his mind tried to understand. Why would anyone want to steal Merit's notebook? "While she was still alive" – so she really was dead now. Where was she buried? Who were the "we" who tried to bring the notebook back to Elijah?. What was the "18.England.Enquiry"? What the hell did this all mean?

He had to fight to calm his mind. He put the mirror back to its box, and into his rucksack, together with the lily and Merit's wedding ring, crushing the lily in the process.

He almost ran through the museum gallery, through the entrance door and down the stairs to the hall. No one at the desk. Impatiently he walked to the church hall, not hearing the beautiful music anymore. Then he saw someone appear from behind a corner and step behind the counter.

"Who has been to the museum today?" His voice was angry and he made considerable effort to silence the energies of his wings.

And older lady this time, clearly alarmed by his approach.

"I am sorry," Elijah forced himself to be calm, "I had a meeting today at the museum, and when I went there, there was no one. I must have mistaken the time. Can you tell me who has been there?"

"Well, no one, as far as I know," the lady answered politely.

"How about the younger lady who was here? Would she know?"

"A younger lady?"

"The one who sold me the ticket to the museum, of course!"

"I am sorry, there is no one here but me. No younger ladies working at this hour."

The woman answered her phone and Elijah took a few aimless steps, looked at the people in the church, but only saw backs of heads - people who had wandered inside the church and stayed to listen to the choir practice. He could hardly go and ask them all if they had been up to the museum.

He turned and walked out of the cathedral.

"Has he left?"

The woman was sitting in the wooden benches of the cathedral, seemingly listening to the music. She did not turn to look over her shoulder.

"Yes, he has gone," her companion, another woman, said. She was watching the happenings of the hall in her hand mirror whilst she pretended to put her hair in place.

"We shall wait for a while, to be sure no one has followed us." The older woman made no attempt to move.

They listened to the beautiful music, seemingly oblivious to their surroundings. Their eyes darted around the church, however, observing everyone in their sight with keen interest.

"It seems we have succeeded," the older woman finally said in a low voice.

"Indeed it seems to be so," the younger one agreed. "Our long quest has finally ended. Our sisterhood can be proud."

"No, it has not ended." The older woman gave the slightest shake of the head. "We have done what our founding mother told us to do, but the danger is far from over. He may find the way, but he will be followed by the dark ones on his quest for certain. The sisterhood must stay alert where ever we are along the Path of the Dead. We may be the only thing that stands between him and peril."

The younger one nodded solemnly.

"After thousands of years of waiting we have indeed reached our first goal, but we were not completely successful. We lost the note-book. But it can be retrieved."

The woman who had been tidying her hair under her hat rose from her seat quietly and unobtrusively. A tourist couple walked through the doors of the church and the man held the door open for the ladies to pass. For a moment he wondered where these two deeply suntanned women came from. They did not look Scandinavian, being short and dark skinned. Their clothes were old-fashioned, their shoes sensible, they even wore summer hats that looked like something you'd find in a flea market, carefully shading their faces and covering their hair. Neither one wore any makeup. He thought they looked like nuns dressed in secular clothes.

When the older one passed him by, he noticed three live bees walking on the woman's sleeve. She clearly saw them but was not afraid.

"Did you have a look at them?" the man asked his wife. "Didn't they look like nuns?"

"Oh they did for sure, very respectable," the wife shook her head. "You should have done something about them bees, though. They could sting the old lady!"

"Looked more like pets of hers," he commented, "as daft as it sounds. Didn't you see how she clearly looked at them and let them be?"

His wife snorted.

"Let them be - that's a good one. Nuns with bees as pets? That would make them the sisterhood of the bees, eh? And the older one was the abbess then? The mother of the bees? Sounds like you've had a touch too much sun, it does."

The man shrugged, amused, and they walked deeper into the cathedral.

In five minutes they had forgotten all about the two women.

40

WEAVERS

That night I had a vivid dream again. I had not continued watching my fingers, or clocks and asking if I was awake or not, but still I began to dream lucidly.

I was standing in a mist, sensing a landscape around me, but nothing was really visible at first. I felt shadowy figures moving and even caught glimpses of them, but they were never close enough for me to make out what or who they were.

Then a figure in the mist came closer. It was Kitty and she looked... scared. When she spoke, I could hear her voice this time. It was like listening to a bad cell phone connection.

"...beware...angel..."

She looked over her shoulder, turned, and vanished.

I woke up with Diana shaking me.

"Dana! Wake up!"

"What is it?"

"You were calling for Kitty, and you sounded frightened. What happened? Where were you?"

I sat up and realised I had a nasty headache.

"I don't know... I was in a foggy area, not very light. And Kitty came to warn me."

"What about?" Diana looked at me, worried.

Suddenly I could not say she had warned me about the angel – because the only angel around was Daniel. If Kitty meant I should keep my distance from him, it would be easy to do, as it was not like he showed much interest in talking to me.

"I don't remember... But she looked scared."

"Scared? That's not usual... Usually dead people look rather happy... They don't have much to worry about anymore, so she must be worried about you."

"That would make sense - even I would be worried about me," I tried to say lightly, "what with all these buffer zones and time walkers and shadows and angels... maybe she was worried I'll go nuts here."

"I suppose that's how we'd be categorised, if we spoke to anyone about this place outside..." Diana smiled. "And you need a pain killer," she continued, seeing my painful expression when I started to rub my aching temples.

She went to the bathroom and returned with a glass of water and a pill. I gulped it down.

"I don't think I can sleep anymore." I leaned my forehead against my hands. "What time is it?"

Diana reached for her alarm clock and turned it so she could see it.

"Five in the morning... You know – a Time Walker group is due back this morning. What do you say if went to have a look at their arrival? You haven't seen one yet, I suppose."

"No, I haven't. And yes, let's do that."

We got dressed, dragged a brush through our hair and tiptoed on our stocking feet to the stairway to the ground floor. There we put our shoes on and went down the stairs. Diana knew where the arriving group was going to enter and led us to the correct room.

We weren't the only ones there. Jason was standing next to the gate, as was Mrs. Olanda and a woman I had seen before, but whose name I did not know. They nodded briefly in our direction, so obviously it was OK for us to stay.

The gate was open in the middle of the room. Jason was keeping the other side like a curtain, and I could see a faint blue glow under his hand when the otherwise invisible side of the opening followed his touch. The misty opening in the air looked unreal against the sharp background of the room.

"They are coming," the woman in the chair said.

I was staring at her hands, because there was something very peculiar happening there.

She sat with her hands on her lap, palms up. There was a misty ball of something wrapping her palms and fingers, and from that mist strings formed and flowed from her fingers like water in slow motion and through the opening in the air. When she moved her fingers the strings would move too, weaving into each other in an intricate pattern. She seemed to be deep in her thoughts, but not in a trance. It was as if she was acutely listening to something the others could not hear. Everyone else seemed to be as quiet as possible, trying not to disturb her.

The strings were not very bright, but clearly of different colors.

We waited. Then - steps approached, without any echo, and a woman stepped through the opening, into the classroom. She was holding her hands in front of her and more strings flowed from her palms and fingers. They were directly attached to the strings coming from the hands of the woman sitting in the classroom, and while she approached her, the strings got shorter and shorter – it was as though the women were drawing the strings back into their bodies as the distance between them grew less.

"Welcome back!" Mrs. Olanda greeted them.

The women pressed their palms together, and when they withdrew their hands, the strings were gone.

"What was that?" I whispered to Diana.

"They are the Time Weavers - they find the path to the past, and direct the group to the correct place and time. Theirs is the hardest skill to learn, they are very rare, and so valuable they are all assigned at least one Guardian who is to be near them at all times. It seems they have to have some Nephilim blood in their family tree to be able to do that. The Nephilim themselves cannot weave through time, though.

They can get in and out of buffer zone on their own, but not weave," Diana whispered in answer.

"So only people can? That's odd."

"Yes, people with Nephilim blood. Old legends tell of good Nephilim who could weave, but they were all killed in the past..."

Diana stopped talking, when others came through the gate in the air. Six people in all. When they had all entered, Jason peeked into the buffer zone and said something quietly. After a short wait three more figures stepped in from the mist. They had similar body build to Jason. Other Gatekeepers, obviously, and all were carrying what looked like short swords. One was about the same age as Jason, the others were maybe ten years older. When they had come through, Jason quickly closed the gate with a few fluid movements. He had to use some force - I could see his muscles working, and there was a clear blue halo coming from under his hands - it seemed the gate had been open for a while. The translucent scar hung in the air for a minute or two, and then it was gone.

I gazed at the six travelers with interest. Their clothes looked Victorian in style to me. The Weaver was wearing a black dress that looked rather costly. On her head she had en elaborate hat of lace, velvet, a few feathers and pleats. With her was a young man, whom I took to be a Hunter. An older man, who was also dressed in the style of a gentleman, followed them, and two servant-looking girls, and then someone I recognized. Professor Reginald Rowan - or maybe I should say Reggie, as everyone else did.

"Ah, Dana and Diana." He bowed, squeezing a book tightly under his arm. "We've found it!"

"What have you found?" Diana asked.

"This!" Professor Rowan – or Reggie – lifted the book into the air like a victory sign. "It's a religious text from a nunnery library. And it's all about angels and Watchers and such. Maybe this is our clue!"

He trotted out of the room almost chuckling to himself with glee. Diana and I stole a sideways glance at each other, and couldn't help laughing. Scholarly enthusiasm was rather a funny thing to observe.

"Was it hard to find?" Mrs. Olanda asked the rest of the group when they sat in the chairs and sighed. Obviously they had been walking a long while.

"Well it took some convincing before the nuns let us into their library." the Weaver stretched out her legs. "But a generous donation to the order made them more cooperative. Reggie pretended to be my scholar of a brother who was finally given permission to study their books – under strict observance, of course."

"Of course..." Mrs. Olanda smiled.

"You stole the book?" I asked.

"We did. The bookshelves were guarded by a railing and a gate, with a very strict looking nun as the gate keeper. Reggie slipped the book under his waistcoat when the guardian of the library went in search of some other book. In its stead he put another book of similar size, so the numbers still matched, when he returned to his pile of books. I trust we were long gone before they noticed – if they noticed at all," the man said

"Indeed," Reggie shook his head, " it seemed no one had bothered to put the books in place for quite a while – there were piles of them on the tables... Unfortunately I could not go to the shelves myself."

"Was that ethical? Stealing the book?" I asked.

"Strictly speaking, no. But history records show this particular nunnery burns down in... well, we can't really talk about days anymore, rather hours after our visit...Its whole library will be destroyed. So you can say we simply saved the book. The only problem was to stop Reggie from taking anything else. Everything else, to be honest. He cannot tolerate the thought of books being harmed, can you? " The well-dressed man, grinned at Reggie. Then he changed the subject. "Are you the newcomer?"

"Yes. I'm Dana," I extended my hand in greeting and he took it and shook it with both hands.

"Welcome! I am Dieter. What's your speciality, then?"

"We don't know yet," Diana answered on my behalf.

"Have you seen shadows with your own eyes?" Dieter asked, placing his hat on the table and ruffling his hair with his fingers. "Have to get rid of these sideburns... I look like an Elvis-impersonator..." he then commented to the mirror on the wall and sang a few bars of Love Me Tender. Jason made a face and covered his ears with his hands.

"Yes, I have seen shadows."

"So you could be a Hunter..."

"We could try weaving right now, " The Weaver who had been sitting in the chair got up and faced Mrs. Olanda, "to see if she's got the knack for it."

"Shouldn't we fetch Mireille first?" the other Weaver in her black Victorian dress asked and started unbuttoning the bodice of her frock. "How women ever agreed to wearing these corsets, I'm sure I'll never understand!" she mumbled to herself. "But if you think it is wise, we could try the weaving. First I'll get rid of this horror, though... I'll be back in a minute, I want to change into something more comfortable."

She walked out of the room, working on the long row of tiny buttons on her bodice.

"Are you sure you can do this?" Mrs. Olanda asked the Weaver.

"I think so. We are experienced Weavers and have been teaching students in Mireille's classes. We will not let her go anywhere, we'll simply do a test to find out if she has the threads in her. Oh, and I am Paris, by the way," the Weaver smiled and nodded to me.

"Dana, " I answered in kind, "pleased to meet you!"

"Likewise," Paris returned the compliment. She looked like someone who had just woken up from a dream.

She was a few years older than me, my height, and a little rounder in shape. She had long auburn hair and grey eyes, and the beginnings of laugh lines around her eyes. I liked her instinctively.

"Have you any idea how time weaving works?" she asked.

"No, this was the first time I have seen it done," I admitted.

The other Weaver reappeared in comfortable jeans and a T-shirt, which made her look rather hilarious – her hair was still combed into an elaborate Victorian hairstyle.

"Anna, " she extended her hand and I shook it. "Welcome to the center."

"Dana, nice to meet you."

With the introductions done they wasted no time. Anna gave me a little embroidered velvet bag. It looked old.

"What's this?" I asked.

"It was my anchor on this journey, " Anna replied. "An anchor is an object from the time the Weaver is trying to reach. It helps you weave your way into the right time. Once you have reached it, you need to adjust your position so that you get out of the zone into the right date. That's another matter, which will be taught to you later, should you be a Weaver yourself. This particular bag was embroidered by a nun at the very nunnery we visited, and more importantly, it was made around the time we needed to visit it – before the nunnery burned down. The nuns earned extra income for themselves doing this kind of needlework. Took us a few months of second hand shopping to find the genuine thing, but it took us nicely right to the doorstep of the nunnery. No need for any extra physical travel."

I looked at the bag closer. It had a design of beautiful cross-stitched red roses and leaves, their colors slightly faded.

"What should I do with this?" I asked.

"Sit still, close your eyes, and listen to the bag. Not with your ears, but with your mind. That should be enough. Tell us the impressions you get."

Though listening to an object sounded an odd thing to do, I took the bag and sat on a free chair. Diana pulled up another chair for herself and sat next to me. I closed my eyes.

At first I only felt the material of the bag, and began to feel a bit silly. I did not have any clairvoyant qualities, it seemed. I opened my mouth to say I didn't "get" anything out of the bag, and the next second it all changed.

I fell. It felt as though I was falling inside myself in a tight spin that made me nauseous. Colors exploded all about me, bright, pure colors. They wafted like smoke around me, but then I saw them condense into strings. I grabbed the string that was the most solid. It was a grey one, pure, bluish grey. I must have used my physical hands, because I felt the string tug at my skin. The other colors swirled around my wrists, but gently. Only this grey string was very tight. I heard what sounded like a whip cracking, and the next thing I knew I flew. Instinctively I squeezed my eyes shut.

"Grab her!" I heard someone yell and opened my eyes.

To my surprise I was not in the room anymore, but surrounded by grey mist much like the mist from which Kitty had appeared last night. I was alone. My sole companion was the grey string that was shining pure silver now. It flowed from my fingers and disappeared into the mist at the height of my hands.

I must have ended up in the buffer zone somehow. I had no idea where I was. I was still holding the rose-embroidered purse tightly in my hands, which were covered in grey mist. I lifted my hand closer to my eyes, and it looked like the mist was seeping through my skin, swirling around the purse, and from there solidifying into a string. An insane sight.

I turned around. Nothing physical anywhere. Only mist that was solid enough to walk on. No gate, no nothing.

I fought fear. If I had no idea where I was, and if there was no gate anywhere near, I could be lost here forever. If I found my way out, I would be in some strange place and time.

"Kitty!" My voice sounded odd, there was no echo. Well, there wouldn't be, not in the mist.

No answer. Kitty was probably in other, higher spheres. I knew I had to be on the lowest level of the buffer zone. The same level where the Immortals and shadows moved. I realized it might be wiser not to try yelling for help again.

Thankfully I had never been the panicking kind. When I met an obstacle, my mind started churning out possible solutions as it always had.

I considered the options and did the only thing that made sense. The string leaving my hands was taut, and it was clearly connected to something on its other end. That something had to be physical. So I started walking in the nothingness towards the direction the grey string was leading.

41

MR. DONNELLY HAS A CLOSE ENCOUNTER

The sketchbook was not quite as well preserved as it had appeared at first. It had clearly travelled a long way - and for a long time - and now Mr. Donnelly understood its worn look, if the book had come through centuries into his hands. Pages were torn, some of them had had some liquid on them - perhaps wine? This had erased much of the writing. It seemed Merit had used a pencil at first, and then some kind of ink that had not survived the moisture that had fallen on the pages. He could see some of the sketches, though. There were people, buildings. Women and babies. The last pages of the sketch book were beyond reading.

But there were a few intriguing passages left to be translated after Mr. Donnelly turned the book around. Mr. Donnelly noticed she had numbered the days from the very beginning of the book - probably in an effort to keep up with time's passing. At date 305 she wrote:

"All is well now. I got fever and they feared I might die, but I survived, much to their surprise. They took care of me and..."

Mr. Donnelly let out a sigh of relief. She had survived a fever. Hopefully it was not malaria.

Then many pages were missing. Day 425 told:

"Elijah, I stumbled across an incredible mystery... Those who kept an eye on us... disappeared... They were doomed to..."

Frustrating gaps in the text again. Who kept an eye on whom? Their parents? Not likely. Surely these were lovers.

"Who disappeared? Who was doomed and why?" Mr. Donnelly said out aloud.

"Doomed? What do you mean?" a sweet voice said from the doorway.

Only because he had been used to the Masters appearing and disappearing out of thin air, did Mr. Donnelly manage to keep his calm. He pulled a paper he had been scribbling on over the sketch book and turned another leaf of one of the Egyptological books, then sighed, and stood up rubbing the bridge of his nose, slipping his Moleskine inconspicuously into his pocket.

"My lady," he bowed, "I do apologize for my appearance. If I had known you were coming to visit me, I would have put on decent clothing and provided you with some refreshments."

The blonde woman in the doorway smiled a beautiful, chilling smile that did not reach her golden eyes. How different her smile had been when he had first met her in front of Westminster Abbey in 1887. She had been so sweet and fragile, and managed to lure him into a life of imprisonment in this timeless place. If only he had known... But no, he had fallen into their trap, hers and whom he had believed to be his brother - he had believed their story and trusted their promises a wonderful life as an esteemed and respected scholar. There was no mention of shadows, monstrous creatures and a threat to his own life if he did not deliver what was expected of him.

"You talked about someone being doomed. Perhaps you would clarify?"

"Ah yes, I was wondering why the subjects of our study were doomed," Mr. Donnelly no longer surprised himself by lying so fluently - the years had taught him to keep his emotions in check to such an extent he almost believed himself when he was lying to the Masters. "What it was that was so dangerous in what they knew that they had to be doomed for all eternity."

"Indeed," the woman observed him with those yellow eyes like a snake observing its prey, "and that is why you were hired. We expect to see results soon."

Mr. Donnelly bowed, his tongue suddenly dry.

"What is that book about? Ancient Egypt?" a slight nod towards Mr.Donnelly's desk.

"Yes indeed, my lady," Mr. Donnelly kept bowing like a cork bobbing about on water, "I expect the Egyptian legends might hide some clue. After all they are amongst the oldest in human history."

The answer seemed to satisfy her.

"Quite so. Do let us know what you find."

She spoke sweetly, but Mr. Donnelly recognized the veiled threat.

"Of course, my lady."

She left and Mr. Donnelly's knees gave way. With a shaking hand he wiped the sweat off his brow.

42

THE NUNNERY

At first I moved like a child, or a young animal learning to walk – erect, exaggeratedly raising my foot high above the ground and then stomping it down carefully. I wasn't at all sure the surface I was walking on wouldn't give way and disappear from under my feet. I had been for a walk in fog before, but then I had had solid ground under me. Now there was only grey... something that resembled mist. It gave way slightly beneath my feet, and fear punched me in the stomach when my brain interpreted it as the ground caving in and told me that I would fall.

The stomp made a definite sound, though, so I decided the surface was solid enough. Also I did not want to draw unwanted attention to myself, so I continued to walk as quietly as possible. I took off my shoes, and shoved them into my jacket pockets. Without them I could move almost soundlessly. The surface under my feet was not warm or cold.

It all felt like an odd dream, and yet the surroundings were strangely familiar. But then again – if this was the zone where we ended up when we dreamed, it made sense that the place felt familiar. I just wondered why I did not lose consciousness, which I had been told happened to people who got into the buffer zone unexpectedly.

What had happened to my hands was the thing I found hard to accept. My hands had always been ordinary, flesh and blood hands, and now suddenly they were capable of creating some kind of a misty substance that appeared from under my skin, and could actually form a solid string... That felt unreal to me. It should not have been possible. No - it was physically impossible. My mind was having a hard time accepting what my eyes were seeing.

Still I could not explain the whole thing away as a dream, I was definitely awake.

After a while I got used to the fog despite the unpleasant sensations of my feet sinking into the mist while walking, and of being almost blind – no solid forms to concentrate on, only the string. I kept my hands in front of me as though I was sleepwalking, but realized soon enough that there was no need for it. Even if I kept my hands to my sides, the string was as solid as ever.

I remembered how Paris had moved her fingers, weaving the different colored strings together. I stopped and raised my hands in front of my eyes again, and did just that. Much to my surprise new, different colored strings flew out of my fingers. I felt like Spiderman – only these strings moved elegantly and slowly and did not shoot forward with lightning-speed. They did move, yes, but so slowly that my eyes could easily follow them.

These new strings followed the direction of the first, silver-grey one. They too disappeared into the mist, and then suddenly one of them, a green one, tightened. It yanked me forward and I had a feeling I was moving faster now – it was kind of hard to tell how fast exactly, as there was no physical object to compare my speed to. It was the impression of the fog against my face that told me I was moving faster – it felt almost like a breeze now.

Then, very fast, all the other strings got attached to something too, and every time one of them got tighter, my speed increased. Soon I could not walk anymore, but had to run – the strings were pulling me forward. My steps became longer and longer, and then the strings simply lifted me up and I flew.

I moved my fingers some more, and the strings braided together and the speed kept on increasing. I felt the shoe in one of my pockets fall away.

It was a curious feeling, wondering if I should be panicking or not, but finally deciding it was of no use. The strings were taking me somewhere, and somewhere was better than standing in the middle of nowhere. And once I learned to relax, this whole flying business felt like fun. The strings tugging at my hands and fingers did not hurt. It was more like someone was shaking hands with me and drawing me somewhere at the same time. Even the fog seemed to clear a bit, and a silvery glow surrounded me.

The stop came abruptly. The strings ceased tugging me and unbraided themselves and the different colors turned from solid to misty and wrapped around my hands again. Only the silver-gray one remained.

I realised I could see something in front of me. Cautiously I followed the string and little by little the forms in the fog grew more solid, and a small room appeared in front of me. The closer I walked, the more solid it became. When I stepped into it, the fog snapped away in an instant, and I stood inside the room in a very physical and real environment. When I turned around, I found that I was now in an enclosed room; the mist was nowhere to be seen.

Now the question was – where was I? And when was I?

There was a small window, and of course I went to look through it first. I saw a pretty landscape – rolling hills, some trees. The building I was in was made of grey stone. It had a high garden wall around it, and there were small buildings both inside the walled area, and outside at a distance. I saw hens in the yard, and two cows in a paddock. The sun was already well past midday, twilight was descending.

Inside the room there was only austere looking furniture without any decorations. A bed with a coarse blanket and a pillow. A small cupboard, and a tiny table, where a worn Bible was the only object. A crucifix on the wall, and an oil lamp. No carpet on the wooden floor.

I was in a monastery. Or a nunnery. Was it the same one where the Time Walkers had come from? It could be – even though I did not know about the laws of the buffer zone, the fact that I still held the little bag with rose embroidery that had led them to their nunnery probably meant I had come to the same place. After all, Anna had said it was her anchor to this time.

This was likely the Victorian era, then. But which country? What language did they speak here? I didn't recall the team mentioning exactly where the nunnery was located. My eyes fell on the Bible and I opened it to see the title page. 1855 was written there. And probably I was in England.

There was no mirror in the room, but I knew I would look very odd in my modern clothes – jeans, T-shirt and a college hoodie. Not to mention the fact I only had one shoe left.

I opened the cupboard door – and there was a nun's outfit, neatly folded on a shelf. Desperate measures, I told myself and dressed myself in the grey outfit, listening for any approaching footsteps. There were no shoes, but there was a type of coarse, knitted socks. I put them on as well. I had no headdress, but I supposed my short hair would remind other nuns, should I meet them, of their own shorn hair. I would have to come up with some explanation about my missing headgear, if someone asked. Thankfully I had not put on any makeup while in my own time – for the obvious reason I had none with me at the Centre. It would have been difficult to explain makeup on a novice's face in a 19th Century nunnery...

I opened the door to the room ever so slightly, just enough to see to the corridor behind it.

No one there. I hesitated for a while, having no idea whether I should stay in the room or leave. Then I figured that if I was in the same nunnery as the Time Walker group I had seen, I might as well go and see the library. Now the question remaining was – where was it?

I could see two stairways from where I was standing. One stairway looked bigger, and was situated in the middle of the corridor, probably leading down to some sort of lobby. The other, narrower stairs looked like something servants might use – the stairway was situated by the wall. I decided to go that way. I ran quickly to the stairs and listened. I heard distant singing.

Of course - the nuns must be at some service, which explained the empty corridors. As far as I knew the monasteries and nunneries had services at odd hours round the clock.

I tiptoed down the stairs, which was not easy - it was a typical narrow Victorian servants' staircase you had to descend almost sideways, because the steps were so narrow. I peeked round the corner. Another corridor, but this time there were bigger, more official looking doors. And one doorway nearby was open. I could see bookshelves.

Feeling lucky, I ran to the door. Just as I was about to enter, I heard whispering voices. My woolen socks were so slippery on the well-worn floor I could not stop when I wanted to but slid right into the middle of the doorway.

Two men were standing in the library. The fact that there were men in a nunnery would have been suspicious enough, but the fact their clothing was from my own age really alarmed me. They had not seen me yet, but as they were looking around, searching for something, they would probably see me in a matter of seconds.

There was a bucket by the door, with a rag hanging from its side. Thankfully it did not reach the water in the bucket and seemed to be dry. I bent down and opened the rag – it was a big one, and not too dirty. I tied it quickly round my head, proper cleaning-woman-style. Then I realized the black embroidered evening bag would look rather odd in the hands of a novice – which I had to be, considering my age. I quickly turned the insides of the bag out, and found the lining was of grey cloth. If I squeezed it tightly, it would go for a rag.

The very same moment the other one of the men turned around and saw me, I had turned sideways to them and took a step past the doorway, carrying the bucket in one hand and the "rag" in the other. I kept on walking back to the stairs I had come from, and heard slight movement from behind me. It took all my courage not to run, but I continued walking with even steps, my eyes downcast, and went back up the stairs. I heard quiet whispering, but no one came after me. My camouflage had worked.

With shaking knees I put down the bucket - and noticed someone was standing in the corridor in front of me. A pair of sensible, worn shoes stood behind the bucket, with a hem of the similar coarse fabric as my own outfit above them.

"What are you doing here?" a woman's voice demanded – in a British accent.

"I am new, I came to clean," I tried to sound as British as I possibly could. "There were two men in the library," I then whispered with lowered eyes.

That did the trick. I was no longer of interest.

"Men? There should be no men here! They must be thieves! They are after our ancient manuscript, for sure!"

I put my hand over my mouth and tried to look horrified, though my sole intention was to cover as much as my face with my hand as possible.

"We shall have to stop them ourselves!" the nun declared, already stomping down the stairs. "The other sisters are at service."

I realized she wanted me to follow. As I could not really do anything else, I did. I might escape in the mayhem that would no doubt follow.

Which it did. The nun had the body build of a rhinoceros and she stampeded into the library with all the grace of the said animal. The two men were now in front of one of the bookshelves, behind a wooden railing that separated the bookshelves from the front of the room. They were pulling precious books down and throwing them on the floor.

"Thieves!" the nun hissed. "Stop what you are doing, immediately!"

The men looked at her, surprised and apparently scared at first, then began to laugh. They saw a short, stocky nun, and a slight, tall novice, who obviously was not very muscular.

"And how exactly are you going to stop us?" the bigger one of them asked and grinned. "Are you going to throw the girl at us? Wouldn't mind that, though. She looks quite pretty, we could have some fun with her."

Obviously that was not the wisest thing to say to a chaste nun with the body build of a weight lifter. With the speed of a cat the nun reached for a poker by the fireplace near the door, next to a reading desk. There was still a huge pile of books on it - probably left by Reggie. Without stopping, the nun charged the men, waving the poker over her head and bellowing at the top of her voice "Thieves, thieves!" She had powerful lungs, all right.

That got their attention. I suppose that it got the attention of everyone within miles. At least the singing down the hallway stopped abruptly.

The men backed away from the nun.

"Protect the manuscript!" the nun yelled at me.

"What...? Where...?"

The poker changed its direction from the thieves to the left of the nun in one wide swoop. I ran to the general direction, between shelves, and then I saw the glass cabinet. Inside it was only one thing – an ancient looking small book. I placed myself in front of the cabinet and then concentrated on looking at the poker ballet performed by the nun who had now advanced to the aisle between the old book cabinets. It was really quite amazing to watch. I wondered if she had been performing in a circus in her younger years.

She surely knew what she was doing. The thieves had to duck and take cover, as she swirled about like a dervish, brandishing the poker skillfully.

Running footsteps approached, and then suddenly the whole place was full of nuns. One of them was holding an oil lamp in her hand. Unfortunately she ran too close to the whirling dervish nun, and the oil lamp took the full force of the poker in her hand. It flew out of the other nun's hand, straight towards a bookcase to my right where it smashed. Burning oil erupted from the glass and metal lamp all over the books.

Dieter, one of the time walkers had said the library would burn in a few hours... I had to get out!

The old books caught fire so fast it was unbelievable. Suddenly I stood behind towering, roaring flames, with my back against the glass case, the heat of the fire hurting my skin. I turned around. I had an odd sensation in my mind, as if I was observing the whole situation through someone else's eyes.

Without thinking I raised my foot and kicked at the case proper karate style. The glass broke. I grabbed the manuscript, cutting myself in the process. Blood dripped on the floor, but thankfully I had only cut my palm, and not my wrists. I swore - what was I thinking? I should have used the rag around my hand...

My brain informed me it was not very wise to stand in the middle of a fire, debating with myself why I hadn't grabbed the manuscript in some other way. How could I escape? Where could I run to?

This time I really panicked. I looked at the bag in my hand. Somehow I had used it to come to this time... It was made here. Could I go back to my time with an object that was from my time? Even without a gate? It had to be possible - from what I had heard I understood stepping down to a time and place did not necessarily require a gate. And the Time Walkers managed to return to their time, with the skills of the Weaver. I had to try. I needed an anchor... My brain was working overtime trying to find a way out.

I did not want to use the old book as an anchor - I had no idea where it would take me.

I lifted the hem of my outfit and put my hand in my jeans pocket. Nothing. No, wait, something... I lifted up the visiting card of Kitty's Divinations. It would have to do. I closed my eyes and tried to block out the panic in my mind. That was not easy, not with the heat of the fire billowing around me, and the nuns screaming. Still, my life was at stake. I did the best I could.

I felt a tug in my hands.

"Lord have mercy! An angel!" I heard someone yell before the heat of the burning library suddenly vanished and I found myself back in the buffer zone.

43

MEETING ANGEL

It took me a while to stop the bleeding. The glass had cut me deeply on the fleshy part of the right palm, below the thumb. I pressed at the wound tightly with the cleaning rag I had used as a scarf, hoping it wouldn't get infected - or that at least I would reach the world of modern medicine soon. I had no choice but to use the rag – otherwise blood would have run into a pool at my feet. Even as it was, my nun's outfit was a mess.

I kept the old book tightly under my left arm, so that my blood would not soil it. I had no idea what it was about, but probably it was some sort of a prayer book, and obviously it was something very valuable, if it was locked into its own glass case. I had no idea what had prompted me to save it, other than the fact that I loved history and books and it had looked so ancient.

My hand throbbed with pain, but eventually the bleeding more or less stopped. I tried to tie the rag tightly around my hand but the cloth was too thick for that. I would have to try to keep it still, to prevent the wound from tearing open again.

I held the visiting card in my teeth until the medical emergency was over. Then I took it in my left hand, being careful not to drop the book under my arm, and took a closer look at the card.

It was tied to my time, or else I would not have ended up in the buffer zone, I figured. Maybe. I wasn't sure, as I did not know about the logic of the anchor-system in time traveling. But as it was all I could use, I would have to try to get back to my own time using it. I could hardly return to the library any more, as it was burning to ashes right now. It was rather strange - if the library had burned in the past, had the two men and I been there to cause it? Or would it have burned anyway? Would the nun in the upstairs corridor have gone down the stairs and seen the men even without me? Would she have reacted to them in the same manner, if I had not been with her, and the men had not made her furious with their remarks about me?

My brain chose the oddest times to try to make sense of this entire time travel thing. I tried to shift my thoughts onto practical matters, such as how the heck to get back to where I should be.

Despite holding the visiting card, I didn't see any strings leaving my right hand. Probably because of the injury, I concluded. So I would need to use my left hand. But I did not want end up in the time when the old book was written. Whenever that was. I wanted to go home, to my own time.

I decided to take off the nun's habit. After a little effort I managed it, without dropping the visiting card or the book. I wrapped the book and the embroidered bag up in the habit, avoiding the blood-stained parts, negotiated the sleeves and hem into a knot and held it away from my body. I figured I needed to physically touch an "anchor" with my hands to be connected to its place of origin. If my logic was right, I was now safe. I had to use my right hand now, though, and it hurt. I turned my right arm at an angle and supported my right elbow to my waist to be able to carry the bundle. I held the weight of the bundle with my wrist, once I had slipped my hand through the opening under the knot.

I squeezed the visiting card tightly in my left hand and concentrated, trying to empty my mind and feel what ever there was to feel. No one had had time to explain the weaving thing to me, so I had to make do with the only thing that had worked before.

After a while I felt a tug, and slowly a misty ball appeared in the palm of my left hand, and from this two strings reached out. The other one was slightly pink, and the other one... It was strange. It glowed with a sinister, golden glow, but it was black. The strings went to the same direction, though, so I just began to walk where they led me.

At first it was slow going – from what I could gather. Again the sensation of speed came from the mist pressing against my face. Then, suddenly, the black string tightened considerably. And then it began to hurt – it shot out of my palm and fingers with such a speed I felt as if I was holding on to a rope that was running through my fingers with too much speed, burning my skin. The pink string kept flowing as it had, but the black one got tighter and tighter, and it yanked me off my feet. Again I flew in the mist.

My left hand began to tingle painfully – like thousand sharp needle-pricks. I did not like this at all. I tried to put my feet down, to slow the speed, but it was as though the solid "ground" had disappeared and my feet dangled helplessly as if I was in deep water.

Then shadowy forms began to take shape in front of me. My flying slowed, and finally stopped. I felt something solid under my feet again. I stood still and listened. I heard distant talking. Two women.

I took a step closer and stopped again.

"No, she has not been here yet. And I haven't forgotten that I will call you when she arrives, just as we agreed before," the voice of an older woman said.

"Thank you! I want to see her after your consultation! Don't let her leave your shop before I arrive. You have my mobile number, " a young woman's voice chimed. A charming voice, as if silver drops were falling on water.

"You are such a good friend!" the first voice commented enthusiastically, "to help someone who is grieving connect with her departed one on the other side."

"Thank you for saying that!" the younger voice rang like beautiful bells. "I want her to be happy again, and this is probably the only way to help her get over the death of her friend."

I felt a strong urge to step out of the mist and see who the owner of this beautiful voice was, but something stopped me. Call it intuition, if you will. I felt as if I was under a spell – like I was about to do something that deep down I did not want to do.

You'll know the feeling, if you ever did anything stupid as a child as a result of someone else's influence. You trusted them, only to find out you were cheated into doing something that was not good for you. The feeling I had was the slightest whisper of a warning, barely there. I hesitated. Then I thought it would not hurt, if I waited and took stock of the surroundings for a while. My emotions tried to convince me I was wrong to wait, that I should approach that bell-like voice, but I decided to trust my intuition instead.

I inched myself closer, and just as it had been when I had approached the nun's cell, the space formed in front of me. I finally figured out I was looking at the interior of a little shop. There were books and all sorts of little pieces of bric-a-brac for sale. By the cash register was a big crystal ball. On the walls were paintings of tarot cards. The young woman was by the door, opening it, starting to leave after having concluded her business. The older woman, the store owner, probably, stood in the middle of the floor.

I sighed. Indeed I had come to the fortune teller's shop, and into my own time. What a relief!

The older woman turned around.

"What was that? I heard someone sigh... There is a spirit here somewhere!"

I looked around and did not see anything. Then the thought hit me - she had heard me. I froze.

"Are you sure?" the tingling sweet voice of the younger woman came from the doorway.

"Quite sure. It came from over there! I think I saw someone there! Come closer, dear soul! Tell us your message!"

I saw the slightly shadowy figure point directly at me. I quickly took two steps back and the shop almost disappeared from sight. But I did not want to go too far, in case I could not find it again, and stopped.

The young woman let go of the front door and started walking towards me. Her movement was so abrupt and so determined I was shocked. This was not a sweet young woman I was looking at, but something much scarier.

"Show me again!" This time the younger woman's voice was not sweet and nice, but steely and hard. The shop owner flinched, and then pointed again at my direction. I could not see her face, but her body language revealed her insecurity in front of the suddenly changed young woman.

I withdrew myself deeper into the fog. Frantically I searched my pockets to find something, anything that might take me to another location. Nothing. Only the book, and the embroidered bag. And the nun's outfit. The book would take me wherever, and the other objects back to a burning nunnery. I considered whether I could use my own clothing, but I'd probably end up in some Far-Eastern factory if I used them as an anchor.

While I searched, the misty atmosphere changed. It became electric – I felt the electricity raise the hairs on my arms, and I knew the young woman had entered the mist. How she had done it, and who she was, I had no idea. But I suspected she was either some kind of a shadow, or one of those who called themselves Immortals. Or worse still - a Nephilim. I stood dead still, hoping the fog would hide me.

Until I looked down and saw the drops of blood floating on the misty surface, slowly sinking through it. They led like the breadcrumbs of Hans and Gretel, from my feet, towards the direction of the shop.

And then she was in front of me. Her body heat enveloped me pleasantly, revealing what she was.

She was beautiful. Her long blonde shiny hair reached her waist. She was wearing tight jeans and a very expensive looking designer leather jacket. Her makeup was immaculate. Her eyes were beautiful as well; they drew you in and held you captive. The look in the eyes was friendly, and slightly concerned. And they were golden yellow.

"Dana, how glad I am that I finally found you!" she smiled and again I felt the enchantment of her silver voice wrap around my mind.

"Who are you?" I fought the voice. "How do you know my name?"

"You really do not know?" she smiled, arching one of her perfect eyebrows, amused.

"I do not know you," I said. Somehow I felt it would be very dangerous to reveal anything about me to her.

Then I felt her inside my mind, literally. It was as if soft fingers were caressing, soothing, playing with my mind. I could sense the direction they came from, and it was coming from her. If I looked closely, I felt I caught a glimpse of dark tentacles floating through the air, reaching out to touch me...

"Come with me, Dana," she purred. "We'll go home, to the place where you belong."

Belong? How could I belong anywhere with this beautiful, dangerous creature? She was certainly not talking about my own home. I felt her mental fingers rummage through my mind and then they touched a place that caused a reaction. The probing stopped. The... tentacles, or whatever they were, could not go past that point. I concentrated on that spot and realised I was not quite as soft as she – and I – had taken me for. I felt anger resisting her touch there, and great strength.

"I'm going nowhere with you," I surprised myself by saying it calmly, from this newly found center of my mind. I even found the strength to become flippant. "Didn't your parents ever warn you about going off with strangers, however charming they were?"

She twitched at my resistance. I felt her try again; her persuasion flowed into my mind and tried to convince me I should trust her. Her only problem was that I had always hated being told what I should do against my will. I felt my resolution get even stronger.

"No. I repeat, I'm going nowhere with you!"

"You - you dare to resist me?" she asked in an unbelieving tone.

"I have no good reason to follow you anywhere, whatever you think you are!" my voice trembled ever so slightly.

"Oh but we are alike," she purred, now clearly amused. "We are so alike, Dana!"

I did not understand what she meant.

"Yes, we are both here in the buffer zone, that much is correct. But I don't like you, and I will not follow you anywhere. Goodbye!"

I took a step away from her, only to find she was already standing behind me. I turned to face her again. The mist was swirling like a storm around me now, proving me she had moved physically and not just beamed there star-trek-style.

"If you will not come voluntarily, I'll bring you in by other means. By any means at my command."

At that she changed. Her voice had taken on a unnerving and powerful tone. She was just as beautiful as before, but her expression turned into something icy. Her eyes were not glowing with warmth anymore. Instead they were like two piercing yellow flames. Her mouth opened into a humorless smile, and I stared at her sharp teeth. She licked her upper lip with her pretty, pink tongue. And then she opened her wings.

They were beautiful – the darkest shade of grey, with golden light pulsing in them. Like thunderclouds with lightning flashing in their midst.

She was one of the Nephilim. And I did not have to guess twice whether she was the good or the bad kind.

"Will you come voluntarily, or do I have to force you?" she asked, with a steely echo to her voice.

"And how would you do that?" I swear, I don't know where the courage to challenge her came from, but it did. I felt the strong spot in my mind turn even harder.

"Well, I could bite you, of course. Surely you already know about vampires? And vampire makers? That would be us." Her tone was almost smug now. "We enjoy the energy blood gives us. Also - we need servants. Win-win situation. For us, that is." She began to smile.

Somehow the perfectly straight, white rows of her teeth behind her carefully painted bright red lips seemed to grow longer, though I did not see any fangs. It was as though the teeth were inside her palate, and she could lengthen them at will by some weird semi-mechanical process. The corners of her mouth seemed to be wider apart than a moment before. It was like watching the smile of a beautiful women turning into a grin of a shark. Repulsive, yet I couldn't drag my eyes from it. Now I understood better what I had been told about the vampire teeth earlier. I was in no doubt that she meant what she said.

"I would only bite you enough for my venom to paralyze you for a while. Of course that would have unpleasant after effects later..." she laughed quietly to herself as if at some private joke.

I had a pretty good idea what that after effect would be. I swallowed.

"You'll do no such thing," I tried to sound as convincing as I could, "because you are not to harm me."

I was playing with fire here. Her eyes narrowed into slits that made me think of a big cat.

"And how do you know that?" she asked, and for a second I thought I caught a note of insecurity there.

I had shot in the dark and hit the mark. Someone obviously had told her to not harm me.

I tried to look relaxed. With limited success, probably, but at least I did not show fear - a fact I could not understand. I was facing a living nightmare of mine, however beautiful, and instead of crumbling into bits, I challenged it. Or something in me did, as if I had a second, hidden trait of personality I had never met before.

"I know all about you," I lied, "I know why you want me. And I know you need me unharmed."

She pondered my words for a while. The lips closed over the fearsome teeth. Then a cold smile spread to her lips. It did not reach the narrowed eyes.

"Then you will also know, what we're going to do to you, if you decline our demands."

"If I choose not to follow someone, no-one can make me do it," I marveled at my calm voice. It was as though someone else was talking through me.

"Oh, but you will do as you are told. I am stronger than you. You have no idea how strong I really am... no one denied me the use of power. A few bruises won't make you any the worse for our purposes," she hissed, taking a step in my direction. Her wings were huge now, and they bent towards me like thunderclouds. Her yellow eyes were piercing, and suddenly I was quite certain she would bite me, just because I had stood my ground. She was clearly used to being obeyed. The look in her eyes was not quite sane.

I knew she would jump at me in a few seconds. I could not think any further than that. Finally I knew I could buy no more time and began to prepare for the inevitable.

She moved closer, her wings bending forward in an attempt to wrap around me.

There was a swooshing sound from behind, and she stopped. Her eyes were all round now, and surprised. Something blue and beautiful extended from behind me and enveloped me before her dark wings had a chance to touch me.

"She is mine," a familiar voice said and I could have cried with relief.

Daniel had found me.

"She is not yours to keep, Daniel," the black-winged Nephilim girl's eyes were hard.

So they knew each other.

"We made her. She is ours. You might not want to know her more intimately than you already do. That would - be against what has been agreed," the girl hissed.

"She is not yours either, Angel," Daniel's hand pulled me even tighter against him, "She is her own being, free to choose her own life. No one is to force her into anything she doesn't want to do. She has not agreed to anything."

"She'll have to choose what she was made for!" The Nephilim called Angel was furious now. "Eventually she will have to choose."

"Choose, yes," Daniel's voice was unbelievably calm, "but not now. And not forced in any way. This is why you're leaving, Angel. Now. I will attack you if you don't. That is a promise."

I had not noticed his wings were that huge. When he pressed me against him with his arm, the blue wings bent forward in an arch above and beyond us – their tips almost touching the black wings of Angel. Daniel had lifted the wings up in stages somehow, so they covered my upper body in two layers. I felt a deep rumble in my body and realised it came from the wings. What enormous energy there had to be in them...

Angel hissed again. Then her hiss turned into a growl that morphed into the most spine-chilling scream imaginable. She crouched into a catlike position so quickly the motion was blurred - she was now at knee-level, mouth open wider than was possible for a human, long teeth exposed. Suddenly she threw herself flat on her stomach. Instinctively I turned my head away. I could feel her spit on my cheek. Like a flash Daniel's hand was on my skin, wiping it off with his sleeve. Angel was instantly a swirling tornado and then was gone.

"Did any of that get into your eyes or mouth?" he asked.

"No, I don't think so..." my voice had suddenly lost all its strength. "Why?"

"Their spit is venomous. It has consequences. Are you sure?"

"Yes. I got it on my lower right cheek, and neck, that's all. I just wonder what the shopkeeper thinks of that shriek. She is bound to have heard it..." I said in a conversational tone and turned to face Daniel.

And then I collapsed into a sobbing wreck against his chest.

44

GODDESS

The sea had been dark and he had felt its breath like a gigantic living consciousness under the merchant ship when they crossed the expanse of water to Astacus, on the western shore of Greece, at the southern edge of the Arcanian mountains. There he left the ship, explaining that one of his father's friends lived there and set off on his long journey to the east.

He still had only his human powers at the time, and so he bought a donkey to carry his belongings. He joined other travellers, to be safe from robbers. He had never walked such a long distance, but he was young and had all his strength. And so, every step took him closer until days later they arrived in Delphi. Ambrogio was very proud of his long journey, and was already creating stories in his mind about what he would tell his siblings when he returned home.

Ambrogio had stared at the temple built high on the folds of the mountain, hidden from the plains below, with his mouth open in amazement. All the way up to the temple he had not been able to see it, and then the road went around a crag of rock, and the temple suddenly appeared in front of him as if by magic.

He walked along the sacred road towards the temple. It rose towards the main building and was flanked by hundreds of statues.

Many of these were given to the temple in gratitude for winning wars, especially after the recent defeat of the Persians. He stared at the three bronze serpent columns with their serpent heads on top of the massive golden tripod and began to understand that he had not seen the world at all.

Six huge columns stood at the facade of the temple, and fifteen at the sides. Never had he seen anything so imposing. Later he heard the Alcmeonid family had paid for the building of the temple, after the original one had been destroyed by fire during the first Holy War, a war that was fought for the possession of the Temple.

The temple was made of Parian marble. On the western end of it were carved scenes of gods fighting giants, and on the eastern side a scene of Apollo driving a horse-drawn chariot. Several other deities were also worshipped at Delphi.

Other magnificently decorated buildings were dotted all over the site as well. There were at least twenty treasuries built there, all containing unbelievable riches, filled with treasures that people and cities had brought or sent as votive offerings.

The temple was run by an independent council, the members of which came from different city states. The Pythia worked here, as did the profetari - the priests who would interpret Pythia's mysterious words. Their job was to guide the consultant so they would ask their questions in the right way. You could ask two kinds of questions: should you do one or the other of various options, or a more general question of what you should do to achieve something. And then there were the possiu, the five holy men.

Priests and priestesses were fully aware of their status, and if Ambrogio had thought he would just walk in and ask for an audience with the Pythia, he now understood he had been a fool. Pythia was not to be approached by outsiders, and kept to herself, protected by the hierarchy of priests and priestesses and the complexity of the ritual.

He could see rich men and women giving expensive gifts to the priests to be allowed to approach the Pythia on the seventh day of the nine months during which Paean - Apollo - was present in the temple, and which were the only days that she foretold the future. Ambrogio had no riches. His father was a mere pauper compared to these people.

He soon learned that to have any hope of approaching the Pythia, you needed a citizen of the local town of Delphi to be your sponsor. You could not approach the Pythia on your own. He also heard that trying to bribe the priests was a capital offence, for which the punishment was execution or exile.

He paid for lodgings nearby and spent his days at the temple, trying to get access to the priests. They did not consider him worthy enough to even talk with. He tried to find a Delphi citizen who might try to arrange an audience with Pythia, but to no avail. He was just not rich enough.

What he did have, though, was his singing voice. Strong and clear, yet soft, gentle and persuasive. And so, when he heard the Pythian games were to be held this year, he knew he had found a way to even try to reach the Pythia. The games had a musical event - singers should sing a hymn to Apollo, the god of the temple. They should also be able to play the kithara while they sang, a musical instrument that resembled a lyre.

The lyre was something Ambrogio had learned to play at home. Surely the kithara was not much different?

He approached the priests yet again, and announced that he was to partake in the games. Now he would need to get a kithara.

He could not get one anywhere. The musicians who came to the games all had their own kithara, and no one was willing to sell him one. Even if they had, the price would have been too much for him.

Then, surprisingly, help came, when he was already certain that his plan to reach Pythia would never work. Ambrogio had descended from the mountainside of the temple to the valley below, and was sitting, desolate, under the shade of a tree near the Kassotis spring, where pilgrims and temple personnel bathed. He knew that if this did not work, he would have to travel back home. Soon he could no longer afford to pay for his lodgings and food. He would have to sell his donkey, if a miracle did not happen.

He heard steps and looked up.

A beautiful woman approached. Taller than any woman he had ever seen, and much more beautiful. Her hair was golden and fell below her waist, her eyes were golden as well, her skin was like the moonlight, and she carried something silvery in her hands. It had to be her weapon, some kind of a bow.

Ambrogio understood she must be a goddess or a naiad of the river, and got to his feet quickly, only to bow back down to the ground in front of her.

She did not ask him to get up, so he knew he had been right. She was a goddess.

"Do you want something?" the woman asked with her voice that rang like silver bells.

"My goddess... I want to sing a hymn to Apollo at the games, but I have no kithara. Could you help me? I shall be your servant forever more," he blurted out quickly, fearing she might disappear.

She laughed.

"Forever more? Are you sure that you wish for such a thing? Beware what you promise to my kind. Eternity is a long time..."

Ambrogio dared one look at her from under his brows, only to quickly lower his gaze again. The goddess was looking at him apprais- ingly. He was a handsome young man, after all.

"Forever more, goddess..." he bowed his head, proud that he would look pleasing to a goddess, but afraid at the same time. The river naiads, the Potameides, were said to be aggressive towards young men.

"Very well. If that is what you choose," she said in a clearly amused voice. "Come here tomorrow and you shall have your kithara."

He did as advised, and the goddess appeared again. She carried a kithara in her hands, as promised.

"Here, do you know how to play it?" she asked, and gave the instrument to him.

"No, but I will learn. I need to win the games."

"Why?"

"So I can ask to see the Pythia. I cannot afford to pay to see her, but if I win the contest, I might have a chance," he said.

"Why do you need to see her?" she asked, still amused. "To learn about your future?"

"Yes, goddess. I know there is more awaiting me in life than being a mere merchant like my father," he said.

"Being a merchant is a good thing in this world," she said. "There are many who have nothing. And merchants can have anything, because they have the means to trade for whatever they want. So do not look down upon your father. You are one of the privileged ones of this world."

"No, goddess. I am sorry, I was stupid to judge my father." Ambrogio understood the error of his ways.

"Well, what can you expect from mere mortals," she shrugged. "Also knowing your future may not always be a good thing. What if she tells you when you shall die? Or gives you an ambiguous oracle that you spend the rest of your life trying to understand? Her oracles are mostly like that. It can drive a man to madness."

Ambrogio had thought about this before.

"If she tells me how and when I shall die, then I shall try to live and experience as much as I can before it is my time."

She laughed.

"And what if she tells you that you'll never die? Will you not grow weary of life at the very thought?"

Ambrogio did not understand the question, but did not dare to ask what she meant for fear of appearing even more stupid. The naiads did live for thousands of years, so she might not have been posing a real question to him. Surely she knew he was a mortal man with only a few decades in front of him at best?

"Well, you learn to play the kithara. And if you win the games, and if you meet Pythia, I wish you luck. I shall return to your promise later."

She stood so close to him that her intoxicating, sweet scent filled his nostrils. Expensive perfumes, the smell of ripe fruit. He tried not to stare at her breasts, barely covered by the thin dress, with poor success. This seemed to amuse her even more. She raised a finger and gently traced his jaw with it. He felt the burning heat of the finger, and looked into her golden eyes. It was as though they sucked him into her mind, and he could not wish for anything else than for her to never turn her eyes away from him.

She looked amused, certain of her power over him, bent and kissed him gently on the lips. When she straightened herself again, he noticed his lips were bleeding as though they had been cut. He tried his lips with his finger and the pain told him that indeed there were two sharp cuts on his lips. An odd tingling made his lips numb.

A drop of his blood was on her lower lip and she licked it slowly with her tongue it as though it was a delicacy.

"Remember, forever more..." she said with a smile that made him shiver.

She turned and left. Holding the kithara, he watched her walk away, his lower lip tingling and numb, and felt an odd sensation that he had agreed to something he could not begin to understand.

45

SONG OF THE RIVER

Mut-Bity and I sailed with the beehives to Mi-Wer. I was surprised at this, because I knew the bees should have been needed further south. But after meeting the odd pale man, Mut-Bity had been very quiet for a long time, and had not said much after telling the captain of the ship where we were headed.

I sat at the prow after the sun had grown tired and plunged down to its underground journey. The stars were rolling quietly from the east and across the sky towards the west. The river took us gently towards the imperishable stars of the north - the stars that never set but stayed above the horizon until the sun was reborn and bleached the sky to blue again.

The crew had already grown accustomed to us, and liked me too, despite my odd looks. Even now, wrapped in the silence of the night, I was eating a honey cake made by the captain's wife in a little clay oven on the deck. When I finished eating and the crunching noise did not disturb my hearing anymore, I concentrated in listening to the singing of the night.

I had tried to explain to Mut-Bity what the song sounded like, and she clearly believed I could hear it, even if she herself could not.

It was like soft waves up in the sky. It caressed the ground below, stroked the shining skin of the river, and made each living thing hum with its own unique note. Like playing a lute, but in such a way that each living thing gave its own, never-ending, never wavering sound. I could only hear it when my mind was completely peaceful, and when the world did not speak with loud noises. And when I did hear the song of the night sky, I could tell where and how far someone was, and to some extent even what they were doing.

Emotions had an effect on how high and strong the note was. When someone was asleep, the song coming from them was just a quiet hum - unless they had a very vivid dream. When a person was awake and felt something very strongly, the song had a louder, clearer voice. I found it very funny to listen how their melodies intertwined, when the captain and his wife retired to rest in the cabin of the boat. Sometimes they could not keep their silence, and I could hear both their muted moans and the song of the world turn up a notch, when their two separate songs reached a peak at the same time. During this last week I had also heard a new, very slight melody, which seemed to grow from the inner music of the captain's wife. It came from her mid waist, still nothing more than a tiny whisper. So I was aware many weeks before the mother-to-be that she was expecting their first child. Mut-Bity had earned us a little extra for many months now, when she had learned I had this skill. Women of the villages loved to gather together to talk, and for a small fee I would tell them if they were with child or not.

I heard Mut-Bity's note humming as she approached me. After a while she sat next to me.

"We have to leave the River," she said quietly to me.

"Why?" I did not need to disagree with Mut-Bity, I knew she was very wise. Still, I was curious.

Mut-Bity gathered her thoughts for a while. I followed her tune as it turned inwards, as it always did when she meditated on matters. This time her tune had a sharp echo. When people were afraid, their tune turned shrill and sharp. And now, perhaps for the first time, I heard Mut-Bity's fear.

"I will not lie to you, even when you are so young," Mut-Bity finally

said quietly. So quietly that no one could possibly hear what she said but me.

I waited. Mut-Bity did not need to explain to me that she would not lie. Of course she would not. Not to me at least. She searched for words, and I waited, concentrating on listening to the songs of underwater beings. They were somehow very quick, and yet very slow - the song reacted to their movements much faster than to the movements of people. There were quick trills, and also slow, meditative echoes from animals living at the bottom.

"You are different, but not just in your looks," Mut-Bity finally said, "you love the stories that people tell about ancient days, as do I. You are becoming someone like one of the people in those tales. You will have very rare gifts, but how they will show themselves, we do not know yet. The song of the world you hear is one of those gifts. You have inherited it from your mother."

"And my sister?"

"She doesn't seem to be going to the same place that you are going. She may never develop similar skills, because you were the first-born. But we may never know for certain. These things are a mystery. In any case, it is important that you know that these skills may be used for both good and evil. Since the dawn of time, the likes of you have existed and have always lived among ordinary people, often undetected, because they - you - are shaped like humans. They have not always managed to hide their gifts, and so many wonderful stories were born."

Mut-Bity was quiet for a long time and I calmed my mind and listened to the stars of the north. They seemed to pull my heart towards them, as if I had belonged there once and they were drawing me back. They felt fresh and invigorating in my mind. I was certain that the cooling winds of the north came directly from them.

"And that man is just like me, only evil,""I said.

"Exactly. And the worst part is, that now that he has come close to you once, he can follow your scent for a very long time - it leads him to you."

"Why would he like to follow me? Because we are alike?"

"Yes... but he would not let you stay the way you are. He would like to make you similar to himself. To bind you to him in vile ways, which you could not avoid, if he once gets hold of you."

"Why?"

"To control the powers you are developing. And he won't give up, now that he has found you and smelled you. We need to cut the trail."

"How?"

"It is harder for him to follow you on water, but he can travel the shores of the River, and even follow the boat, if the wind comes from the right direction. And in this case it does. He is very, very fast. Still - a bee-sting is a very bad thing for him, and it will take time for him to heal. But as he knows we are carrying beehives, he will come looking for you in the places where bees are currently working. That is why we are now traveling directly to Mi-Wer and leaving as soon as we can, in a direction he won't immediately guess. Somewhere where you cannot take bees. And we have to stay away for a long time."

I swallowed. Mother and sister were in Mi-Wer, at the house of the king's women. Would I have to say goodbye to them? I felt a choking feeling in my throat and the song of the night vanished. I felt very small and very lonely.

"We have to leave so that your mother and sister remain safe. Your mother is like you, but she is so strong that she can protect herself and keep your sister safe, once she has been warned. It is important, though, that we don't lead the pale man to them and cause them danger. This is why we cannot leave your scent near them for a long time."

I could not answer her, because I felt like crying. So I stayed quiet and just watched the cold stars warped by my tears, with my knees against my chest. The sky had turned mute.

46

THE PLACE OF THE NETERU

Merit had clearly discovered information about some mystery that Elijah knew about as well.

"I am traveling in search of answers," Merit's journal told him. *"There are many ancient writings preserved here that we have no idea about in our time. They have vanished in centuries in between, but they still exist here. I did learn to read some hieroglyphs at home, but those were mostly offering formulas in tombs. I have taken on the task of learning to read this writing properly. Thankfully I am at a position where I can do so. I have become one of the children of the kap, it seems, despite the fact I am an adult."*

"The kap?" Mr. Donnelly scratched his ear.

Frantic leafing of the Egyptology books brought Mr. Donnelly the answer.

"Ah, the royal nursery... Children of the royal palace learned reading and writing and other skills in the kap... So she is a member of the court! Learning hieroglyphs and reading and writing. Well done, Merit, well done..."

Pleased with Merit's progress in ancient life Mr.Donnelly kept on translating the last pages.

"And I finally found my clue to the location of the neteru. It was

written on a piece of papyrus in the House of Life of Inbu-Hedj, or Memphis. I do not dare write the clue down as it may get into the wrong hands. I know no one can read this yet, because the language does not even exist - what a curious feeling that gives me! But if this book ends up in the wrong hands in the future... And I admit I tore that part of the papyrus out and took it with me."

Mr. Donnelly sat absolutely still, numb with shock. The place of Neteru... Could it be...

With shaking hands he searched his books which were now literally towering around him on the floor. He found a book about reading the hieroglyphs.

Neteru. Gods. The abode of the gods. And now he understood he had mistranslated earlier. *"Those who kept an eye on us..."* The Masters used another term completely.

This could not be a coincidence. Merit had found the clue he was seeking for the Masters. It had to be.

His lips felt numb as he mumbled the last sentences.

"And I have found there are Immortals here as well. I do not know how long I can keep myself hidden from them. I think my looks will raise their suspicions, if they haven't done so already. I have to retreat to Mi-Wer and keep in hiding there, out of sight, protected by the guards of the royal harem, and trust that there are enough light-colored ladies there so that I blend in. Otherwise I shall draw doom over those I love as well. But rest assured, Elijah, I will do everything I can to find you again. If I cannot enter the mists of the buffer zone, then perhaps others near me can and they can lead me through the mists of time back to you... However, to find out if that is the case, I might need to wait for many years yet. They are still so..."

A hole in the paper again.

"Who are? What are they?" Mr.Donnelly wailed.

Mr. Donnelly closed his Moleskine and the sketchbook. He would have to hide them from the Masters. But where could he hide them? How could he keep them from the eyes of the Masters? If only there was a way for him to leave the City of Immortals...

47

TRUTH WILL OUT

My memories of returning to the Time Walker Center are fragmentary. I only remember moving through the mist, then rising higher until a real landscape formed around us. What it was, I have no recollection. I recall Daniel's strong arms carrying me, and I was barely conscious. I was in a state of mental collapse because of the shock. His body heat felt calming and relaxing and I must have finally fallen asleep - or fainted.

When I woke up, I was in some sort of hospital room. My hand was bandaged and there was a strange taste in my mouth. And I had a fever. I could feel it.

My eyelids weighed a ton and I could barely manage to keep them open for a few seconds. I was lying on my side, with my bandaged hand in front of my face. There was someone sitting beyond it. My vision was blurry, but I felt the warmth emanating from the figure.

"Daniel..." I thought to myself before falling asleep again. I think I felt someone gently touch my cheek.

I woke up to whispering voices. People often think they cannot be heard, when they whisper, when in fact all the s's hiss so loudly you are bound to pay attention. Groggily I remembered reading in one of the Narnia books when I was a child that if you don't want to be overheard when you're whispering to someone, replace every letter "s" with an "h". That makes the whispering difficult to hear from a distance, according to this character in the book.

These two were certainly hissing like two snakes...

"We shall have to tell her now."

"I wish we didn't have to... not just yet."

"Well you can hardly explain away what Angel told her. It's better she knows in advance. Besides – it may already have started!"

Lilith and Grandma, I recognized their voices.

"She is awake," Daniel's voice announced.

I opened my eyes with difficulty, just in time to see him leaving the room. Still avoiding me, then. The worried faces of the two women blocked my view.

"Dana, are you awake?" Grandma asked, looking into my eyes to see if I was present.

"No, I'm only pretending," I mumbled, "and would someone please tell me who dumped cat litter in my mouth?"

The women laughed in a relieved way and Lilith gave me a glass of water. I found swallowing hard whilst lying down, so I sat up to empty the glass. For a while the world spun around me, but eventually my surroundings settled into place.

"And now I want explanations." I faced the ladies once the surroundings were solid again.

"What do you remember?" Grandma asked.

"Everything until Angel left. What did she mean, when she said they had made me?"

The glance between Grandma and Lilith spoke volumes. I suppose they had hoped I had somehow missed that part.

"First of all we want you to know we only suspected. We were not sure if you would be... what you probably are. We had strong indications because of your bloodline, yes, but these things are never certain," Lilith said cryptically. "You surprised us all by being such a strong Weaver. Truly, we had never seen a human Weaver make an opening to the buffer zone by herself by simply... well, weaving. All the others needed an opening made for them before they could enter the buffer zone to travel in time. But you proved to be different from the human Weavers."

"Wait. What do you mean by human Weavers? Am I not human, then?"

Lilith opened her mouth, but Grandma beat her to it.

"It's probably best if I explain it from the very beginning. Be patient, Dana, and you will have all the answers you're looking for."

The door opened and to my surprise Daniel walked back in with a tray.

"You've not eaten in a while, so you'd better get this soup into you before listening to anything." He placed the tray on my lap.

"Thank you..." I was almost embarrassed about thinking he was still avoiding me. I took the spoon and ladled the warm soup in. It tasted wonderful.

"You are explaining it all to her now?" Daniel asked.

"Yes, we have to," Lilith sighed.

"About time," he commented and dropped back into the chair in which he had been sitting when I woke up. He did not look in my direction, but stared into the distance like a statue.

"This will shock you, I am afraid," Grandma said, "and as that is bound to happen, I won't sugar-coat this for you. The first thing is – you are adopted."

I gasped. Daniel turned his head and looked at me. Really looked at me, deep into my eyes. I knew he had known.

"You were born during the Blitz, in London, England. The year of your birth was 1940."

"What?" The spoon fell onto the half empty plate and splattered soup onto the bed.

Grandma nodded.

"You were born as the illegitimate child of a young servant girl and a soldier. You were chased by the shadows from the start because of your genealogy."

I did not say anything. I could not. My mind was empty.

"I'm going to show you a photograph. It is the only photograph of this person."

Lilith held out a print of an old photo. I took it into my hands. A tall, dark-haired man was standing outside what looked like a medieval palace. His clothing was old fashioned – from the beginning of the twentieth century.

"This is Cain. He is the leader of the dark Nephilim. And he is your grandfather."

Everyone sat still, observing me with keen interest, while I tried to digest what I had just heard. I felt like someone had just knocked me down and forced the breath out of me. My scalp was tingling with shock and I leaned backwards, against the pillows, as all my strength left me.

"You are saying... What are you saying? Who is this Cain? What is this Cain?"

Grandma sighed.

"Like I said. The leader of the dark Nephilim."

"So you mean I am... I am... a..."

The world began to spin.

"Stop it, you two," Daniel's voice was harsh, "you are not handling this very well. Leave us."

Much to my surprise Lilith and Grandma did not object. They rose from their chairs and walked out of the room. Daniel walked over to the bed. He sat down on it and took my hands in his.

"Yes. You are Nephilim. You are the granddaughter of the leader of the dark Nephilim. And you are the result of a long... I am sorry to use this term, but there is really no other way to put it: you are the result of a long breeding program."

I could only stare into his bright blue eyes. The golden spots were still there.

"But... I cannot be! There's nothing out of the ordinary about me!"

"Oh, but there is. It may take a Nephilim at this stage of your development to recognise it, even if it is not yet physically visible. I knew the second you touched my wings. They resonate in a special way to the touch of another Nephilim."

"Is that why you have been acting so strangely?" I surprised myself by being curious about this.

Daniel looked out of ease.

"Well, yes... And it was so clear you had no idea of who you are. I felt sorry for you – you were about to face a very rough ride, accepting the truth about yourself."

I had a strong feeling he was not quite honest with me, but I wanted to learn more about my genealogy, to ease the turmoil of my mind. So I did not express my doubts.

"Was Grandma serious when she said that I was born during the Second World War?"

"You were. Your father was the eldest son of Cain – he, too, the result of a long breeding program. A wife had been chosen for him for that end, but he escaped his family and ended up in London. Quite by chance he happened to meet another Nephilim - a girl who had no idea what she was. She had been in trouble already because of her Nephilim powers which manifested early as a child. Extremely rare. Usually a Nephilim grows into their power around the twentieth birthday, at the earliest around eighteen years of age."

"What powers? Breeding program to what ends? What...?"

"It is best if you listen to me first. Afterwards, you can ask all the questions you want. OK?"

"OK..."

"Your mother, it seems, was the last in line of one of the purest Nephilim lines, if I can put it like that. The dark ones have hunted their kind... my kind... our kind... for thousands of years, trying to wipe them off the face of the earth."

"Why?"

"Because we do not share their ambitions of ruling the earth and having the people as slaves, basically. People have no idea of the battles we have fought to protect them from this fate."

"Oh..."

"Your grandparents from your biological mother's side hid her, when she was born, by giving her up for adoption. However, they followed her life close by, ready to step in when she matured, to explain to her what she was. She moved to London, and her real mother followed. She was close by when the young ones met. They fell in love. The girl got pregnant, and that is when the dark ones found him."

"My... father?"

"Yes. The son of the mighty Cain."

His voice sounded bitter. No wonder, if this Cain was responsible for killing Daniel's kind.

"They found him and took him captive. No one has heard of him since. They probably killed him because he disobeyed Cain – there is no bigger offence amongst them than that. The good part was that the dark Nephilim did not realize at first that your mother was pregnant and that she was Nephilim too.

"She was about your age when she got pregnant and did not show her true heritage at that point. If Cain's family had known, they would have kidnapped her, or at least tried to steal the baby – you – immediately after your birth so that your mother would not have had a chance to nurse you. That would have been the easiest way to get you, but it would have had consequences later, should you have tried to get children of your own...

"Mother's milk is essential for the development of the Nephilim baby into a full-grown Nephilim. If the mother is human, the Nephilim child cannot develop to his or her full potential. And most often the baby has the tendency to be what the mother is, in the case of a mixed breeding between bad and good Nephilim. This is something the dark ones have used to their advantage through centuries to strengthen their kind... They seem to have problems conceiving among themselves - getting pregnant can take years, if they are successful at all. If they had managed to steal you right at birth, they would have given you for breast-feeding to one of their own kind who had managed to give birth, to increase the probability of you willingly turning into one of them. And of course, they would have had other means of making you "convert" as they put it, if you did not ask of your own accord to be... turned to their kind."

"You mean some Nephilim actually choose to become.... bad?"

"Yes. There is great power to be had and near immortality."

Daniel rose to his feet and walked to the window.

"So I am a mixture of the dark and good Nephilim?"

"Yes, but there have been several such ones in the course of history. You are not unique in that respect. And you should not feel the temptation to turn to their ways so strongly; thanks to the fact your mother had a chance to nurse you. Also we suspect your father was not committed to their ways when he met your mother." Daniel did not turn to look at me.

"When Cain learned his son had fathered a child, he sent all the shadows he could spare in search of your mother. It was not easy – she hid her power the best she could, and did not use it. Also she stayed indoors most of the time, looking after an old, blind woman. But sometimes she had to venture out, and that is when one of the shadows caught up with her, smelling that she was a Nephilim. There is the cinnamon-like undertone in the smell of the good Nephilim. What's more - because of giving birth to you, your father's scent was all around her too, and so they knew they had found the mother of Cain's grandchild. The shadow followed her home, where she killed it, just as it was about to steal you. That was the first time she spread her wings fully out of her own free will, and took control of her power."

"How do you know this?"

"We observed her from the buffer zone. We found her around the same time as the shadow did, and we were planning on coming to her rescue once she was alone and no one could see us."

"What happened then?"

"Before we had the chance to save you, your mother took you out, and an air raid destroyed the house where you were living. So you could say it was a lucky thing the shadow tried to steal you and scared your mother out of the house with you – you would have been killed otherwise. But Cain knew now who she was, and came to claim you as his heir."

"His heir?"

"Yes. None of his other physical children have managed to bear children of their own. It seems there is something fundamentally flawed in his genes, and he has been working for centuries to find a way to overcome this, and to develop the perfect offspring. You are the last of his carefully bred line, just as you are the last of your mother's line."

"Bred to do what?"

Now Daniel turned to me. He looked very tired.

"To find the Book of Watchers – to claim all its power, so they can learn all the ancient secrets that they lost, when the original Nephilim race had to flee. All Nephilim were being hunted down and killed after the downfall of the Watchers."

"How can you breed anyone to find a book?"

"The word is misleading," Daniel said, "it may not be a book as such. We don't know exactly what it is, but the dark ones seem to think it would be a powerful weapon in their hands. As to your breeding - you have already witnessed the effects of it. Somehow they have managed to develop the perfect Weaver – you don't need gates to enter the buffer zone. Still, even in that respect, you are not the only one. I can do it too, should it be necessary. Nephilim of pure blood can.

"But then - you went directly to the time of the embroidered bag. You seem to move effortlessly through time which other Nephilim cannot do. And you move very fast. That is not a given – other Weavers may get lost or land in a wrong place and time, no matter how carefully they weave. And they never make it the first time. Also the farther back in time you go, the greater the chance that the Weaver will lose her way. Your hands, on the other hand, connected immediately."

"Why is this weaving so important to them, then?" I wanted to know.

"It could be that they have in their possession something - an object, or knowledge - that would lead a Weaver of your kind directly to the place of the Book of Watchers. That is why they need to have you before you turn into a full Nephilim."

"Why don't I go get it then? Grab the book and then return here instead of them?"

"They would not let you. They would turn you into one of their kind, to make sure you would not jump ship."

"Turn me... how?" the memory of Angel's teeth must have shown on my expression, because Daniel was by my bed instantly. He touched my hand reassuringly.

"It only takes a small dose of their venom. They can turn good Nephilim into their own kind easily, they simply add the lacking ingredient to their blood, and their bodies start producing the venom in a matter of weeks. It seems to be inherent in all Nephilim - this principle that is ready to be turned dark - which has made us fear that the Watchers were not of the good kind.

"After the body starts producing the venom, it changes the physique of the infected Nephilim, and they become different, or dark as we call them. Angel was just about to do that to you, when I found you. And she tried to do that by spitting the venom, when she could not get physically to you through my wings. I was careless and my wings were too high up, when I tried to protect you. Luckily you turned your head. If it had reached your eyes or mouth, you could have been lost to us."

"Can it be reversed? The effects of the venom."

"No. There are many of our kind now in their midst, turned into monsters after being infected by them. It doesn't even take a bite – they may put venom in your drink, and that does it, if you have the tiniest cut in your mouth or anywhere in your digestive system."

I felt I had no hope anymore. I could never eat or drink anything safely again, nor walk in crowds.

"What does it feel like... Turning into a Nephilim?"

"You develop a high fever, but it doesn't make you sick, only stronger. Then all your muscles begin to ache, and you feel like someone was carving your spine out with a knife."

"Nice..." I grimaced.

"That is the worst part. After that you grow in height. And then, one day soon after that, you shall have your wings. It is as if the body needs to grow in length to make space for them. You feel them inside you, and you know how to open them, intuitively."

I thought about this. I had a fever already. I remembered the look Lilith and Grandma had exchanged.

"Has it already started?" I had to ask.

"Let me see..." Daniel spread his wings slowly and touched me with their tips, gently like a butterfly.

A shock of electricity zapped me. It felt as though my heart would bounce out of my chest. Chills ran up and down my spine. I felt something happen to my eyes, and they locked with Daniel's. We looked at each other for a long while, not moving, not talking. Not breathing. I felt myself melt into his energies, which were warm, strong, frightening, wonderful, and suddenly I noticed I was crying again.

My body began to hum as if a current of electricity went through it. I could feel it in my teeth, feel the buzz in my temples.

And my heart... I felt a warmth I had never experienced before. I felt strong and weak at the same time, utterly defenseless and burning, when something in me anchored itself into him. I felt it like a physical jolt, and he responded, drawing in a deep breath. I saw his eyes turn dark with emotion, and he did not turn away from me.

"Yes, it has begun..." Daniel finally whispered, and I felt his words resonate deep inside me.

He bent and kissed my cheek so lightly I thought I imagined the whole thing. I felt his lashes touch my left temple. Then he took another deep breath, hid his wings slowly, and walked out of the room, taking my heart with him.

48

MY PAST

It took all the self-control I could muster to be able to face Grandma again, who walked in just after Daniel left. I had no doubt she had been listening outside the door.

I tried to remember if anything Daniel and I had said would reveal what had happened between us, when we had forgotten ourselves in each other's eyes. But I could not remember either one saying anything.

"We have been in contact with the pure Nephilim ever since this Centre was established, though never directly from here. We have kept its location a secret from them," Grandma explained. "They tend to stay among themselves, but in the last hundred years or so, the dark ones have been waging a real war against them. Before this there had been animosity, and some skirmishes, some killings too, but mostly that happened in the distant past. The two groups had stayed separate from one another, avoiding too much contact. What prompted the new era of aggression, they have not told us directly."

I lay down on my bed; utterly exhausted from all the mental turmoil I had been experiencing. I wished she would go away, and leave me to sort out my emotions. But she continued her explanations, despite my closed eyes.

"The situation turned so severe that the dark Nephilim started killing or infecting all the pure ones they could find. They also started stealing their children, and increased their numbers by infecting these children with their venom, and then returning the babies to their mothers - often without them realizing what had happened. They managed to get some mothers this way - if a child has teeth and is breastfeeding, it can bite. Some did, and so they infected their mothers.

"Around the start of the Second World War the good Nephilim began to go underground whenever possible, in order to survive at all, or they withdrew into their castles in remote areas of the world. Many live in cities still, but their homes are veritable bunkers, and they guard their own without ceasing. If only people saw the Nephilim soldiers patrolling the edges of our reality... they are a mighty sight..."

In my mind's eye I created an image of angelic soldiers flying above cities in the darkness, holding swords. A very Hollywood-like image, I am sure.

"Do they protect this place too?" I asked.

"No, as I said, this is a human center, and the secret of this gate has remained within these walls. We cannot trust the information even with pure Nephilim, in case they are infected and turn dark. We would have all the dark Nephilim of the world attacking this place if they knew. Their servants, the humans and vampires who call themselves Immortals, living in the buffer zone, would love to control our gate. Some Nephilim know how to open temporary gates of their own, but that skill runs only in very few bloodlines - like yours. Others, whose blood has been diluted with too much human blood, need ready-made, stable gates just like humans."

"How about the people using the gates? Would they not tell it to the dark Nephilim, if they were caught? Or turned into vampires?" I wondered.

Grandma did not answer at first, but then she sighed and lifted a little amulet hanging from her neck. She opened it, revealing a little liquid-filled capsule. It took me a full minute to understand.

"That is... poison?" I stammered.

"Yes." Grandma turned the capsule against the light for a moment, then put it back into the amulet and closed it with a snap. "It's unfortunate, but it's the only way to guarantee that the infected won't talk. If a human vampire bites them, most likely they will be killed. The vampires aren't exactly searching for new family members, if you get my point. They only want to feed, and the ones bitten don't hang around to discuss it. If they are bitten by the Nephilim, who are not just feeding, but creating a new servant, the infected one has at least a few hours to take this pill before the change."

"Has anyone..." I could not finish the sentence.

Grandma nodded.

"And they were all bitten by the Nephilim. The change is so painful to most that taking the pill is a relief. They all took it voluntarily. Also anyone taking part in the time walking makes an oath to use the pill if necessary. But no one is forced to do so. If they do not wish to do this, they can stay in the Centre and work on other things. Research, for example, or training others."

She looked away and I saw tears in her eyes. Clearly she had known many, if not all, of those who had taken the pill.

"But what about Daniel? He is a Nephilim, and he knows of the gate. And if I am one too... How can you trust us?"

Lilith, who walked through the door just then and heard me, answered.

"The few Nephilim, who know of this place, have also made an oath. If they are ever infected, they are to be killed before the infection takes hold. They have stronger immunity systems than humans, and so they have a few weeks before the venom begins to function. During that time they will either take their own lives, or they will come here to be killed."

I swallowed.

"But we do not want to kill anyone. That is why we have cells underneath the Centre. So far we have not had a single human who would have survived as a vampire. Even those few who were left alive by vampires or dark Nephlim chose to use the pill so they would not turn into those creatures. And if one of our Nephilim turns bad, and is not of a bloodline that can enter the buffer zone alone, they may be kept alive in the cells. They need physical contact with each other to amplify each other's power, and only then can they freely move in the buffer zone. If such Nephilim were to be imprisoned here, they would never gain their freedom again. However, if an infected Nephilim is one who can enter the buffer zone on their own... Well..."

She did not need to say any more. I understood. I realized I would be one such Nephilim. And Daniel was one too, as was his brother.

"You have a... prison? Have you any Nephilim prisoners, then?"

"Thankfully, no," Lilith shook her head, "And hopefully never will, because of the small number of Nephilim who know of this place. You must understand Daniel has not even told the Council of pure Nephilim about the gate. The Nephilim of this Centre are a true secret society. Still - we are prepared to keep the infected ones alive, if possible, in the hopes that a cure will be found one day. We hope the need never arises. It would be a cruel thing to keep a living creature prisoner for centuries."

I nodded, understanding. Or rather - not understanding. I suddenly realized what she had said.

"What did you say? Keep them prisoners for how long?"

"Centuries. The Nephilim live considerably longer than humans. There are stories of Nephilim who are thousands of years old, especially the dark ones. Cain must be one of the oldest," Lilith explained, "Some say he is from the times when the Watchers still lived here..."

Grandma intervened.

"But back to your story... Cain found out about you and came to claim you. We were aware of your birth very soon after it happened, and searched for you, so we could come to get you and your mother ourselves. I was there, together with a Time Walker group, when Cain tried to get you. We received word about you from the pure Nephilim. They had followed Cain and knew he was going to steal you from your mother. You would become yet another of their stolen children. They did not want to lose you, all the more so when they learned that your father was Cain's eldest son, the only one of his offspring, who had managed to father a child. You."

Grandma felt my forehead, which was burning. Her hand felt blissfully cool against my skin.

"We almost came too late. The shadows were within grabbing distance of you. We were just about to step down from the buffer zone, even though I was the only Hunter among us, and we would have been severely overpowered. Still, we could not leave you to them without a fight. It was right then that the bomb exploded. The pressure wave blasted the shadows away. Your mother managed to open her wings just enough to protect you, when the explosion threw her into the air."

Grandma was silent for a while, searching for words.

"Your mother, unfortunately, did not make it. Her wings broke when she fell on the debris, and her blood ran out. We took you, and brought you to this time."

"How did I end up with my family, then?" I asked, eyes still closed, my emotions now dulled to numbness.

"I took you to my own daughter, who is your mother as much as anyone can ever be. Your parents could not get a child of their own; they had tried for years, and gone through expensive treatments while trying. They got a message from an adoption agency that they had found a baby girl for them - an agency I had recommended to them. They never knew this adoption agency specialized in rehoming Nephilim children... As far as your family goes, I am an ordinary, yet a bit eccentric old woman. They have no idea of what I really am."

I opened my eyes and looked at her in amazement.

"Yes, you heard right. We often have to hide the children of the remaining pure Nephilim. When they are hidden among ordinary people, in ordinary human families, unaware of who they are, they are much safer than when they are raised by their own kind.

"This is sad, but necessary, because the dark Nephilim soldiers circle in search of these children constantly. They have problems having children of their own, so they increase their number mostly by stealing pure Nephilim children. Only after Nephilim children have grown their wings, can they protect themselves against the venom. The wings have such an energy field it prevents the venom from functioning - if caught before it enters the body's bloodstream. Angel almost caught you, because Daniel had not quite managed to wrap you. He was threatening Angel with his wing tips, and that left an opening to Daniel's cocoon, for Angel to try to reach you."

"But how did Daniel find me in the buffer zone?"

"He flew in as soon as we found him and could alert him of your disappearance. He knew your scent, so he followed that. Also, you dropped a shoe on the path the Time Walker group had just used," Lilith said. "Daniel found it and guessed you were headed to the same library the group had just come from. He reached the library just as you escaped it. The nuns were scared out of their wits at the sight of an angel in their burning library... I am sure, if we now searched for the annals of the nunnery, we would find a reference to this - and it would not have been in the annals yesterday."

Grandma chuckled. I remember the cry I heard just as I entered the buffer zone - someone had cried about an angel... If only I had remained a few seconds longer, Daniel would have taken me to safety and I would never had met Angel.

"And because you had hurt your hand, it was even easier for him to follow the smell of your blood right to you. You will be surprised how acute your senses become, when you turn into Nephilim. Because of these heightened senses they can hunt down anyone whose blood they have smelled. And it gets even easier, if they have tasted the blood."

Suddenly I realized I had dropped my blood all over the place where Angel had appeared.

"That means Angel too..." I whispered.

"Yes. She is a formidable opponent, never ever underestimate her." Lilith's eyes were serious.

"But who is she?"

"She is Cain's daughter. How she found you in the buffer zone, I am not sure..." Grandma looked at me inquiringly.

I explained about the visiting card.

"You said you found it in the street after the shadow attacked the drunken man?"

"Yes."

"Sounds like it was placed there on purpose... It was meant for you... Why would you follow it then..."

We both guessed the answer.

"Kitty..." I breathed.

"They knew about Kitty," Grandma said, "they knew you grieved for her, and would perhaps use the card to try and contact with her..."

It seemed the dark Nephilim knew all about me. The thought made me squirm with discomfort.

"So they knew about Kitty's death...knew enough to set a trap for you. This is something we need to examine. Unfortunately you arrived in the shop when Angel was still there. If Daniel had not arrived when he did, you would be lost to us now." Lilith had been standing quietly by the window until now.

I felt fever shivering in my spine. All my muscles ached.

"I need to rest..." I whispered.

"Of course. You are heading for a very hard patch. No pain killers will help you, I'm afraid," Lilith sympathized, "best you know what to expect in advance. But the pain will not kill you, remember that. The fever will awaken powers within you that will help you endure the suffering. And it won't last forever. Every Nephilim has gone through the same ordeal."

The women rose and headed to the door.

"One more thing..." I said, and they turned back, "How did Daniel come to be trusted with the information about the gate, if the Nephilim should not know of it? I mean... who told him?"

Lilith smiled.

"It's the other way around. He trusted us with the information. You see, he is the one who found the gate, stabilized it, and he is the one who had this Centre built."

I remembered the wrought iron gate of the center. And the year in it.

"He... built this?"

"Yes. He established this place at the end of the 18th century," Grandma said over her shoulder, already out of the room, "But for a

Nephilim he is still rather young. Only a little over three hundred years old."

49

THE DECISION

Daniel read the piece of paper and then the note card with the picture of the bee on it. He glanced across at his brother, noting how the visit to Finland had changed him. There was an eagerness, but also a sense of anxiety about Elijah. Let his hopes not be raised in vain, thought Daniel.

"Show me the mirror," he said, placing the card on the table.

Elijah handed him the mirror. Daniel lifted it so it caught the light and the tiny writing showed more clearly.

"This writing is in Finnish..." he said.

"Yes, it is. It reads: 'I am in Amenhotep's court. I do not know how to get back. Help me, Elijah. Merit.'"

Elijah's voice was thick.

"She ended up in the past somehow. And she never had time to learn how to travel in the buffer zone, let alone how to travel through time. None of us has ever traveled that far back in time. But we need to go and get her, Daniel. Once she is out of the buffer zone time keeps on going at its normal pace. She might still be alive there even now!"

There was desperation in his voice.

Daniel said nothing for a while. Then he pointed at the note card.

"That tells us that she kept a notebook while she was still alive. But it doesn't tell us when she died in the past."

"No, but her notebook would give us a clue – it would say how many years she lived there. We might still have time!"

Elijah's voice was filled with wild hope.

"But who stole her notebook? It had to be Cain's servants. And why? What was so important about the notebook? And if it was so important, why was it simply placed in a library and not taken to Cain immediately? Because they did not understand the language? Did they forget about it later?"

"How should I know?" Elijah banged his fist against a bookshelf.

A few researchers sitting nearby in their own library lifted their eyes from their work.

Elijah managed to control himself.

"And what does the 18.England.Enquiry mean?"

A head lifted at a nearby table. An old woman who seemed to be in the library always.

"I do apologize, gentlemen, but I could not help overhearing," she lifted her spectacles and blinked a few times while her eyes adjusted, "if you are talking of an old library, then I think that is a hint to the location within the library. 18 could be 18th century. And England might mean the country... But you said the last word was enquiry?"

"Yes, it was," Elijah nodded. "You have some idea what that might mean?"

"Of course I cannot be certain, but it just might be a book written by George England in 1737. It was called 'An Enquiry into the Morals of the Ancients'. So, what you are looking for would be in the 18th century literature section, a book by George England. If you cannot find it, there must be a librarian there who can help you."

"Thank you!" Elijah hugged the old lady, who blushed, hurriedly put her spectacles back on the bridge of her nose and returned to her studies.

"Very well, then." Daniel spoke quietly, as he led Elijah away. "We are going to the City of Immortals. And we will find try to find Merit's notebook, or what is left of it. If needs be, we'll find that librarian and force him - or her -to help us."

Elijah drew a deep breath.

"I could go alone," he said, "perhaps I should go alone. Merit is my wife. We are in great danger in the City of Immortals. Dark Nephilim go there often and you know how thrilled their servants would be to get their hands on Nephilim of our kind - and you also know what they would do to us. It is very dangerous."

"I know," Daniel said, "but Merit was your twin soul. It may be too late to try and rescue her, but if there is the slightest chance to learn about her fate... still, it might be best if we keep this to ourselves for now."

Elijah wiped a tear from his eye and nodded.

"So why wait," Daniel smiled grimly at him, "let's go as soon as possible."

When the researcher looked up again to rest her eyes, the Nephilim brothers were gone.

50

THE BOOK OF MESSENGERS

"What does it feel like?" Diana wanted to know. "Turning into an angel, I mean."

I rolled my eyes at her.

"Like hell..." my muscles were aching so much I could not sit still but had to walk around non-stop. If I sat, I needed to rock myself back and forth all the time. When I stopped for a second, the ache hit me. The last time I had been this sick was when I had influenza. It wasn't a dull ache. It was sharp, and it was intense, as if someone was tearing my muscles from within.

"And it's not angel, it's Nephilim. Half-angel, or something like that."

"Must be awesome... Imagine - you'll have wings! You will be able to fly! You can reach the upper levels of the buffer zone."

"Really?" that stopped me for two seconds. I remembered to continue my rocking very quickly.

"Yes, the pure Nephilim at least are able to go to the higher levels. Don't know about the bad ones - haven't had the pleasure of meeting one, thankfully... They - and we ordinary humans - usually tread the lower levels, where the mist is, because it is a good hiding place. It takes a lot of effort to learn to reach the higher parts of the buffer zone."

"Could I meet Kitty then...?"

The pang of pain was right there - I missed Kitty so much... the brief glimpse I had seen of her in the buffer zone had only made me miss her more.

"Everything's possible, if Kitty wants to meet you. I would think so, as she's already showed herself to you once, and has come into your dreams."

I concentrated on managing the ache in my limbs for a while. I felt as if someone was trying to stretch me on some medieval torturing device.

"Am I the only person around who had no idea what Nephilim even were? All the angelic beings I ever saw were pretty angel pictures and statues. No one told me about angels mixing with humans or fathering children with them. And now I am told I am about to turn into one... This is not exactly the easiest thing for the mind to accept, I can tell you!"

"We've all heard of the ancient giants of the Bible... they were the Nephilim, I suspect," Diana explained.

"Giants?" I looked up in horror. "I hope I won't grow through the roof at least!"

"You're Nephilim, not Alice in Wonderland," Diana retorted with a grin.

We were sitting in our room - there was no point in keeping me in the hospital room anymore, as I would not infect anyone with any illness. Also, I knew Grandma and Lilith were keeping a close eye on me, because of my impending change. They could help me, should the need arise. But Daniel, who knew all about this process, and might have helped me better than anyone, was nowhere to be seen. He was definitely staying away from me again.

I did not say a word to Diana about what had happened between me and Daniel. Maybe nothing had. For him, that is. But I knew I was changed forever. Something had shifted, a door had opened that I could no longer close, and I knew I was now totally in love with him. Even the fact that he was three hundred years old did not matter to me. Three hundred! To him it obviously mattered - I must be a real baby in his eyes.

I also still had to come to grips with the idea that I was going to live way past my expected human years. Everyone I knew would be dead and I would continue living - if I could avoid being killed by the bad Nephilim.

I did not want to even consider the other option - being infected and turning into a dark one. I could not imagine what their life would be like, but I knew that it did not include respect for other living beings. I could not see myself killing others, drinking their blood... wings and spitting venom had never been part of my idea of vampires, but it seemed I'd been clearly uneducated in the matter. I'd never had any desire to think that vampires were real. For me they had been just figures in stories, the produce of someone's imagination with the aim of selling books.

Grandma had made me call my parents.

"You can't go home now, not for some weeks or even months. Reggie and I have already called your parents, and they believed us when we told you had secretly applied for a place in Reggie's university, and had been accepted as a student there. You will be studying ancient history - Egyptology to be exact. And, surprise surprise - we have an intensive course in Egypt for a few weeks at the end of this summer. We leave tonight, so you won't have time to meet your parents before that. That's the story. We'll return after your transformation is over and you are in control of yourself."

"You mean they will let me go?"

"Reggie is very convincing in his role as a professor. He actually is a very well known professor in his field, with so many titles after his name he'd need two visiting cards to show them all. Studying in the buffer zone has its advantages... besides - most of Egypt has been totally peaceful and quiet all this time, despite recent upheavals. The unrest has mostly been in Cairo around Tahrir square - and we will not be going to the Egyptological Museum located there, we promised your parents that."

"Will we actually go there, to Egypt I mean?"

"We might pop in for a few photos, so our story will be more believable to your parents. It will be easy to arrange - we won't be needing airplanes, after all! But now you need to call them, and sound very excited. Remember - do not tell them you know you are adopted. It was very important to your mother you never knew. It has never been easy for her, not being able to be a biological mother."

My mother... now I could finally understand the distance between us, the feeling that she really tried to love me, but somehow just couldn't. I knew she did care for me deeply, but we never did quite connect.

So I made the call, and sounded as enthusiastic as I possibly could with the pain throbbing all through my body. They both talked to me on the phone, Mom and Dad, and Dad especially was very proud of me.

"How did you manage to keep your application such a secret?" Dad wanted to know. "You really surprised us!"

"I know... I surprised myself too!" I said to the phone.

"How did you get into university already without getting your exam results?" Mom wanted to know. Was it my imagination or did she sound a bit suspicious of the story?

"It's a special program they have - I can sit my exams there while I already begin my preliminary studies in the history department. They can do that for specially gifted students," I repeated fluently what Grandma had written on a paper for me. She had assured me Reggie had actually promised that there were scholarships and support available for special cases.

We continued talking for a while, and I was totally exhausted after the call. The pain seemed to concentrate more on my back now. I wasn't sure I liked that any more than the feeling of someone forcefully stretching my limbs.

I took off my shirt many times in the following days, to look at my back in the mirror. Nothing special there, just my skin looking completely unchanged.

One day - maybe three days later - I wandered into the hallway, still not being able to stand still, and ended up in Lilith's office where I found her with Reggie.

"Dana!" Reggie beamed. "Do you have any idea what kind of service you've done for us?"

"Erm... no..."

I hadn't a clue what he was talking about. As far as I knew I had only scared everyone out of their wits and nearly been grabbed by a dark angel - funny that her name actually was Angel. Twisted humor...

"The book you brought back with you from the nunnery... to think that it might have burned! I had no idea it was there in the library, as that nun would not budge from behind the railing so I could never see what lay on the far side of the shelves..."

He stopped talking and just smiled at me as if I should now understand everything.

"Yes?" I had to prompt him.

"Ah, oh... yes... It is the only known copy of the Book of Messengers - an ancient Greek book about the origin of angels. The word angelos meant messenger," he clarified. "This is a copy from the times of Saint Dionysius the Areopagite, the second bishop of Athens. Written on parchment, and in amazingly good condition... Miraculously it survived all the turmoil of Western civilization as it grew and developed, hidden away somewhere that no-one would ever find or steal it. Perhaps the lack of jeweled covers meant that it attracted no unwanted attention... it has survived for two thousand years!"

I began to understand his enthusiasm.

"I've spent the last few days translating the ancient Greek - and this book references the Nephilim as well as the Book of Watchers. This is the very book we have been trying to reach in all our travels through time. We knew there was a book that that would provide the explanation for much that we needed to know and you brought it to us!"

"Really?"

What were the odds that I would weave my way accidentally to the very place where such a book was being kept? And that I would get it, instead of the Time Walker group that was sent in search of it? And what was the impulse that made me break the glass and take the book so it would not burn? I had no idea what made me do that. Was this the Weaver breeding of the dark Nephilim in me, the work of Cain?

"We knew that there was an important book in the library, but we thought it was the Book of Angels, the one we took home. It was quite educational, certainly, and valuable too, but there was nothing new in it. The Book of Messengers is another thing entirely!"

Lilith beamed too.

"We believe that we finally have some knowledge about the Book of Watchers. The Book of Messengers talks about the gates, and we think that they have to be the gates we have found. They couldn't be anything else, really. Indeed they seem to have been the very gates the Watchers used, when they still walked among humans before their fall, after having taken human wives and fathered the Nephilim. We all know the story that the Watchers were thrown into a deep cave in Tartarus to wait for the punishment that would come at the end of times. The gates remained where they were. So it seems the Watchers reached the human world through the gates either from the buffer zone, or used it as a path from some other place or level."

Reggie was too excited to sit still. He took a few steps, and then pushed his hands into his pockets as if to ground himself.

"The book you brought back tells us that the Book of Watchers is not just any book! It is a map! It is a map to the place where the Watchers came from. It is called the Abode of Angels in the Book of Messengers. We think the dark Nephilim want to find the ancient Abode of Angels!"

I did not know what to say, except "Why?"

"We do not know... the fact that the captured shadow threatened that evil would follow for us when they found the Book of Watchers isn't exactly encouraging, though. Daniel has gone to find out more about that," Lilith said.

"Gone where?" I could not help my voice rising nervously.

"He has gone to the buffer zone, to the City of the Immortals, to see if he can discover more information. He suggested it himself as soon as we told him about what this little book revealed. "

"Oh..." I had to find myself a chair where I sat down heavily. "Is that safe? Will they not infect him?"

"He is not alone. He has his brother Elijah with him. They are very good at camouflaging, hiding their energies. Their plan is to try to capture an Immortal with some knowledge, and bring that one back here. They already have some indication of who this person might be, it seems. The Nephilim don't spend too much time in the City of the Immortals, so if Daniel and Elijah are quick, they should be able to escape. The Immortals cannot follow them to the higher levels, and by the time the other Nephilim are alerted, the boys will be up and away, long gone."

The boys... didn't exactly sound like the word I would have used of someone who was three hundred years old. How old Daniel's brother was, I had no idea. I wondered if Lilith was putting a positive spin on their task in order not to let me know how dangerous it really was.

"When do you expect them back?" I rocked on the chair to keep the pain at bay.

"Any time now. They have been gone since you woke up. Five days."

I felt a band of fear squeeze around my heart. Five days in the middle of the enemy? Maybe they were dead or infected already...

"Here, have a look!" Reggie gestured me to approach.

His fingers dipped into the pockets of his loose jacket and pulled out a pair of cotton gloves. With these on he carefully opened the cover of the small book on Lilith's table. I bent closer.

"This must be one of the oldest codices in the world," he explained.

"I'm sorry... you mean book?" I wasn't quite sure I understood.

"Yes, indeed, a book in book form as we know it," Reggie nodded, "It was a revolutionary invention! Consider the scrolls that people had been using for thousands of years. They could be very long and clumsy to use of course. And then someone realized that papyrus could be cut into pages that were attached to each other at one side. The earliest books, as we know them, come from the first centuries of the Christian era. And this - I have never seen an older book than this!"

He was so overtaken by emotion that he pressed the backs of his hand to his eyes for a while. After a deep breath he gained enough composure to continue.

"You see this book is written on papyrus. The covers are made of simple boards, which I think have been covered later with leather. All these are perishable materials - it is a wonder it has been preserved!"

I nodded.

"This is written in Greek, and it has illustrations as well!"

Delicately, as though he was touching a butterfly's wing, Reggie opened the book at a place where we could see an old drawing.

It was beautiful and clearly made in Greek style. It depicted a male figure with huge red wings. In his left hand he held a scroll, which he was opening with his right hand. There was tiny writing on the scroll.

"Now, here... look through this," Reggie's deep pockets produced a magnifying glass.

Through it I saw Greek letters I did not understand, and another drawing on the scroll. I had no idea what it was supposed to depict - it looked like a torn leaf.

"What am I looking at?" I asked.

"The drawing is a map. It appears that the artist here had an actual map in his hands, which he copied onto the scroll. We haven't yet been able to identify where it is precisely, but its most likely location is somewhere in the Mediterranean region. Our researchers are working on it on their computers as we speak."

"And the text?"

"That's the very clue to the Book of Watchers!"

Again Reggie had to take a moment to control his emotions. He looked at the ceiling and breathed deeply. I observed his scholarly excitement with interest. Then he returned his gaze to the book:

"The text says: The scroll of iyrin, the path to their abode."

"The word iyrin means "the Watchers" in our language," Lilith said, "so now we know that the Book of Watchers is a scroll, a map that leads to their place of origin."

"To...heaven?" I asked.

"We don't know. It could be a place in the buffer zone realms, it could be the place where they are now, or it could be a physical place on earth - after all according to legend they lived here with their human wives," Lilith said, "and that is what Daniel and Elijah are trying to find out."

There was a knock on the door. One of the Guardians, whose name I did not know, opened the door. His eyes were wide with shock.

"Come quickly. Daniel and Elijah are back! And - "

He didn't have to say anything more. The expression on his face said it all. I was out of the room ahead of everyone else.

51

THE PROPHECY

The Pythian games were held only every fourth year, and Ambrogio understood that he had been lucky to come here just now, when the games were about to commence, beginning on the seventh day of the month of Boucation, at the end of summer.

Six months earlier the theoroi, nine messengers chosen from among the citizens of Delphi, had left on their round of visits to every city in Greece to announce the start of the festival. During this time the heiromenia, a truce, was observed. No city could attempt to invade the sanctuary at this time, or they and their citizens would be excluded not only from entering the sanctuary, but also taking part in the games, or asking the advice of the Pythia.

The Delphi temple area was restored with great expense. The theoria, or official missions from the participating cities, arrived. They included not only leading athletes, but also the elite and officials of all the participating cities, and they gave rich offerings and animal sacrifices to the temple.

Ambrogio had only a few days to practice on his kithara. It did resemble the lyre, but had certain differences. Its sound box was of wood, and it had two horns that were attached to a horizontal tuning bar. There were seven strings. The horns were flexible, and when the strings were plucked, the horns made a wavelike sound. The instrument sang with a strong and deep voice.

Ambrogio had the instrument hanging from his shoulder on a strap, and played it with two hands, with closed eyes, to really listen to the different notes. His fingers were too clumsy, so he made a little plectrum out of a flat piece of wood.

If anything, he had always been musical. Learning to play the lyre had come naturally to him, and so he soon found confidence in this new, yet difficult instrument. He knew he could not win over the musicians who had played the kithara since childhood, so he decided that instead of trying to play a difficult tune, he would use it only to support his singing voice.

The song he chose was one his mother had sung to him when he was a child. It was not a lullaby. His mother had a remarkable voice and he had inherited his musical talent from her. This song was long, and had a variable melody, which took the singer from deep bass to high trills, and the intensity of the singing voice varied. He only needed to rephrase it, turning it into a song to honor Apollo.

He never saw the golden-haired goddess, while he practiced. He felt a shiver of fear, when he heard, that a musician had been found dead in the valley where the spectators of the games had set up their camps, his throat cut, but no blood anywhere on the ground around him. Because he still was wearing his jewelry, it was decided no one had broken the heiromenia, and a wild animal had attacked the man. If Ambrogio suspected where his own kithara came from, he did not dare to voice his suspicions even to himself.

The games began. The first two days were religious. On the first day a great number of animals was sacrificed in the temple, and their meat was eaten. Then a holy play was enacted, to show how Apollo killed the horrible Python snake that harassed human kind. The god threw the body of the snake into the chasm over which Pythia now sat, and the fumes caused by its decomposition made her go into trance and predict the future.

The next day people feasted on the sacrificed animals. People from different city-states got to know each other. Ambrogio also got his share of the delicious meat, and ate to his heart's content.

Then the third day of the Games came, the day of the music competition. The singers gathered in the Theatre, and performed their songs, one after the other. They had travelled from far to participate in the games, protected by the Holy Delphic Peace. There was a competition for playing the autos, the flute. And then there was the singing contest in which the singer accompanied himself on the kithara.

When Ambrogio's turn came, he closed his eyes, and sang like never before, playing the kithara only as far as he had become familiar with it. He was not as good a kithara player as the other singers, but his voice beat them all. He had never sung so well.

He won. He was crowned with the laurel wreath, which was sought and cut by the same actor, a young boy, who had played Apollo slaying the great Python in the holy play. Suddenly Ambrogio was lauded by all.

The athletic contests were in turn on the fourth day. There were foot races, like the hoplitodromoi - running a race in full armor - boxing and wrestling and the pentathlon. On the fifth day he watched the horse races.

When it was time for Pythia to give oracles again, Ambrogio was told he would be one of those allowed to approach her. The sacrificed goat's entrails showed the Pythia would be safe. She had already fasted, and on the seventh day of the month she bathed at dawn. This she did in the very same ravine where Amrogio had met with the goddess, situated between the Phaedriade cliffs, the shining ones. The spring where she bathed was sacred, located where Apollo had killed the Python - the Castalian spring, near the statues of Gaia and Themis. She then drank the holy waters of the Kassotis near the temple – and now Ambrogio also heard it was the place where a naiad, a water nymph with magical powers, was said to live. He understood it was she he had met.

Pythia then returned to the temple with her retinue. She burned an offering to Apollo - barley meal and laurel leaves, and spoke words of worship. Priests sprinkled cold water on a flawless goat, which shuddered as a sign that Apollo was willing to answer questions. The goat was then sacrificed outside the temple so all could see the day was favorable, and Pythia would prophesize.

A priest sprinkled the temple floor with holy water. Ambrogio, having purified himself with the water of the springs of Delphi, stood in awe at the temple entrance and read the words written there. "Know thyself" and "Nothing in excess". A big letter E was carved there too, but he did not know what it meant and did not dare to ask.

Ambrogio had bought the required pelanos, the sacrificial cake you could only buy from the Delphians. Inside the temple he was required to make another sacrifice, a goat again, on the inner hearth of the temple, accompanied by a Delphic citizen, who had been chosen as his proxenos - the local representative. Anyone who was not Delphic, had to have a proxenos to enter.

The Pythia then descended the steps into the place where her tripod seat was placed – the adyton, the inaccessible place. She was the only woman allowed to enter here. She held laurel leaves, and a dish in which holy water of the Kassotis spring formed a mirror. Near her was the omphalos, the navel of the world in the form of a decorated stone. Two golden eagles were on both sides of it, to remind them of how Zeus had sent two eagles to flight from both ends of the world. Where they met, was the center of the world, and this is where the omphalos was placed. The stone was covered by a carved, thick net on its surface, the agrenon. Two statues of Apollo filled the place - one wooden, the other golden. Apollo's sacred armor and lyre filled the rest of the space, leaving only a small amount of room for the Pythia.

Ambrogio tried to see the chasm from which the vapors of the decomposing Python were supposed to rise, but he only saw a limestone floor. Maybe they had covered the chasm with a floor of stone... under the tripod on which the Pythia was sitting was an incense burner and she was enveloped by the thick veils of smoke that emanated from it. This was the breath of Apollo, which entered into the Pythia and came out through her mouth as divine words.

They were not allowed to approach Pythia too closely, and only one could come and ask their question at a time. She sat on her tripod, staring into the bowl of water with glazed eyes. Her head began to bob.

Ambrogio had the honor of having the first turn. He observed the Pythia from a distance, from the entrance of the adyton - no one was allowed to come too close. The Pythia was no longer young, even though she wore the dress of a maiden. He had heard she was chosen from among the families of Delphi and, once selected, could no longer have a normal family life. She dedicated herself to be the vessel through which the god Apollo spoke directly, and lived a chaste life, taking great care of her purity. If she had been married and had children, she was to leave that life behind.

Ambrogio had been told that he should ask Pythia a question that had two options. So he had written down his question. "Should I return to my home and become a merchant like my father, or should I leave ordinary life behind me and seek for my happiness elsewhere?"

Ambrogio had been told he might not understand a word of what Pythia said, and that priests would interpret her words for him later. After this he was to think about the answer on his own, because only he could know the truth. This is why "Know thyself" was written on the entrance of the temple – if you did not know your own mind, you could not understand the cryptic answer.

But it was not so. The Pythia sat in a hunched position, listening to the question the priest quietly read to her, her face near the water. Suddenly she declared loudly in a clear and ringing voice:

"The curse. The moon. The blood will run."

Nothing more. Ambrogio was led out of the temple repeating these ominous words.

52

THE CHANGE

There was a silent ring of people standing in the hallway in front of the gate. Lilith pushed them aside to get past, and the rest of us followed through the opening she had made.

Daniel was standing, his magnificent blue wings spread, holding a frightened-looking middle aged man in a tight grip by the arm. Next to the man crouched a dog-like shadow, its movements reflecting the nervous twitching of its master. Still, it seemed to have a will of its own, and tried to move away, whilst the man did not try to escape.

On the floor lay a dark-haired Nephilim, whose features resembled those of Daniel's. This had to be Elijah.

He lay there with open wings and closed eyes, fighting for his breath. The rasping sound of his labored breathing echoed from the walls. And his wings... they were torn into horrible shreds. Originally they seemed to have been bluish, but the shreds were turning darker as we watched. They shivered and crumpled as Elijah tried to breathe, and a pool of blood spread slowly across the tiles.

"Oh no!" Lilith gasped. "Who did this?"

"A Nephilim fighter was in the Immortal City and followed us. He caught us before we could reach any higher planes. We had to fight the man's shadow and that slowed us down, giving the Nephilim time to reach us."

Lilith knelt by the young man. Despite the horror I felt, I did not freeze. Instead my legs had a will of their own and took me right next to him.

The young man opened his eyes, and they were cloudy with shock. For a second they locked into mine, even though I could not be certain he actually saw me, and I felt a sudden wave of deep compassion flow through me. The depth of the emotion made me sway.

"Take the man to safekeeping," Lilith ordered, not diverting her gaze from Elijah.

Several Guardians stepped in to surround the shadow and the man standing in Daniel's grip. Daniel cut the cord between the shadow and its master in one inexorable and deft motion, and the shadow fell into a shivering heap on the floor. The man was left gasping for air as if someone had hit him in the stomach. People drew back, not wanting to touch the remains of the shadow as it crawled aimlessly and pitifully along the floor. Soon it stopped moving and turned into a pile of grey dust like a deflated balloon. The Guardians led the man away, and he did not try to fight.

Daniel had eyes only for his brother, and he too knelt on the floor.

"Was - is - he bitten?" Lilith asked, not daring to touch Elijah.

"I fear so, but I do not know. There will have to be blood tests," Daniel said. "They clashed wings in the most vicious fight I'd ever witnessed, whilst Elijah tried to give me a chance to escape with our prisoner. I hope he managed to protect himself."

He extended his wings and carefully slid them under Elijah's limp body. With the help of his wings and strong arms he gently lifted Elijah off the floor and headed towards the sick ward. Lilith and I followed. Reggie and Grandma were nowhere to be seen. Elijah wailed in a thin voice, barely conscious.

All the way to the ward big drops of blood fell on the floor. They were red, but had an odd glittering shimmer to them. The remnants of Elijah's wings trailed along the floor in Daniel's wake.

I could not watch that. I stepped closer, bent, and carefully lifted the shreds so that I ended up holding them in my arms as if I was carrying the train of a wedding dress. The shreds gave me slight electric shocks, and were slippery with blood. Only then did I realize I might have put myself in danger. I tried to remember if I had any scratches in my arms so that Elijah's blood might get into my bloodstream. But no, I did not remember having any cuts in my skin.

Elijah screamed when I touched his wings and Daniel looked over his shoulder.

"What are you doing?" he asked, but did not slow down.

"His wings... I'm afraid bits will fall off..."

Daniel did not say anything, but now we had already reached the ward. The word had spread, and there was a whole medical team waiting.

Daniel carefully lowered Elijah onto the bed so that he lay on his back. The bed was T-shaped, and when they spread out Elijah's wings I understood, why. Both wings could be stretched out and treated at the same time as his body.

We moved aside to the wall and watched them do whatever they could for Elijah. They cut off his clothes, and saw deep marks in his body, as though someone had burned him with a hot blade. I could see scorched tissue, and deep cuts.

I understood that if the other Nephilim had managed to spit into those wounds, or had caused them by biting, Elijah would be infected.

There were four doctors. Two worked on his body, and two on his wings.

It is an amazing sight - to see how the angel wings were treated. The wings were transparent, but not immaterial. The shreds were carefully straightened to their proper place. The darkened edges were then handled with some kind of liquid that shone bright yellow – it reminded me of honey. It seemed to glue the bits back together.

Then they had to turn Elijah around to treat his back. Daniel stepped in to help, and with the help of his strong wings they managed to keep Elijah's wings supported as they spread them out widely during the process. Despite all their efforts Elijah screamed with pain. His voice hurt my whole body, and I felt it like a stabbing pain in my bones.

A little sob broke out of me when I saw his back. I couldn't help it. I could literally see his ribs, the cuts were so extensive. I had to put my hand over my mouth; the sight made me want to vomit.

Daniel stepped closer, and to my surprise he put his arm around my shoulders and drew me to him. I felt my skin prickling at his touch. Against his steady hand I noticed I was shaking.

What surprised me even more, came as a shock almost, was the realisation that I had grown in height since I had last met Daniel. Before, my head was at the level of his shoulder, but now I reached his cheek.

"Will he... die?" I managed to form the difficult word.

"It could be. I have never seen a Nephilim this badly injured," Daniel said with a thick voice. "When the results of the blood test come, we'll know whether ... he'll even be allowed to live..."

I had no words. Daniel's answer confirmed what I had already suspected - Elijah was one of those who could travel between the buffer zone and our world on his own. All I could do was to squeeze Daniel's hand on my shoulder, and he turned his head and met my eyes. I saw tears in his.

"Oh, Daniel!" I turned to face him and hugged him before I even knew I was doing it, "I am so sorry!"

He wrapped his arms around me, making my heart sing even in the midst of all the horror. We stood locked like that for a while. I could have stayed like that forever, but I understood this was not the right time. This was not about me. No matter how I felt for him, this was not the place to tell Daniel about my emotions. So it was I who let go first, and we continued watching the doctors working on Elijah.

Elijah was a sorry sight, when they were done. His whole body was covered in huge cuts and quickly emerging bruises. His skin had been stitched together with hundreds of sutures. His wings lay by his sides; the torn edges glued together, dark patches dimming their usual glow. They had tried to take away his necklace, a scarab, but he had been conscious enough to stop them. It was wiped clean from blood and now lay against his chest.

He was wrapped in bandages, and an iv-drip kept on feeding his body with the odd yellow, glowing liquid they had used on his wings. He was so pale I wondered if there was enough blood left in his body to keep him alive.

They could not cover him with blankets, as they would have pressed on his wounds. Instead they raised the temperature of the room.

"Go now," one of the doctors, a middle aged woman, said to Daniel, "there is nothing you can do here. Elijah needs to rest."

"I'm going nowhere," Daniel said in a voice that accepted no objections, and the doctor let us be.

"The test results will take a day to be ready," was all she said, "then we'll know."

I could not leave either. I stood there with Daniel, feeling the room become more comfortable by the minute. It took me a while to understand it was because of the quickly rising room temperature, which matched my own body temperature.

One of the doctors stayed with Elijah. He sat in an observation room with a big window onto the treatment room. He was keeping an eye on the monitors there.

Daniel pulled up a chair for me, then one for himself. We sat side by side, our eyes on the still unconscious Elijah. I had never been religious, but now I prayed. Whatever higher force there was, surely it would want to save an angel?

I could not face the thought that Elijah might be infected and would have to be killed. I had a very good idea who would have to do the killing. Could there be anything worse than being forced to kill one's own sibling?

There were no windows in the room, but I felt the day turning old, and eventually night came. The clock on the wall measured time, silently. Daniel never withdrew his wings - he seemed to be on alert all the time.

I began to feel very odd around midnight - as if a swarm of bees buzzed in my body. I had to get to my feet. As I did, a spasm of pain ripped my back.

"Oh!"

No matter how I tried, I could not keep silent.

"What is it?" Daniel asked quietly.

"Pain...!" I bit my lip. This was not the place to complain about my own aches.

"Where?"

"My back! OH!" now the pain left me no option to stay silent - I screamed when it stabbed me with such a force my legs gave way and I fell on the floor.

Hurried steps. Daniel lifted me from the floor, I noticed the doctor behind him.

"Is it happening now?" he asked Daniel.

"Has to be - but it should not be happening yet! This is too soon, neither her body of her mind are prepared!" Daniel said with concern in his voice.

I was paralyzed. Suddenly I was a prisoner inside my immobile body. I felt nothing but terrible pain, as if an invisible knife carved my back, but I could not even scream anymore. Only my eyes could move.

"Put her on the bed, on her right side, it is easier on her heart," Daniel's voice commanded.

They did. I was staring at Elijah on his bed. Then Daniel was sitting next to me.

"Shhh... try to calm down," he said when he saw the panic in my eyes, "The paralysis will last some time, maybe a day or two, but it will pass. And you will be taken care of while it lasts."

He stroked my cheek gently, and I locked into his eyes, desperately searching for relief, but none came.

I don't know if you have ever been gripped by extreme and constant pain, and I hope you never will. It stops time, leaving you in an unbelievable bubble of existence that is straight from hell. There is no pause from the agony, just searing, constant never-ending pain. You would do anything to make it stop. You would kill yourself. You would hope your heart would stop beating, because every beat is thundering through your body, multiplying the pain as blood rushes through your veins.

But I could not kill myself. I could not move. All I could do to try and stay sane was to look at something. So I looked at Elijah, and I looked at Daniel.

Before sunrise Daniel fell asleep in his chair, despite trying to stay awake. I could hear Elijah's labored breathing. The doctor behind the glass wall was looking at a computer screen, clearly forcing himself to stay awake.

I heard a loud crack. It must have been in my mind, because Daniel did not wake up. It felt like I had been cracked open vertically, from my toes to the top of my head.

And then, suddenly, the pain was gone. I took one huge, careful breath, afraid to move lest it came back. It didn't.

I felt an odd sensation on and in my back and turned my head. Nothing there. Then I realized I had moved. The paralysis was gone.

I sat up on the bed. No pain. I stepped down, and to my amazement Daniel did not wake up at the sound of my stepping down. I looked down and understood why. I was not standing on the floor - I was floating at a finger's width above it.

I understood what must have happened.

I concentrated on Elijah's face, and without taking a step I glided to his bedside.

I stood there, not knowing what to do, but then I felt something unfurl on my back. It was a very strange feeling. I could feel a new part of my body that had never been there before. It was like being aware of a new arm, or leg. It was definitely there, and somehow I knew exactly how to use it.

I heard Daniel draw a breath behind me.

"Dana..." he said quietly.

I turned around. He was standing, with amazement in his eyes. He looked wary of me, which was strange.

I, on the other hand, was oddly calm. I listened to the strange sensation on my back, and in my mind, and concentrated. I breathed deeply and slowly, and surrended to whatever was happening.

There, by the bedside of an injured Nephilim, facing another, I turned into one. My wings opened like the petals of a blossom and filled the room with their glow.

"Silver..." I heard Daniel whisper, "you have silver wings!"

I thought about moving my wings, just a little, and a new energy rushed into my body when the wings obeyed. It was as if I was breathing with all my body, not just my lungs. I closed my eyes and enjoyed the delicious feeling of unhindered breathing, the like of which I had never experienced with my human lungs.

I turned and looked into Elijah's eyes, feeling the same surge of compassion as before, when I saw him lying on the floor, only now the emotion was ten times stronger. I bent over him, and kissed him on the forehead. I did not think consciously about what I was doing; it was as if a wordless consciousness was functioning through me. I did not obey it, I was it.

Then Daniel was by my side. He said something, but I could not hear what it was because I was so concentrating on Elijah. I felt my wings spread out around me. Gently as feathers they bent down and matched the shape of Elijah's torn wings, covering them completely, and I bent down as close to his damaged body as I could without touching his skin. I realised that I was humming, but it was not a song, just an unchanged melody that emanated from deep inside me. I wasn't even sure the voice came from my vocal chords - it was more as though the cells of my body were producing the sound from invisible strings inside me, each resonating with their own voice, creating a mesmerising melodic drone like that of a beehive. My analytical mind vanished into the sound and my being spread out to levels I had no words for.

I stayed out of human consciousness for a long time. I do not know what happened physically, but my mind was traveling in odd realms. I could see beautiful colors, mingled with gold and silver. I felt total happiness, yet I could sense sadness, compassion, and fear somewhere underneath. But I was above them, safe.

I saw darker veins of energy. I approached them, and touched them with my mind, and they dissolved, and returned to beauty. I could have stayed there forever; I had never felt anything like this weightless joy before.

Then there was a sliver of beautiful, electric blue, and I followed it with my mind, eager to touch its beauty. It became bigger, and finally enveloped me, and that is when I became aware of my physical surroundings again.

I was still standing at the ward, and Elijah was still lying on his bed. My wings were no longer touching his.

The odd thing was that Elijah's wings were now whole, healed. He was staring at me with unbelieving eyes, which were... fearful? Longing? Daniel... yes, Daniel was there too, holding me, in fact, with his beautiful, electric blue wings.

"What happened...?" I whispered, not quite back in my mind, closing my eyes at the deliciousness of his blue energies.

"You healed his wings," Daniel spoke as if he could not have believed what had happened. "You used the power of your wings, and you healed them."

I moved and Daniel stepped back. I felt as if I was falling, when his wings let me go.

"How...? Where was I?"

"You need to calm down first. Your energies are now so high you could electrocute someone," Daniel stepped even further back.

I wondered why his eyes were so carefully hiding any emotion. I looked back at Elijah, and his eyes were now full of emotion when they locked with mine. There was definite sadness there, and longing. For the briefest moment I remembered seeing a vision of a young, tall, blonde woman, when traveling in the odd realms of the mind, but I might have imagined it.

Then I noticed there were others in the room too. Lilith. Grandma. Somehow Diana had also appeared. Reggie was there, squeezing the old book against his chest, his mouth half open with excited wonder.

They all looked at me with round eyes. Like they were... scared of me? Only Diana was looking at me with a wide smile, clearly liking what she saw.

"Oh stop it, you!" I tried to say lightly, but my voice shook. "I seem to have become Nephilim, then. But it's not like you weren't expecting it, and it's not as though you've not seen one before!"

"Oh we've seen Nephilim before. But we haven't seen one like you before. You should not exist," Grandma said with amazement in her voice. "In the Nephilim world you should be a genetic impossibility."

"Great. Are we going to start talking in riddles again?" I sighed.

"No riddles any more, dear," Grandma decided. "But food. You need to eat a lot more now that you have your wings. Come, let's go to the cafeteria."

My stomach growled loudly and Diana stifled a giggle. I smiled back at her, and suddenly felt like a normal teenager again, feeling giddy and light - and hungry. I was glad she was there. It made me feel less spaced out, less different.

"Would you withdraw your wings before we go, dear?" Lilith asked, "they are quite a sight, and might scare some people."

I had not really even looked at my wings, and peeked over my shoulder, and then up. Way up.

"Oh... Oh wow..."

They were beautiful! They were huge, their tips brushed the ceiling, and they were white and silver. Strong pulses of silver liquid pumped in the see-through veins. They glittered in the light.

"I look like a Christmas angel!" I laughed, still feeling giddy with the high energies I had experienced, and Diana giggled in agreement.

"Well, it's not Christmas now, so close them." Grandma sounded surprisingly grandmotherly.

"It is to me..." a quiet voice said in my mind.

It was Elijah's voice, but I did not see his lips moving. Surprised I looked into his eyes again. They were full of wonder and that inexplicable longing I had sensed in him. And then I saw Daniel's eyes, which were carefully emotionless.

I had no idea what had caused his aloofness. I would ask later.

"Let's go eat!" Diana opened the door to the hallway. "You must be famished."

She was right.

53

BEAUTIFUL EVELYN HARPER

William Donnelly had been quite happy with his work in his London bookshop. He enjoyed arranging his bookshelves alphabetically, listing each author on a separate list with the correct shelf location, keeping statistics of the books he had sold, and serving his regular customers. He ordered special books just to please his academic clientele, and was well appreciated for his expertise.

He had managed to build a good reputation as a man of letters, whose passion was books. Even to an extent his clients thought he kept his little bookshop only as a hobby, to be around his beloved books, and to fund his own research.

They were right. But they did not know how expensive his research was for him. He had to buy very rare books and manuscripts, which were often hidden in monasteries, or in private libraries whose owners knew their value full well. He was up to his ears in debt, and saw no way out of his predicament, other than selling his pricey books. And he could not force himself to do that.

William Donnelly was at his wits' end. Another letter had arrived from his major creditor, demanding payment in quite impolite terms. He had no idea how he could ever pay the sum he owed. He had even received pre-payments from his customers for books he had not yet bought – and now had no money to buy either.

Then came Queen Victoria's Golden Jubilee. On 21st of July in the year 1887 Mr. Donnelly was standing near Westminster Abbey in order to see the arrival of the Queen. She arrived in an open landau, but much to Mr. Donnelly's disappointment she did not wear a crown. Instead she wore a bonnet. But no one could deny the sight was magnificent – the handsome Indian cavalry, the Queen's cream-colored horses – the guests... such a fine spectacle!

He tried to distract himself from his gloomy thoughts by joining the cheerful crowd. Suddenly someone stumbled against him. He turned and saw a young lady who was about to fall to the ground. She was clearly fainting. He had no other option but to grab her and hold her up – the throng was such that he could not do much else.

After a while the lovely young woman came to. She stared at him with her beautiful golden eyes, not knowing for a while what had happened to her.

"I am so sorry," she blushed, "I fainted! I hope I did not do any harm?"

"Oh no, by no means, I am happy I managed to catch you before you fell to the ground, Miss...?" Mr. Donnelly stammered.

Because he was. Happy, that is. The young lady was quite beautiful – pale creamy skin, amazing yellowish brown eyes, and beautifully coiffured, thick hair that brought to mind fields of wheat. She was quite tall, and he was quite short, but it did not matter. She blushed and managed to make him feel like a medieval knight who had just saved a damsel in distress.

"Evelyn Harper," the young lady extended a dainty hand and he almost did not dare to touch the fingers.

"William Donnelly, at your service, my lady," he bowed.

"Not the William Donnelly who specializes in ancient myths, and has a bookshop?" Evelyn exclaimed.

"The very same," he bowed again; cheeks slightly blushing because of being called the William Donnelly.

"Such a glorious coincidence!" the young lady's smile made Mr.

Donnelly's heart miss a beat. "My brother has antiquarian interests, including the acquisition of rare books. He would greatly appreciate your advice and would pay you well for your services. Indeed, he has intended to contact you for some time. How would it be if I invited you for afternoon tea as a thank you for your gallantry today, and you could discuss my brother's requirements with him then? Shall we say next Tuesday?"

"Indeed, I would be honoured."

Mr. Donnelly could not believe his luck. He almost fainted when he saw the address on the pretty visiting card that Miss Evelyn Harper gave to him. Her family clearly had a lot of money.

Next Tuesday, dressed in his very best and spruced up in a way that his shop clients would not have recognised, he lifted the gleaming and ornate door knocker at that imposing address. A thin, very pale butler escorted him in. Mr. Donnelly couldn't quite decide his background - his hair was very shiny and black, and his skin an odd pale yellowish color. For a while he thought he might be Chinese, but his features were Mediterranean. Before Mr. Donnelly could make any more observations about him, the butler was leading him into a drawing room on the ground floor and announcing his name. Mr. Donnelly briefly noticed that the house was a small palace – there were statues, paintings, marble, gold, embroidery, and tapestries... and many of those were in the entrance hall, so the rest of the house must be even more magnificent. He was certain the tapestries were originals and centuries old.

Miss Evelyn Harper rose to her feet. She wore something light-colored that flattered her lovely form and her wonderful blonde hair was lifted into a high knot and dressed in curls on the forehead. Her beautiful golden eyes smiled warmly at Mr. Donnelly.

"How glad I am that you found time from your busy schedule to come and visit us," she said to her guest with a voice that rang like silver bells, and he could only bow and mutter compliments.

"Please, do follow me. My brother will arrive shortly."

And arrive he did – Mr. Donnelly did not know how to show his respect for this impressive man. He was very tall, had broad shoulders and black hair, and the same golden eyes as his sister. His movements were so fluid he seemed to be gliding through the air. He did not shake hands with Mr. Donnelly, but simply presented himself from across the room as Cain Harper.

Mr. Donnelly could not help but notice that the body temperature of the siblings was quite high, but they did not seem to be ill in any way and they were not perspiring at all. They discussed matters in an educated manner, and seemed to know a great deal about Mr. Donnelly's line of expertise, which was ancient myths and cuneiform script – a writing only a few could translate as yet. Mr. Donnelly was most impressed with the fact that a young woman such as Evelyn Harper was so well educated in ancient knowledge and could talk about it with the confidence of a distinguished scholar.

Cain Harper explained to Mr. Donnelly that he had come into possession of old manuscripts relating to his very field of study. He told Mr. Donnelly about some clay tablets that he had bought. They were from Mesopotamia, and written in cuneiform. An expert had told Mr. Harper the tablets were about the Annunaki, the gods who had created humankind. Would he be interested in reading and translating them? Any costs would be covered, of course.

The cuneiform tablets themselves would have been enough, but the sum Mr. Harper offered to Mr. Donnelly almost made him weep. Never had he imagined that luck as great as this would arrive so suddenly and in such measure.

He tried not to show his emotional turmoil, whilst he pretended to consider the offer. He asked a few deliberate questions in order to give the impression that he wanted to be sure the work matched his scholarly ambitions. After this he accepted, of course, and left his generous hosts with lavish hopes for fruitful cooperation in this exciting task.

Poor Mr. Donnelly – little did he know what future had in store for him.

54

SAVING ELIJAH

I spent that evening with my back turned to the big mirror in the bedroom I shared with Diana, holding a smaller mirror in my hand. Through it I watched my reflection in the big mirror, and learned how to open and close my wings. I knew instinctively how to do it, but as I was a beginner, my own wings tended to snap open like Daniel's had, that first time I had seen them. I sent the hanging lamp flying the first time I opened mine. It barely missed Diana's head and caused her to duck down in a corner of our room.

"Hey, watch out, Birdie!" she yelled.

"Sorry..." I made an apologetic face, "it isn't every day a girl gets her wings... not quite used to these yet."

I fluttered my new silvery extensions. I have to admit I was excited about the wings, even with Elijah awaiting his fate in the ward.

"You'd better not try flying without Daniel..." Diana shook her head and lifted the lamp to examine any damage to it. "You'd probably break the sound barrier with those if you tried flying now..."

It was absolutely fascinating to watch how I could will the buds of the wings out of my back, and with little more concentration unfurl them. They reacted to my will so quickly that most of the time they just shot out like a bullet. It took great concentration to be able to slow the process even a little.

The color was what I found most beautiful. I could stare at it endlessly – when I practiced my wing breathing, the wings expanded and withdrew ever so slightly. Though the movement of the wings was barely noticeable, the silver pulsing in the veins moved so fast it gave an almost glittering effect.

Diana looked at me admiring my wings. She shook her head, amused.

"If you keep up with that much longer, I swear I'll place you on top of the Christmas tree this year. Snap out of it. We have other things to do. Or I do, at least." She picked up a book on ancient Egypt - just one of the subject areas we had in common, which had brought us close together - and curled up on her bed. Soon she was immersed in her reading.

I had to admit she was right. I needed to focus on something else. I closed my wings, feeling the odd sensation of them finding their place somewhere inside my back, and pulled on a shirt. I decided I would go see Elijah on the ward. I did not know how my wings had healed his wings, but I was glad they had. I felt happy about that at least.

If only I'd realised how quickly my joy was going to vanish.

I knew from the moment I walked into the ward. Elijah was sitting slumped on his bed. He had withdrawn his wings. Daniel was standing by his bed, no wings visible either, his face ashen. Lilith, Grandma and a doctor were there too, and their stunned expressions on their faces said it all.

Elijah was infected.

He looked up, when I stepped into the room and the pain in his eyes was like a physical blow to my heart. I seemed to hear a sad faint musical note in my mind.

"Will you do it quickly, Daniel?" he whispered, "Now. Before I... change..."

"No!" Daniel said through gritted teeth, "I refuse to do it! I will not kill you!"

"But you must... As soon as I change, I will escape to the buffer zone and our secret about the gates will be out. The human we brought here cannot create a shadow whilst he's out of the buffer zone, so he can't leak the information. But I can, and I will, you know how the mind of a dark Nephilim works! I will have no loyalty to you anymore. And I have already lived for centuries, so I cannot complain about dying young."

Daniel withdrew away from Elijah and saw me. His eyes were so full of despair that tears welled into my eyes. I felt the same huge compassion I had felt when seeing Elijah lying on the bed with his broken wings.

"Isn't there anything that can be done?" I whispered, not really directing the words to anyone in particular.

The doctor shook his head.

"The infection will spread, it is like aids, or any other serious virus. Once you have it in your system, it will never leave. And there is no medication that could control it. The Nephilim have tried to find a cure for thousands of years, but there is none."

Daniel stormed out of the room, swinging the door open with such force it shattered into two pieces, each hanging from its own hinge.

"Elijah – we need to check your blood a second time to be sure..." the doctor approached him warily.

"What good will that do? Maybe I should simply commit suicide right now..." Elijah spat the words out, angrily. "That way no one has to take responsibility."

"If there is even the slightest chance..." Lilith pleaded. "Please, let us take another blood test."

Elijah extended his arm in an angry gesture, as though he was going to punch a hole in the air. The doctor reached for a needle. I felt dizzy. It was as if I was being drawn backwards deep into my mind, through a long and narrow tunnel. I was there, but suddenly I felt as if I was far away. Then the tunnel ended and in a split second my mind expanded to reach the whole universe. There was a low buzzing there, like a swarm of bees heard from a distance. It was a kind of speech, but without words.

"Oh..." Grandma looked suddenly in my direction and stepped back in haste, almost tripping over a chair.

The huge emotional turmoil in my heart erupted in a single feeling - compassion - and my wings shot out under their own will, without me telling them to. I looked at them up and around me with slight wonder, and felt a new, warm pulsing sensation in my chest. It was not my physical heart; it was more like a second pulse. I looked at Elijah, and suddenly found myself on my feet, gliding to his bedside again, as I had done when I healed his wings. The doctor withdrew hastily when I raised my hands to touch Elijah.

My hands had changed. Suddenly they, too, began to glow with the same silvery colour as my wings. I stared at my fingers with mild disbelief – they turned transparent, whitish, and I could see the same silver pulsing in the small veins as in my wings. I could see my bones as slight shadows inside the whiteness. Then the whiteness spread to my palms, hands and wrists. I felt the second pulse within me strongly; it was beating so hard it felt as though my skin would burst. It could surely not contain it... it got stronger and stronger, and then... my hands started to sing. There was no other way to describe the sound that emanated from them – it was a constant, slowly pulsing melody, soft and pure. My fingers started to form silver strings that slowly began to weave their way through the air, bridging the short distance between my hands and Elijah's. They resembled the strings leaving a Weaver's hands, only there was no mist around them. These strings came straight out of the tips of my fingers, as though my fingers themselves had stretched forward. Or as if my very veins had suddenly extended beyond my body...

"Impossible..." Lilith whispered.

I don't know how Daniel knew to come back when he did, but suddenly he was there too. He saw how the strings wrapped around Elijah's arms and in a quick thrust pierced the skin in several places, and penetrated into his veins. Elijah seemed unable to move, but his eyes were round with surprise and suddenly alert.

I was oddly detached from it all. I saw how Elijah's blood started pumping through the silver veins and into my body and I observed it as though I was floating inside my body, not quite present.

"No!" Daniel yelled and tried to grab me. "Dana! No!"

He fell to the ground as if he had run into an invisible force field. Elijah and I were wrapped in a silver cocoon of my wings that Daniel could not enter.

I do not recall everything clearly after this; I only remember Elijah's big eyes merged into mine. The power looking through my eyes held him still. Others told me later how they had seen Elijah's blood rise into my left hand, disappear from sight under my human skin, somewhere mid-arm, and then appear again at the root of my wings, rising in the veins as a dark red, which slowly turned to a lighter color. The blood returned to Elijah through my right hand. While this happened, Elijah was paralyzed, unable to move, as was I.

I felt the pain of his blood in my system. It was as though my own veins were fizzing with sparkling mineral water. I was experiencing searing pain, but it was bearable and not as bad as the pain in my back had been during my transformation into a Nephilim. In this state I only observed the sensation, but did not react to it. Despite its strength the pain was only an echo of a reality that seemed to be far away.

Then the second pulse eased, the singing sound became subdued, and the silver tentacles withdrew from Elijah, leaving tiny droplets of blood on his wrists and arms, glistening as if they had crushed diamonds in them. The several tiny cuts the tentacles had made closed almost immediately.

I fell unconscious onto the floor, my wings breathing so deeply they banged on the floor in spasms, making the bedside table fall and sending the chair next to the bed flying towards the glass wall, which shattered, something I only discovered afterwards. I cramped on the floor so hard at one point only my heels and head touched the floor. The... tentacles... withdrew back into my fingers, and my hands returned to normal again. Only then did my wings relax enough for others to touch me.

I woke up on the floor. A blue-winged angel had his arms and wings tightly wrapped around me. I did not remember anything; I did not even know my name or who I was. I only felt the uncontrollable twitching of my wings. Little pearls of sweat on the beautiful young angel's forehead revealed how much strength it took him to bind my wings and my hands.

I stared into his beautiful blue eyes for a while, wondering what magnificent color they were. Like the deep blue ocean – or the evening sky, with tiny golden speckles swimming in the blueness. My feet kept kicking the floor.

"Dana..." he repeated, "come back, Dana!"

Absentmindedly I wondered what a dana was.

"Leave us!" the blue-winged one said to the others, "you are in danger! She does not know who she is, and now she too may be infected."

I saw several people quickly leave the room, closing a door behind them that was in two pieces. How strange.

I turned my focus on the beautiful blue eyes again. Those little golden dots swam in the vastness of them, mesmerizing me. I felt a strong emotion, much stronger than anything I had ever felt. I did not know who I was, but what I did know, was that I had never felt anything this beautiful before. I raised my head and kissed him, wrapping my arms around his neck. How I managed to free them first is beyond me. They seemed to float free from his restraining hands as if we were immaterial beings.

His lips were hard at first, unresponsive. He tried to withdraw himself, but couldn't, my grip was so strong. I wondered why he tried to struggle, when it was so obvious he wanted it too, his eyes had revealed it to me. I looked into his eyes with wonder, not fighting him, but not letting go of him either.

We looked into each other's eyes for an eternity. And then he suddenly responded. He took my head between his hands and kissed me back, with hard, demanding lips.

I melted into him, and his touch turned gentler. His lips brushed mine and we wrapped around each other for a long time, our bodies matching totally. My wings relaxed inside his, finally, and he stroked them with a gentleness I did not know could ever exist. My wings answered his touch with a low, content hum.

I could feel his heat through my clothes, and I knew he felt my burning as well. I sensed the beat of his strong heart against my chest. My heart answered back, and then we seemed to only have one heart, so tuned in unison that they beat with the same rhythm. His hands were holding me tightly now, one stroking the small of my back, one behind my neck. I could sense them trembling as he tried to gain control of his emotions. I did not want to control my emotions or myself. I pressed myself even more tightly against him and would not let him draw away from me; I wanted him to remain forever like this, tightly pressed against the whole length of my body.

I closed my eyes, my cheek safely against his burning neck, and fell into a deep, happy slumber, still not knowing who I was.

55

CURSED BY A GOD

The words of Pythia haunted Ambrogio that night. He could not sleep after the celebrations. The warnings of the goddess he had met came to his mind.

Shortly before sunrise Ambrogio finally decided to head back to his lodgings in the village. He held the kithara in his hands, and walked slowly, admiring the waking world. Then he saw someone walking up the road leading from the town to the temple.

She did not notice him standing there in the shadows at first, and he had a few uninterrupted moments to admire her innocent beauty. She was still very young, barely a woman. She had long black hair and delicate eyebrows. Her lips were curved into a slight smile, reflecting something she was thinking.

Then she came close enough to see him, and stopped, scared.

He did not move, but smiled in a friendly way at her.

"You are out early," he said, "and I am out late."

Her eyes registered the kithara and the laurel wreath on his head - Ambrogio wore it every day, enjoying the reaction of people when they saw it. Suddenly she smiled, recognizing the winner of the Pythian musical games.

He lost his heart right there and then. He had never seen such a breathtaking smile. It transformed her face into something other-worldly in its beauty.

"Be still, my heart!" Ambrogio whispered, "a living goddess!"

She laughed aloud then - a shy, joyful laughter.

"Where are you headed at this hour?" he asked,

"To the temple," she answered and only now did he pay attention to the good fabric of her dress.

She was one of the priestesses, then. He bowed to her respectfully, and let her pass.

After this he was in no hurry to head back home. He suddenly found the village a pleasant place, and the people also wanted to hear him sing now. The elite families invited him to their houses to hear his beautiful voice, and even paid him for it.

And each morning he woke up early so he could meet the beautiful girl on the road to the temple.

He soon learned her name was Selene, and that she was the youngest sister of Pythia. It was her job to take care of her sister after she gave the oracle in a trance, and before she had quite come back to her senses. At other times she served the temple.

He had never met a kindred soul like her. It seemed they had known each other forever, and he did not dare to touch her in a disrespectful way.

After two weeks he finally kissed her, and her innocence was obvious. She withdrew quickly, with a beautiful blush on her cheeks.

Ambrogio noticed that someone at the temple had begun to pay attention to them. He was a nobleman, but Ambrogio did not know from where he came. He had stayed on at the temple after the end of the games.

Obviously he was well off, because he was in no hurry to leave the temple. He was very tall, as tall as the goddess had been, and Ambrogio often saw him looking at Selene with lust in his eyes. He warned Selene never to be alone with the man, as it seemed clear what he would do. Selene said no one would dare touch her, because she was a priestess, but Ambrogio doubted this man would care about such things.

Then Ambrogio received a message. His father had heard where his son resided, and sent him a letter ordering him to come home immediately. He threatened to disinherit Ambrogio if he did not comply.

Ambrogio decided it was time to act. He waited for Selene in the evening when she headed back to the town, as he had done for weeks now, for fear the tall nobleman would follow and attack her if he found her alone. Whilst they walked, Ambrogio asked Selene to marry him and to come back with him as his wife.

They were very much in love by that point, and she agreed.

They kissed, and he felt the passion in her body and was tempted to have his way with her. But he would not. Instead he asked her to walk to the temple at dawn the next day, as she had done these few weeks. He would wait for her on a specific turn of the road with his donkey, and what provisions he had gathered, so that they could leave together immediately.

Selene left him reluctantly, and he returned to the town alone.

Ambrogio remained standing where he was until she had disappeared. Only then did he notice someone standing under a tree, next to a boulder by the road.

It was the stranger - the nobleman from the temple. And seeing his eyes Ambrogio knew immediately that he was in trouble.

The man looked at him with an expression of contempt.

"She is not for you," he said in a cold voice, "and you will leave her alone."

It took all his courage, but Ambrogio managed an answer:

"She has promised herself to me, and we shall be married. You can go and find yourself another girl."

"No, it is you who will find another one. She will be mine."

His voice bore almost no emotion. Ambrogio had the unpleasant feeling he cared less about him than he would about an ant. He wondered what the man would do next.

What the nobleman did surprised him. He moved so fast Ambrogio did not have time to blink. He was suddenly in front of him, grabbing him by the shoulders, and he quickly spat into Ambrogio's eyes and face. A surprising amount of saliva wetted his face. He only had time to realize he was staring into strange golden eyes before it happened. Eyes similar to those of the goddess.

Then the man simply let go of him, and stepped back. Ambrogio did not understand. Why show contempt by only spitting into someone's face? He had expected a physical attack.

For a while nothing happened. Then came a slight tingling sensation. It intensified into a horrible burning in his eyes, and the skin on his face felt as if it had been torched. He screamed and fell to his knees, rubbing his eyes. He heard amused laughter.

"I will let you keep your worthless life - for now. If you stay away from the temple, I will allow you continue living. But a word of warning - I have now taken the light of the sun away from your life; from now on you can never let the sun caress your skin ever again. It will get worse over time; every moment will be torture when your skin is touched by light, until you shall be a creature of the shadows. And your precious maiden will not want to have anything to do with you anymore, because you will have turned into a monster. So you shall spend the rest of your wretched existence in darkness. No maiden will follow you there."

It took ages before Ambrogio managed to open his eyes. In disbelief he stared at his hands that were covered in blisters. He had no way to see his face, but he guessed it must look the same.

The tall stranger must have been a god... a god who had taken a liking to a beautiful mortal maiden, and would not accept any competition. And now he had cursed Ambrogio so that he could never walk under the sun any more. Ambrogio had no reason to doubt he had been telling the truth.

A horrible thought rose in his mind. The man must have been Apollo himself in disguise... That would explain his healthy, tall, muscular body. And his power to deny the light of the sun from a mortal. He was the god of light, after all.

What could he do now, having been cursed by a god?

"The curse. The Moon. The blood will run," he whispered to himself. The Pythia had known.

He looked up into the sky, water running from his burned eyes, its salt stinging his damaged skin. There was a strange smell of fruit around him. Much like the smell of ripe fruit around the goddess, but in him the sweet scent had turned bad. Rotting fruit.

The sun was setting. He could not meet Selene in the morning, because he could not face daylight any more. He would need to find a shelter - preferably a place where people would not see him.

And yet, in the midst of his horror, he felt his love for Selene becoming even stronger.

How could he ever win her now?

56

SILVER ANGEL

"You're quite an act to follow, I'll give you that!" Diana sat by my bedside on the sick ward.

"Oh God... I'll never be able to look him in the eye again!" I groaned, burying my face in my hands.

Diana laughed.

"Quite an interesting reaction, I'd say. It was so obvious from the moment you arrived, that you had a crush on him. And now that you have actually kissed him, you are embarrassed? Unbelievable... every female in this Centre would have given their right arm to be able to kiss Daniel! He is Hot! And I won quite a decent sum - we had a bet going on how long it would take you two to fall into each other's... erm, wings. Lets just say I won."

"Oh God!" I repeated and reburied my face in my hands, Diana's laughter ringing in my ears.

It had taken an hour or so before my memory returned. Unfortunately I discovered that the short-term amnesia had not erased our embrace from my mind. I was so totally embarrassed at my behavior that my face was as red as a fire truck.

Daniel had sat by my bedside until I got my wits back. I pretended to be utterly exhausted to make him leave. After that I had tried to think where on earth I could fly, so that I wouldn't have to face him again.

I withdrew my wings, and the doctors took many tubes of my blood to see whether Elijah's blood had infected me. Then they took even more blood from Elijah, who now seemed to be in amazingly good condition.

Our test results came back at the same time. I was not infected. And - neither was Elijah.

They couldn't keep Diana off the ward as soon as it was clear we were out of danger. She burst through the door with a wide grin and announced that everyone knew Daniel and I were an item.

"How, what... who...?"

"Well, Daniel kindly broke the door, if you remember, and the pieces hung on their hinges at an angle so that one could peek through quite conveniently," Diana declared, sending me to the depths of shame.

"You mean everyone saw..."

"Oh yes, honey. Or rather, just a few people. Elijah was most interested, but you cannot blame him, really. After all, you had just healed him. And the doctor, Lilith and Layla, who were concerned for your safety. So, a nice little audience there. And me too of course. Word travels fast."

When I finally dared to take my hands off my face, Lilith and Grandma had appeared.

"Darling girl!" Grandma ran to hug me so that my ribs cracked. "You healed Elijah!"

"Don't thank me... I have no idea how it happened," I said. "All I know is that I am seriously odd... what on earth was that all about?"

"That, my dear, is who you are. For the lack of a better term, let's call you a silver angel."

"Silver angel?"

"Well, Nephilim. Silver Nephilim. You are something that hasn't existed in thousands of years. We thought the silver gene had vanished from Nephilim blood - the Nephilim history books say that the dark Nephilim created a formidable Hunter who could find and destroy the

Silver Nephilim. At that time they were a family group, all related and probably staying in close proximity to one other. That was a mistake that cost them their lives.... The Hunter from the dark Nephilim found them, and killed them all, so they would not pose a threat to the power of the dark ones. Or so the dark Nephilim believed," Grandma explained.

"Silver gene - what is that, exactly?"

"Maybe I could explain it to you," Lilith began, then fell silent for a while, searching for words. "As you know, much of the Nephilim blood has been diluted in mixing with ordinary human blood. But there have remained some bloodlines that are purer than others. Mostly because it is very tiring to pretend to be human to your spouse - not to mention living hundreds of years longer. If you wanted to hide your true identity, you had to arrange your disappearance after a few years - people started to realise how young the Nephilim looked and wondered about it. So it was easier to find a spouse among your own kind than to hide your identity from ordinary humans."

Diana and Grandma were nodding in agreement behind Lilith's back.

"Well, Cain did his best to breed the ultimate Weaver, to find the Book of Watchers. What he did not take into account was that his own son would turn against his heritage and manage to escape, or that he would father a child without Cain knowing of it. Probably Cain would have given him a very high position, and could not understand why he chose not to take it. He could have been Cain's second in command. But as it turned out, that person is now Angel."

"So my father was dark?"

"We suspect he wasn't yet infected when you were conceived. Cain usually infected his children once they had developed into Nephilim, not before. It has to do with their ability to procreate. And your father had not been Nephilim for long," Lilith told me.

"Also your mother was the end of a very pure line of good Nephilim. Probably your genes are a unique mixture of two pure bloodlines, which both carried the recessive silver gene."

"And what does it do - this gene?"

I avoided their eyes and observed my fingers closely. They appeared to be completely ordinary now.

"It is the gene of a healer. You have the power to heal injured Nephilim, and humans too. One of the forms of healing is by blood exchange. Your wings are like a huge dialysis machine. The same skill that you use for weaving, is obviously connected to the healing part - you spin silver threads into the sick person's veins, suck out their blood, your wings clean the toxins from their blood and neutralize it, and then the silver threads return the purified blood back to the sick person's body," Lilith's hands drew imaginary wings in the air, and then pushed something down - probably she wanted to show how the blood returned to the sick person.

"So you could say I am a sort of a vampire after all..." I cringed, "or...or...a flying dialysis machine...I didn't realise that was what I was going to turn into!"

"Well, not really a vampire. Of course the sucking of blood part is true, in a way, but you don't drink it, you just clean it and give it back." Diana looked and sounded enthusiastic as she said this, as if she was describing some fantastic creative gift that I had, like being a concert pianist or world class opera singer or something.

"I bet your grandfather did not know that he had actually managed to breed the worst possible weapon against himself," Elijah said from the doorway.

"Weapon? I am no weapon!" I felt slightly hysterical, "and if you think I will ever meet him face to face, you can think again!"

"It may not be a choice for you to make," Daniel appeared from behind his brother, and I duly blushed again. "But he has no way of harming you now, other than killing you."

"Is that supposed to make her feel better?" Diana asked. "Such a great choice of words..."

"No. But I very much doubt Cain would want to kill the last offspring of his long line," Daniel said, "So Dana should be safe."

Safe was the last thing I felt at that moment.

57

CAIN AND ANGEL

"Well? Did you succeed in your task? Is she now ours - one with us?"

Cain's voice was emotionless. His high-backed, carved chair was set on a platform, below which thick oriental carpets muffled the steps of anyone approaching. He was the epitome of luxurious living and gave the overwhelming impression that this was his natural state.

Angel stood in front of him.

"I spat into her face, when I found an opening in Daniel's defenses." Angel's voice was respectful. "He wiped it away, but - with luck - some of my venom got into her eyes. We shall have to wait."

Cain observed his beautiful daughter, who showed no fear in front of him. He liked that.

"Luck? Ah, yes. A very human concept, my sweet. She is your niece. She belongs to this family. She will be one of us."

"Yes, Father. Of course, Father."

"She should be our pride and glory, not theirs. She is the ultimate Weaver. And why is that?"

Angel kept silent, because she knew that he wasn't really waiting for an answer.

"That is because I have used the bloodlines correctly." Cain paused before continuing. "I myself sired all the original foundation stock used in this breeding program in ancient times, and before that, I spent years in devoted study, examining the family history and skills of every Nephilim before permitting them to breed."

Angel waited, watching him warily, taking advantage of his apparent disinterest in her to wonder how this - project - might affect her own future. She did not even dare to think what had gone wrong after those ancient times, why Cain's direct offspring could no longer breed.

He continued, speaking softly, as if almost to himself. "I know she is the strongest Weaver yet. She must be ours!"

Angel had heard this talk many times over, but she knew well enough not to show any disrespect towards the subject or his commitment to it. She nodded in agreement and stood still in attentive silence.

"I have heard disturbing information, Father," she finally said when Cain had fallen silent for a time. It would have been dangerous to interrupt the Patriarch.

"Yes?" Cain's eyes seemed to grow sharper as he focussed on her intently.

"Two Nephilim came to the city of Immortals and stole one person, together with his shadow."

Cain's eyes narrowed.

"Why?"

"We suspect it was because the person who was taken is our librarian. He knows about our search. This would suggest the secret...is no longer secret."

Cain rose to his feet. He was very tall, and very handsome. His body was that of a young man, and his skin had a pale glow. If you looked closely enough, you could see tiny wrinkles on it, which revealed that in fact he was no longer young. But no-one looked too closely at Cain. Ever. You kept a respectful distance, and you were wise to be afraid of him. He was staring intently at Angel when he next spoke.

"We know of the - unfortunate incident - of the shadow who talked to one of their Hunters."

"Layla," the name came from Angel's lips without thinking and she had to concentrate on not showing her fear whilst Cain continued to look at her. She had interrupted him. She bent her head in shame, and after a while Cain spoke again.

"Yes. Layla. She is one of their most experienced Hunters, so she would have taken the words of the shadow seriously. So they have heard of the Book of Watchers. But they do not know what it is. Does this librarian know? Do we know?"

"No. No one knows what the book actually is - there are no known references to it anywhere in any ancient text, as far as we - or anyone else - knows. There was once a book called the Book of Messengers, but we have destroyed every copy of it after searching for any clues within it - it was said that in one of them the key was hidden. We never found it in any volume we discovered. The last copy was kept in a nunnery in England. Our men went in search of it. They did not find it, as they were interrupted, but the whole library burned down because one of the nuns dropped an oil lamp. That was fortunate for us even though we lost that book, because now that copy, or any other, can never reveal the secret to anyone."

"What does this librarian know? Which one of our librarians was it?"

"The one we brought from London. He knows we are searching for a trail of clues leading to the Book of Watchers. At worst he knows the likely starting point, because that was his field of research. But nothing more, of this I am certain. I have spoken to him on many occasions, asking what he has learned. If a mortal lies to me, I'll know."

Cain closed his eyes and stood like a mighty statue. Slowly he opened his magnificent wings, which were much like his daughter's, only much darker and more impressive. Angel knew he revealed his wings inside only when he was angry. They reached up and out as though they would fill the whole world.

"Ah yes, I do remember our little librarian now. An inconsequential fellow, though much devoted to you, my pet. I greatly suspect he had found the starting point, or was very near finding it, and was too afraid to reveal his information. Most likely he thought he would be useless to us after that. Probably he was right too... Thus we can draw the conclusion that they will try to go to that starting point, using our Weaver. We might be able to catch her there... Why did I not force the librarian to tell me what he knew, the last time I met him? Or why didn't I ask you to do so? A missed opportunity..."

Angel waited until she was certain Cain had finished talking.

"May I suggest something, Father?"

Cain's cold eyes turned back to his daughter. He enjoyed looking at her beauty. He had considered taking her as his wife, but as he was careful about the strength of his bloodline, he did not want to risk it with inbreeding. Shame, though, as she was as shining an example of a perfect Nephilim as any other he had created. Her only fault was she had not managed to produce children yet with the Nephilim he had chosen for her. But she was not alone in that. The lack of reproduction in his children was Cain's greatest disappointment.

Angel enjoyed the appreciative look of her father and looked him straight in the eye. She had learned ages before that even the slightest sign of fear could throw anyone out of Cain's favor.

"If we catch her, she will fight us. And Daniel will do all he can to stop us."

"Of course."

"And that is simply a waste of time. Why fight them now? Why not let them do the work for us? We know the librarian will be of great assistance to them. Why stop him from helping them? Let's follow them, and if they find the Book of Watchers, then we'll attack with all we've got. There are so many of us, and so few of them, that we should win easily..."

"So you mean we should lull them into false feeling of security, and let them do the work for us? Daughter, you make me proud."

Angel bowed her head.

"And if I managed to get my venom into her, then she will come to us anyway somewhere along the path of their search. Even if they haven't found the book by then, we'll get all the information she already has, and can continue on our own. If she doesn't transform, we shall get the information we want anyway, but indirectly. We have our spies."

Cain smiled. His teeth were perfect, white, and straight. His beautiful smile mesmerized his victims, giving him ample time to attack them. Most of his human servants were his own victims, who now happily served him, and spread terror in the human world in their transformed state.

Cain never doubted his power. There was no need to. What he wanted, he obtained. His war to turn all the Nephilim into his own kind was progressing well. It would take time to achieve his vision, but eventually they would draw them all, and this unnecessary and unpleasant - friction - between the two groups of Nephilim would vanish. They would be one, at last, the way they should be.

He could wait for that day; he already had, for years too many to count. One day, soon, they would have all of humankind as their cattle and servants, without any need to hide their true form. This world would belong to the Nephilim, as it should have done from the beginning of human history. The thought made Cain feel content.

"Daniel will be ours soon, too, if all goes well." He looked at Angel. "You may keep him, if you still wish," he added in an unexpected moment of generosity.

Angel bowed her head, but not before Cain had seen the lust in her eyes. Well, who was he to blame her! Despite Daniel breaking the word of his father, he and Angel were perfect for each other – strong, young, and beautiful. Their offspring would be a valuable asset to Cain. He felt almost elated at the thought. Daniel's bloodline was something he had wanted to get his hands on for a long time. It would be worth a try to see if he could manage to produce an heir to Cain.

"We managed to get Elijah," Angel dropped the good news almost casually. "One of us fought him when they stole the librarian, and bit him - the venom went straight into him."

"What? Really?" Cain clapped his hands and laughed out loud. "This is perfect news! You could have him as your spouse instead. Why wait for Daniel when we already have his brother with such similar genes? Maybe you'll finally succeed in making beautiful Nephilim children for me!"

Angel clearly had not expected this. She looked shocked. She had wanted Daniel only. Cain enjoyed her disappointment, and the fact she could not protest. To him it did not matter. Either one of the brothers was good for his plans, and Angel must try to breed with anyone he ordered. Yes, she would do it and finally produce another heir to his line.

"Go now." Cain waved his hand and Angel turned and walked out.

58

HADES

Ambrogio remembered the path that led from Delphi to a sacred Corynthian cave. It was situated higher up on the same mountain, a long walk from the temple of Delphi. It was a place where since time immemorial local people had gone to seek answers from the gods, with no need for an oracle. They used dice with the names of the gods to ask for advice.

He would need to go there, to be in a place where the sun would not reach him. But how could he leave a message for Selene? He had no writing equipment with him.

He looked around. Maybe he could use small stones to write a message on the path for Selene... He knew that Selene knew how to read - a rare thing for a woman.

So he reached for palm-sized stones with his blistered hands, wondering how many stones he would need to write in big enough letters "Selene, I will be back. Wait for me."

Where should he write it so Selene would see it? If he wrote it across the road, any people and donkeys passing by before Selene arrived would walk all over the text. If he wrote it on the roadside, she might not see it, if she was looking the other way.

But he had to try. He decided to write the text on the side of the road, following the direction of the road. Maybe that way his text would remain untouched. He would also make an arrow out of stones to lead her gaze to the text.

Darkness fell quickly after the sun had disappeared, and soon he could see nothing. He had to feel the shape of the letters with his fingers, and desperately grope in the dark for small stones. He did not dare to stop his efforts, to think too deeply about what had just happened to him. His mind could not comprehend that the gods actually walked among ordinary people, and that he had raised the wrath of one by falling in love with a maiden so beautiful even a god lusted after her.

Then, suddenly, he heard the sound of something moving behind him. He froze. There were wolves in the mountains.

"Who is Selene?" a slightly curious male voice asked. A pleasant, strong, scary voice.

Ambrogio was so on edge he yelled aloud and fell to the ground, totally startled. He had not heard anyone approach. Whoever was standing behind him must have appeared out of thin air.

He turned around, but could barely see a human figure in the darkness.

"How do you know about Selene?" he managed to ask.

"You have written her name on the ground with stones," the voice observed.

Ambrogio turned to see the ground, and saw nothing. He could not even see his own toes.

"But you cannot possibly see it!" he said.

"Oh but I can," the man sounded amused.

Ambrogio just stood there.

"You smell strange. Has one of us attacked you?" the man asked

Ambrogio took a step back, messing up his carefully laid stones while doing so. The odd metallic scent of rotting fruit wafted in the air as he moved.

"Are you a god too? Why are you all here now? First the beautiful naiad, then Apollo, and now you... Who are you? Are you here to curse me too?"

"The beautiful naiad... What did she look like?" the voice asked, now sounding genuinely curious.

"She was beautiful. Very tall, she had golden hair to her waist, golden eyes. She carried something made of silver. Maybe a weapon. She gave me a kithara so I could take part in the Pythian games. And I won..." Suddenly, winning the contest felt like nothing and Ambrogio fell silent.

A sharp intake of breath from the darkness.

"Indeed? And what curse are you talking about? Why were you attacked?"

"I love a maiden of the temple, Selene. She is the sister of Pythia. But Apollo has fallen in love with her too, and does not want her to leave, and he cursed me so that I can never enter daylight again. We were supposed to leave tomorrow morning with my donkey, Selene and myself. She agreed to be my wife... And now I can never see her again..."

A long silence. The man did not move, and for a while Ambrogio thought he was alone again.

"What if I help you? In return for a favour," his voice suddenly pierced the darkness.

"How could you help me? Why would you help me? Who are you?"

The man did not answer, but instead something strange happened to the darkness around him. It began to glow. First a faint glow, in a semi-circle around the man. Then two huge black, yet glowing wings appeared around the figure, making his form visible as a shadow against the glow. Golden light coursed through the wings like blood in veins, and the same golden light seemed to shine from his eyes too. Ambrogio fell to his knees at the sight.

"You are Hades... the god of the underworld!" he shouted, understanding why this god moved in the dark and had black wings. He fell to his face on the road only to exclaim in pain and rise up again when his cheek and hands touched the ground.

Ambrogio thought he heard amused laughter. Probably it was

because of his wriggling on the ground. How silly mortal men must look in the eyes of gods...

"I can offer you a safe place where the sun does not touch you, where your skin can heal from its blisters, and where you can live your days out in comfort. You may bring your Selene there too."

Ambrogio fell onto his face again, disregarding the burning of his skin on his hands and face.

"How can I ever thank you enough, o mighty Hades?"

"Come. I will show you," the god said. "You need to take my hand."

Ambrogio hesitantly held out his hand, and the god took it into his. The god's skin was burning hot and the heat on the blisters on Ambrogio's skin made him almost faint with pain. The world around began to fade, and turned into a grey mist. Only then Ambrogio understood that if he was holding the hand of Hades, the place where he was taking him, had to be the afterlife - the joyless place where souls were doomed to reminisce about their former life in the world of sunshine for all eternity.

So he was dead now. He would never see Selene again except in his memories, not until she died too and they could meet in the afterlife. And he had heard the afterlife was a dreary place, where lovers did not recognize each other anymore, where a mother would not remember her own child.

Mute with despair he hardly looked around him, not even caring about the pain in his hand. The god did not seem to be moving his mighty wings, but there was a feeling of moving forwards nevertheless. They were in thick grey mist. It was very dark at first, but then the mist began to get lighter. A landscape began to form. And it was nothing like Ambrogio had expected the world of the dead to be.

First of all - there was light. It seemed to come from every direction simultaneously, but you did not see the sun anywhere.

Secondly - there were buildings. And people, who quickly bowed down when they saw Hades with his wings stretched. And then there were odd shadowy, distorted creatures, which did the same. Ambrogio had never seen the likes of them. They had to be some kind of demons.

"Is this your kingdom, oh mighty Hades?" Ambrogio asked with a shaking voice.

"This is where my servants live and are not touched by time," the god said. "Or the sun, for that matter," he added, after a quick look at Ambrogio's face.

He let go of Ambrogio's hand and strode forward. Ambrogio wondered why he did not use his huge black wings, but maybe they were for the human world. He did keep them open, though, but moved forward with his long legs.

He had to run to keep up with the black-winged god. He could not stop staring at the amazing wings and almost tripped on his own feet because of it. They were nothing like a bird's. They were formed like wings, sort of. But they were transparent, and looked almost... liquid. The golden blood pulsed in the see-through veins, up on the back of the wings, and down at the front. From the wings emanated a clear hum.

Hades entered a big palace-like building and strode up the steps two at a time to enter. Ambrogio trotted after him.

They walked over the stone floor of the entrance hall, and into a smaller room with a few chairs.

"Wait here," Hades said.

Ambrogio bowed deeply, and the god disappeared through a doorway. He did not dare to sit - chairs were for the nobility.

When the god came back, he had hidden his wings and Ambrogio stole a short look at his face.

He was handsome. Very tall, dark-haired, and golden-eyed like the goddess had been.

"This is for you," the god said and gave him a bow and a quiver full of odd-looking arrows.

Ambrogio took the weapons, which surely had to be magical, and waited.

"You are to kill the silver winged ones with these," the god said.

Ambrogio did not understand. Which creature had silver wings?

"Swans, oh Hades?" he hesitantly asked.

"Yes, you can call them that. But I will explain better: they are my kind. Human in form, and they have wings. Silver wings. I do not want to leave even one of them alive in this world."

Ambrogio bowed down, not daring to ask why.

"How do I find them, oh Hades?" he asked.

"With this," the god said and extended his hand.

A silver... something - not like anything Ambrogio had seen before. It was a curving piece of metal, with leather straps attached to its ends.

"You sing with this and they come to you. When they do, you are to kill them with your arrows. One arrow for each silver winged one, so do not miss! Forty five arrows in all, and no more can be made. These arrows kill them, no matter where they hit. And you are to take their blood, and write to me with it that you have killed one of them. You can then write another note to your girl."

"But the sun, oh god..." Ambrogio's voice trailed off.

"You shall move by night. And I shall have you brought back here every sunrise. Before that you shall have to present the body of the silver one to the beautiful goddess you have met."

Ambrogio looked at the bow in his hands, and the metal piece with straps. To kill the likes of Hades, and then give the bodies to the goddess?

"These silver ones are a threat to us, they can destroy us. They are our enemies, willing to destroy the balance of the gods, and of the human world as a result," Hades said to Ambrogio. "This is not work that I would give to anyone lightly. But you told me you can sing, and this instrument will draw them near. And these 'swans' are a gift to the goddess you have already met. She has something that belongs to me."

The silver... something she had been holding came to Ambrogio's mind.

"Her silver weapon," Hades confirmed. "She has stolen it from me, and I want it back. Your mission is to win her trust with the bodies of the silver ones she too hates, and when you get the chance, you will steal her weapon and bring it here. When you do, you and Selene can come here and live under my protection. No other god will dare to hurt you here, in my domain."

Ambrogio bowed, wordless again.

"Here..." Hades had parchment and a quill in his hands; "You will write your messages with these, using the blood of the "swans". You will discover that you cannot fool me with any other kind of blood. And if you fail..."

His voice was suddenly hard and menacing, when he towered over the much shorter Ambrogio.

"If you fail in this, I shall make sure your Selene suffers. I shall give her to Apollo myself. He is not known for being gentle with the girls he fancies."

Ambrogio could only stand with a bowed head, too scared to say anything.

"And if you plan to escape, know that I can follow your scent easily, and find you no matter where you go. If, however, you succeed, you shall be my loyal servant and well rewarded for it. You shall have this palace, or any other you'd like to live in."

Ambrogio swallowed. Something moved past him. He turned and saw one of the demons looking at him. It looked like half man, half... predator of some kind. Its eyes were dull, lifeless, its movements dreamlike, slow. He could see through it.

"Look into its eyes," Hades commanded.

Ambrogio obeyed, still holding the bow and arrow tightly.

Something strange happened. The more he looked into the creature's eyes, the more alive it seemed to become. And soon it was as if something opened in his mind and part of him could... see through its eyes. Not as a clear visual experience, but like a picture that appeared in his thoughts. He stepped back and felt a tug in his chest.

"This is your shadow now. He will help you to hunt, and you can see through his eyes and hear through his ears. If you try to escape, he is to come to me and tell me where you are. Because he can also see through your eyes and hear through your ears," Hades said.

Ambrogio's limbs began to shake.

"Oh come now," Hades laughed, "once you get used to your shadow, you will see it is a great help to you in hunting. It moves much more quietly than you ever do, because it is not quite solid. If you wish to make him more solid, concentrate and give him more of your own power. If you wish to make him more transparent, draw your power back. You'll learn it soon enough."

Ambrogio took a step backwards, and the shadow followed him like a dog, mimicking slightly his movements. If he lifted his hand, the hand of the shadow twitched. If he took a step, the shadow did so too. Still, it moved on its own as well, and Ambrogio felt a slight tug at his chest when it did so.

"And now it is time. It is midnight in the human world, and you need to hunt one of the silver ones for me before the night is over. Come, I shall take you there."

Hades extended his hand and Ambrogio had no other option but to take it. The afterworld began to darken around them, first into dull grey mist, and then it was pitch black, and they stepped out into the starry night of the human world.

59

SHADOWS AT THE GATE

The faint light of the night sky was visible through the window. Diana slept on her back, snoring lightly, her long curly hair spread across the pillow, but I could not sleep.

I stood by the window, staring at the eternal stars of the north, the Ikhemu-sek – the stars around the North Star, which was the star Thuban in the constellation of Draco in ancient times. The Egyptians used to call them the undying stars, because they never set during the night. Before their worship turned from stars to the sun, they believed the souls of their pharaohs travelled to the northern stars after death. That was probably why the pyramids had these tiny tunnels, stellar shafts, towards the north sky, reaching upwards from the burial chamber. The soul of the pharaoh could use the tunnels to travel to the night sky.

I never understood why I was so interested in ancient Egypt. But ever since I was a small child I had dreamed about the place and I wrote the dreams down. Much to my surprise many of the names and places in the dreams turned out to have actually existed. I never told my mother this, knowing how she would react, but I did begin to wonder at an early age whether there was truth in reincarnation stories.

It was very quiet, even though I knew the Centre was functioning all around me, operating in secret alongside a luxurious spa. It was heavily guarded, and within its safe walls researchers worked, Time Walker groups were trained – and now, prisoners were kept. All because of the war between the good and the bad Nephilim. I felt like a character in a fantasy novel.

I tried to wrap my mind around all the things that had happened to me. A few weeks ago I thought I was a normal sixteen-year-old girl. And now I knew I was Nephilim – I had wings, and I could heal people. I still did not think it was me – the energy seemed to come from an unknown source I could not yet identify with.

I turned my hands in the faint light of the stars. They looked perfectly normal now, and I could not see any special spots from which the odd strings of light and color could come out. There were no tiny holes anywhere, just smooth, soft skin.

Who was I? What was I? Where had the Watchers come from? Was the story true that they took human wives and created my kind? Were they an alien species from space? Was I an alien, then? I sure felt like one...

Standing there, looking into the night, I felt very lonely. I could never again be an ordinary human and the only ones of my kind around were Daniel and Elijah. And there were so many dangerous, dark Nephilim out there in the world. The likes of Angel. Even if I did manage to keep safe, I would lose all my loved ones and live on long after them. Somehow I was not able to feel joy about being given such a long life span. What if I grew tired of living? What if everything began to feel like meaningless, endless repetition?

I lowered my hands and looked at the stars again. Were the dark Nephilim flying there even now? How about the good ones? Where did they live? What was the council of Nephilim I had been told about?

And then there was Daniel.

I felt almost physical pain when I thought of him – my soul and my whole body longed for him, and all my defenses were down – I had read about what falling in love felt like, but I had never expected an emotion this strong: as if I had a hole in my chest where my heart used to be and a throbbing, raw, delicious and painful emotion was drawing me in like a moth to a flame. At the heart of that flame was Daniel. And I did not even try to stop myself from burning up in it.

After healing Elijah, when I had lost the remembrance of who I was, I had been pure emotion and my love for Daniel had revealed itself in its full force. Maybe I had driven him away from me for good with my behavior? Yet he had answered to my emotions in a way that made my knees buckle when I thought of it. The crushes I had had at school felt like pitiful jokes compared to this.

What was becoming of my life?

The stars did not answer. I leaned my cheek on the window frame. It felt cool against my hot skin. It was strange – I could feel that my body temperature was oddly high, but I did not feel ill. I wondered how high my temperature actually was – it felt somewhat similar to the time I had influenza. It was definitely higher, but obviously not high enough to cause coagulation in my body.

My senses were getting sharper too. Even though the window was closed, I could hear the little sounds the animals outside made. The rustlings of mice, the calls of the night birds – and if I listened closely, it was as though I heard a slight background sound to all of this. It seemed to come from above, as if the stars themselves were singing. And oddly enough this... song for the lack of a better word... seemed to resonate back from Diana. Still, this impression was so slight I probably imagined it.

Also the night did not look dark to me anymore. It was as though I was looking at it through some sort of infrared binoculars. I could see that living things gave off a faint glow – the branches of the trees against the black sky were clearly visible to me. The light of the stars was much stronger than it had been before – and the whole sky had more stars than I had ever seen. The lights of a nearby city formed a strong semi-circle on the horizon to the left.

I put my fingertips on the window glass and traced a distant tree's outline on it. My fingers began to glow faintly, and the silver strings began to form as a mist on the tips of the fingers. Curious, I let them appear, and kept drawing the tree onto the glass.

I began to feel slight vertigo, but did not stop doodling the tree onto the window. Then I felt that I was being sucked into a tunnel again, this time forward and suddenly I was outside. I was not standing safely on the ground – oh no. I was standing on a tree branch, and the Centre was across the field. Quickly I hugged the trunk before falling down.

Wow. I had transferred myself to the same tree I had been doodling on the window! It had to be so. The threads seemed to connect into things I was pointing at! I hugged the tree trunk and felt a bit giddy. What if I tried again?

I looked at the scenery. Then I started to trace the outline of the roof of the Centre. It took a while for the strings to appear from my fingers, but I learned they seemed to respond to thought just like my wings. When I concentrated on the thought of flowing energy through my hands, they appeared. They did not shoot out with the same speed as the first time, so maybe I had learned to control them a bit.

I kept tracing the roof and chimneys of the Centre, and after a few strokes the strings began to set to the form of the roof in the air – much as though I had been drawing with a white pen onto a dark paper. I began to feel the same vertigo as before, and suddenly the world seemed to run past me while I stayed in place.

I was on the roof. I understood that maybe this was not the wisest place to be – it was steep, and slippery. I grabbed the chimney next to me to stabilize myself.

Better get off the roof, I decided. For a while, I considered trying flying down, but that would probably not be a very good idea. Firstly: I did not know how to fly – or even if I instinctively did, with my uncontrolled weaving skills I might end up anywhere. And secondly: I had no idea how visible my wings would be in the middle of the night. The last thing I wanted was to draw attention to myself. Who knew how many spa guests were looking out from their windows with their cell phone cameras at the ready. Thankfully the chimney was between me and the windows of the spa.

I looked across to the other side of the wrought iron gate and decided I'd go there. Only I did not want to draw the gate with my fingers – I might end up on top of it, and the spikes were veritable lances. I decided to go to the little hill behind the gate and started drawing its gently sloping side with my hands. Its outline soon appeared as a silvery line in the air, and in a second I was standing on top of the hill, behind the bushes facing the gate.

Only I wasn't alone. When I looked at the bushes at the foot of the hill, I could clearly see three shadows there. With my sharpened senses they might as well have been decorated with Christmas lights. Now that I saw easily in the dark, I also saw the lack of light more clearly. And these shadows were like holes in the lighter fabric of the world. I could even see clearly the cord that left their bodies from their neck and vanished into the air after a few inches. Their lifeline to their masters.

This was the third time that I'd seen shadows (or fourth, if I counted the short video), and I understood full well where the stories of werewolves came from. These crouching figures reminded me of wolves. Still they had a definite human quality about them – there were clearly waists and hands. Two had snouts like a wolf or a dog, and one had a head that looked completely human.

They had not noticed me and I wanted it to stay that way. Luckily the wind blew from the direction of the shadows, towards me. I stood absolutely still, so as not to draw attention to myself, and only moving one finger I began to draw the outline of the balcony on the facade of the Center. I knew it led to the hall on the upper floor right next to Lilith's office.

I was there in an instant and tried to open the door. Closed, of course. I had seen a light on Lilith's window, and so I tried to stay in the shade by the doorway and knocked on the balcony door.

Someone with ears just as keen as mine opened the door. I looked into Elijah's eyes.

"Quick!" I pushed him inside, stepped out of the balcony, and slammed the door shut.

"Wow! What happened?" Elijah observed me with an amused look in his bright eyes. "You were smoking out there and someone saw you?"

"Shadows. Three of them."

"Shadows? Here?" Elijah turned serious in an instant. "Where, exactly?"

"On the other side of the gate. They are hiding in the bushes at the foot of the hill on the far side of the gate."

"And how did you happen to see them?" Elijah's eyebrow rose in exactly the same way as Daniel's did.

I waved my fingers and he noticed the silver threads flowing weightlessly in the air and nodded in understanding.

"Oh, I see. You wove out threads and... but you'd better draw those back in before you end up somewhere without intending to..."

"Oh, right."

I concentrated for a while and imagined withdrawing my energy to the center of my chest. My fingers stung a little, and then the silver threads vanished.

Elijah was already knocking on Lilith's door. She opened it as if she had been standing behind it, and I began to wonder if she ever slept. She was always in her study. Reggie was also in the room, by a side table laden with books, with a faraway look in his eyes.

"Three shadows, outside the gate," Elijah said.

Lilith walked to the window and closed the curtains. Then she picked up her cell phone.

"Layla? There are three shadows outside the gate... Where exactly?" she asked Elijah.

"In the bushes at the foot of the hill, opposite to the gate," I replied.

Slight surprise in Lilith's eyes revealed she had not expected me to answer, but she did not ask anything.

"You heard that? Ok. Come here, and we'll do what needs to be done."

In two minutes Grandma was there.

"We should kill them now." Grandma voiced her opinion without hesitation.

"I'm not sure..." Lilith hesitated. "Perhaps we shouldn't..."

"Explain." Grandma looked like a horse chomping on the bit - I could see she wanted to go right after the shadows.

"Maybe we should invite Daniel in here first." Lilith picked up her mobile phone.

Somehow I found it rather hilarious that angels needed cell phones. Or half-angels, if you will.

Daniel came through the door almost immediately. Lilith told him about the shadows.

"Should we kill them or not?" she asked, "If we do, they will know that we know they have found us. If we leave them there, we may have more time to prepare, if they are planning an attack."

Elijah and Daniel stood side by side, equally tall and equally handsome. One dark-haired, the other blonde, both with slightly wavy hair, broad shoulders and lean bodies. I only had eyes for Daniel.

"Wise words," Daniel said, adding "Truth is, I can only wonder how it took them so long to find us."

"They may have found this place when they were chasing me and Dana from the university," Grandma tapped her finger to her cheek. "Reggie did open the car window for a while, and with the shadows' keen sense of smell one of them must have caught our trail."

Daniel nodded, and did not seem angry with this.

"And because I rescued Dana from Angel, she knows that I will be where Dana is too. Yes, I suspect they know about us now. We must warn everyone against leaving this building. The guards are up as we speak because we have always been on alert. I still think they do not know about the gate, or we would have seen an attack by now."

Daniel thought for a while.

"We shall have to leave, Layla, Dana, myself and Elijah. We shall show ourselves to them in some distant location and draw their attention there. And this place will stay as quiet as possible, except for the spa."

Everyone else was of the same opinion. I had no opinion. If I could leave with Daniel, I would go anywhere.

"But first, we'll go and have a little discussion with our prisoner from the city of Immortals." Daniel opened the door and stepped out.

"We need some information, and I am not sure he will talk to ordinary people. Come, Elijah."

They turned, and we all followed them as if his invitation extended to us too. We went out of Lilith's office and down the stairs to the hall, where Lilith went to speak to the guards. We continued down another flight of steps, and then to the floor below the ground, to the prison level.

60

MR. DONNELLY'S PAST

Mr. Donnelly's face was the picture of confusion as he glanced around his prison once again.

This welcoming room did not resemble in the slightest the miserable cells under the council hall in the City of Immortals. In comparison, this prison was a luxury apartment, save for the fact that it was windowless.

He had a bedroom with a decent - no, a very comfortable - bed and coverings, a living room with a sofa and also a little kitchen. He had a fridge with beverages, and a book shelf full of novels. And as for the bathroom – that was the height of luxury. A real bath tub, a machine for shaving, and a water closet. And a shower. This was so novel to him that he spent a lot of time turning it on and off and adjusting the heat of the water, even chuckling to himself when the spray splashed the tiled walls or floor.

The strangest thing was the treadmill in the corner of the room. He had figured out how it worked by standing on it and pressing "start". Thankfully the machine had been set to such a low speed he managed to stay on board when it began to move. Mr. Donnelly liked it; his thoughts had always been keenest when he walked and that was something he used to do all day along the long corridors of the library in the City of Immortals.

Looking back, he realised that he had been incredibly naive to accept what his masters had said at face value. This was not at all what he had been told to expect if the "others" caught anyone from the City of Immortals. According to his previous masters, he should have been in chains in a wet cellar with rats, eating mouldy bread. If they gave their prisoners food at all, that was – starving them was something they were all told to expect if caught by the others. The meals he had been served on a tray here were excellent and nutritious and he was coming to like the mincemeat steak in a bun, with salad and cheese and mayonnaise on it and chips - they called them "fries" - on the side.

He sat on the sofa, immersed in the book called "The Fellowship of the Ring" that he'd started a few days earlier. He knew there were two more volumes to come and was looking forward to continuing the adventure. Somehow the world in the book resembled the world of the Immortals. The wizards and elves could make things happen by uttering the right words, just as they could in the City of the Immortals, using the material of the buffer zone. After thousands of years the Immortals had created a fantastic world - in every sense of the word - on their own level.

He thought back to that fateful first meeting. When he had learned the true nature of his benefactors, he had fainted. For an analytical mind like his it was not easy to take in the huge wings they opened up in his front of him one day.

Cain and Evelyn Harper had revealed that they were not siblings, but father and daughter. Their youthful appearance meant that their true relationship to each other would not have been believable in the human world, hence their pretence to be brother and sister.

It was flattering that they had revealed their secret to him. He had been a religious person all his life, and this proof of the existence of angels had, at first, made him thank the Lord and begin to read his Bible with renewed enthusiasm in the evenings. The only thing that left him wondering was that angels could have children. Surely that required certain... behaviour...not usually connected with angels.

Then they had told him they came from another world, and he believed that too. Of course they did. When they said they could take him there, and he could live there and never die, he almost fainted with joy. He sold his book shop. It meant nothing to him now, when he thought of the immense knowledge and time that would be available to him in the City. He paid all his debts just to keep his good name (even though his debtors could never have found him again), packed his bags and arrived at the Harper house on the day of departure. And what a departure...

His arrival in the land of the Immortals, holding the hot hand of the beautiful Evelyn Harper, was indelibly etched on his memory.

A whole new world opened up in front of him, right at the edge of ordinary reality. There were fields, mountains, lakes, rivers... and the City....it was like no earthly city and yet it sometimes reminded him of places that he knew. Different ages were reflected in the blend of architecture, from medieval towers and turrets, to modern city houses. He soon learned that this was because the inhabitants were from different ages of human history, and as they did not die, it was natural that they should create the appearance of their own age and place in their immediate surroundings.

At first he viewed everything in a state of wonder. He was given a position as a librarian, and enjoyed his research into ancient myths. Books were brought to the library all the time, so he never lacked work or resources.

Of course he noticed the odd-looking shadowy figures on the streets of the city. He asked about these, and was told they were the servants of the Immortals. And the weirdest thing was – people living in the city could create them themselves!

Mr. Donnelly was eager to learn, and with the help of his library assistant, he learned to "mould the clay". Wonderingly, using only his mind, he slowly learned to create physical things from the material he simply scooped from the ground.

He was told that this whole world of theirs consisted of mouldable energy. And that the solid structures stayed solid only because of the attention that was paid to them. If an object was created, and people lost interest in it, it slowly disintegrated and disappeared. Renewed focus to it brought it back into a more solid form. To begin with, Mr Donnelly found this endlessly fascinating.

Now Mr. Donnelly understood those houses and statues in the city that had become shadowy. Their forms had faded. Their colours were not as bright, and sometimes you could almost see through them.

Mr. Donnelly was given an unoccupied house and he spent many hours wondering how simply looking at it made it rebuild itself.

He started with the walls, obviously, and after he had been looking at them with keen attention for a few days, they had definitely become solid. He then continued with the floors, the door, the roof, the windows... until he finally had a very cosy little house of his own, only a block from the huge library building.

He did not know who had originally created the house and, as he was not yet skilled enough to form one out of nothing, he was happy to "renovate" an already existing "ghost house". That's what these uninhabited, fading houses were called and sometimes the shadows took possession of them too. People stopped occupying houses once the shadows had arrived. You could see the shades moving about inside, through the semi-transparent grey walls. Shadows within shadows.

There were real workshops in the City that specialised in creating the creatures that they simply called "the shadows". Mr. Donnelly was repelled by the forms they produced, which were all monstrous, like wraiths or werewolves. He wondered aloud why they could not be pretty maidens, and it was only later that he began to understand. It was because of the energy level of this world. You could make magnificent things, but because the city was situated at the lowest level of energy around the human world – the level where thought energy was heaviest. Everything was somehow tainted by that energy. No matter how hard you tried to create a human looking shadow, it would change into a twisted form on its own.

He watched what was happening with a growing sense of unease. Perhaps it was due to the inexperience of the people using energy to create things. He found that logical – his own feeble attempts did not create much beauty either. If he formed an apple, it looked appealing for a short while, but the next day it was wrinkly and had lost its color. This was the start of his disillusionment with the City and its inhabitants.

The most alarming things were the angels that he began to see every once in a while. At first their beauty overjoyed him, but soon learned they were not at all the angels of his imagination or belief. He heard the whispered term "Nephilim", and learned what it meant. These were not angels at all, but abominations. He found an old book that described the offspring of angels and men as terrifying creatures – without empathy and without any positive emotions. They showed no remorse when they killed people – and worse, they drank their blood, turning them into horrible monsters of the darkness. Half human, half shadow, these Nephililm-created creatures needed to drink human blood to survive - the blood seemed to return some of their humanness for a while. This they sought constantly, living in a state of endless misery, unable to satisfy their appetites. He learned from what he read that there were other kinds of Nephilim, good ones, but he had never seen them - of course, why would they come to a place like the City of Immortals, with its superficial attraction and underlying decay and shadows?

And if any of the Immortals should fall from grace with the dark Nephilim there was rumoured to be an even lower level of energy, where these unfortunates lived in their transformed state. Their domain there was so low they could move straight into the human world to kill and to drink blood. Mr Donnelly viewed it as the gutters and sewers of the energy world and tried not to let it into his imagination at all.

In time he learned even more – how the Immortals transferred part of their own energy into the shadows, so they could control them on their journeys. One task of the shadows was to be sent to the human world to steal things the Immortals did not have the skills or the desire to make.

One day Mr. Donnelly learned to do this himself. He found that, with intense concentration he could connect with a ready-made shadow figure, and make it move. He started to see with its eyes, and hear with its ears in a curious way. It was a strange feeling – as though he was in two locations at the same time.

"Do not make too close a connection with your shadow." That's what they warned him. If he didn't follow the advice not to bond too closely, he risked transforming into his shadow and his physical body would die. Mr Donnelly had seen a few such people in the City of Immortals and every time he had found the sight deeply disturbing.

Mr. Donnelly never really learned how to feel comfortable with, or successful at, dividing his consciousness between two places at once. If he sent his shadow on an errand, he had to lie down or at least not do anything that required concentration afterwards. He used his shadow only to steal books, and withdrew from it as soon as it came back. Once the connection had been made, he could never detach himself completely from it, though. The only way to do that was to kill the shadow. And soft-hearted Mr Donnelly, who had always captured spiders under a drinking glass in order to release them, could not bear to think of killing a shadow, however monstrous it was.

As the human years passed Mr. Donnelly realised he was not getting much older. Not as much as should be expected, anyway. He was advised that he could use his shadow to steal energy too, which would invigorate him, and replace the slowly depleting energies of his own physical body. If he ran out of energy, he would die; but here, that would be a matter of hundreds of human years hence even if he did not steal energy from others. Nonetheless, this world was close enough to the human world that time did have an effect, however slowly, unless action was taken to prevent it. Mr. Donnelly could not bring himself to use his shadow to steal the life-force of living people. He considered it as abhorrent as drinking their blood. And - after all, was not a few hundred years of life enough?

He barricaded himself in the library and, wisely, pleased Evelyn and Cain whenever they came for a visit. As time passed, he began to see them for what they really were and cursed himself when he realised how deeply he had been taken in by their glamour. In time he learned what they were really looking for – the mysterious Book of Watchers. There were clues to it, he learned, but these clues were well hidden and no one knew where. No-one had succeeded in finding any so far. This is why they had brought him to the city of Immortals.

The task was complicated by the fact that they were sure the clues had to be found in a certain order. The correct starting point had to be found in order to reveal the next step on the path.

Mr. Donnelly had once sneaked down to the lower level of which he'd heard rumours. There was a gateway to it in the castle where the Council sat. Inhabitants of the City who broke its rules were sent straight from the Council chambers down there. As the library was connected to the Council building, no one stopped him or commented on the fact he was loitering about with books and scrolls in his hands.

Slipping through the gateway, he had entered what looked like an underground world. It was dark and misty, and full of vague and horrible figures. He had only moved a few steps inside the gate, but his presence drew the attention of creatures that chilled his blood.

Then he recognised one of them – it was his own library assistant who had slept on his job, and as a result tipped over a candle that had caused some books to burn. He had been taken away by the Council guards and then - simply vanished. Now he was there, still identifiable in this horribly pale, grey, and ferocious being. His mouth had changed – he had grown some kind of a snout and had a very unpleasant row of sharp teeth. His appearance had a new familiarity about it though and Mr. Donnelly realized with shock that he had been forced to become one with his shadow permanently.

This is surely the end, thought Mr Donnelly, cursing himself. These creatures would tear him apart. Suddenly his old assistant spoke in a snarling voice.

"Back! Get back, all of you!" He snapped his jaw and raked out his upper limbs at the other encroaching shadows, revealing sharp claws at the end of each finger instead of nails. The other shadows stepped back reluctantly as he growled and slavered ferociously at them. Then he turned to Mr Donnelly and said, in a voice that was angry and yet filled with anguish, "Leave! Now! Never return. This is the place of the doomed. Next time - even I might view you as food!"

Mr. Donnelly turned and for the first time in years, ran.

His one thought now was to escape, knowing for certain he had made a horrible mistake in falling for the superficial charms of Evelyn and Cain and in coming to the City of the Immortals. He began studying anything he could find about the world he was living in, trying to discover some hint about possible gates back into the human world, ones he could use without the need to go to the shadow world underneath the City.

His hosts were greatly pleased by his endless hours of work, not realising he was using many of them to try to find a means of escape. Mr Donnelly kept a tight control on his emotions and imagination and practised for hours so that he would reveal nothing in his face or movements. When he finally realised that it was his shadow that anchored him to the world of the Immortals, preventing him from getting back to the human world, he fell into depression. He still could not bring himself to destroy it, although he knew he must in order to achieve his freedom. After a few days he understood his work was all he had left now, and he threw himself into dedicated, almost feverish research.

In his new enthusiasm for research he had indeed found a clue as to where the path to the Book of Watchers would start, but he held the information closely to himself, fearing that if he told anyone about it, he'd make himself redundant. And if they didn't need him any more....and then he had found Merit's notebook.

They had become impatient, the Nephilim, and one day Cain appeared in the library, where Mr. Donnelly now held the position of librarian in chief.

"Still no results, my esteemed librarian?" Cain's voice was cool and indifferent. He had been standing so close to Mr. Donnelly that sweat had started to trickle from the scholar's neck because of Cain's body heat. With one burning finger Cain had simply drawn a line on Mr. Donnelly's neck, and he understood the gesture for what it was - a threat.

He would have to reveal his findings.

The night after this, he had sat in his study clearly marked with the sign "head librarian". He sat with his shadow, having lost all hope. And miraculously, hope came.

Suddenly there were two young men with him in the room. The door was locked, and yet they appeared standing behind Mr. Donnelly. He realised that they were Nephilim and almost fainted with fear. Cain must have sent them to take him away...

Then he noticed the difference – these ones had bright blue eyes, not yellow. He had learned about them in his studies – they were the other kind of Nephilim, the unspoiled ones.

So he had not objected at all, when they grabbed him and bore him off. He lost consciousness along the way, and when he came to, he was in the hallway of an unfamiliar building.

Everything felt more solid than it ever had in the world of the Immortals. Mr Donnelly realised with a relief that almost brought tears to his eyes that he was back in the human world!

The dark haired Nephilim was lying on the floor, his wings horribly torn and bleeding. Mr Donnelly was escorted away, and he felt a sudden snap of energy that hurt his stomach, and knew his shadow was dead, and he had all his own energies back for himself.

He could have cried for joy. Finally, he was back among the living. His shadow was dead and could no longer pull him back into the dreaded world of Immortals. He was free.

61

NEPHILIM SEARCHING

I don't know what I expected to see, but it wasn't this. My idea of Immortals was much colored by fantasy literature and films. I'd have expected an Immortal to be young, muscular, and wearing something that looked like a Roman soldier's outfit.

Instead I saw a thin, bald man in his fifties. He was wearing a worn jacket with leather patches at the elbows. His trousers were straight, and his old-fashioned shoes were well polished. It looked as though he had been to an English pub with old friends, to eat shepherd's pie and perhaps have one pint.

He had round spectacles on his nose, and a kind and tired look in his eyes.

When we entered the room, he immediately closed the book he was reading, put it carefully on the table, folded his glasses and put them in his vest pocket, and rose to his feet, facing us. I had a glance at the book. It was the first volume of Lord of the Rings, I noticed, one of my childhood favorites.

"Good - ah - morning," the man bowed slightly and I realised that he'd probably lost all sense of time. "William Donnelly at your service."

I could see Daniel had not expected this either. He had probably planned on scaring the man into talking, but now it would have been out of place.

"Good day, Mr. Donnelly," he answered politely instead. "Do you know where you are?"

"I do not, but it is enough to know I am back in the ordinary world. I cannot begin to thank you enough for it. But why you chose to save me, I can't imagine. May I ask what this is about? And - will you let me stay here? I don't need to go back to the Immortals?" he asked, clearly nervous.

Lilith stepped forward.

"You are our prisoner, but indeed we have no intention of returning you to the buffer zone."

Mr. Donnelly smiled, and then surprised us all by starting to cry. We stood there, not knowing how to react to this sudden show of emotions. Then Grandma moved gracefully forward, put her hand around Mr. Donnelly's shoulders and led him back to the sofa.

"There, sit down Mr. Donnelly, and we'll have a talk."

"Indeed, indeed... I do apologize.. I am simply so happy to be free again!"

What an odd thing to say - to consider oneself to be free in a prison.

With shaking hands Mr. Donnelly dipped his fingers into the pocket of his vest and took out a pristine clean handkerchief, dropping his glasses onto his lap. He dabbed his eyes with the handkerchief, and took a deep breath.

"You were held there without your consent?" Lilith asked.

"Yes. But it is not so straightforward, I'm afraid. I did enter the world of the Immortals willingly, you see."

Mr. Donnelly told us his story, beginning with meeting the apparently delightful Miss Evelyn Harper, and ending with being snatched away by Daniel and Elijah.

"Evelyn... Angel, more likely," I heard Elijah mutter to Daniel.

"But how can it be that you are so well healed, young man?" Mr. Donnelly directed his words at Elijah. "You were severely injured the last time I saw you. I was afraid you would die, the attack on you was so fierce."

He swallowed, still clearly shocked by the fight he had witnessed in the buffer zone.

"We have very good doctors," Lilith hastened to say.

"Yes, maybe the Nephilim heal faster," Mr. Donnelly mused as if he was making a mental note for a research subject. ""I see there are three of you here. All of the unspoiled kind. How happy I am to see you. I thought the dark Nephilim had killed you all. I am aware of their war against you - it has continued since antiquity."

So Mr. Donnelly had immediately marked me out as one of the Nephilim too.

"They do try," Daniel commented dryly, "but no, they have not killed us all."

"Tell us what you know of the Book of Watchers," Lilith interrupted. "Why do they want to find it?"

Mr. Donnelly collected his thoughts for a while.

"They are very interested in their history, the dark Nephilim. There is some ancient truth in that book they need to find, or so they said to me. They did not tell me what it was, but I think I have worked it out on my own."

"Yes?" Lilith was careful not to reveal anything, and managed to sound only mildly curious.

"I may look like a quiet scholar, but I keep my ears and eyes open, and I have the mind of a researcher, even if I do say so myself. I overheard Evelyn and Cain talking to each other once about a Book of Messengers, and how all the copies needed to be destroyed so that no one else would find their way to the Book of Watchers."

Reggie stepped forward, eagerly. Lilith's gesture made him stop. Mr. Donnelly clearly recognised a fellow scholar (they looked quite alike, with the only difference between them being Reggie's bushy hair and eyebrows, and tall frame), and the rest of his words were directed at Reggie.

"I had heard of the Book of Messengers while I was still living in

London. And as it happened, while studying angelology, I had come across the very book. It was located in a small nunnery in Kent. They were very proud of their little library, and had this ancient manuscript in their possession. It took me years of correspondence with the good mother superior, but finally, one Christmas, I was invited to see the book."

"Really?" Reggie could no longer stay quiet. "What was it like?"

"Quite small. And I have to say, the oldest, and most magnificent book I have ever seen. The very first book, in book form as we know it, that was ever created! It was beautiful!"

Mr. Donnelly forgot himself in his memories for a while, looking very much like Reggie in the same state of mind, smiling to himself, and sighing.

"And...?" Lilith prompted.

"Oh, yes, quite, begging your pardon... There was an illustration there, of a red-winged angel. He was holding a scroll, and on it was drawn something I could not quite get. The words revealed it though, it said: The scroll of iyrin, the path to their abode."

"Ah! Yes!" Reggie beamed.

"So I came to understand that the Book of Watchers is not a book at all, but a map that leads them to wherever they came from. I never revealed to them that I knew what the book was. I tried to remain as inconspicuous as possible, and not draw any unnecessary attention to myself."

Lilith nodded.

"Indeed. It is a map. But what of the clues to it?"

"Now that's the interesting part. It seems there is a chain of clues; each needed to understand the next one. If you find a clue, but don't have the previous one in your hands, you don't know in which order you should proceed."

"Hands? You mean they are physical things?" Reggie inquired.

"So I gather," Mr. Donnell nodded. He looked slightly embarrassed and it was a few seconds before he continued, "My shadow was very good at stealing books. That may be because our shadows do reflect our personalities, even if they are twisted in their form. I often sent it to the human world to steal books, as I was not given permission to go there myself. I never understood why it could enter the world, but I could not. It was one of the curiosities of my existence there. I never sent the shadow to steal the Book of Messengers, though. It was too fragile, and shadows have no respect for fragile things... If the book had been damaged in the process..."

Reggie was already sitting by Mr. Donnelly on the sofa.

"So what are these clues?"

"One of the books that my shadow stole was in another monastery, in Germany. This book was from the early middle ages and had been brought to the monastery from Italy. It was safely locked inside a wooden box, mind you, so the shadow could not harm it. This was probably because of the beautiful bejeweled bees on its cover... It was written in Latin, and there was a reference there to the Trail of Angels. It sounded like a spiritual path for a believer to follow, to achieve enlightenment, but I found the wording a bit strange."

"What did it say?"

"Well, in modern language - as some of you may not understand Latin - it said that if the reader were to follow the Trail of Angels, they would find their way to the Creators. And that's the odd part. Plural. Not Creator, not God, but Creators."

"I see..." Daniel looked at Elijah, who nodded.

"Yes?" Mr. Donnelly looked at them eagerly.

"It's obvious, of course!" Reggie jumped to his feet and literally took a few excited hops around the room on his long legs. "Of course! This only confirms what we had already concluded."

"Do tell," Mr. Donnelly pressed his round spectacles even more firmly onto his nose.

"The Book of Watchers is a map to the abode of the Watchers. And what you just told us reveals that the Trail of Angels will take one directly to them. They might even be the same thing under a different name. Cain's Nephilim want to find the physical location of the ancient Watchers, the forefathers of the Nephilim! The very same Watchers, who sired the Nephilim in the first place, and according to legend were thrown into eternal damnation as a result."

"The actual Angels?" Grandma asked, "the forefathers of the Nephilim?"

"Yes, or Watchers, as they are called. What they are, we don't know. But they were here to help human kind evolve. They revealed too much information to human kind too soon, and married human women, producing the Nephilim. For this their power was taken from them, and they were imprisoned for all time. Religious literature the world over contains hints about them."

"So what are they?" I finally opened my mouth and it was Elijah who answered.

"Some kind of beings who had possession of a higher intelligence than humankind. Why they were here to observe humans, we don't know. Why it was dangerous to give knowledge to humans, we don't know either. Religious writings may be corrupted efforts to understand what happened. As religious writings often are - they are expressions of man's limited understanding attempting to explain something that is way above their current state of intelligence. Trying to explain the inexplicable."

"Are we some sort of aliens, then?" I asked.

"We don't know what we are. We appeared in human history thousands of years back, and when we go in search of information about our ancestry, all we have to go by are limited sources in old religious documents. People have twisted these writings to their own ends throughout history, taking away some parts and adding others. Mostly, it was done to fit whatever suited those in power. So we do not know the truth," Daniel explained. "What we do know for certain, however, is that we have been here for thousands of years, and as such should have a right to be here. But we cannot reveal ourselves to ordinary people. That would cause havoc. Imagine what would happen to world religions, if we began to walk - or fly - about, showing our wings."

I couldn't imagine, really.

"It would throw the whole world into turmoil. It is best that ordinary people don't see the other reality. Nephilim, vampires, shadows... if their basic beliefs of the structure of reality are shaken too much, it may lead to wars, and destruction. The balance of the world is a delicate thing," Daniel explained. "Fear is the emotion that tips it."

That I could understand. If my Mom were ever to see a shadow, or my angel wings, she would surely lose her mind.

"So... The Trail of Angels is what they are looking for. Do they have any idea where it might begin?" Lilith asked Mr. Donnelly.

He shook his head.

"No, as far as they know it could be anywhere. And the first clue is what they need to follow that trail in the right order."

"So... we would need to figure out what the first clue is..." Reggie rubbed his chin with his fingers, deep in thought.

"Well, not quite. I think I have - ah - figured - it out already," Mr. Donnelly announced.

62

THE CLUE

We stared at Mr. Donnelly, surprised.

"You know where the path starts?" Daniel finally put the question into words.

"I cannot say I know where the path starts, but I have found a description about the location of the first clue, which will tell where the Trail of Angels begins. A clue to the clues, if you will."

"Let's hear it, then." Elijah moved towards him.

Mr. Donnelly's hands twitched nervously.

"Patience, Elijah." Lilith raised her hand as if to push Elijah back. "Remember that our guest does not have good experiences of the Nephilim."

Elijah muttered apologies and stepped back.

"It was the oddest thing, the way I found this clue... It was a shadow that told me about it not many days ago."

"A shadow?" Grandma's voice revealed she could not believe her ears.

"Yes, a shadow. But not like the shadows of the city of Immortals. This one was more like a... ghost. Someone who had really died."

"A ghost?"

"Yes, the ghost of a young woman," Mr. Donnelly nodded, "I was sitting in my study, doing some... translation work... when she materialized in my room. I have to say that in my old life I would have been scared out of my wits, but after a while one gets used to all sorts of creatures in the city of the Immortals. I knew she was not an ordinary shadow. She was beautiful, not at all like the twisted shadows on the City."

He searched for words and drew something into the air with his hands.

"She was visible only from waist up, and tried to speak, but I could not hear her voice. I do not know who she was, maybe someone who had died in the city, and was now bound to it forever..."

Lilith wondered about this.

"You know, no one is bound forever anywhere after their death, and can move on. If they are stuck, they can be advised further. But not all want to move forward."

"Quite. The murderers, criminals and such," Mr. Donnelly nodded, "I have seen them. I went to the lowest level under the Council hall... and I have seen some in the City as well. They cling to their old environments, and try to get the attention of anyone or anything nearby, so that they will pay attention to them and so feed them energy. That makes them more solid."

"So people die in the City as well?" Grandma asked, "but not likely of old age?"

"They do die, as people live there in their physical bodies. Physical bodies can be killed," Mr. Donnelly replied and shivered. Obviously he had some unpleasant memories of the subject.

"But this young lady did not have the feeling of desperation about her, as had the other ghosts I had seen. She was quite pleasant to look at. So I looked at her, to give her more substance with my attention, but it did not work. That is when I understood she must come from the upper levels of existence and my lower energies were not needed for her to materialize."

"You mean her energies were higher?"

"Yes, higher than mine, which is why my energies did not have an effect on her - do you understand? The ones who die in the City share the energy of the ones still living there. They are of the same level, if you will. A bit hard to explain, but it's similar to creating things from the material of the City with your thoughts."

"Yes, I think we understand," Grandma assured him. "It seems you had a visitor from the higher levels then. What did she do? Why did she come?"

"She understood I did not hear what she said, so she beckoned me to follow. She led me out of my study, and into the library. She took me to a part of the library I had not visited much, which was the Coptic section."

"You had ancient Coptic manuscripts?" Reggie got excited. "How old?"

"Very old. She took me to a shelf and pointed at an old script. I took it with me. Then she took me to a more modern part of the library, and pointed at one of the most recent acquisitions. I took that too.

"The Coptic manuscript was a fragment only, but it talked of one of their churches in a most peculiar way. A Christian hermit had written it, and it was found in the deserts of Egypt, being preserved by the dry climate. It said that in the city of the Sun a church was built, inside a heathen tomb. An Angel appeared and told him that the key to a path to the Creators was hidden in the church - notice the plural form - and then disappeared. The angel had three pairs of wings. The portrait of the Angel was painted there in the church as a reminder for the congregation of the heavenly visit."

Reggie and I spoke at the same time.

"Panhesy!"

"Pan... what?" Grandma looked like we were talking utter nonsense.

"Panhesy! It is the tomb of Panhesy!" Reggie shouted.

"The chief servitor of the Aten in the city of Akhetaten!" I continued, "In Christian times the Copts built a shrine in his tomb."

"And there, at the semi-dome of the apse, are the remains of a painting. What kind of creature, we do not know, as the central part of the painting has been destroyed. But the wings are still there!" Reggie's hands were flying through the air when he first drew the apse into the air, and then used his hands as wings, and stuck them first high up in the air, then a bit lower, and finally at his sides, in depiction of three pairs of wings. "Anyone have a computer with them?"

No one had.

"To the office." Lilith rose to her feet. "Mr. Donnelly can come too."

When we came to the hall, the gate had been hidden. A big painting of the Centre, obviously made around the time the building had been built, now hung on the wall covering it. Gentlemen and ladies on horseback, wearing old-fashioned clothing, were riding in front of the building. No wonder the gate had been surrounded by a decorated frame. It just looked like any big old painting now.

Mr. Donnelly looked around him in awe.

"We had nothing of the sort in our City." He pointed at the lights, and almost wrung his neck trying to figure out what the computers were at the central desk.

The City sure sounded like an old fashioned place. That led me into complicated thoughts about time and technology and questions that I couldn't answer, so I concentrated again on what was actually happening.

Lilith wrote her password and opened her computer screen.

"Go on, Reggie, you show us," she gave way to Reggie who eagerly reached for the mouse.

"Let's see... The Amarna Project... Recent Projects... Survey.... Christian Settlements...."

We waited when he searched and scrolled.

"Here!"

Everyone tried to see the screen simultaneously, and in the ensuing congestion I ended up right next to Daniel. Our arms touched and I felt my knees melt.

I tried to concentrate. I looked at the picture. "Six-winged creature in the semi-dome of the apse" the text said.

And there they were. Six wings. Red wings, just like in the Book of

Messengers. The center of the painting had been destroyed, and only the wings on their blue surface remained.

"Indeed!" Mr. Donnelly clapped his hands. "These are the very wings that were shown in the modern book! And the book also told that Panhesy lived in a city where the king worshipped the light of the sun, a long time before the birth of Christ. So he was a heathen, then."

"Akhetaten," Reggie and I said simultaneously.

"The clue to the path leading to the Book of Watchers is in the tomb of Panhesy in Amarna," Reggie clarified.

"How did the Copts know the king of Amarna worshipped the Sun?" Grandma asked. "They lived 1400 years apart in time, after all."

"Panhesy's tomb is full of well-preserved reliefs about Akhenaten worshipping the sun, and the sun's rays ending in little hands, which bless the king and the royal family," Reggie explained. "Not hard to draw a conclusion."

"Panhesy, Second prophet of the Lord of the Two Lands Nefer-kheprure-Waenre. That would be Akhenaten." Lilith searched the net, "Overseer of the double granary of the Aten in Akhetaten, Overseer of cattle of the Aten."

"That's where we'll be going, then," Daniel nodded.

I did not dare to move, because for a fleeting moment he stroked my fingers with his. And then it was over, and I stood there, with my heart beating like a drum, not sure if he had done it intentionally or it was just an accident.

I hoped not and told myself to concentrate on what was happening in front of me.

"Can you tell us anything more about the ghost you saw?" Grandma asked. "What did she look like?"

"She was quite young, and very attractive and pleasant looking. Her hair was cut to her shoulders, and was brown in color... And she was wearing a necklace - a white little cat's head with a pink bow on its head. Something a child would wear, really..."

I knew who had hair like that, and who had been buried with a Hello Kitty necklace around her neck.

"It was Kitty!" I whispered.

Grandma smiled. I noticed Daniel and Elijah briefly exchanging glances.

"I told you she wanted to contact you! And now it seems she is involved with our mission of finding the Book of Watchers!"

I could not help tears of joy filling my eyes. Kitty was still around.

63

MEETING KITTY

We left the following morning. Grandma sped away first in her red sports car, alone. Another hunter, Tinky, a short Asian girl, spied on the shadows, and returned to let us know that one of the shadows had followed Grandma. Two had remained in the bushes.

I had not been able to sleep for the most of the rest of the night. Instead I had spent hours standing at the window of our room. Diana had stayed up with me.

"What does the world look like to you now? I believe the senses of the Nephilim are different from ours?"

I explained to her how I could see more light in the darkest night, so that even in total darkness I could see my way - how beautiful the starry skies looked now that there was double the amount of stars I was used to seeing. How I could see little animals moving in the grass and forests, and spot anyone approaching from far away because now their body heat was visible to me.

"Can you see ghosts now?" Diana wanted to know.

"I have no idea. I haven't seen any that I know of. Wouldn't mind seeing Kitty, though..."

"I don't think you can call Kitty a ghost. As I understand it, ghosts are souls that have not left this earthly plane, but have remained here, wandering near places that are important to them. Kitty, on the other hand, has travelled to higher levels after her death, as she should have done. She's not a ghost."

"But she showed herself to Mr. Donnelly."

"Showed, yes, by her own free will. Think about it. Surely you don't think she haunts the land of the Immortals because she can't leave? And she had trouble expressing herself in the lower buffer zone level, if she could not make her voice heard. That means she doesn't belong there."

Diana had a point there. I remembered my own dream where Kitty had warned me about the shadow under my window and I could not hear her voice.

"There's just one thing I don't get," Diana said, "Kitty's death. Everyone seems to think they tried to kill you, and hit Kitty accidentally. If you are such a valuable Nephilim to the dark side, why on earth would they want to kill you?"

I shook my head.

"No, I'm sure they killed Kitty on purpose, to catch me. And then they planted the medium's visiting card in my path, trying to lure me to her shop so Angel could kidnap me."

"That makes sense," Diana admitted, "and is yet more proof of how little they value human life, the dark Nephilim. And how dangerously clever and manipulative they are."

Diana helped me pack a small bag. I still had no makeup, and was getting accustomed to it already. Turning into a Nephilim had given my skin quite a nice glow, and I did not mind my blonde eyebrows now. Before I had looked eternally surprised, without clearly defined eyebrows, and used a lot of time creating them each morning with a brow pencil. Now, however, they were still very light in color, but they seemed to define my face more than before. Also my blue eyes had become more intense in color. I had no golden dots in them like Daniel, though.

The Centre had its own costumiers and Diana took me there because my growth spurt had made all my previous clothes too small.. I had been once before to the costume department, and it was a real hall full of clothes rails.

"Different teams travel to different times and need clothing that enable them to immerse themselves in the times they are visiting."

"You must have quite a few Time Walker teams, if the amount of clothing is anything to go by." I swirled around. "You could clothe a small town with these!"

"We sure do, because certain teams specialize in certain times for obvious reasons – it takes them years even to learn the language and habits of a particular time, and even with the buffer zone stopping people from getting older, it is a lot of work. If a team stays in a specific time for a longer period they try to buy clothes made in that time and bring these back to our modern times. They can then be used as models in creating new dresses of the age."

Diana took a medieval-looking dress from one of the racks.

"This looks like a genuine dress - look how coarse the material is. This seems to be a dress for poorer folks."

I touched the fabric and had to agree not many people in today's world would put it on voluntarily.

"And now, let's get you something more fitting to wear, you look rather hilarious in those jeans - not that your ankles aren't pretty, but still..." Diana grinned at my skinny legs exposed by the short trousers.

Luckily there were other tall people as well, so I managed to get something to wear.

"You certainly won't fit into the past," Diana shook her head, looking at me after I had my extremities properly covered with clothes again, "you are way too tall now. Women were much shorter then."

"Thanks. Now I feel like a clumsy giraffe."

"You're very welcome," Diana smiled, "but – with your skills on weaving and moving to and from the buffer zone, you are perfect for short pop-ins. Very handy on occasions, if we need stealth-attacks. Not to mention what an effect your silver wings will have, if necessary."

I was certain Diana saw me in her mind's eye me scaring some bishop in the middle ages about to burn some unfortunate midwife for witchcraft. I had learned to know her enough by now to know she felt very strongly about injustice against those who could not defend themselves - probably because of her own slave background.

We met in Lilith's office after sunrise. Daniel, Elijah and I.

"We shall go somewhere, where you can practice your skills," Daniel spoke first. "And after that you need to be introduced to the Council of the Nephilim. It is the custom so all will learn to know you."

"And as you need to prove your parents we are visiting Egypt, that's where we're going. We'll follow you after a few days," Lilith declared, "to take photos. Layla has already sent them some, without you in them, and they want to see photos of you too."

I couldn't help but smile happily.

"Egypt? Great!"

Lilith laughed.

"Something good in all of this, then. Hold Daniel's arm. You have your bag? Good. Have a safe journey!"

Daniel offered me his arm, but did not look at me in the eye. I didn't wonder, not after I had attacked him like that after the healing-episode.

We did not step anywhere. I only felt Daniel's energies intensify, and Lilith's office melted away from around us. Then we were in the mist of the buffer zone, but did not continue in it. Instead we shot right through it. There was a clear sensation of moving upwards. We went higher and higher, and different landscapes appeared and disappeared. I guessed we went as high as we could, to a level where the shadows or dark Nephilim could not follow us.

We did not begin our descent immediately. Instead we stopped on the ledge of a mountain overlooking a green valley. Light came from everywhere, and it was so beautiful I could have stayed there forever. I did not ask why we had stopped. I only enjoyed the scenery.

"Beautiful...makes you wish you would never have to leave," I sighed

"Not even we can do that." Elijah breathed in the air deeply, "or we would have to be dead. This is the highest we can reach while still in our physical bodies."

Daniel did not speak. I did not dare to let go of his arm for fear of falling down to some lower level, but I felt uncomfortable for his lack of attention, even when I was holding his arm. He was keeping his distance from me again.

Something appeared on the ledge next to us. A foggy shape which became more solid. I recognized her even before she was fully formed.

"Kitty!" I almost screamed, half laughing, half crying.

"Dana!" she yelled, and now, finally, I could hear her loud and clear. How I had missed that voice!

I wanted to run to her, hug her, but I did not know if I could let go of Daniel's arm.

"Go on." Daniel pushed my arm gently away from his.

I yelled proper teenager style and ran to Kitty. We hugged each other, and cried and screamed and jumped up and down with joy. I heard laughter, and realised both the Nephilim brothers were laughing out loud at us.

"How are you?" Kitty asked. "I see you have become something else entirely! You have wings now! Without having to die to get them!" she continued in her typical humorous style.

I looked at my back and to my amazement my wings had opened without me noticing - perhaps caused by the energies of the highest level of the buffer zone. They were shining with such light it blinded me too.

"No, it turns out I am a Nephilim. Half human, half angel. Or a descendant of them."

"I know... and I never even suspected my best friend was an angel. I didn't remember!" Kitty laughed.

That last sentence didn't make any sense to me. She was so real, so totally solid in form. Only she looked much happier and healthier than she had ever been in physical life, even though she had been perfectly healthy then. She had a real... glow to her skin, like she was lit from within.

"But you are involved in all of this – we heard you had visited the land of Immortals, and showed their librarian the clue to the path. To find the Book of Watchers. How did you know about it? And how did

Daniel and Elijah know to get that very librarian out of the City of Immortals?"

Kitty got serious.

"Yes. We all know about the search for the Book of the Watchers on this side. Some of us have followed your quest, and agree with you in that the dark Nephilim want to wake up the Watchers, and gain control over human kind. Your world will fall into chaos, if that happens."

"But surely you already know where the Watchers are. Can't you simply tell us? Why all this tedious finding a path and clues and all that... and why would the Watchers even help the dark Nephilim?"

"We don't know. And maybe they wouldn't. That is forbidden information for us as well. Maybe there is knowledge of this in the upper levels of existence, but not in ours. Also the situation that led to the punishment of the Watchers is hidden in such ancient history we don't know how to go that far back to see what happened. Things change constantly and we are completely different energy beings now. Everything expands and you cannot bring back what was, because the world and people have... expanded past those ancient events. It would be very difficult for us in the energy worlds to stay in the past energies even if we did manage to reach that far. Maybe those in physical bodies could, because they are still of denser energies. And most of us don't even want to get involved. Most souls don't feel like connecting to the human world any more, and are not much interested in its history now that they have reached the higher levels of existence. But those who wish to intervene have their free will to do that, within the laws of the spirit world. Which makes it a bit difficult, because most people cannot perceive us in denser energy levels, and communicating is difficult."

I could understand that.

"We observe the goings-on of the City of Immortals and found Mr. Donnelly because of his job, and because he was not like the others. He did not want to harm anyone, and he wanted to get out. And the dark Nephilim would not let him go visit the ordinary world at all. They had tied him to the city of Immortals through his shadow much more strongly than was usual. His shadow was literally instructed not to let him go to the physical world at all. Obviously he was too valuable to them. So I told Daniel and Elijah where to find him, when they told me they were looking for a librarian in the city of Immortals. I knew he had to be important in all of this... Whatever this is. Otherwise the dark Nephilim would not have kept him prisoner," Kitty then explained.

"So you three have met for this purpose?" I asked.

"Yes. We planned this together," Elijah answered, "Kitty was hovering all over the place, eager to contact you after her death, so it was easy for us to talk to her and plan the whole thing in the buffer zone."

"But why do you want to come back...down?" I asked Kitty.

"Remember the letter I wrote to you before I died? That I felt my true purpose was only just beginning? Well, it was. I was born to protect you, Dana. I should have turned into a clairvoyant, who saw beforehand any dangers waiting for you after you turned into a Silver Nephilim. But they killed me before I developed into my skills and would have remembered the deal we made before you were born. You were not supposed to be found. Not during the Second World War, and not in present time either. When you were brought to the present time, I had to die in the bombings of London and be reborn with great haste to be with you again. Thankfully my mother in this time was already a few months pregnant, and living in the area where you would move - I could see that, because your Grandma had already decided to give you in adoption to your mother, and also to give her house for the new family to live in. So I chose her to be my physical mother - it could be done because no soul had yet attached itself to the baby permanently."

Now this was something completely new to me. That we chose our own parents at our own free will? That we made agreements with others about fulfilling our life's purpose even before we were born?

Before I could continue thinking about the philosophical issues around these choices Kitty continued talking.

"Also you were supposed to get your wings much later. Maybe it was Elijah's need for help that hastened the process. You were to become a healer, after all. And a Weaver with extraordinary skills."

I had no words, I was just trying to understand how the rules of the spirit world worked.

"So, before you were born, we knew that you would be a Nephilim, of course. We knew the dark Nephilim would try to get you, because you were the Weaver who could travel time like no other, and connect with the Book of Watchers. We had to protect you from getting into their hands, from getting infected and turning dark."

"But why? Why would you... or they, in the upper levels, even care? If there was no need for them to ever come back down again? You just said most souls don't care anymore what happens in the human world."

"Don't you see? If the dark Nephilim wake up the Watchers, and the Watchers are what they clearly expect... evil, that is, and if such evil Watchers regain their power over human kind, the dark Nephilim can do as they please. This means the human kind is doomed for slavery, possibly for good. That is not the way that was intended for human souls. It takes away the most important lesson of all - that of free will. If the dark Nephilim find the Gates of the Watchers – and the dark Nephilim are aware of their existence, trust me on that – they can move their troops anywhere they like using the buffer zone."

"Troops? What troops?"

"The transformed ones, or the human vampires, ghosts and shadows have their ways of moving in and out of the human world from their own level. And the purebred Nephilim simply step between realms as they please, reaching as high as their energies allow. But the people, ordinary physical people, who are willing to work and fight for the Nephilim – they need the gates if they want to move independently between the physical world and the buffer zone. As do the half-Nephilim, whose blood is so diluted that they are stuck in the physical realm. If the Watchers awaken, and are released from their prison, the knowledge of the exact location of the gates is out. War troops can be marched into any location using the gates. Many of which have not yet even been found."

Kitty started to fade a little. I could see the forest by the river through her now.

"This sounds like a war of the heavens almost," I said.

"It is," Daniel was suddenly next to me. I looked around, and Elijah had disappeared.

"Daniel," Kitty smiled, "good to see you again. Thank you for bringing Dana to meet me. You shall have to protect her in the physical world for me now. I failed in that mission."

"You would never have had any chance against the forces of the dark Nephilim, not without your skills fully developed." Daniel shook his head. "We have talked about this before. We should have protected you from them, until you turned into a clairvoyant. So you can say it is we who failed. We had no idea they would pay attention to an ordinary human, or that they knew about your mission in life."

"So you met Daniel after you died?" I asked Kitty the obvious.

"Yes, Daniel was there when I stepped out of my body," Kitty said, "he helped me through the buffer zone. People in shock can get stuck there, you see. And despite my forebodings about the coming death - it must have been the first signs of my clairvoyance developing - I was in shock. Daniel appeared out of nowhere, took my hand and lifted me to a level where I could meet my own guides and proceed to the afterlife. He saw I did not want to go, and we talked for a long time about you, and our intended life on earth."

I remembered the dream I had the night Kitty died. I turned to look at Daniel, who met my inquiring gaze calmly, clearly expecting the question that would follow.

"Are you some sort of an angel of death, then?" I half joked.

Daniel smiled, and this time the smile reached his eyes. His beauty hurt my heart.

"Yes," he replied, "many of us are."

If the afterlife- or at least this upper level of the buffer zone – hadn't been so beautiful, and if I hadn't been so overjoyed at meeting Kitty again, I might have been shocked. But as it was, I was taken only mildly aback, and asked:

"Explain this, will you?"

"Not now. I'll do it when we are back in our world. Elijah has gone on ahead to make our camp ready for us."

I had another look at the wonderful hilly scenery. Beautiful lilac flowers grew on the mountainside.

"Shall we see each other again?" I asked Kitty.

"When you learn to rise up here on your own, certainly. I will try to come to the lower levels too, when necessary. I lose a little more of my solid form on every level downwards. That is why it may be you only see a part of me, or can't hear me. I do hear you, though, when you think of me, and speak to me in your mind," Kitty hugged me, "and I will continue my job, protecting you, from this level, as best I can. You can see pretty far when you are up here. And now I am able to see probable futures easily. I only had to die to reach my potential," she smiled.

She began to fade even further.

"If you can, tell my family I am still alive. I try to do that too. Tell my mother that every time she smells roses where there are none, it is me."

"I will, Kitty, I promise, when I see her."

Kitty smiled, waved her hand and vanished like the smoke of a candle. I stood there, feeling pure joy.

"Thank you, Daniel... and I am sorry," I stammered

That took him by surprise.

"Sorry? Whatever for?"

"For behaving like that after Elijah... healing Elijah..."

I don't know what I had expected, but not this roaring laughter.

"I am sorry..." Daniel found it hard to stop laughing, "did you actually think I did not like what you did?"

I blushed so hard that I felt like a tomato flying on silver wings.

"My darling Dana..." he took my hands and smiled into my eyes, "any Nephilim would fight for your love. Have you any idea how beautiful and pure you have become? I am sure I did not deserve all the... attention you gave me there at the ward, after healing Elijah, because you did not know who you were. But I assure you it was one of the top moments of my life. It was quite hard not to take advantage of the situation."

"Take advantage... Oh..."

If possible, I blushed even more.

"I promise I will behave." Daniel smiled at me, laughter sparkling in his eyes.

He bent forward and kissed me gently on the lips and in a snap I was on fire. I wrapped my hands behind his neck and kissed him, and not so gently.

"I wish you wouldn't. Behave." I whispered to him, pressing myself against him.

For one precious moment he kissed me back, and then he gently pushed me away.

"Dana..." I could feel his hands tremble, and I saw how his eyes had turned almost the color of the night sky with emotion, "we cannot."

"Why?" I gasped for air, not wanting to stop. He held me by my arms, not allowing me to come closer.

"You are too young for this."

"No, I am not," I knew I sounded like a pouting child, but Daniel did not hurt my emotions by treating me like one.

"In human years you are what... sixteen?"

"Seventeen next month."

"I have been around for a lot longer." He looked at me seriously.

"I know. Around three hundred years."

He looked surprised. Obviously he had not known I knew.

"And that doesn't bother you?"

"No. In a few hundred years I am sure we won't even notice the difference."

He let out an almost desperate laugh.

"Do not tempt me, Dana... because you do, you have no idea how much you do..."

"I do? You haven't exactly shown it to me. It seems to me that you've tried to distance yourself from me."

"You are right, Dana, I have," he fought to gain composure, but his eyes remained almost black and his breathing was hard, "but that is only to protect you."

"I don't need to be protected from you..."

"You have no idea about the forces between the Nephilim. You have no idea how we choose our mates. It is not an easy deal, and once you have bonded with someone..."

He did not continue any further, but stood there, holding me at an arms length. I forced myself forward despite his hands, and pressed myself against him again, feeling his delicious warmth.

"Dana...!" he groaned and stepped back.

The old, sensible human Dana inside me felt ashamed. The new, Nephilim Dana, did not. It was as if someone was acting on my behalf - a wild and passionate creature I had never known before and who knew exactly what she wanted.

I managed to get the old Dana to the surface with considerable effort.

"I'm sorry, Daniel... I cannot help myself..."

"Young Nephilim are like that," he had to clear his throat to be able to speak, "their newly born power is so strong they cannot help themselves. They are all emotion and energy. I should have remembered. Right. We are going down to Egypt. Now. Close your wings, so we don't draw attention to ourselves if there are people around."

My wings were trembling, when I willed them out of sight, feeling them curling back inside me, along my spine. Daniel let me gain my composure in peace, and stood at a distance. When I had calmed down, he extended his right hand, and I took it into my left, wrapping my fingers tightly around his.

When we descended to the deserts of Egypt together with the light of the rising sun, my heart was singing. Daniel cared for me!

64

KISS IN THE DESERT

The solitude of the Egyptian Western Desert, vast and silent, stretched away in all directions. There, under the guidance of Daniel and Elijah, I learned to fly.

I'd had my share of flying dreams in the past, but the real thing was a thousand times better. Much to my astonishment, the basics were the same as in my dreams.

There was no beating of wings involved. We did not fly like birds. When I wondered about that, Elijah burst out laughing.

"That bird-wing thinking is the human way of seeing how anyone could fly in the first place: flying means wings, and everyone knows how wings should work, don't they? I would think we'd look just plain funny if we went flapping about. If we needed to move our wings in that way, our chests would have to be huge just to accommodate all the necessary muscles. We would stand out in crowds like a sore thumb."

Nevertheless, we did need the wings to move for the flying part, to overcome the gravity of the earth. First Daniel and Elijah taught me to fly with wings open, even though it could be learned to do so without showing the wings. With wings open moving about was more accurate, faster and safer, they explained.

"When we fly with wings open," explained Daniel, "it's the connection between our minds and the tips of the wings that holds the key."

So we opened our wings to their full extent. First up and then out to the sides, so they formed a semi-circle behind us and cocooned our legs. And then we used our minds to connect to the upper tips of the wings. This wasn't as difficult as it might sound - it was as though the tips drew our attention to them automatically once the wings were open. Like a tiny tug inside the mind. You know when you feel itchy – your mind goes to the location immediately.

With our attention concentrated on that point, the pulsing of our veins intensified towards the tips. It felt like a slight tremor in the wings. Then the rest of the wings turned around us from back to front like a transparent cocoon, and gravity no longer existed.

The sensation was the same I remembered from my dreams - I had simply willed my energies upwards, and flew. In the air the breathing of the wings was so strong it made me elated, light, and dizzy.

The first time I managed to rise above the sands of the desert I got so excited I forgot to keep my attention focussed in my wings, and started to tumble back towards the earth like a stone. Elijah, who had been flying under me, caught me mid-air and laughed. He laughed a lot these days, I had noticed.

"Keep your focus on flying, young lady!" He shook his forefinger at me after putting me safely down on the sand. "Knights in shining wings aren't always near to catch you when you fall."

Then he gave a smacking kiss on my cheek, which made me giggle and Daniel look at him under his eyebrows sternly.

"Oh come on, Daniel!" Elijah smiled. "She's so cute you can't blame a guy for stealing a kiss from her!"

Daniel muttered something and rose higher, followed by Elijah's laughter. He also winked at me.

I learned to like Elijah a lot during those days. With his wings extended he was just as fierce-looking as his brother, but Daniel was much more serious. When they stood side by side, blonde and dark, with their wings extended, they looked like true angel warriors – tall, muscular, handsome, and... lethal. That really was the only word I could think of. The power in their wings was pulsing like distant thunder – you could almost hear it, and you certainly felt the rumble and electricity around them much as you feel an approaching thunderstorm.

After a few scary moments of plunging down through the air, I finally learned to keep a small part of my mind in my wings all the time, while I flew. The rest of my mind was free for everything else.

I loved looking at the desert. The golden dunes, slowly making their way across the desert plain with the deep blue sky beyond them took my breath away. There were strange rock formations. There were oases.

Once Elijah and Daniel took me on a flight to the southern end of the Great Sand Sea near Gilf el-Kebir. There, they showed me some strange stones lying in the sand. They were light yellowish green, and the light shone right through them.

"They look like glass." I raised one in my hand against the sun.

"That's because they are," Daniel said, "silica glass, formed by the impact of a meteorite some 29 million years ago, or so it has been estimated."

"Did you know that one of Tutankhamon's pectorals has this same glass in it?" Elijah asked, "a light green scarab."

I nodded. Now I remembered the pectoral.

"How on earth did they get the glass? We are in the middle of nowhere! Surely no one can survive in this environment for the time it takes to get back to the Nile valley on foot!"

Indeed we were in the middle of nowhere. Huge sand dunes were all around us like solid waves of a golden ocean. Wind constantly blew sand into the air. You could see the green pieces of desert glass in the dunes, being polished by the power of these elements.

"They had their sand-dwellers in ancient times, people who lived in the desert," Daniel said, "and anything this beautiful would have been valuable in trading. Silica glass is rarer than diamonds."

I noticed the little jewel – or piece of glass – on my necklace was the same color as this meteorite glass. Of course! Grandma had told me my necklace was made of this very same glass in the distant past. For the Shadow of Isis... Shuet...

One day Daniel disappeared for a few hours without telling us where he was going. Elijah and I spent the hottest hours sitting in the shade of a mushroom-like rock formation in the Egyptian White Desert. The blinding whiteness meant it was like sitting in a snowy landscape – only this was rocks and hot sand. We did not talk much and didn't find the silence uncomfortable. Instead we watched the day turning into night. After sundown, it looked as though the sky was on fire; it was of such an intense golden color. Then it changed into deep blue, and slowly softened into black. The moon rose, and the glow of the white rock formations looked unearthly. A little desert fox appeared out of nowhere and observed us for a while, alert. The next time I blinked my eyes it had vanished, like a small ghost from another dimension.

I looked at this unbelievable beauty with my new sense of sight, my heart feeling like bursting. I could clearly see myriad stars despite the strong moonlight. I sighed, content.

"Do you love him?" Elijah broke the silence.

I looked at him in surprise. I was even more surprised when I saw the look in his eyes. They were calm, but the depth of sadness in them made tears well up in my own eyes.

I glimpsed a vision from the time I had healed him - a tall, blonde woman was looking at me with serene eyes. While I was still trapped in the vision, Elijah suddenly bent and kissed me. Tenderly, for a long time.

I was so surprised I did not even fight it. He felt so comfortable, so trustworthy. I felt myself answering his kiss, tentatively, listening to the emotions the kiss caused in me. A surge of sadness hit me and I withdrew.

"Elijah..." I did not know what to say, "I... Why....?"

He did not say anything, just questioned me with his eyes, and clearly got his answer, because he got to his feet and walked away. I turned my gaze to the desert, wiping tears, breathing in with a ragged breath. When I could see clearly again, I saw Daniel standing nearby in the white moonlight.

He must have seen it all. He might have been chiseled out of stone, standing on the white sand, with the moonlight pouring over his tall figure. He did not move any closer. His blue eyes glowed eerily in the darkness as if they were lit from within. I looked at him, and began to cry for real, burying my face to my hands.

He vanished in an instant, withdrawing into the buffer zone.

Only he did not stay there. Suddenly I heard the brothers on the other side of the rock formation, arguing. They kept their voices down, but with my enhanced hearing I could still hear them.

"If you ever touch her again..." Daniel's voice was icy.

"Then what?" Elijah sounded tired. "You will attack your own brother? You two are not married; no one has given any promises to anyone. She is free to choose. It is only fair to show her she has options. Young Nephilim have a tendency to fall in love with the first Nephilim they meet after their transformation. Her own mother did so, when Cain's son approached her."

"Which is exactly why you should have left her in peace!" Daniel snapped. "She is not yet of age to make such decisions. She transformed too soon and her mind is not ready! And what of Merit?"

A long silence followed.

"Yes, I know what you think. I shall always love Merit. I hope I can save her, but it maybe I cannot. I am confused and I am lonely, and I have my weak moments too. You cannot blame me for admiring her beauty. When she merged her energies into mine, healing me, I saw into her soul and it was beautiful. How could I not be drawn to her, when it felt as if it was my heart she was healing too? I thought no one but Merit could do that, ever. If I did not know she is Nephilim, I would have taken her for a real angel. But I have also seen the way you look at her. You should take your own advice and not take advantage of her newness either!"

"I know." Daniel's voice was icy. "And I will not. And I expect you to do the same. No one is to try to claim her, until she is old enough to make such decisions for herself."

Silence. Then Elijah spoke in so low a voice that I almost missed his words in the soft whisper of the desert wind.

"Daniel – do you love her?"

He never answered out loud.

65

KILLING SWANS

Hades tied the metal against Ambrogio's neck. The silvery piece rested tightly against the skin of his lower throat, the straps tied to the nape. Then he tightened a bracer to Amrogio's left arm, and gave him a finger tab to protect his drawing fingers.

"I leave. They do not come anywhere near when I am around," Hades said. "All you need to do is to sing, and keep your bow at the ready."

"What shall I sing, oh Hades?" Ambrogio asked.

"It doesn't matter. It's the voice itself that will bring them to you. Cease singing as soon as one is near enough. You don't want more than one at a time, because they move too fast for you to kill both of them. When there is only one, others of their kind won't be warned. They usually fly alone, so only one should come at a time. Do not try to attack, if there is more than one. The other one will kill you."

At that, Hades disappeared and Ambrogio was left standing in the dark. Nervously, he pointed the arrow with its strange transparent tip towards the ground, and placed its shaft on the arrow rest, so he would be ready.

It was a peaceful night. He was standing up on the mountain, above

Delphi. Not a soul was in sight. Only the stars like droplets of milk thrown across the sky.

He drew in a breath and began to sing a lullaby his mother had sung to him when he was a small child. And that is when the miracle started. His voice suddenly had many layers - as if he was singing with many voices. It had a lingering echo that was caused by the device against his throat, not by his voice bouncing back to him from a distance.

And it was beautiful. So beautiful... His voice had never reached these depths, these heights. Tears welled into his eyes at the beauty of it.

Then he saw the silvery one. It was human in shape, just as Hades had said. A man. His wings were green, and the light pulsing in them was pure silver. There was no mistaking that this was one of those he was hunting for.

He was beautiful, and obviously very curious about the singing voice. He came through the air and landed near Ambrogio.

He almost could not do it. But then his stinging skin and his love for Selene won. He stopped singing, and quickly pointed his left shoulder towards the silver-winged one, and raised his bow to aim. He was right-eyed, and the bow was right-handed. He held the bow with his left hand so he could aim with his right eye. Somewhere from the back of his mind he heard his father explaining how eye-dominance was everything in archery.

His hand rose to his anchor point, the corner of his mouth. The movement was automatic, from years of practice. Just as automatically he relaxed the fingers of his bow hand, before his movement alerted the winged creature.

The arrow flew straight and hit the silver winged man in the middle of the chest. His mouth opened in surprise and a strange voice rose towards the stars. For a short while Ambrogio wondered if he himself had continued singing, but no. The same strange echoing song that had come from Ambrogio's throat, came now from the winged creature.

He fell to his knees, and something very strange happened to his chest. Cautiously, ready for any sudden movement, Ambrogio stepped closer to see.

There was a hole in his chest. Not just a small hole created by the arrow, but a really big hole, as if someone had slashed the man with a huge knife and carved him open. The edges of the wound had an eerie bluish glow. Ambrogio could actually see through the hole. Silver blood gushed from the wound onto the ground.

The man's blue eyes stared into his, in a silent question. And then he slumped forward, and swayed for a while. In the end he did not fall onto his face, but on his back. Something white, like mist, rose from the wound and when it was gone, the winged one was dead.

Ambrogio's knees gave way and he fell to his knees and vomited until only bile came out. With shaking hands he placed his bow on the ground, and leaned over the dead body.

The wings were darkening fast. The silver blood wasn't. It pooled on the ground, which began to absorb it.

With great haste Ambrogio fumbled through his clothing, in search of the parchment and the quill. He found them, and trying to stop his hands from shaking so the quill would not break, he dipped it into the silver pool on the ground. With care he wrote a note.

"I have killed the first swan."

He could not think of anything else to write, and put the note on the ground. Then he took another note, and wrote on it.

"My beloved Selene. I cannot meet you as promised, because Apollo does not wish you to leave his temple. I am afraid he wants you to himself. Try to stay away from him; you will recognize him as the very tall man with yellow eyes. He has cursed me so I cannot walk under the sun, but I have found a way for us to be together. It only takes some time. If you are willing to wait for me, make a spiral of stones on the roadside where we were supposed to meet this morning. I will write to you every day so you will know I am here. Ambrogio."

He stood up, watching the dead creature with wonder. His wings were almost gone now, melted into the ground, and he looked like an ordinary, tall man, if not for the strange glowing silver blood running in tiny rivers from under him. Ambrogio hesitantly reached for the arrow and pulled it away. Its transparent tip had partly melted. He dropped it, and it seemed to draw a bluish line into the air, which glowed faintly for a while, and then vanished.

Then Ambrogio turned and made haste towards the Delphi temple. He would have to place his letter on the spot where they were supposed to meet with Selene, before the sun rose. The eastern horizon was no longer totally black, you could sense dark blue color there. He would have to hurry.

He ran when he could, and he did make it in time. He placed the letter on a stone, and put another stone on top of it. His shadow appeared next to him.

"You will guard this so no one else takes it but Selene. She is a beautiful maiden who comes here searching for me. You will not show yourself to her, but you will scare off anyone trying to get this letter. Do you understand?"

"Yes, master," the shadow bowed.

And then Hades stepped out of the darkness.

"Well done," he said. "Next time you can simply ask your shadow to leave your note for your girl. And your shadow will also take you back to my realm before sunrise. Now you need to go back and call for the goddess so you can give the body of the silver one to her."

Hades touched his hand, and quickly they travelled through the grey mist to the body of the dead man.

"How do I call for her, oh mighty Hades?"

"By name. Sing."

"Her name...? I am sorry, I do not know her name."

"Artemis. Do not let her see the singing device." Hades said and disappeared.

Ambrogio closed his eyes for a while, feeling nauseous. He had never killed anyone before. But he was also proud - he had served a real god, and served him well.

He opened his mouth, and began to sing Artemis's name.

66

THE PYRAMIDS

I had fallen asleep at some point, because the next thing I was looking at was the sunrise. I could not see Daniel or Elijah anywhere.

Still half asleep I jumped to my feet. In dreams emotions are strong, and raw, and for a while I was certain the brothers had fought one another, and were lying wounded somewhere. The nightmarish sight of Elijah's torn wings flashed in my mind.

"Good morning!" A cheerful and familiar voice greeted me. "Perfect timing – coffee will be ready in a moment. Just enough time to clean your teeth!"

"Diana! What are you doing here?"

Because it was Diana. And behind her, Grandma was sitting by a small fire, boiling water in a kettle, measuring the horizon with a content look on her face. At her feet was a tin of coffee. And to top the scene off, Jason appeared somewhere from behind the rock.

"Top of the mornin', as they say," he grinned, "slept well?"

"No, not very..." I yawned and stretched myself. "Where did you all come from?"

"Daniel picked us up during the night, while you slept. Your father has been calling, and wants to speak to you on the phone. We better get ourselves to some touristy places and take some photos, and call your parents," Grandma commented.

I took the bottle of water Diana handed to me, and my toothbrush. Cleaning my teeth made me feel better, even though I could not use much water here. There's nothing more valuable in the desert than water, that I had learned very quickly. It seemed that even the Nephilim could not go on without water.

I sat down for breakfast, looking around. I had to ask, or else they would have begun to wonder.

"Where are Daniel and Elijah?" I tried to sound as casual as possible.

"They have gone ahead to meet the Council of the Nephilim. You're about to be introduced to your own kind, after we have taken some appropriately touristy snaps," Grandma said matter-of-factly. "We also need to vanish from here, after we send photos of you in Egypt to your parents' email. We are certain the dark Nephilim are spying on it, and will appear here as soon as they see where the photos are taken."

I chewed on the sandwiches they had brought with them. They tasted delicious after a few days of camping food.

"And now you need to change clothes to look like a tourist," Diana said. "I brought some for you from our dressmaker."

She handed me a duffel bag full of clothes. A very nice pair of khaki jeans, a T-shirt with a picture of the Sphinx, a baseball cap, sunglasses, socks and sneakers. I went behind a boulder to change. Diana followed me.

"OK, so what has happened?" she asked immediately.

"Happened? How do you mean?" I tried to sound innocent.

"Oh come on... your eyes are all swollen, which means that either you are allergic to something here, and the only possible thing would be sand, and no one is allergic to sand - or you have been crying. Daniel was as cold and distant as an iceberg when he came to fetch me. One plus one. Math, my dear, math."

I said nothing, just pulled the T-shirt slowly over my head, to buy some time.

"Don't try to pretend I'm wrong, Dana," Diana stood with her arms folded. "Tell me."

So I did – it felt such a relief to tell someone of my age.

"No way..." Diana sighed with round eyes, "they are both in love with you? How on earth did you manage that one? The girls in the Center are drooling after them both, because they are..." she poked her finger at her thigh and made a hissing sound, "...hot! But neither one shows any interest in us mere mortals, and we were already beginning to wonder if they were... erm... otherwise inclined, if you get my point. Not towards each other, of course, but still."

I shook my head, but couldn't help a weak smile.

"And in marches Dana, and has both the brothers smitten? Wow, I wish I was Nephilim!"

"It was not a very pleasant situation," I said. "Elijah kissed me, and Daniel saw it, and they had a fight over it."

"Fight? As with fists?" Diana bent eagerly forward.

"No, just verbally... And now they are obviously not talking to me either..."

"Oh, how delicious!" Diana beamed.

"I don't think so..." I felt miserable.

"So, which one do you prefer? Can I have the other one?"

I had to laugh. Diana was such a cheerful character.

"Oh I know, it is Daniel," she nodded a few times, "it is so obvious. Elijah is gorgeous too, but I have seen the way you look at Daniel. Not to mention the episode on the ward..."

"Oh don't remind me!" I blushed. The old Dana was now dominant, and she would never take the initiative in kissing anyone.

"OK, OK, I'll shut up. For now. But I expect the full story later." Diana winked at me. "But now, let's get to the pyramids!"

Even more people had appeared while I had changed my clothes. Reggie and Lilith now stood admiring the desert view.

"Ah, Dana," Lilith smiled, "I trust the boys have taught you the use of your wings?"

"Yes, they have," I said. "Quite an experience!"

"I am so envious," Diana sighed. "If you ever find out how I could become a Nephilim, do let me know, will you?"

"I promise," I laughed, "but as far as I know, it is genetic, so I'm afraid there's not much hope in that sector!"

"Ok, girls," Lilith clapped her hands like an elementary school teacher, "we're going to the pyramids now. Dana can weave us there."

"Oh, how?"

"Well, our Weavers usually move to locations within their own time, using photos of their target location. So here. But wait until we are all in the buffer zone."

She handed me a magazine. There was a picture of the famous three pyramids of Giza. There were over a hundred pyramids in Egypt, some quite small, some totally eroded, but people usually knew nothing of them. Most people only knew of these three.

Lilith raised her hand, and slashed an opening into the air. We all walked through it, and she closed it behind us.

We stood in the grey fog – you could barely see the forms of the rocks in the White Desert, looming through the mist.

I remembered my past adventure at the Center, and started tracing the picture with my finger. Not a single pyramid, because I was afraid we'd end up to the top of one, and straight into the worldwide news. I figured that if I traced the outline of the picture, we'd end up at the general location of the photographer who took it.

I was right. Only I did not take into consideration that I instantly zoomed physically to the spot where the photo was taken, but the others didn't. They probably should have touched me to follow me.

I shot out of the buffer zone like a bullet and fell to my knees in the sand. I quickly rose, cleaning my jeans, checking out if anyone had seen me. There were a few people, but they were all between me and the pyramids, and thankfully looking at them, not me.

So there I was - standing on my own, facing the huge pyramids, wondering what to do. I would have returned to fetch the others, but obviously I had no idea how to do that, as I didn't have the foggiest where we had been.

Someone touched me. I looked down, and a little boy raised a necklace for me to see.

"Please miss, buy cheap!"

And suddenly they were everywhere, as though they'd grown out of the sand. Little children, trying to sell me the trinkets they were holding. I looked around – hardly any tourists to be seen. No wonder – people considered Egypt a dangerous place, after the uprising of the Arab spring. Families who had survived on tourism for years were desperately poor now.

"Please, miss!" they circled me.

I pulled my pockets out to show the children I had no money, and they withdrew, disappointed. They did not go far but observed me just in case I had hidden some money somewhere and would pull it out.

I had no idea where to go to. I could only hope the others would find their way here soon, as they surely knew where I had gone. I just stood there, waiting, and looked at the enormous structures.

The pyramids loomed in front of me, just the latest tourist to observe them in their four and a half thousand years of history. They had eroded and also been deliberately damaged in the process, but they still remained. The white casing stones that had once covered them, were now gone. I could see the big hole on the side of the Cheops pyramid – created by the workmen of Caliph al-Ma'mun in the 820's.

The sheer mass of the ancient monuments had me humbled. You really could not understand how huge they were, looking at pictures. Only when you stood in front of them, feeling like an ant in comparison, did you understood how enormous they were.

"How on earth did you do that?" Diana's voice right behind me made me jump.

I turned around to see the rest of the group around me. Daniel and Elijah included.

"I just wove my way here..." I tried meekly.

"No, that was no weaving," Lilith said stressed each word, "because I saw no strings coming from your hands. You just took the photo and vanished! We were afraid that you'd got yourself lost in some other time again, I had to go get Daniel and Elijah in case they needed to track you down again."

I tried to look Daniel in the eye, but he pretended to be looking at the pyramids. Elijah was busy fishing coins from his jeans pockets, surrounded by the children, who had not benefited from my presence. I wondered how our team had arrived without drawing attention to them, but looking at how the children paid no attention to anyone but generous Elijah, I figured no one had noticed.

"What exactly did you do?" Grandma wanted to know.

I told them how I had managed to move from one place to another by drawing the outline of the destination with my finger. Everyone was speaking at once.

"That has never happened before!" Grandma said.

"Some kind of supersonic weaving!" Jason commented.

"Show us how you do it!" Diana grabbed my arm eagerly.

"No, she can't," Lilith said, "we are drawing enough attention to us as it is, without Dana disappearing into thin air."

"Right, let's take a photo then," grandma took out her phone. "Stand in a row, and say cheese. The tall ones at the back, please."

That meant Daniel, Elijah and me. The brothers did not speak to me, or look at me, but I noticed how Daniel made sure he stood between Elijah and me. Daniel did not touch me, though, even though he stood close. In fact he seemed to very carefully position himself so that we would not touch. I forced a smile onto my face, and Grandma took a few photos, making a show of asking us to smile, and taking extra photos just in case.

"Right, I'll send these a bit later to your parents," she said to me, swiping her finger across her cell phone screen to see the photos. "Now, call them with my phone."

She handed me her phone. It was already ringing at the other end. I took a deep breath.

"Hello?" Dad's voice, which seemed to come from the bottom of a barrel. Suddenly I missed him so much my eyes welled.

"Dad?" I yelled into the phone.

"Dana! Honey! Dana is calling!" Dad shouted at the other end. "How are you? Are you having fun?"

"Yes, it's been great! We have just come here to see the pyramids of Giza! Grandma took some photos for you!"

I don't remember much about the things I chatted about with my parents, because I was so confused by my feelings and the obvious distance the Nephilim brothers were keeping from me. But I suppose my parents were convinced we were having a great time. The voices of the children selling their trinkets to tourists were a good thing - they clearly told them we were abroad. Grandma took the phone after a while, and talked with my Dad for a few minutes.

I walked slowly toward the pyramids. Diana appeared next to me.

"Come on, Dana, try to look more cheerful!"

"It's hard," I said. "Can you see how they both avoid me now?"

"Well, what would you expect. They are behaving themselves now, just as they said they would. It doesn't mean Daniel doesn't care for you."

I saw the brothers at a distance. Daniel glanced my way ever so briefly, and I wondered if he had heard what we were talking about, with his acute Nephilim hearing. I tried to listen to their discussion and couldn't. So he probably hadn't heard us either. He turned around, and kept on walking with Elijah.

Diana and I kept on walking too. Then I began to feel there was someone behind us. I did not hear anything, but the feeling of a presence was so strong, that Diana and I turned instinctively, at the same time.

"Hello, sweetie," Angel's voice was dripping with honey, "fancy finding you here!"

67

ANGEL AND DANIEL

"Get behind me," I said to Diana and she obeyed without questioning.

Angel laughed – that lovely laughter, like silver bells tingling. She did not have her dark wings out. She looked so beautiful that some tourists started aiming their cameras at her – thinking she was some supermodel, no doubt. Because that's what she looked like. Tall, lean, with her almost white blond hair gently blowing in the wind.

"What are you doing here?" I asked, not diverting my eyes from her, not even to see if others had noticed what was happening.

The last time I had seen them, our human entourage was involved in buying necklaces and plastic sphinxes made in China from the children. And Daniel and Elijah had been walking at quite some distance, with their backs towards us. It might take a while.

"Oh, I came to see how you were doing," Angel smiled sweetly. "Who is your friend?"

Diana said nothing, but I saw her shadow in the sand – she was standing without showing any signs of panic. Either she did not know who Angel was, or she had nerves of steel. I suspected the latter.

"I am sure you did not come to socialize," I said, surprised at how calm I sounded.

"One has to have manners." Angel smiled sweetly. "It's only polite to say hello to a relative. I am your aunt, after all."

She looked at me with eyes narrowed against the sun. She was standing in very relaxed position, hips forward, hands in her jeans pockets as if she was posing for a photo shoot. I remembered how fast she had moved last time to attack me, and was prepared for anything. I felt the electricity increase in my spine, but willed my wings to stay hidden. I hoped the presence of ordinary people would make her behave.

Angel sensed something, though, and looked at me with her head tilted to the side, speculatively.

"My my... it looks like you have grown..."

She stood very still for a few moments.

"Surely you haven't grown your wings yet, dear? It's way too soon."

I did not reply, but willed the rising power in my spine back down. She saw that her words did not surprise me, so she obviously knew that I was now aware of what I was.

"How did you know where to find us?" I asked.

"That wasn't hard," Angel said lightly, "after all you did call your parents some time ago, with the nice story of being accepted as a scholarship student to a university even before you'd even passed your exams. And that you would go to Egypt with your study group. After that we simply placed one of ours in the vicinity of the most famous tourist sites, to keep an eye out for a group like yours appearing. You'd need to convince your parents you really were in Egypt, and so there was a pretty good chance you would appear here by the pyramids. Every layman knows where these pyramids are. Of course, we have some more people in other nice locations. Karnak, Luxor, Kom Ombo, Abu Simbel. Quite the little tourist itinerary. When you all suddenly appeared here, it only took one phone call. I was in the vicinity, and thought I'd come in person to talk with my niece."

"And what do you want?" I asked.

"Oh, I want plenty of things. But mostly I wanted to check, if I had managed to turn you into one of us. I see I have failed in that. Your reflexes were surprisingly fast, considering how scared you were, and not yet Nephilim. Maybe I should try again?"

She smiled, a breathtakingly beautiful smile that also managed to be pure evil.

"That might not be wise." Elijah appeared out of thin air right behind Angel, hugging her closely as if she were his adored girlfriend and he was giving her a loving surprise.

Angel's body remained upright, but I saw how the muscles on her back and hands tightened, as she tested his strength. He laughed and held her easily.

"Now now, Angel, surely you won't make a spectacle out of this?" Elijah murmured into her ear, "not with all those tourists filming you, wondering which movie star you are. I am sure Cain would not appreciate such antics, not with all the care he's taken about keeping the Nephilim hidden in the midst of people for thousands of years."

Angel smiled sweetly and looked over her shoulder as a girlfriend in love would.

"Elijah," she cooed, "how lovely to see you. I have been waiting to hear news about you."

"Yes, I think you might have heard rumors of some sort about me getting ill. Well, rest assured, I am well recovered."

Angel turned her head even more, so that her neck was at an almost impossible angle, and looked up into Elijah's eyes. Elijah let her stare, because the angle was impossible for Angel if she was planning on spitting in his face. She stared at Elijah's blue eyes, unbelieving. Elijah stared back and wiggled his eyebrows in an amused way.

"This cannot be," she said, and for the first time her voice revealed emotion. She sounded uncertain.

"What can't?" Elijah smacked a kiss right onto her ear, probably causing it to ring for a long time.

Angel let out a growl that froze my spine.

"You were bitten. You cannot be healed!"

"Yet, here I am, and not the least bit ill. How very frustrating for you, wondering how that happened..." Elijah winked at me over Angel's shoulder when she could not see it.

Oddly, I felt a rush of relief. That little gesture showed Elijah at least connected with me, even if Daniel didn't.

I saw Lilith, Grandma, Reggie, Diana and Jason standing near us now, staring at the scene. They had placed themselves between us and the group of tourists who were now shooing the trinket-selling children away. A camel driver approached them, the tassels in the camel's blanket and bridle swinging in rhythm with the animal's steps.

"You're leaving now, Angel." Daniel's voice came from behind me.

"Daniel darling!" Angel was all sweetness again. "How wonderful to see you, my love."

Something must have shown in my expression, because Angel's eyes turned to mine in an instant.

"I do hope you are not much smitten, dear niece. You see, Daniel is spoken for. Always has been."

I forced myself to be calm, and looked back into Angel's yellow eyes as coolly as I possibly could. Obviously I was not very successful, because Angel laughed, and this time she sounded almost triumphant.

"He hasn't told you about our engagement? Oh dear... it's a long-standing one, too. We were engaged to be married in... now, when was it, love?" Angel looked at Daniel from under her long lashes adoringly.

"I am not your love, Angel." Daniel's voice was totally calm.

"Oh but you are. We were promised to each other in... when was it again? Oh, now I remember, it was January 24th in 1742, the same day Charles VII Albert became the Holy Roman Emperor, if my memory serves me well. And trust me – there is nothing wrong with my memory."

"I never made any promises to you, Angel," Daniel said in a quiet voice, but there was a threat in it now.

"No, but our fathers did. They betrothed us to each other, and to me that is just as binding."

"To me, it isn't," Daniel said. "To make an engagement binding, both Nephilim must be of age, and give their consent, aloud, in front of witnesses. No such ceremony ever took place. We were not present when our fathers discussed our possible future marriage."

"If Cain says I am betrothed to you, then I am. His word is law!"

Angel's face began to distort with odd emotions, but she quickly gained control of herself. Still, before she did I had detected anger and... fear?

"Yes, I suppose you must believe that. Or you might face the same fate as your mother," Elijah said coldly.

Angel lost control. She shrieked with anger like a bird of prey and began to fight Elijah's grip. I saw the group of tourists stop and stare at us, trying to see what the voice had been, from behind Lilith, Grandma, Reggie and Jason. With so few tourists in the country we did not blend into the crowd. There was no crowd for starters. And Angel's shriek had not sounded human at all.

"If I let you go, will you go nicely?" Elijah asked, still holding her from behind with amazing strength.

"Oh, I will go. But I will return. Soon you shall all be converted." Angel forced herself to stand still, and directed her words at Daniel and me.

"And you, pitiful humans," she spat towards Diana, who was too far away for any danger, safely behind my back, "you will be our slaves, our cattle!"

"If you won't calm down, we will not let you go," Daniel said with no emotion in his voice, "and we don't have to, you know. We could kill you too. We don't want to, as we are not like you. But should necessity rise, we can."

Daniel's voice was pleasant enough, but Angel understood he meant what he said. I observed her with interest, not feeling threatened any more. She was looking at Daniel now, and I saw a new mixture of emotions in her eyes. Fury, and longing. Suddenly I surprised myself by feeling empathy towards her. In a short time span I had learned to know what it was to be tormented by love. And what was already a painful, demanding emotion was almost unbearably strengthened by the complexities of being Nephilim.

Daniel stepped between me and Angel.

"Have you calmed down now?"

Angel did not say anything, but maybe she nodded her consent. I could not tell, Daniel's tall frame blocked my view.

"Elijah will let you go, and you will leave immediately. You will not linger near us in the buffer zone, or I promise I will kill you. I know your scent, so I will know if you are there. This is the only warning I'm going to give you. Do you understand?"

Behind Daniel's back I heard no reply

"Say it aloud."

"Yes." The word clearly came through gritted teeth.

"Let her go." Daniel kept moving so that he stood between Angel and me.

I stepped a little sideways too so I could see what happened. For my own part I also blocked the view of the tourists. Also I wanted to be in front of Diana, in case she needed protection. So there we stood in a line, Daniel, me and Diana.

Angel stood still for a second after Elijah let her go. I could feel Daniel's force field intensify, when she did not vanish immediately. She looked at Daniel and opened her mouth as if to speak. Daniel's energies were positively humming now, and she changed her mind. She began to fade. A few seconds and she was gone.

"We need to leave immediately," Daniel said, not looking at me.

We gathered together and started walking away from the pyramids, and into the eastern necropolis, where Cheops's sons and daughters were buried in their mastaba tombs. There, sheltered by the solid stone structures, Lilith slashed a gateway for us and we stepped into the buffer zone when no one was around.

"Take hold of us," Daniel said over his shoulder.

Reggie and Lilith took Elijah's arms, Diana took mine, and Jason and Grandma took Daniel's.

"Open your wings," Elijah said to me, "we'll go to the upper levels to get away from danger. Angel cannot follow us there. Despite her promise we cannot trust she'll keep her word."

We all opened our wings to their full extent, and began rising through the levels of the buffer zone, higher and higher.

"Wow!" Diana almost wrung her neck, looking at my wings, "your wings are still amazing!"

"Erm... thank you. I guess..." I concentrated hard on keeping up with "the boys". I had only just learned how to fly, and still didn't trust my skills. And now I had the responsibility of keeping someone else up in the air as well.

"That Angel character is creepy..." Diana whispered as landscapes formed and vanished around us. Most were of pure nature, but in one I could see a village too. "I almost peed my pants!"

"I know... me too!"

Diana giggled – an odd sound in an almost echoless world.

"Well I couldn't tell. You stood just like Daniel - prepared for anything, with royal posture, and you were humming too!"

So she could hear my wings. No wonder Angel had observed me so intensely.

"You were pretty cool-looking yourself," I said to Diana, then, "I did not want to show her my wings, but I would have, if she had attacked."

"Glad to hear that," Diana said.

"What was that talk about Angel's mother?" I asked, not directing my question at anyone in particular.

It was Elijah who answered, holding Lilith and Reggie securely by the arm:

"Her mother was of the pure Nephilim - all the mothers of Cain's children are. She tried to raise her to be one of us, and hide her from her father, but Cain sought them out, and infected the little girl himself when she was only a child. And then he tore Angel's mother to bits for objecting to his rule."

"Good Lord...!" I felt sick.

I did not understand, why a good Nephilim woman would want to carry Cain's child. Unless, of course, it wasn't voluntary... the thought made me even more nauseous.

I wanted to ask why Daniel's father would have considered marrying his son to the daughter of the leader of the dark Nephilim, but I knew this was neither the time nor place. I would ask him about it later, when the time was right.

68

ANGEL CHILD

"Were you successful?"

Cain stood by the window, observing the horses training on the racetrack that lay beyond his stable yard. He was a skilled horseman, and bred the finest thoroughbreds, as his forefathers had done. Only he had been all of the forefathers, conveniently sending their son away to a relative or school and "dying" before the "son" returned some years later as an adult, looking amazingly like his father.

Angel stood at the center of the room, calm and poised.

"Yes. I threatened them, told them that they would soon all be converted, and insulted the humans by calling them our cattle and slaves."

Cain laughed quietly.

"Well done, that should do it."

Angel nodded, even though her father could not see it.

"I am sure this will speed up their search as a result."

"Very good." Cain was paying attention to one of his new stallions, which was giving a hard time to the lad on its back. He smiled, amused at the animal's power and will to test its rider. He enjoyed strong characters.

After a while Cain noticed Angel was still standing in the room.

"Do you have something else to tell me?"

"Yes, father. Something very strange... Elijah... He was infected by one of our soldiers as you know..."

"Yes, indeed. Has he changed yet?"

"I saw him. He was there with their group."

"How odd – usually they drive away the infected ones, and we wait to offer them a home."

"I looked into his eyes, and they have not changed. They were bright blue. There were some yellow specks, but to me it looks there were even fewer of them than normal."

Cain stared at Angel.

"How can that be? Are you certain Elijah was bitten?"

"Our soldier swore – he managed to get several bites through to Elijah's skin. He is completely trustworthy. And I saw his injuries after the fight. They were so extensive he is still out of duty."

"And Elijah has not changed?"

"No."

"There must be something very strange in the genes of that family, then... We need to find out more. Can he be captured? It might be a mutation that only affects him and not Daniel. We need to make sure it doesn't spread. He must not breed before we catch him. The first child of a Nephilim usually inherits the strongest traits and abilities. We do not want him to create a child who cannot be infected."

There was a tiny flash of hope in Angel's mind, but she was very careful not to show it. This could mean she would not have to take Elijah as her husband. The thought of Nephilim children who could not be infected was on top of the list of Cain's fears.

"We will try, but it's not very likely that we'll do it easily."

"I don't care whether it is easy or not." Cain's voice was cold. "I only care that it is done. Sooner or later. I do understand the challenge, but I demand results."

"Yes, father." Angel had long practice in keeping her expression emotionless.

"Anything else? The girl?"

"I did not manage to infect her. She is still normal. But she has grown a lot in height – and I could already hear a silent hum from within her. She should be having her wings soon."

"That is a bit early... It should have been another year at least... But it could be that these are just the first signs, and the actual wings won't develop until later. It has been known to happen – the wings taking several months to develop."

"Her family has a history of early development..." Angel said. "I studied her bloodline, after Lilith's Time Walker group stole her as a baby. It took a while to find her mother's adoptive family, because she did not use her real name in London. But eventually I did find the small country village, where she was raised, before moving to London. I heard some wild stories about her."

"Really? What did the stories say?"

"I talked to those people who had been children at the same time. I found some of them still alive in old people's homes. I took a job as a nurse for a few weeks to get to them."

Cain stepped away from the window. He looked amused.

"This is interesting. You nursing feeble humans to find information. When were you planning on telling me?"

"As soon as I had interviewed enough of them, to be sure the stories were not simply old minds losing their touch with reality before death... I was writing my report when the news came she had been found, and Kitty's death had to be arranged. That became my primary responsibility. And after that getting Dana to us."

Cain nodded.

"Very well, acceptable. And what did these people tell you?"

"They told me that Dana's mother was bullied as a child. She was very tall already when she was young, and very shy. That is all it took for children to pick on her. She tolerated them, and tried to be accepted. But once the children went too far, pushing her face down in the mud when she was wearing her best dress, because her family was leaving for a wedding. She lost control, and her wings opened when she was only ten years of age."

"Ten? I have never heard anyone getting their wings at ten years of age!" Cain was openly surprised.

"She possibly did not remember much about what had happened either, because her mind wasn't ready for the wings yet, so she probably forgot about it afterwards. But like any new Nephilim, her emotions were very strong. Let's just say that she punished the children so severely they never even talked to her again. They were too scared to do so. After that her wings disappeared."

"I can imagine their horror..." Cain chuckled, "being beaten by an angel..."

"The children told their parents, of course, but no one took them seriously. The girl wasn't exactly angelic, after all. Especially having beaten the other children. Also the parents did not believe a little girl could beat their children so badly and came to the conclusion they had all been fighting with each other. Still, after this she became an outcast."

Cain laughed.

"Sounds like she would have been a very good wife for Nathaniel, after all. If we had known of her pregnancy, we could have infected her, or the baby at least, and all would have been well. But, as it was..."

Angel stood upright and showed no emotion for the fate of her half-brother. It was not permitted to grieve for those who had fallen out of Cain's favor.

"So, what are your plans next?" Cain asked.

"We shall wait and see where they will go for the clue. Surely they must have figured it out already. The clue has to be in our time, if the prophecy is right."

Even while speaking she knew she had said the wrong thing, but the words were already out. Cain's hands were round her neck so fast she did not even register their movement.

"NEVER doubt the prophecy!" Cain said quietly and squeezed, so that she began to choke.

She could not speak, could not nod to show that she agreed. She only had to wait to see whether he would kill her or not. And she could not show her fear in any way – that would awaken Cain's killer instincts instantly. He had no control over himself, when that happened, but killed anything and everything that stood in his way.

He did not kill her. After a while he dropped her on the floor.

"I apologize, father," Angel managed to whisper, "will you forgive me?"

Cain was trembling with fury, but forced himself to calm down.

"I understand you are still young. I forgive you. You must study the prophecy again. And again."

"I will, my father." Angel stayed on her knees on the floor.

"Go. Arrange to have them followed, so we may learn what the clue is. And when they leave for the Trail of Angels, have them followed even more closely, no matter what it costs."

"It shall be done." Angel rose to her feet, her head bent submissively so that her long blonde hair obscured her face.

Cain dismissed her with a wave of his long fingers and returned to his position by the window. The lad now had the stallion under his control. Cain was satisfied.

69

DIVINATION

Our boat navigated a channel of the river that would take us to the Great Lake. We passed the pyramid of the great king Senwosret, and continued towards the lake of the sacred crocodiles.

Mut-Bity had told me the story of the lake. King Menes, who unified the upper and lower Kemet into one kingdom, had been hunting near the lake. Suddenly his dogs, excited by the chase, turned against him. They could have killed him easily, but a crocodile came and scared the dogs away. The crocodile had carried the king over the lake into safety. To thank the crocodile, king Menes decreed that the lake would be a safe haven for crocodiles for all times. The king established the city of Shedt, the city of the god Sobek, which became the center of crocodile worship. All temples in this area were dedicated to Sobek.

When we finally came to shore one morning near Mi-Wer, Mut-Bity took me to the cabin of the boat.

"Stay here. Do not show yourself on the deck. Stay away from the wind."

Mut-Bity climbed on the pier and left. The captain pushed the boat away from the pier and the shore. Then we waited. I sat in the cabin on deck, and peered at the goings-on through the slits in its woven walls.

Because Mi-Wer was the summer home of the king's Great Royal

Wife Tiye and the royal children, many of king's wives were living there. I knew quite a few of them, and I had learned many languages, because most of them came from far away kingdoms. Either their fathers, the kings, had sent them as wives to our king, or they had followed in the retinue of a royal bride to Mi-Wer, and became minor wives themselves.

The king travelled here once in a while, when touring the country, and often spent every night with a different wife. He liked to make love to many women. Still, there was no threat to Tiye as his main consort, the Great Royal Wife, and she was the mother to the heir of the throne. I had often sat with my mother and watched her as she told what she saw in the future to the Great Royal Wife.

On one such time I had been watching the big, flat water bowl. Mother had poured oil on top of the water. Mother and Tiye had been discussing something, and I forgot myself, watching how the oil moved slowly on the water. I must have dozed off, because the next thing I knew was that I was on my back on the floor, and mother had bent over me.

"Shuet!" she said and slapped me softly on the cheek, "Wake up!"

I sat up, scared. It was very impolite to fall asleep in the presence of the Great Royal Wife.

"I am sorry, mother. Forgive me!"

For some reason the Great Royal Wife was looking at me with an odd expression, and her servants were staring at me with round eyes.

Soon after this the same servants began to bring me little gifts. I did not know how to react, because before they had mostly avoided me. I was certain it was because I was so ugly. But now they started to bring me little cakes, and wooden dolls with real clothes, even jewelry.

My sister began to be jealous of all the attention, and she showed it by spending more and more time in the daylight sun with the children of Mi-Wer. I could not follow them there. I was alone most of the time, listening to their laughter and play, and one day I did not want to sit in the shadows anymore. I went out and joined the children.

As before they looked at me as if I was strange, but did not go elsewhere. And I sat in their midst and played with dolls and balls, and played games in squares drawn to the ground with a stick. I could have cried with joy. I had friends!

My skin burned so badly I nearly perished. My skin was in big blisters, and I got a high fever. I sat and howled aloud. I could not lie down because of my burned shoulders, and neck, and scalp. The oldest of my mother's servants, Mut-Bity, took it as her duty to take care of me. She had seen more than I had realised and she scolded my sister.

"This is your fault!" she said angrily to my sister.

"I did not force her to go into the sunlight..." my sister tried to explain.

"Shut up! You were envious of the gifts she had received. You knew she cannot bear sunlight, but did not bring her in when you saw her outside, or bring your friends inside to play with her. No one wants to be abandoned and alone. Of course she wanted to play with you. But because you knew what the sun does to her, and did not act on it, it is your fault!"

"Mother!" my sister began to sob, "listen how your servant is speaking to me!"

"I hear," mother said from the next room, where she was making a poultice for my burned skin. "Firstly, she is right in what she says. And secondly, she is not my servant."

Her words were balm to my hurt feelings, and my sister grew quiet from sheer surprise.

"Mut-Bity saved my life once, and from her own free will she became our protector," mother's voice came nearer and she stepped into the room, "and you will address her with respect."

Mother's poultices helped slowly, but my skin remained angry and red for a long time. I thought I looked like a red and white cow. I withdrew into my own world even more, slept during the day and spent my nights on the roofs of Mi-Wer. Mut-Bity often kept me company. She seemed to have developed a special interest in me, and it felt good. I was a child, and she was old, but it was comforting to have company.

One night I finally managed the question that had been in my mind for many days.

"What is it you are protecting us from?"

Mut-Bity did not smile.

"From evil. You especially need to be protected."

I was too young to understand real evil yet.

"Why did the servants bring me presents?"

"They believe you are a great seer like your mother, and want to be in your favor so you would scry their future."

This was surprising.

"But I am no seer!"

Mut-Bity turned to look at me. The stars were so bright that even on a moonless night they cast her shadow on the roof next to mine. The world seemed to be all black and white and there was no sense of depth.

"Do you remember the day you fainted in Tiye's rooms?"

"I did not faint, I fell asleep," I corrected.

"You looked into the vision bowl of your mother, and it was as if you had fallen asleep with your eyes open. You spoke with an odd voice, and you predicted the future."

"What did I predict?"

"Two deaths. First the death of the crown prince Tuthmoses. And then the death of the king. You told to the day he would die, and you told everyone who was listening how even the gods would die with the new king."

"But the king is not dead..."

"The day has not yet come. Word about you has spread, however. I am not sure you are safe here."

"What would threaten me here?"

I did not find it odd that I spoke like an adult to Mut-Bity, even though I was only six years of age. Mother always said I was born old. I learned to speak at two years of age, but I spoke full sentences from the beginning.

"Evil. Evil in human form, which could use a good seer to further their own purposes."

I did not understand. But when a messenger from Inbu-Hedj, the city of White Walls, came with the news that prince Thutmose had died of a strange disease after a few brief days, my mother did not hesitate. She and Mut-Bity packed my belongings quickly.

Mut-Bity fetched her bees from a nearby garden, and we were on our way to the harbor before the news had spread. We heard the first ululations of grief over the walls of Mi-Wer when our boat had already left the pier. And on that journey we had been until the pale man appeared.

70

COUNCIL OF NEPHILIM

It was Daniel and Elijah together who introduced me to the Council of the Nephilim.

The image the phrase had originally conjured up was a dozen of them sitting cloaked in a semi-circle in some ancient crumbling castle, but the truth could not have been further from that.

Instead of a tower, I found myself standing in the south foyer of the extremely modern London Convention Centre. I was looking down at a carpet with grey, blue and red squares, while Daniel and Elijah collected our nametags from people sitting at a low table near to an enormous glass wall opposite the theatre. To my surprise the nametags were ready and waiting for us. Then I realised that this was probably what Daniel was arranging when he disappeared briefly from the desert.

Daniel handed me my nametag. It said that I was a participant in a convention of Nubian studies relating to the Middle Kingdom period of Egypt.

We walked through wooden double doors that were flanked by two very muscular Nephilim, who would not let us pass until they had looked right into our eyes. Everyone had to take off glasses or sunglasses before gaining entrance into a lecture hall that was filled with Nephilim.

"Wow..." I whispered.

They were all tall and visually arresting. Everyone looked young, or if they were clearly older, their appearance was still very youthful. The massed concentration of high body temperatures gave the theatre a mildly tropical atmosphere. A female member of the convention centre's staff was standing in the doorway, reassuring everyone that they would do their best to find the fault in the air conditioning.

"Oh, we are used to hot climates," a man reassured her and she gave him a grateful smile and no doubt wondered if she could ask him out. He looked extremely handsome, of course.

We sat at the back of the theatre. Some of the Nephilim turned to stare at me with open curiosity; others paid us very little attention.

The doors were closed and the room hushed in an instant.

A dark-haired man stepped onto the podium.

"I bid you welcome to our seminar," he began, "and to begin with I'll present the latest news... First of all, three of us were infected during this last year. One committed suicide after learning the fact, two left and joined the other Nephilim, as was their right. We shall miss Tabitha Jackson, Maria Angelos and Jonathan Rossman."

The silence was deafening.

"The good news is that we have learned of fifty pregnancies worldwide amongst us. Our adopted children have been taken good care of, and three have gained their wings this year. We did not lose a single child this year."

This time the audience applauded. They did not look happy, though. But how could you - if you knew all the babies were taken from their birth parents and given as adoptive children to other people? I now began to understand how heartbreaking it was for the Nephilim.

"And - " the presenter paused for effect "- in our midst today is one of the three who have now grown wings. Daniel Archer has been her Guardian for reasons that will be revealed soon."

There was a slight murmuring and then an air of silent expectation fell across the theatre. I blushed in horror. Was this meeting held because of me?

"We have received information that Cain's Nephilim are now certain their Prophecy is to about to be fulfilled. Those of you who are attending this Council for the first time: the Prophecy can be found in an old manuscript in their possession. It relates how all the Nephilim could inherit the earth - with the knowledge of the Watchers."

There was some mumbling from the audience, when the new members of the Council were filled in.

"This last hundred years' persecution of our kind can now be better understood. Cain wants the dark Nephilim to be in power. Supposedly the reason for this is the wording of the Prophecy that says 'the Nephilim shall inherit the earth.' If only Cain's Nephilim were left, he wouldn't need to worry about sharing power."

"But that's insane," I whispered to Daniel. "Who in their right minds would believe some vague prophecy?"

"Cain would," he whispered back.

"Daniel - please step forward and tell us more about the prophecy and the latest developments." The chairman's voice was controlled, but something in it caused the air of expectation to intensify.

Daniel rose and walked to the front. He exchanged a few whispered words with the chairman, stepped to the front of the stage and began to speak. His voice was so clear and audible he did not need a microphone.

"It's as our chairman said - I have been guardian to a young Nephilim, who was hastily rescued from Cain's hands in the midst of the London Blitz in 1940. Rarely has a more desperate rescue been attempted, but the child was saved and brought to our time. She has been well hidden within a foster family - the daughter of one of our very best Hunters, who had kept the child's true identity a secret from her family. Thus they had no idea of the parallel world of the Nephilim, shadows and the afterlife.

"Without our realising it, somehow the shadows found her in our time, but Cain's Nephilim did not attack her. This was surprising, but we think we know why - they were not sure of her heritage and waited for a time, to assess if she was truly Nephilim. When we kidnapped Cain's senior librarian from the City of the Immortals, we discovered even more."

This was news to me. They had to be talking about Mr. Donnelly.

"He had read the Prophecy and recited it to us. There was one part in particular that caught our attention. I'll repeat it here."

Daniel took a piece of paper from his pocket and began to read. As he spoke the words, my spine began to tingle.

"The time shall come, when the offspring of the bloodlines of Cain and Seth is born, who will be called She of the Silver Waters. Her companion is a white lioness, who sees the future. Together they can walk the Trail of Angels, and old times shall be once more. You shall know her from what she weaves. "

My mouth opened in astonishment.

"We think now we know who this person is. Dana, please join me here."

There was nowhere to hide. Every face turned towards me and oh yes - I blushed.

"Go on, Dana," Elijah nudged me, "they don't bite. Pun intended."

I managed a shaky smile, and rose. I walked to the stage with wobbly knees.

"This is Dana," Daniel introduced me, "my protege, and the last offspring of the bloodlines of Cain and Seth."

Astonished whispers from the audience.

"Her father was the eldest son of Cain, Nathaniel. He escaped when Cain approached him, after he had grown to his Nephilim state, whilst he was still living with his mother. Cain declared that he was to be changed and to marry a bride of Cain's choice. Nathaniel was one of us, as many of you may remember."

I did not understand this. Did Cain keep a harem of unchanged Nephilim, then? And did the act of lovemaking in itself not cause an infection? It had to do with venomous spit only? How else could my father be still unchanged as an adult?

"He had a brief affair with the daughter of the Seth line, and Dana was the result of this relationship. Nathaniel was found by Cain's

Nephilim and taken before he learned of the pregnancy, so Cain did not know of a coming child either. This is probably why Dana's mother had a chance to give birth to her - and nurse her."

The audience stared at me intently - all those bright eyes were unnerving. I noticed two Nephilim with darker complexions in the audience as well, and their eyes were not blue but of a cool yellowish shade. Not like Angel's oily bright yellow, no, but more a mixture of gold and silver. One pair of eyes staring at me at the front row were brown, and I could see the yellow specks in them as well.

"We sought knowledge as to what the Prophecy meant by the One of the Silver Waters. When we fetched the main librarian, we were attacked by one of Cain's angels. He fought with Elijah, who was severely injured, and also bitten."

Voices rose in argument. Angry glances in Elijah's direction, confused looks towards Daniel.

"Elijah, come here."

Elijah rose and walked up to us on the stage. I noticed how the Nephilim avoided touching him as he passed.

"Anyone is free to come up here and look into his eyes."

No one moved. Just as the situation was beginning to feel awkward, the chairman himself stepped up and walked to face Elijah. They looked into each other's eyes for a long time.

"His eyes show no change," the man finally said, "and the number of yellow specks is very low. How can this be?"

"Dana, time to show your wings," Daniel murmured to me, and smiled at me. Warmly, with emotion, clearly with the intention of calming me down.

When my knees were firm again, I drew in a deep breath and opened my wings. OK, I admit it, I shared some of Daniel's sense of drama, and I popped them open fully extended, so that everyone could see them well.

Total silence. Absolute, total silence.

"These are silver wings. Both of Dana's parents must have carried the very rare, recessive silver gene. The silver gene is the gene of a healer, and you cannot have silver wings unless both parents carry the gene. She has used her healing powers twice now - first to heal Elijah's wings, and second, to purify his blood. She did this by weaving silver threads straight into his veins. You shall know her from what she weaves."

The chairman stepped in front of me and stared at me in the eye. Looking into his stern eyes I knew that he was capable of killing me, if he did not like what he saw. But I did not flinch, or back away. I felt this was a decisive moment in my life.

Finally, he withdrew and turned to the audience.

"She is pure. And what's more - there is no yellow at all in her eyes. They are totally blue. Daniel has spoken words of truth. We have a silver angel in our midst..."

The chairman turned and addressed his next words to me:

"Silver Nephilim were thought to be extinct after Cain used the calling device of the Watchers, and lured them all into a trap and had them killed in ancient Greece. We thought their whole line was destroyed, but somehow, miraculously, the genes still existed, and created you. The mass murder of the Silver Nephilim is when the war among the Nephilim really began. That device was intended to call upon Nephilim healers in desperate situations. He used it to kill the healers who could themselves cure mortally wounded Nephilim."

"Why would he want to kill such healers?" I asked.

"The virus that infects the Nephilim and turns them dark, is so strong it keeps them alive for thousands of years, if they are not killed in another way. Cain's Nephilim had no need of the Silver Wings to heal their kind any longer. And he wanted to take our healers away from us so we would be weakened. Our life span is shorter."

While he spoke, people rose from their seats. They stared at me as if they had seen a miracle.

"Close your wings," Daniel whispered.

I did. And just in time, too. The doors to the theatre opened and the lady who had been talking about the air conditioning came in. I wondered what would have happened, if she had seen my wings...

"And indeed the fortress of Buhen is now lost to us. It is now submerged far beneath the waters of Lake Nasser, and we are only left with the excavation reports. Today we shall be exploring some of those excavation reports from the Egypt Exploration Society," the chairman was by the microphone in an instant.

After the member of the staff had talked again with the man to whom she had been promising improvement in the air conditioning system, she left. By that time the audience had calmed down.

"But that is not all," Daniel continued his speech immediately, "we have also learned more about the Trail of Angels. It seems that this is a trail where clues are hidden which lead to the City of Angels, or the Abode of the Watchers. Cain's angels want to wake the Watchers and return the old order. Humanity would be enslaved. We need to stop them."

"Why?" asked someone in the audience, a man.

Daniel turned to look at him. For a while he said nothing, and his unwavering look made the questioner squirm slightly.

"This world is not ours only, it is shared with humankind," Daniel stressed his words. "No one is to enslave anyone. Also - we do not know what the Watchers are, and whether it is even safe to wake them up. Or to release them from their prison, if the old legends are true."

"Shouldn't we be too fearful to find out?" a woman asked. "Would it not be safer to let them be, wherever they are?"

"No. We have to find out, because if we don't, Cain's angels certainly will. We have received information as to where the clue is that leads to the beginning of the Trail of Angels."

"Where is it?" the same woman wanted to know.

"That will not be revealed here, in case anyone here might be infected in future and reveal the information to Cain. We have gathered a Time Walker team that will travel there, and if at all possible, walk the Trail. The Trail might not be in current time, given the ability of Nephilim and Angels to travel throughout time, so Time Walkers are necessary."

"Many of the Time Walkers are humans. How can you be sure they are strong enough for the task?" the chairman asked.

"The ones we've chosen certainly are up to the demands of the task. And before you ask, I won't give their names. They will accompany me, Elijah and Dana. They are needed not only because of their skills, but because of their humanness. The Nephilim don't blend in with crowds well, particularly so in the past, when people were much shorter. Even if we did, people still sense our... differences, especially when there are several of us around."

Agreeing nods in the audience.

"And Dana will be your Weaver?" the chairman asked. "She is an ordinary Weaver as well, if I have understood this correctly? All the Silver ones in the past have been Weavers."

"Indeed she is," Daniel nodded.

"Can I ask... who or what is the white lioness in the Prophecy?" someone asked.

"She was Dana's best friend Kitty. They made a deal to live together in this day and age. She was to develop into a clairvoyant, who could use her skills to protect Dana from any forthcoming danger. She was killed by Cain's people before she could grow into her skills."

"So she is gone..." the chairman said.

"Yes and no," Daniel said. "She has returned to the lower levels of the buffer zone, to help Dana as they have agreed."

"She has not proceeded to her level in the afterlife? She has chosen to stay?"

"Yes, she has chosen to stay and to do her best from where she is now, to help Dana in her mission, because this was the agreement between her and Dana before they were born."

The Nephilim discussed the information with each other in low voices. Their conversation did not give any impression there was anything new in this. To them talking about the dead as if they were still here didn't seem to be anything special. Well - obviously to the Nephilim they were still here, sort of, because the Nephilim could move in the spiritual realms as well, and meet with the dead ones.

"Very well," the chairman finally said. "Of course we respect Kitty's decision, and hope she truly can help you, because you must surely understand that Cain will do anything in his power to stop you from reaching the goal and finding the Watchers before he does."

"Yes, we are fully aware of this," it was Elijah's turn to speak, "but

Dana is our strength. They can't harm her by infecting her, and she has the means to cure those who are infected. As long as Dana is amongst us, we can take risks."

"I hope you will avoid risks, though," the chairman said.

"Cain's Nephilim do not know yet of Dana's abilities in healing, so I wish this to remain secret as long as possible. We understand it will be revealed sooner or later, but hopefully later, after we have left," Daniel said.

There was general agreement in the audience, even if it was easy to read between the lines that Daniel expected someone here to get infected, and eventually leak the information out.

"You have our blessing, and our help," the chairman said, "seek out our kind in the times where you travel, and show them this."

He pulled his necklace out from under his shirt and handed it to Daniel. I did not have time to look at it, because he carefully kept the pendant in the cup of his hand.

"This is the seal of the Nephilim council. It has remained the same throughout the ages, and each council has a similar one. All the pure Nephilim will obey this seal, no matter in which time or place they are dwelling."

"We thank you," Daniel bowed, "and now it is our time to leave."

"We'll leave right away too as our presence here is bound to draw the attention of Cain's spies," the chairman nodded. "The first ones will leave soon after you."

Daniel took my left hand, and Elijah took the right one. The physical world faded away around us.

71

HIS MOTHER IS RE

"Where are we going now?" I asked.

"Back to the Centre," Daniel said. "We need to research the tomb of Panhesy. It may not be safe to actually go there, not if Angel's spies are all over the tourist attractions in Egypt. Perhaps we shall find the clue by some other means."

Daniel had no problem in finding his way to the Centre's library in the higher buffer zone. I had no idea how exactly he did it, but we appeared there among the shelves after some flying through the mist. Daniel walked along the corridors, clearly knowing where he was headed. After a while an opening appeared in the midst of the bookshelves to reveal a round space, with the corridors spreading out in all directions. There were several desks, and people were sitting there with their laptops, typing notes.

"Do they have an internet connection here?" I asked, not believing my eyes.

Elijah laughed.

"No, of course not. And we would not use it, even if it were possible to have one here. Where there is internet access, there is a risk of hacking. Cain's Nephilim know their way around the net, and hacking is their favorite pastime when they try to track us down. These researchers write their notes here, and then the laptops are connected to the central computer of the Centre, which is not linked to any net either. It is a completely closed system. The researchers then work on the material in the Centre. No memory sticks or cell phones are allowed either."

"Of course we have normal computers, connected to the internet, and we feed information through them about the Magellan spa, for Cain's spies to see," Daniel continued. "Since the shadows appeared outside the spa gate, it seems there has been a lot more interest in the Centre's website. And a few hacking attempts, but they have so far found nothing suspicious. Because it isn't there."

"Aren't the people here in danger, then? If Cain's Nephilim know about this Centre now, then surely they will follow the people who visit here..." I worried.

"I wouldn't let that bother you too much," Daniel answered. "As you will have noticed, one of Centre's wings is in actual spa-use. So ordinary people who have nothing to do with the Centre, visit here all the time."

"Aren't they in danger, then?"

"A few shadows have followed them, yes, but when they have proved to be ordinary people, and not exactly the kind who would mope about their lives over drink so their energies would be easy to steal, they will soon begin to doubt if they have drawn the right conclusions. They followed Layla, but they know nothing of what happens here. As far as they know, she might have been visiting the spa with you. They never saw you leaving this building, they only knew your scent was along the highway that led to this place. You might have left before they arrived."

I somehow doubted the shadows or Nephilim were that stupid. Of course they would suspect I was here.

"All our Hunters keep strictly indoors now and only leave through the buffer zone. The shadows and dark Nephilim are not certain about this being our meeting place, so they haven't approached us. If, however, one of their Nephilim should arrive here, things may change. Still, it is more likely that they will try to send an ordinary person here as a guest, to see what this place is about. That's the way they work. It wouldn't be easy, though, because to enter you need to be recommended by existing customers. The treatments here are very expensive, and we don't advertise. Word of mouth brings our customers here. And we only accept the very richest, the crème de la crème, if you will."

"And they pay for the running of the Centre," I concluded.

"Indeed," Daniel agreed.

"Also the hall, where the gate is, is protected. Remember Reggie's bronze bowls? He told me you weren't exactly enthusiastic about them," Elijah continued.

"How could I forget!"

I could still recall the humming, vibrating sound that had almost driven me crazy on our drive to the Centre.

"The walls are fitted with a sound system that repeats the same ringing sound. You cannot hear it inside the central hall because of sound proofing, but the walls, the ceiling, the floor - they are all "booby trapped" with loudspeakers on the outside. If the system recognizes the vibration of a dark Nephilim nearby, the speakers start playing the sound of the bowls," Elijah grinned. "A most unpleasant experience for an unsuspecting dark Nephilim. The sound goes straight to their wings and it feels like a bad toothache. Or wing-ache in this case. Not one of Cain's followers can function properly in the midst of that noise. It's all about differences of vibration. And we have an emergency power generator in the basement, so cutting our electricity wouldn't have much of an effect on our sound system, should they try that."

He chuckled, put his hands on his ears and made anguished faces, and I had to laugh. Even Daniel smiled. I felt so relieved they were behaving normally with me.

"How old are you, exactly?" I asked Elijah.

"A wee bit older than you, I'm afraid. But younger than Daniel."

"That figures," I said. "You behave like a teenager."

"Yes well, we don't mature very fast, as you can see, looking at our physique," Elijah made a sweeping motion from his head to toe. The in-between was exceedingly handsome.

"Good job she can't see into your mind... the level of immaturity would shock her," Daniel smiled crookedly and gave a mocking kick towards his little brother's back and Elijah turned around and made some boxing movements at Daniel.

Thank goodness, they were on speaking terms again. It was clear they were keeping a polite distance from me. I understood that. My heart was aching for Daniel, but I understood.

"OK, you kick boxers." Diana appeared carrying a pile of books. "Here's Panhesy for you to study. Dana, you have been reading about ancient Egypt for a long time, so you're going to participate too. Sit at that table and start going through any info about the walls at first. Look at them and try to find anything that doesn't fit into the overall picture."

"Well, that's kinda hard, considering that the clue was left by the angel a long time ago, when the Copts had their church there," Elijah said.

"Less talking and more application to the task! You of all people have enough knowledge of ancient Egypt to help with this," Daniel slapped him softly on the back of his head.

"Yes, mother..." Elijah grabbed a pile of books, steering my vivid imagination in the direction of what their mother had been like. Or was like. For all I knew she could be alive still.

It was hopeless. We leafed through the pages of the books, but the photographs and drawings revealed nothing. If there were photographic images of the actual wall reliefs of the tomb, you could barely make out the outlines. The drawings themselves revealed nothing to us, nor did the translations of the hieroglyphic texts. We had no idea what we were trying to find.

There were many depictions of Akhenaten and Nefertiti and their daughters. They were worshipping the Aten, and nearly always had a substantial entourage around them. They rode in their chariots. They gave gold to Panhesy. As in any Amarna tomb, the scenes were not about the gods, but about the royal family, whom everyone was supposed to worship. The royals were the only ones who could approach the Aten and so no ordinary person could have direct access to the sun disk.

They were interesting scenes and it was easy to get absorbed in them, but I didn't see anything that would have given a hint about the Trail of Angels. No one with wings was fluttering around. And there was definitely no X to mark the spot. The only wings were the three pairs of red wings, between which the grey plaster had fallen down, and there was certainly no hidden clue or hint.

"Oh, I need a break!" I put down the last one of the books. "I'm finding nothing here!"

"Maybe the clue has already disappeared - destroyed a long time ago," Elijah rubbed his eyes. "If it was anything of value, it's bound to be long gone. Despite all those elaborate preparations for death, many of the Egyptians didn't exactly respect their dead, and looted the tombs often right after the burials. Even the pharaohs stole whatever they could from their predecessors, or reused it, perhaps we should say. Statues, grave goods, temples... And it still continues, right across the world. Some people have no respect for history - they destroy in the name of religion or steal for financial benefit."

"No, it can't have been anything of value like gold. Whoever left the clue must have known that it would have to be inconspicuous," Daniel sighed. "But I agree, let's go and have something to eat."

We found Reggie and Mr. Donnelly deep in discussion at the cafeteria. Both had pushed aside half-eaten plates of food, and spread out papers all over their table. Their hands were flying in the air when their heads did not almost bang together over some interesting piece of information. Reggie's laptop also seemed to be an object of great fascination to Mr. Donnelly, and he pressed a key occasionally, and let out a delighted laugh. Reggie tried to keep the machine away from him, but the curiosity of the latter and his inquisitive mind meant that his long fingers kept reaching for it when he could.

"Good evening!" Daniel greeted the scholars.

They both almost jumped as they suddenly realised the presence of other people.

"Oh, good evening, good evening..." Reggie looked like someone who had been forced to wake up from a pleasant dream. "Any success with the Panhesy search?"

"None whatsoever," I sighed, "lots of pictures and text, but nothing in the least that gave us a clue."

We took our food to another table next to Reggie and Mr. Donnelly, as our drinking glasses were not safe near their animated discussion or flying hands. Diana moved up from a nearby table and shook her head.

"It's been quite an experience to listen to those two having a discussion." She placed her tray on the table. "I am sure the only people on this planet who have the faintest idea what they are talking about are they themselves. That's partly because they kept dropping into various obscure ancient languages. Their versions of them, anyway."

"Do you remember the exact wording of the Coptic script that was found in the desert?" we heard Reggie asking.

"Not exactly, no... but it said an angel had appeared and told people the clue was hidden in the tomb."

"Was hidden? I understood earlier the angel hid it. As in an activity by the angel."

"No, no... the Coptic language is perhaps not my forte, but I am certain now the text said the clue was already hidden in the tomb."

"Hmm... so it was there already, and the angel came to tell people it was there. Why, I wonder..."

"So that they would write it down, of course, and so that the knowledge would become part of their religious tradition." Mr. Donnelly voiced his opinion. "It was crucial to this winged creature that the knowledge of the clue would be saved. And if a Nephilim showed themselves to ordinary people, who already had a religious tradition of angels - well, wouldn't you say they would write that down?"

"Yes, of course... material vanishes with time, but stories are immaterial and keep on living throughout the ages..." Reggie mused and pointed at something on the table with his fork, barely missing Mr. Donnelly's fingers. I wasn't quite sure whether it was intentional, as the said fingers were again reaching for the laptop. "So it is somewhere there... was there anything else, anything at all?"

"Well, yes... Come to think of it. An odd sentence... allegedly the angel said that 'His mother is the sun, and the king's wives live forever'. A heated theological discussion must have developed from this.

Doesn't exactly fit Christian theology, now does it?" Mr. Donnelly seemed amused.

"Ahha! Haha! Marvellous! That's it! That's it!"

Reggie could not contain his enthusiasm, but jumped up so that he knocked his chair over and did a little victory dance by their table. We forgot our dinner and just stared at his long arms waving in the air, and his long legs kicking to an unknown rhythm.

"Mutefre! Hemetnisu Weterneheh!" he sang rhythmically while he danced, snapping his fingers.

"Does anyone else suspect he finally lost his marbles?" Elijah asked, staring at Reggie with a wide, amused grin.

"Erm... now that you mention it, the thought does arise..." Diana mused.

"Uh-huh." We all added our various agreements.

"Seems studying history has its disadvantages. I think his hard drive finally reached maximum capacity..." Diana observed with a tilted head.

"Follow me!" Reggie bolted at a run.

For a second we stared at him, then exchanged glances, and ran after him, leaving our food behind us. Suddenly we weren't hungry any more.

He ran to Lilith's office, of course. Only Lilith wasn't there.

"Lilith!" Reggie galloped past us and along the corridor that led in the opposite direction from the one where Diana and I had our room.

He knocked on a door at its other end, hollering Lilith's name. The door opened and Lilith peeked out. She had obviously been asleep (so she did sleep, after all), but was immediately awake and alert.

"What is it?" she asked. "Is there danger?"

"No, no, but Mr. Donnelly did indeed find the clue to the beginning of the trail. His mother is the Sun! King's wives live forever! Haha!"

Reggie turned around and trotted towards Lilith's office again.

"Where is it... I'm sure I have it..."

We followed. Suddenly he stopped and swerved to his right, into a room. Thumbing noises and muttering were to be heard. We looked inside, and found our good professor rummaging through a huge pile of books. There were several piles surrounding the bed, and towering on the table, but he seemed to know where it was - whatever it was.

"Davies, where are you..."

Daniel was standing by my side, and I enjoyed every moment, feeling his physical presence. Elijah was peeking over his shoulder and in the process pushed him against me. I tried to stand as relaxed as I could, so I would not scare him away. I so wanted to touch his hand, but didn't. I only swallowed and pretended to be looking at Reggie with interest, but it was difficult, when what I wanted to do something quite different, which involved Daniel...

Then I noticed Diana grinning. She winked at me and I made a face at her as inconspicuously as I possibly could. Right then Reggie pulled at a book, causing all the other books above it in the pile to collapse on the floor in a small cloud of dust.

"Sorry, sorry..." he said to the volumes, "Davies, found you!"

"What did you find?" Lilith wanted to know.

Reggie beamed.

"The Rock tombs of El Amarna by Davies. A book by the Egypt Exploration Fund from 1905!"

He clearly expected some sort of applause, which did not come.

"Could you clarify a bit?" Lilith asked.

"Yes, here..." he frantically flipped through the pages, "the plates, where are the plates... Here! Do you see? The lintel of the door..."

We all bent forward to see the picture he was holding towards us. Akhenaten and Nefertiti stood giving sacrifices to the Aten, with their hanging bellies and round thighs marking typical Amarna art. They stood next to an offering table filled with food for the god. Behind them were three of their daughters, shaking their sistra - sacred rattles - and beyond them were court ladies in bent positions. Behind these were two even smaller figures, standing upright. There were two similar scenes, mirroring each other, with the offering table in the middle.

"You see it?"

"Well, no... what are we looking at?"

"These here!" Reggie pointed his finger at the two smallest figures behind the court ladies.

"They look a bit... odd," Diana said. "They are not children... their toes are pointing inwards. Like they had bent feet?"

"No, no, of course they are not children. They are the two dwarves that are often shown together with Nefertiti's sister. Mutbenret, or Mutnodjmet - the spelling varies."

He looked at us, clearly enjoying his moment. Then he finally told us.

"Their names are: Mutefre and Hemetnisu Weterneheh. Translated as: 'His mother is Re', and 'King's Wives Live Forever'. The very thing the angel said to the Copts when he appeared to them in Panhesy's tomb. And this picture is from Panhesy's tomb!"

Now we finally understood, though Mr. Donnelly seemed to be more concerned about how Re could be anyone's mother, being a male god.

"The beginning of the Trail of Angels is not a thing - it is a person. Or two people!" Daniel said. "The royal sister's dwarves have the knowledge we need! In Akhetaten, the royal city of Akhenaten and Nefertiti."

"Built in the 14th century BC..." I said, "the birth place of Tutankhamun."

"So," Lilith smiled, "now we know where to start. It seems we have a lot of planning to do for a time walk some three and a half thousand years back into the past!"

72

DEAL WITH A GODDESS

Ambrogio sang the name of Artemis, but without the device on his throat. He had hidden it on the advice of Hades. But he would not have needed it anyway. The pool of silver blood at his feet seemed to remain alive, swirling slightly where the dry ground had not drunk it up. When his voice cut the darkness, the blood seemed to sing along – a faint, but clear echo, much like the voice the throat-device had created.

And she came just like Hades, appearing out of nowhere. Ambrogio could see her form in the silver glow of the blood on the ground. Her yellow gaze met the torso lying on the ground, and then turned to the shaking Ambrogio.

"You did this?"

"I did, oh mighty Artemis."

"Why?"

Ambrogio was not prepared to answer this. He had only been told to give the body as a gift to Artemis, and he had not thought about it any further.

"Someone told you I hunt for these?"

"Yes, my goddess," Ambrogio stammered.

She laughed.

"I can imagine who this someone was. Trying to win my favour back..."

She left it at that and Ambrogio was glad she did not press the subject.

"I am glad. You have repaid well your debt of the kithara. We shall discuss the forever in my service later."

Artemis bent down and dipped her fingers into the silvery blood. She smeared it in her fingers. It shone beautifully in the increasing morning light of the eastern sky. She laughed at the sight. And then she raised her other hand, where she held what looked like a small silver bow and slashed the air with it. A gap appeared, behind which was grey mist. She stepped into it, turned around, and the cut in the air vanished.

Ambrogio stared in disbelief. Artemis had a weapon that could slice through the air itself.

"Master..." a hoarse whisper behind him made him swirl around.

It was his shadow.

"We can return now," the shadow bowed, "the girl came and found your letter and read it."

"What... How did she react?" Ambrogio almost grabbed the shoulders of the shadowy form, but could not make himself do it. It looked too much like a demon of his childhood nightmares.

"She looked around, searching for you. I did not show myself but observed her from the misty place."

Misty place... That had to be the reality behind the human world, behind which the afterworld and the abode of Hades were situated.

"Yes? And then?"

"She folded the letter, hid the bundle she was carrying under an opening on a rock by the roadside and continued towards the temple."

The shining rim of the sun's disk appeared on the eastern edge of the sky. Ambrogio felt the pain on his face increasing. The shadow grabbed his arm and pulled him into the mist. They did not move as easily as Hades had. There was an unpleasant feeling of being stuck into a sticky substance that did not allow Ambrogio to move. But the shadow pulled and pulled, and the resistance eased slowly. Then the mist cleared, and

Ambrogio could move again. A landscape appeared, and soon they were walking towards the city of Hades, across the rolling hills, that appeared almost solid and real. There was an occasional thinning here and there where the grey mist showed through, but the shadow did not seem to find these alarming and kept walking, leading Ambrogio ahead.

The sun had bruised his skin into a dull grey color, but his exposure to its light had been so fleeting, his skin soon began to return to normal.

Hades kept his word. Ambrogio got the palace for himself, and rested there every day, waiting for nightfall in the world of humans, while staying in the eternal scattered light of the afterworld. He never managed to work out where the light came from. It could not be the sun, because it did not harm his skin.

He learned to know some of the people in the eternal city. They were ordinary human beings, but every single one possessed some skill Hades found useful. Someone was an expert in poisons. Another was a skilled armourer. Yet another a talented thief. And there were hundreds more. They all had some mission given to them by Hades, and they did it gladly, in exchange for a chance to live in a place where they were not touched by time. They called the place the City of Immortals and considered themselves above ordinary mortals.

He met the oldest citizen of the city during his stay. He came from Egypt, and his name was Thutmose. He had been a sculptor and an artist at the royal Egyptian court in the distant past. He practiced his skill still, creating the most beautiful statues out of the material of this strange world. Ambrogio often sat at his studio, and observed him working, scooping the ground and forming his art from it.

The strange statues of the king and queen of his own past at first came out beautifully, but after a while their features changed. It was as if they were made of wax that had its own will. Nothing could stay the way they had been created.

"Does this not bother you? That your work changes?" Ambrogio asked once, when he sat with a goblet of wine, watching how the sculptor worked.

"No, it is quite fascinating," Thutmose commented, "I have noticed that this material responds to the way I feel. If I am angry, the statues become distorted into an unpleasant form. If I am in a good mood, the change can be sometimes quite beautiful."

Today Thutmose had been in a good mood. The male statue he had made distorted itself into a laughing dwarf. The men chuckled at the sight, sitting amicably side by side, enjoying the good wine.

Thutmose's paintings, however, remained the way he had painted them. The reason was obviously the fact that he used real paint and brushes, and real papyrus to paint on. These were the materials of the human world, already solid. Ambrogio admired the way he painted beautiful women out of memory. They had elongated necks and long skulls with no hair, but they were beautiful. None as beautiful as Selene, though.

Every night Ambrogio went to the human world, every time to a different location, and using the calling device lured yet another silver winged one to him. He became very skilled at killing them before they realized what was happening. They all had the same kind, concerned look on their faces when they approached him and then the expression of utter surprise when he killed them.

And they all sang, beautifully, when they died. Ambrogio began to call this music the song of a dying swan. He bent closer to see how they made the eerie sound, but it did not seem to come from their throats. It came from their whole body.

Every night he wrote a note to Hades with the silver blood as proof of yet another kill, and after that, every night he wrote a note to his beloved Selene. He began to write poems to her and his shadow told him that she read every one of them.

All in all Ambrogio killed forty-four of the swans, as he now called them. He gave them to Artemis, and she was satisfied. She always came when he sang her name; and she always expressed her joy at the sight of the corpses.

And then the unthinkable happened. The last of the silver winged ones approached, and he shot the arrow- and missed. The creature vanished in an instant, and he knew he had lost the last of the swans for good.

He stood there, on the mountainside, with his bow, without arrows. Hades had not appeared in a long time, and had not given him more arrows. And he had promised that after forty-five nights he could come and take Selene to a safe place where Apollo would not find them.

He sat down on the ground and cried. Surely now, when he could no longer send letters to Selene, she would think he had abandoned her, and would not wait for him any longer. He could not use any other blood for the letters. He was certain she would not believe they were from him, if they were not written in silver blood. And Hades would not let him return to the afterworld with Selene, because he had missed the last swan.

"What's wrong?" a familiar voice asked.

Artemis had appeared. She was carrying her magical weapon in her hand, and behind her was a slit in the air. Ambrogio knew now was his only chance to ever get Selene to himself. He had decided to try this tonight anyway, and now his mind quickly changed the plan from trying to grab Artemis's weapon.

"Oh mighty Artemis... I have run out of my magical arrows... I still have one swan to kill and nothing to do it with. I see you have a mighty weapon in your hands. Could I ask to borrow it so I could kill the last remaining silver swan?"

There was silence. The longer it stretched, the more certain Ambrogio became he had been too impudent and the goddess would punish him for talking to her so disrespectfully.

To his surprise the goddess answered:

"I don't see why not. But I will stay with you and see how you lure them to you. It will be a great joy to me when I see the last descendant of the Shadow who created the silver ones disappear."

Ambrogio had no idea who or what this shadow, this ancestor, might have been.

For the first time Artemis now spread her wings. Ambrogio had suspected she had wings, but she had never shown them. They were not half as impressive as those of Hades, and they had a greyish hue.

Still, their veins pulsed with vibrant red, and the light that emanated from them was red too. Despite being smaller in size, they were mighty and their hum revealed she had great power in them.

In the reddish glow of the wings he saw her extending her hand towards him, holding the strange small bow-like weapon. He bowed respectfully and took the weapon, trying to hold it as Artemis had.

"I would not recommend pointing the blades towards yourself," Artemis said in an amused voice, "you will only split yourself into two."

Ambrogio observed the strange weapon. It consisted of two metal pieces. One was straight, woven out of three thin, intertwining bars of some silvery substance, like a woman's plait. It shone like silver, but was much lighter. In the middle the metal bars looped away from each other, leaving enough space for Ambrogio to slid his fingers through, making it possible for him to squeeze the weapon into a tight grip.

The other piece was of thick flat metal, and curved like the crescent moon. It curved away from the keeper's hand, and on its outward curving side it had what looked a lot like the arrow tips Ambrogio had used on his magical arrows. They were tube-like, translucent, and narrowed into needle sharp tips. It was as if he was holding the jaw and teeth of some magical creature. The weapon felt hot in his hands and he could feel a slight tremor in the blade, as though it was alive. His arrow tips had never felt this... alive. He looked at them closer, and they had a slightly different color from the arrow tips. These were of pale red color, though totally transparent. Like glass.

Artemis vanished somewhere in the background and Ambrogio made his move. Having observed Artemis for forty-four nights he knew what to do. He raised his hand and quickly slid through the air. An opening appeared like cutting through flesh. He ran forward, and into the opening. In his haste he did not think of calling for his shadow to help.

He did not have a chance. Two grey and red wings curled from behind and enveloped him, yanking him back to the world. When they touched his skin they burned him so badly that he had to scream. He dropped the weapon and fell to his knees at the feet of the furious goddess, on top of the bow. He could feel it snap under his weight. A pale hand snatched it away from under his legs.

"Tell me one good excuse why I should not kill you right now, thief, " her voice hissed above his head.

"Selene!" Ambrogio's voice broke in tears, "I will lose Selene if I don't bring your weapon!"

That took her by surprise.

"Why would you lose Selene if you don't steal my weapon?" she asked.

"Apollo cursed me so I could never walk under the sun again. Selene and I were to leave together to live as husband and wife... How could I take her anywhere if I cannot be touched by the sun? Then Hades came and said he would give us a safe place to live in, away from the sun, if I gave him your silver bow... I had no choice but to obey..."

Ambrogio did not dare to lift his head. He saw three fallen blades from Artemis's weapon on the ground, under his knees.

Artemis pulled him up on his feet.

"So, I see the one who asked you to do this was after my weapon, and not trying to win my love back. All the worse for him..."

Artemis looked at him in the eye. Then she pulled something from a pouch hanging on her neck. It was a little bottle, made of precious glass. And it had silver blood in it.

"What if I give you this blood to write a letter to Hades and to your girl? And you shall then be the servant you promised to be for ever."

"I would be forever grateful..." Ambrogio whispered, "but why would you do this? Why not kill me now?"

"I need faithful servants also. Hades would have given you immortality in his city, where the sun would never touch you. I can give you immortality in this world, and heal the curse of Apollo, so the sun will not harm you. There will be no need for you to hide in the mist at the edge of the world. You can be together with your girl. But there is a price to pay."

Ambrogio felt hope rising.

"Anything, my beautiful goddess, anything! I shall worship you forever!"

"Indeed you shall. As a result of your promise, you will be eternally young, but you will not be like normal people any longer. You will become the best hunter and no prey will be able to escape you, because you will outrun them all. And you shall hunt for me and kill whom I ask you to kill. For food you will drink the blood of the animals you catch, because no other food will ever be accepted by your body. It will be like intoxicating wine to you. And you will need lots of it."

"I can accept that, goddess," Ambrogio was eager to accept the terms.

"But this is not all. You shall have your Selene, but not in the way mortal men would want. You cannot touch her, you cannot kiss her, you cannot make love to her. Because if you do, your changed body will be the death of her. You will give her an illness that will turn her into a shadow. Your sweat or saliva will do the same to her as Apollo's spit did to you. If you two can live together on these terms, I will help you."

Ambrogio fell silent.

"I shall have to tell her this," he said, "and if she agrees, I am happy to accept."

The goddess smiled and gave the bottle to him.

"Here, then. This blood is from last night, so it should still be fresh enough to write with."

Very carefully Ambrogio opened the bottle and dipped the quill into the liquid. He then wrote to Hades "I have killed the last swan". And then another note to Selene, in which he told he had met a goddess, and explained the terms of Artemis to her, following the dictation of the goddess: "If you agree to do this, come to the Kirrha docks by the sea. I shall wait for you there."

Artemis stepped back.

"Your shadow will come soon. I shall have to kill it so it won't reveal our plan to Hades."

And sure enough the shadow came. It looked around suspiciously.

"Where, oh Master, is the body?"

"It is behind that bush," Ambrogio waved in the direction where Artemis had disappeared.

The shadow did not have time to realize what was happening. Artemis hit it on the neck with her weapon, and the shadow disintegrated in front of Ambrogio. He felt an unpleasant snap as if something had hit him in his pancreas.

"There. Now we shall leave your final note to Selene."

The goddess slashed the air, and taking Ambrogio's hand pulled him into the grey mist.

The slash closed and all was quiet. Then, from the darkest shadow a figure stepped out. His eyes glowed faintly blue in the darkness, when he bent to look at the note written by Ambrogio. His finger traced the silvery writing and an angry hum filled the air around him.

Then he noticed something on the ground. He very carefully picked up the three transparent tubes that had fallen from the weapon from the ground, and vanished.

After a while another dark form materialized from the pre-dawn darkness. A hand picked the note from the ground. A low chuckle was heard, and then the figure was gone.

73

THE TEAM

If I had thought we would just take off and head for Amarna, I was very much mistaken. Instead of leaving we were effectively sent to school.

"You need to know as much as possible, before embarking on your journey. You need to know the history, the language, and the cultural background of the times," Lilith began. "You're going to stand out from the crowd, and you will not learn everything in time, so you will need to act as foreigners coming on a visit to the royal city."

We were sitting in a classroom, with our pens, papers and laptops at the ready.

"We have chosen your team carefully," Lilith said. "Firstly, of course, there are the Nephilim. Daniel, Elijah and Dana. You're going to be foreign royalty from a faraway country in the north. And you're bringing with you something that's greatly coveted by Egyptian nobility."

Lilith opened a box on the teacher's table. It contained unformed lumps and also beads in warm golden, orange and yellow colours.

"Amber. Reggie will tell you more in a while."

"Then we shall have Layla, of course," Lilith pointed at Grandma. "She is well tanned, and of the right height to fit right in.

Short hair isn't a problem - the Egyptians often cut their hair short or shaved it off for hygienic reasons. She is to be your servant. We want to have a good Hunter keeping an eye on any threats coming your way."

Grandma smiled across at me and I suddenly had a flashback of the day she had picked me up on the road. It was so clear and yet it seemed to be light years away now.

"Diana too. She has African ancestry, which was usual in ancient Egypt, as it was and is an African country. The Egyptians never considered skin color as anything of real importance, that is an unfortunate later invention. Ancient Egyptians were of every color and some came from far away lands - they were still all Egyptian - that's what counted. You were a dweller in the valley of the Nile, the major power in the ancient world for millennia. Diana will take the role of a worshipper of Hathor who has taken up a position in your retinue after the closure of many temples as the worship of the Aten came to prominence. Having a temple worker on the team means that we can get to places that ordinary people can't - such as into the inner sanctum of the gods and goddesses. It also means that you may have access to the secret conversations and thoughts of the elite and find out what is happening behind the scenes. So, you'll need to intensify your language skills, as will the rest of the team."

Diana looked both thrilled and slightly overcome at the thought of the responsibility of the role.

"The religious work of a temple priestess, even a minor one, is also very demanding. They dance and sing before the deities, to please them," Lilith smiled at her. "I know that you have the skills to fulfil that role. It keeps you in good physical form, being a Guardian. You must be ready to fight as well."

Diana nodded.

"I like that too."

I had never seen Diana fight, and never really considered her a Guardian, but looking at her cat-like, alert posture, I could well believe that she had mastered some Oriental fighting techniques that would take any ancient would-be assailant by surprise.

"We shall have our researchers too," Lilith went on, "and who better than Reggie?"

Reggie stood up and bowed to our applause.

"Delighted to join you, truly delighted... to be able to study the times up close is a great honor. Thank you, thank you."

"You'll need some soldiers with you, or no one will take your story of being royalty seriously," Lilith continued. "So: we have Jason and Aemilius here."

Jason grinned at me and Aemilius nodded gravely.

"Jason has been taught at the Centre here to be a Gatekeeper, but has asked to join you in the role of a Guardian. He has great strength and fights well, so we agreed."

"Aemilius's strength is his knowledge of ancient battle techniques - in 31 BC they used swords and spears and Aemilius has trained many of our people in those ancient fighting skills. He will be carrying an ancient sword as well," Lilith said.

"My own sword." Aemilius lifted a sword to the table in front of him. "This is a gladiolus. I used in the naval battle in which Octavian defeated Marc Anthony and Cleopatra. Right before I was brought here. And it has served me well in many an occasion after that."

He stroked the big scar on his cheek, a response to some fighting memory, no doubt.

Reggie whistled.

"That's going to cause quite a stir. There was no steel yet in Akhenaten's time. Iron was virtually unknown, because the Egyptians did not know how to use it, nor did they appreciate its strength. They thought there was no one to threaten the country at that time, not seriously with the deserts protecting it from east and west, and Nubia was held off behind a row of fortresses in the south. Though, come to think of it, Tutankhamen was buried with an iron dagger. It was a royal thing to own. That sword alone will assure everyone we are royalty."

"If all goes well, no one will be seeing this sword at work," Aemilius said gruffly.

"Let us hope that will be the case," Lilith said. "Now, I have one more thing to ask you. There is someone who is willing to come along, but who may not be strong enough for the part. We'll need to vote, to see whether he's allowed to join your team. He wishes to study the creation myths of the time. There was a great conflict in Egypt when Akhenaten chose to rewrite religious history according to his beliefs regarding the light of the Aten. Our proposed team member would like to research this conflict."

"I can guess already..." Elijah said, "Mr. Donnelly, if I am not much mistaken."

"Indeed," Lilith nodded. "The question is: do we trust him?"

"I do," Reggie said enthusiastically, "he is a true researcher. And he also learned hieroglyphs during his stay in the City of Immortals. His Coptic studies, though he modestly says he is not an expert in the language, are an asset too. The ancient Egyptian language's pronunciation is unclear, because they only wrote in consonants, but the Coptic language was a direct continuation of it, and as such is used as the basis of the pronunciation we use today."

"What harm could he do?" Elijah wondered. "If we notice any trouble, or that he doesn't have what it takes, we can bring him back."

"Is it agreed, then?" Reggie asked enthusiastically.

"Let's vote. Raise your hand, if you agree he can come," Lilith said.

All hands rose.

"Good, you can let Mr. Donnelly in."

Jason was closest to the door and opened it. Flustered Mr. Donnelly walked in.

"Welcome to the group, Mr. Donnelly." Lilith smiled at him. "Do take a seat."

Mr. Donnelly looked so happy he made us smile.

"I'm honored, truly honored." He bowed to us many times.

"And then we have our Gatekeepers and Weavers at this end. Anna and Paris are the Weavers we have chosen. We will need to send one of them with you, because Dana has not yet been taught the skill of staying connected to another Weaver in our time."

"I shall stay at this end for a change," Anna said, "I've been traveling so much these last months that I am exhausted. Paris will go with you."

She did indeed look tired - there were dark rings around her eyes and her whole appearance was somehow subdued. Shocked, almost. She had been working too hard, obviously.

Paris on the other hand smiled so that little laughter lines appeared from the corners of her eyes.

"I love anything to do with ancient Egypt, so I volunteered when I heard Anna needed a little vacation from traveling."

"Well, there we have our group then. Daniel, Elijah and Dana. Diana, Layla, Reggie and Mr Donnelly. Jason and Aemilius, Anna here and Paris with you. Eleven in all."

"How about you?" I asked.

"I hardly ever travel across time," Lilith shook her head. "I keep the Centre running, and travel in the dreamscape, and it is safest if I stay here for those reasons. If I need to contact you, the Weaver on this end will help me get my message through. The Weavers can send thoughts also, using the strings."

There was obviously a lot more to Weaving than I had realised.

"Now, you need to start seriously researching the times. Reggie - you could start with the amber, perhaps?"

"Ah yes, amber!" Reggie darted to the front of the room. "The amber we talk about comes from the coasts of the Baltic Sea. It is pine tree resin. We know amber was used right at the time we shall be traveling to - the famous shipwreck of Uluburun which dates from around this time shows that. Several amber beads were found there - amazing that they were still there, as normally they float on water... also Tutankhamen had a breast ornament of large Baltic amber beads. So it is a fact we know that the royal family appreciated amber."

He lifted one of the beautiful, polished lumps of amber and looked at it admiringly.

"The Egyptians believed that amber was the tears of the sun god Ra. It was also connected with Ra's daughter, the horrifying lioness Sekhmet who almost annihilated humankind because of their disrespect for her father. Amber was considered to have protective qualities, and it was sometimes inserted beneath the skin on the hands of

Egyptian mummies - they believed it protected their way in the afterlife..."

"How did all that amber then come to Egypt? The Baltic Sea is a long way from Egypt..." Jason asked.

"The so called Amber Road was the ancient trade route used. At first the route crossed the Alps, but later the Vistula and Dnieper rivers were used to reach the Mediterranean countries, and from there it was transported to Egypt," Reggie's hands were drawing lines in the air. Most likely he was sketching out a map of Europe, "and our story is that this is the route we've taken to see the famous King of Egypt in his Horizon of the Aten. Akhetaten. His city," he explained further.

"Now, let's start the history lesson. First of all... the country was not called Egypt. That is a later word, from the Greek word Aegyptos. The Egyptians called their country Kemet. The Black Land."

"Black? But there's nothing black about it," Jason looked baffled, "or at least I have not seen any black sand in the deserts there."

"Yes, there is black land," I interrupted, "Kemet refers to the black silt the river Nile brought during inundation. It's fertile, and the reason for the prosperity of Egypt."

"Indeed!" Reggie was pleased, "and now we're going to study the history of the Eighteenth Dynasty, so you know the background of what led to Akhenaten abandoning the old gods, and beginning the worship of the Aten..."

74

DESTINATION REVEALED

"We have received news from our informant." Angel walked into Cain's office.

"Yes?" Cain lifted his eyes from the computer screen.

"They have a Time Walker team in training for the journey. They know now where the Trail begins."

Cain's eyes were shining.

"Where?"

"We - are not sure yet. Our contact is discreetly trying to find out more, but the word Egypt was definitely mentioned. Also we have another possible source of information now. Much more accurate information - one of our newest servants is going to arrange that. Through him we believe we can get hold of someone who knows everything."

"Good, very good... find out where and to what time they are going. We need to be ready."

"Consider it done, father." Angel turned and left.

Cain appreciated his youngest daughter. She was no-nonsense, beautiful, lethal, and obedient. A good replacement for Nathaniel, whom Cain had planned to be his second in command. Also she showed no fear. If Cain had been an Egyptian pharaoh, he could have married her in an instant. Not that anyone would dare to oppose him, if he chose to do it now.

But no. He would keep the bloodline pure. Purebred Nephilim were needed in the new world order. Maybe it was time he looked for another daughter of Seth to be his concubine.

75

LONGING

"Wow, Diana - you certainly don't look all that respectable!"

"Me? Ha, look who's talking!"

We were inside one of the vast wardrobes in the centre's costume department, having our Egyptian clothing fitted. We were taking several coffers, all made especially by a carpenter who had researched ancient Egyptian woodwork. These would be crammed full of breathtaking clothing and jewellery. We'd been wondering how all this would be carried when we arrived there and had learned that finding a boat wouldn't be a problem. The Nephilim who lived in ancient times in Egypt would help our group as soon as they saw the seal of the Council. The seal was so ancient that it even predated Old Kingdom Egypt.

While I had been trying on some of my clothes, Diana was already in front of the mirror dressed in... well, nothing much. She was wearing a revealing temple costume. She swirled around, made swaying movements with her hips, which were decorated with an embroidered belt and jumped up and down in a way that revealed she was a gifted dancer. She laughed at her own reflection in the mirror, then stepped aside so I could see myself too. I stared at the person that I had become.

I was wearing the thinnest linen dress, which almost showed everything underneath when I moved. Only the clever pleating hid my nakedness when I stood still, but at the slightest movement I made, my skin showed through the sheer fabric where my body pressed against it. I knew this was the fashion of the nobility of the time, but still the sight made me feel slightly embarrassed.

I had grown to my full Nephilim height, and the dress emphasized my slender waist and long limbs beautifully. I had never been round, and my breasts were firm and small, barely covered with fabric. I turned sideways in front of the mirror, lifted my hands and pushed my breasts into a better place inside the sheer fabric, much to Diana's delight.

"Looks like there's not much to choose between us as far as revealing clothing goes! They left only just enough to the imagination back then," she laughed.

I did a few dance moves, and the sensuality of my movements and the flowing dress elegantly swaying around my long legs made me stop in embarrassment. I had left home a teenager, and now I looked like a woman. I wasn't used to seeing myself look so... sexy. And I was embarrassed by the fact that I enjoyed it.

My hair had grown a lot these last few weeks. It had been quite short when I had met Daniel at the bookstore. Now it was almost reaching my shoulders in wheat-colored locks.

I had no makeup on, and my skin was a beautiful pale shade, which emphasized my blue eyes.

Suddenly I felt the now familiar tingling in my spine and skin that meant a Nephilim was near. I thought I saw the slightest movement in the shadow of the cupboard, but did not turn to watch. Instead I kept looking at myself in the mirror, trying to see out of the corner of my eye whether someone really was there. But nothing moved in the shadows.

Daniel! The thought came to me in an instant, raising a warm glow all over my body. The idea that he might have seen me moving, dancing even, in this beautiful and revealing garment raised mixed emotions. A part of me wanted it so badly to be true. I wanted him to want me, to come to me, to press me against him, and kiss me until I melted into him, and let nature take its course. I wanted it so badly my whole body ached. And the hardest part was that I knew he wanted the same. I could read it in his eyes, I could sense it in his vibrations when he was near.

Why did he not give in? Was...was he afraid of the strength of my emotions? Why had he not answered out loud to Elijah when he asked him in the desert if he loved me?

Diana saw me staring at the mirror and could sense that somehow my mood had changed.

"Ok, enough shopping for clothes now, it seems," she said. "Let's change back into something more respectable and go have a coffee or something."

I tried to ignore the sadness and longing that was sitting in my chest in a lump as big as an iceberg and changed quietly back into my jeans and T-shirt without a word. We walked past the cupboard when we left costume, but there was nothing - and no-one - there. Well, of course not. If he had been there, he would have taken care when he left to ensure that we wouldn't see him. But - I was sure that it had been Daniel.

Diana led me to the cafeteria and found the most private table she could find – it was in a dark corner behind a big monstera plant. This made an effective hide-away - you could see through the gaps in the leaves of the plant if anyone was approaching while still remaining hidden from general view.

"I'll be right back." Diana left.

She came back with two steaming mugs of cocoa and more pieces of chocolate on a plate. These she dropped unceremoniously into our mugs for some additional sweetness.

"Heck, Diana - what's this? This has to be about a month's worth of sugar for the average person..."

Diana ignored my attempts to avoid what I knew was on the way.

"Now. What is bothering you? I saw a pretty young woman flirting with the mirror, and then suddenly her shoulders slumped and she withdrew into herself. Speak."

By now I knew there was no point in trying to keep secrets from

Diana. She was observant and sharp-witted and after all, we'd been room-mates for a while. I sighed.

"OK: Here goes. I think Daniel was watching us just now."

"Well, I wouldn't wonder," Diana shrugged, "we could have sold tickets to the male population of the Center this afternoon, what with us in those see-through outfits. Does that bother you? You feel embarrassed by it?"

"No... yes... I mean..."

"You mean why did he not show himself? Is that it?"

It was more of a statement than a question, and I had to nod. I felt a familiar blush rising up my neck and cheeks.

"Ok, here's the deal. You are wondering if he loves you. No need to nod, I know that's what you're thinking. And here's my theory. Are you sitting comfortably?"

I sipped my cocoa, wiped the cream moustache off, and sighed.

"Ok, let's hear it."

"You remember when you touched his wings in the library when you arrived? How he behaved so oddly?"

"How could I forget..."

"Well, the wings of a Nephilim are extremely sensitive. You have noticed their energy hum, of course. OK. So. Have you ever heard of twin souls?"

"Yes..."

"I have been working with Nephilim long enough to know what happens if a twin soul touches the wings of a Nephilim. And I mean Nephilim soul, of course. Two Nephilim. I'm not putting this into words very well, I'm afraid, but you know what I mean?"

"Two Nephilim who are twin souls, yes, I get it."

"Well, the thing that happens is...if the Nephilim in question is dumb enough not to recognize a twin soul, the wings do their very best to inform him or her of the fact. They get an electric shock if a twin soul touches their wings - you with me? Not a painful one but so pleasurable it takes the breath away. And every Nephilim knows only a twin soul can cause this kind of shock. I looked at Daniel and I have never seen an expression like that on his face. He was shaken to his core, in a way he obviously had not expected. If I had known at the time you were Nephilim, I would have booked a date for your wedding in my calendar right there and then."

"Oh, cool it, Diana..." I was glad of the shelter the plant gave us, because by now I was as red as a tomato.

"Oh no I won't. You need to know that twin souls - Nephilim who were meant for each other – feel as though their blood is singing to one other. Even their hearts begin to beat in unison, when they are near each other. It is an attraction that defies any laws of logic. And twin souls bond for all eternity, not only in body, but also in mind. If one dies, the other one can't go on living alone. "

I stared at my cocoa mug, watching how the whipped cream melted.

"The connection is too total, too strong. If it is broken, the one left behind often loses their mind - as though half of their being was gone for good. Most such Nephilim simply waste away, or commit suicide. All their will to live is gone. The effect is exactly the same, if it's the other one who is infected. It changes their mental makeup to such a degree, that the connection is severed. And so, the infection of one often causes the death of the other."

Diana took a long sip of her cocoa, maybe to give me some time to take in her words, and after a while continued.

"Daniel knows Cain's Nephilim are hunting him. He thinks it is more than likely he will be caught at some point, and we all know he would not give in to being infected. He would fight until death, or kill himself. And knowing what would happen to you as a result makes him keep his distance. He has seen that the pain Elijah went through and has kept him from killing himself after his wife vanished - yes, I did know about his tragedy, but it was not my place to tell you about it until now. After having seen his brother's suffering, Daniel does not want you to experience the same."

I could hear my blood ringing in my ears. So Elijah had gone through what can only be described as hell...

"If I know anything about Daniel, I think he almost hopes you might find someone else who is not your twin soul. If you made promises to such a Nephilim, and he was infected, you would survive. So there. I think he is very much in love with you, and fights it with all his willpower. Which is formidable, I have to tell you."

"Do you mean he could... deny his feelings for me completely?" I whispered.

"Deny? Oh no! He cannot deny his feelings. None of us can, not really. He may push his emotions back, keep his distance from you, but he can't deny what he feels for you."

"What will happen, then?"

"That, my dear, is not up to me, but to you two," Diana said bluntly. "I just had to fill you in about Nephilim love affairs so you aren't walking blindfold into something. I wish I could console you and say that of course you two will get each other, but I am no magician. Like I said - it's up to you."

We finished our drinks in silence.

76

DREAMSCAPE

Days of intensive study immersed us completely in the Amarna period until we felt as though we were living in that time. For hours each day we examined every detail; the people of the period, their religion, clothing, food, skills, warfare and beliefs in the afterlife. We studied the geography until we felt we had walked every inch of the landscape under the intense heat of Akhenaten's god Aten, the sun disk. We knew how the inhabitants of Amarna had built their houses, how they hunted and fished and how they tended their livestock and crops. We knew how they viewed their neighbouring countries and the royal family.

Taking only brief breaks to eat and rest, I realised that I did not seem to need as much sleep as when I had been an ordinary teenager. Diana slept like a log. She said she had learned to fall asleep anywhere and anytime, when she was a house slave. She was expected to serve the family on an instant's notice and had learned to grab a few minutes of sleep any time that she could, if necessary.

No one complained about having to do research, though. We knew we had to understand as much as we possibly could before leaving. Our very lives might depend on it.

My seventeenth birthday came and to celebrate we all ate birthday cake during the coffee break, before going back immediately to our studies. I made a phone call to my parents during which I chatted cheerily and promised to come visit as soon as I could.

To my great surprise Daniel walked up to me, as we were leaving the cafeteria, and asked me to wait. I had a feeling Elijah was in on the plot because he seemed to almost herd the others back to the classroom. Daniel seemed lost for words, and without saying anything, put a little object into my hand when the others were out of sight. It was a tiny wooden box.

I looked at the box and then at him, surprised.

"What's this?"

"It's a little trinket that my mother used to wear," he said, and seemed slightly embarrassed. "If you don't want it, I will understand. I... Dana, I don't want you to think I don't care for you. But it is... complicated. Still, it would make me very happy, if you chose to wear this."

My discussion with Diana had taught me more about the relationships of the Nephilim than Daniel knew, but I said nothing. I opened the box. A small brooch was in the box. It was a silver crescent moon inside a golden sun. The rays of the sun resembled those of a flower.

"It's... It's beautiful!" I stammered. "I would love to wear it. Thank you..."

I stood there, not knowing whether I was allowed to touch him or not. It was so awkward. I was certain I saw desire in his eyes, and knew my eyes were revealing my emotions as well. I took half a step towards him, and then stopped.

"Here, let me put it on," Daniel moved right next to me. It took him a few seconds to attach the brooch to my shirt and I touched it gently. I managed to touch his fingers also, and he did not withdraw his hands immediately. For a few seconds our fingers kept their contact and we looked into each other's eyes. I saw his pupils were dilated, which made his eyes almost black. I am sure my eyes looked just the same. I just stood there, listening to the humming in my head, trying my very best not to kiss him. I was surprised I did not see sparks flying from our fingertips.

Then he stepped back.

"We'd better go now. Happy Birthday, Dana..." he whispered hoarsely, and his words felt like a caress.

I felt so happy I could have cried, but instead I just smiled at him, trying to appear as though everything was normal to anyone who might be watching us in the cafeteria. I have no idea if I was at all successful, if Diana's words about the whole Centre knowing about us were true. And why wouldn't they be? Rumors travel fast.

In the evening I sat by the window, looking outside, listening to Diana snoring lightly. I caressed the little brooch with my fingers and turned it around so I could peek at the back. There was an engraving there.

I held my breath, when I saw what it was. There were two letters. D and D, entwined into each other. Daniel had given me a message about how he felt... I kissed the little brooch and let the tears run. Why did love need to be complicated? Why could it not be simple? Why did he not trust me enough?

Tears turned into anger, and then to frustration. I had just decided I should try to sleep a bit, when there was a knock on the door. I walked to it and opened it just a little, hoping that my eyes didn't show I'd been crying.

It was Lilith.

"I think it is time for you to see the dreamscape," she announced. "It might be a skill that could come in useful for you in Amarna."

"Oh! That's wonderful... are we leaving right away?"

"Yes. I have the Key, but I would like to see you gain access to the buffer zone yourself, while I'm here with you. So I'm going to take hold of your arm..." which she did, firmly, "...and off we go."

"Where to?"

"Just to the buffer zone first. I know the way from there."

I concentrated and the hum in my back intensified. I did not need my wings to open for this, but I needed to activate their energy nevertheless. I directed my thoughts to my back, and then backwards from there. Slowly the physical world turned misty; it was like falling backwards into water in slow motion, and then we were in the buffer zone.

"Well done," Lilith said, "now, we need to go one step down from this level. It's your turn to follow me."

She concentrated, standing still, and to my surprise threads started forming from her fingers.

"You are a Weaver!" I exclaimed.

"Yes, didn't anyone tell you?" She looked amused.

"No... But with what are you weaving? What is your anchor?"

Lilith's hands were empty.

"Dreams. It's enough that I remember one of my own dreams, and it takes me to the dream level."

The mist around us began to lift, and we descended to a level the like of which I could not have imagined.

Think of a hundred curved cinema canvases side by side, overlapping, and all with their own movie running. Behind the screens you could see others, and behind them others, until they disappeared into the distance. They had no sharp edges. It was more like holograms hanging in the air, brighter at the center, more transparent at the edges. Like transparent thought bubbles.

The bubbles were interacting with each other too. I saw a young girl eating an apple in one hologram, and a young boy right next to it becoming aware of the apple and trying to reach for it. An office worker looking out of a window into a beautiful landscape, which was another bubble behind it.

"Now, let us see if anyone is lucid dreaming," Lilith said.

She walked through the transparent edges of the dreams and kept on looking for something. I ducked when a horse suddenly appeared with a girl on its back and jumped a fence right towards me.

"Don't worry, they are only thin veils of thought energy. If they touch you, you can walk right through them," Lilith said over her shoulder, "but if you are not careful, it may happen that an especially strong dream carries you away with it."

"What happens then?" I looked at an old man reading an antique Bible with a young woman standing by his side, trying to get his attention.

"You fall asleep into their dream. You wake up later, but it is a strange sensation to be caught in someone else's dream... oh, you see that young woman with the old man?" Lilith realised what I was looking at.

"I do."

"She is not a dream, she is dead. Let's talk with her."

Lilith turned to the old man's dream.

"May we talk with you?" she asked, and the woman turned towards us. Now that we were close, I could see she was more solid than the dream bubbles were.

"Of course," the lady said.

"Are you trying to wake him?"

"Yes. We were married, and I died quite young. He never got over it, but began to blame himself. He is very religious and convinced himself that his sinful ways caused my death. I would like him to know I am just as much alive as I was with him. Or more alive, if that's possible to convey..."

"We can perhaps help you there?"

The woman looked at us.

"You have a winged one with you?"

I had a quick peek over my shoulder, but my wings were not open. She could sense what I was by some other means.

"Yes, she is new. I am teaching her how to move in the dreamscape. She is a healer."

"Perhaps she could then help my husband, to heal his pain?"

The discussion was taking an unexpected turn. I looked at Lilith.

"How would I do that?"

"I'll try to lift this man into a lucid dream. He is religious. You know what to do."

Lilith walked to the man and put her left hand on his shoulder, and her right hand to the nape of his neck. Her hands went straight through him, but he twitched a bit.

"What's his name?" she asked the dead wife.

"John. I am Elsa."

Lilith turned back to the old man and began to talk into his ear.

"John... your wife is here... John, look around and you will see her..."

The old man looked around with unseeing eyes, then returned to his Bible.

"John, an angel has brought your wife to see you in this dream. Open your eyes and see the angel..."

The word "angel" caused the old man to suddenly become more solid. He opened his eyes and began to look around.

"Wings, Dana..." Lilith whispered.

"Oh, of course..." I concentrated and opened my silver wings softly, not wanting to scare anyone. I moved right in front of the man.

The old man's eyes wandered a bit, but then his gaze locked onto me, and I could see how he became aware of his dream state. He began to become more solid.

Elsa moved across to stand beside me, and now he saw her.

"Elsa, my Elsa! You are here! You are not dead!" he whispered.

Elsa left my side and went to him. She gave him a hug.

"Oh, but I am! I am physically dead, but I am here. I am alive in spirit. I am here waiting for you, when your time comes. You must give up your anger and bitterness, and live the years you have left. It was my time to go, and nothing you could have done would have changed that. And nothing you did caused that either."

"Elsa..." the old man began to cry, and it was as though the strong emotion somehow pulled him back towards his physical world and he began to fade. "Elsa, don't go!"

"I won't go anywhere, John," Elsa smiled, "I will be here in your dreams until it is your turn to come here to me. I love you, John."

The dream bubble vanished in an instant. Like a soap bubble bursting.

"He woke up," Lilith explained.

"But he had time to see me and recognize me. I thank you, angel," Elsa said and took my hands, looking at me in the eye. Her touch felt strangely immaterial... Much like touching a Nephilim's wings.

"Oh I am no angel," I felt almost embarrassed. "I am Nephilim."

"I don't care what you call yourself. You helped me, and that was the deed of an angel. Thank you."

Elsa let go of my hands and began to fade too. In a few seconds she was gone.

"I was glad to help," I whispered and withdrew my wings.

Lilith smiled. New dreams formed about us and old ones disappeared. Colors and forms danced all around. It was eerily beautiful.

"Your first good deed using your wings," she said, "and there will be more, I am sure."

"What do you mean by more good deeds? The healing?"

"Yes, healing will be a part of it, but you can also help in other ways. Ask Daniel and Elijah to take you with them on their food aid tours sometimes."

"Their what?"

"There is so much hunger in this world, yet there is enough food to feed those who are hungry," Lilith said. "The boys have amassed a considerable fortune in their long lifetime, and they use a lot of it in buying food."

"Food?" I repeated like a parrot.

"Yes, they buy food, and then they travel in the buffer zone to those areas where there is none. They give the food there to those in need. Also medical equipment. Direct aid at its best. There are no middlemen stealing it along the way. They don't have much free time, but what they have, they use in that way."

I did not know what to say. I had not even thought I could use my wings to help others like that and I didn't realise that there was also this practical side to Daniel and Elijah. It was odd, thinking of beings that were half angel yet involved in charitable activities that were so down to earth. I immediately knew I wanted to join in this work, whenever possible.

"Now you have seen this place, you can use your memory as the anchor and come here whenever you wish."

"But if I want to see a specific person and what they are dreaming, what should I do?"

"Ah, yes. Let's try that. Hmm... we could start with Diana."

"OK, sounds good. Are you sure she won't mind?"

"Most likely not. She is not the kind who would take offence at my teaching you, even if it meant peeking into her dreams," Lilith said.

"True, she isn't."

"So, when you are here in the dreamscape, all you need to do is to think about the person whose dreams you want to ... hey, wait!"

I was suddenly zooming off with increasing speed in some direction. Dream bubbles flashed by, and then suddenly stopped. After a while Lilith appeared next to me.

"You sure are fast!" She shook her head in disbelief. "I'd better keep hold of you next time."

"Sorry."

"No need to be sorry for being faster than an old lady..." she smiled.

"You're not that old!"

"I should say I am... I was born at the end of the 18th Century. Spend most of my time in the buffer zone, which explains the way I look."

"Oh, I see...No one seems to be their right age around here."

"You can say that again... But now, here is Diana..."

I could see that. I saw Diana swirling in an Egyptian dress, dancing. Around her a landscape was forming that was clearly ancient Egypt. I could see how her mind was working on today's lesson, which was wine making, because suddenly she was stomping grapes in a huge vat, holding onto a horizontal beam above her head, so as not to slip. She was singing. The sound came out oddly, like a radio channel that faded on occasions, only to return clearly again.

"This harvest will make an excellent vintage ... here in Kemet ... ...where we are going to find..."

Lilith froze. Then she pointed at something behind Diana's dream.

A shadowy figure was crouched on the far side of Diana's dream bubble. It stretched out its arms into her dream and seemed to be weaving too - shadowy tentacles were swimming in the air around her, trying to grab her.

"...When we go...we are going..."

Lilith jumped right through Diana's dream, causing her to disappear. The shadow did not have time to do anything, before Lilith had severed the lifeline at the back of its neck. It fell down and vanished, sinking down into the mist while it disintegrated.

"I should have thought of this!" She turned to me shaking her hand as if it was hurting. "Of course Cain wants to know where we are going. He cannot come to the Centre, but he can send his spies to see our dreams! Come on, we have to get to Diana to find out if she's revealed anything about our destination in her dream."

Lilith grabbed my arm hastily.

"Think of the Centre."

I did, and the thought formed strings out of my fingers and began to reel us back in to the Centre with ever increasing speed.

77

KIDNAPPED

"So we can't even sleep in peace anymore?" Diana rolled her eyes. "They are spying on us even in our dreams?"

"They are. And this means you need to leave as soon as possible, before any one of us falls asleep again." Lilith looked around at us - we had woken up everyone quickly after our return.

"But we haven't learned everything we need to know yet!" Reggie looked desperate.

"There is no more time. They are out there, lurking in our dreams, fishing out information. They must know already that we are leaving for Egypt." Lilith lifted her hand as if to bang her fist on the desk, but did not. "I only hope no one has dreamed specifically of Amarna... Does anyone remember doing so?"

Everyone shook their heads.

"Do the shadows even know who the members of this team are?" Elijah asked.

"I hope not," Lilith sighed.

"Why pick out Diana, then?"

"Of course they would seek out Diana..." Daniel said, "she was standing right next to Dana, who was protecting her from Angel at the pyramids. That's why. She was a good guess on their part. If we had looked around us at the pyramids, we'd probably have spotted a Hunter of theirs with a shadow. Maybe amongst the tourists. We just weren't paying enough attention to anyone else but Angel. One sniff of Diana's scent and the shadow could easily navigate to her dreams in the buffer zone, if they knew her approximate physical location. They probably guessed it easily enough, after the shadows found the Centre by following Layla and Dana. They wouldn't approach Dana, as she might be heavily guarded now, so Diana was probably a safer bet."

"So they probably know about the other members of the team as well... maybe now the shadows know everything. How could we have been so stupid, not taking the dreams into account!" Grandma pressed her forehead with her fingers as if she had a headache.

"We need to leave as soon as possible. We can still get away in safety, though; we just have to mislead them. We'll leave in pairs," Daniel said. "I'll work with Weavers to take the members of our team to different locations, very quickly, and return immediately. And I'll then come and pick everyone up from their chosen location. We need to temporarily scatter all over the world."

We made our spur of the moment plans. Grandma and Reggie would go to Toronto, Mr Donnelly and Jason would be sent to Edinburgh and Diana and Aemilius to Rome, Elijah and I were going to Paris. Specific hotels in these locations would be used.

"Why these particular hotels?" I asked.

"Because we have our own people working there. We only need to appear, and they will give us a room without entering our real names on their database. Also they will not ask for our documentation."

We began to pack our things immediately. Everyone fetched their clothes. All modern jewelry and watches were left behind. We would have to leave our regular clothing as well, but at our rendez-vouz-point, which was for Daniel to decide. He did not tell anyone about the location of this point, other than Elijah, in case we fell asleep and were spied on. Elijah was not likely to fall asleep - I knew from experience now that the Nephilim did not need much sleep.

If we got out of the Centre without anyone noticing, we would be safe from dream-spies. They would need to know our physical proximity to find our dreams, the "dream bubbles" were only visible near the physical location of the dreamer.

Our major problem was taking our big coffers with us. Daniel and Elijah would first carry them through the buffer zone and to our secret rendezvous point. When they had moved everything, they would return so we could start our travels.

"Nervous?" Diana asked me after we had nothing else to do but wait in our room.

"Yes... to actually go to ancient times... What if we get lost? What if something happens to us there? We can die in another time, can't we?"

"Yes, we can. We have the same physical form there as we have here, so we can get sick, and die, and be harmed. But we have you with us, so what's to worry about? Besides, we've been vaccinated against cholera, plague, smallpox and what have you..." Diana cringed at the memory. She wasn't exactly fond of needles.

"Has anyone ever gone that far into the past?" I asked.

"Well... No. I think Aemilius and Rome is the furthest back we have ever gone... and the destruction of the Alexandria library... The farther back we go, the more... vague the paths become. Especially if we are talking about a time that is not well researched."

"Why is that?"

"It's quite simply those laws of energy once again... what you concentrate on, gets stronger. I am not sure we could even find our way to any "lost civilization" if there was no historical record about it, and we were only going by legend or rumors. Like the myth of Atlantis, for instance. But if we think about Amarna, so much has been written about it, and so many objects found, that its energies should be strong enough for us to find it easily."

"No one has told us in exactly which year we're aiming to arrive..." I observed.

"True... Maybe we should go and ask Lilith about that..." Diana rose from her bed.

"Yes, let's." I just couldn't stand the small room any longer. "If anyone wants us we'll be in the Center, if we chance to be away from our room."

It was a relief to walk down the corridor, and towards Lilith's office. We knocked on the door, but she was not there. Reggie, on the other hand was, with his nose buried in a big book about Amarna. Mr. Donnelly was feverishly writing something in his notebook beside him, with his index finger pointing to the page of a book to his left.

"Ah, young ladies! What can we do for you?" Reggie smiled.

He had red dots burning on his cheeks, and you could tell he was happily anticipating our time travel. Mr. Donnelly looked just as pleased.

"We were wondering... do you know to which time we're planning to go, exactly? In Amarna I mean. Any specific year?" Diana asked.

"Well... I'm not sure we should really be telling you..." Reggie scratched his ear.

"Oh come on – we're going in a few hours, and we promise we won't take a nap before that!" Diana insisted.

"Well, that is true..." Reggie considered for a while. "OK, we have chosen Akhenaten's year 12. That is when he arranged a great show in Akhetaten, and royalty all over the ancient world traveled to attend it. He wanted to show off his newly built city, and display his riches and power. The city will be full of strangers then, so a few more won't draw too much attention to themselves."

"Great!" Diana clapped her hands "We shall see a real spectacle then!"

"Yes, indeed. But there is one unpleasant thing about it..." Mr. Donnelly raised his head, looking very much like a nutty professor.

"Yes? What is it?"

"The guests brought an epidemic with them, which caused havoc in the city. Many of the royal family also died of it. Some of Akhenaten's daughters, maybe Nefertiti as well. And the king's mother, Tiye. Probably Akhenaten's favorite second wife, Kiya as well. It may have been cholera, or plague. So we need to be careful out there..."

"Oh..." Diana became serious, "but thankfully, we have Dana with us, in case the vaccines don't work!"

"I think you trust my abilities a bit too much..." I said. "I don't know exactly how to heal..."

"Nonsense. You're our medicine on wings, dear! You don't need to know. It seems your Nephilim side is on automatic mode on this matter," Diana smiled. "OK. Let's get back to our room and wait..."

That we did. To spend the time we played cards.

While Diana was picking up her hand of cards, I felt something. A slight electric current shot through my spine. I had learned that the feeling meant a Nephilim of our kind was near. It was like a vibrational hello.

"Time to stop playing! I think they are coming." I took the pack of cards from the bed and replaced my card hand on top of it. "I sense a Nephilim presence."

"Great!" Diana jumped to her feet. "All ready to go!"

She turned to grab the sack which held her clothes. It was carefully made to look genuine in ancient Egypt. I turned to get my belongings, still holding the playing cards in my hands.

The Nephilim who suddenly appeared in our room holding one others' hands were neither Daniel nor Elijah. There were three of them. One immediately grabbed Diana's neck, and she slumped onto her bed.

"Don't worry, she will be unharmed." The Nephilim responsible for making Diana unconscious turned to me.

I could see they were my kind. Bright blue eyes. I didn't understand.

"What is this? Who are you? And - why did you do that to Diana?"

"No time to talk," a tall red-headed woman answered bluntly. "You're coming with us - now."

"I'm not going anywhere without..."

"Oh but you are. If you don't, your friend here will die. No one wants to see that happen, but we are ready to kill her if we must," another Nephilim woman with an olive colored skin said. "I'll stay behind to make sure you leave nice and quietly."

The other two grabbed my arms and tugged me into the buffer zone in an instant. They did not seem to do any weaving, but simply opened their wings – ochre and grey in color - and rose out of the misty zone into a level that looked like a desert. I remembered what Lilith had told me - that Nephilim touching each other physically amplified each other's power, which is how they could enter the buffer zone if they were not able to do so alone.

I held on to my sack all the time, and noticed I still had the pack of playing cards in my hands. The moment we arrived at the level of the desert, I carefully moved my fingers so that one of the cards fell down. The Nephilim did not notice - they were looking straight ahead. I could only hope that Daniel would follow us to the right level and would be able to hunt me down with the help of my scent on the cards. I knew first hand what an amazing sense of smell the Nephilim had. I could not bear to be near people who used perfume anymore. Any man-made scent was almost painful. Only natural floral scents smelled good.

We flew for a long time, and I dropped the cards, one by one, every once in a while. My escorts were in such a hurry they never looked back to see the cards flying in the air. After I had dropped the last one we flew for such a considerable distance I began to fear my little leads would be left too far behind, and I would never be found.

And then, finally, we began to descend, and entered the misty zone. From there we emerged a totally featureless room. There was one door, heavy, made of metal. No furniture, no window, no nothing. Only a surveillance camera attached to the ceiling, and loudspeakers in the corners.

They yanked my sack from my hands and rummaged through it. The only contents were plain linen clothing, a toothbrush and a hair-brush - and nothing of value.

"You can keep it." The man dropped the sack on the floor.

They left the room, the man and the red-haired woman. Immediately after this the loudspeakers began to play a sound that I remembered and hated - that of the brass bowls.

Elijah had been right – the sound shot right through my very core, in a quite different way from when I was still a "normal" person. It did not cause actual pain, even though it was definitely unpleasant. But when I tried to use my wings, they were paralyzed.

I fought panic. I stood up and breathed deeply a few times. When I finally managed to find my anger, it became easier. I walked to the corner of the room, under the old fashioned surveillance camera, so they could not see me, and leaned against the wall. I carefully built up my rage so that I would not be paralyzed by fear as well. They would tell me soon enough what they were after. And at least they were my own kind, so I probably was not in danger of being infected. If I even could be infected with my silver wings...

I did not have to wait for long. The door opened, and the olive-skinned lady came in dragging Diana with her. Diana's eyes were dilated, and she was groggy. I guessed they must have drugged her. She blinked her eyes slowly, and tried to focus them, but you could see she wasn't really present.

Then the two others walked in as well. I could see a corridor with fluorescent lamps behind them. For a while I considered attacking them, because the music had to have an effect on them too. But in all likelihood I was not a match to the muscle power of three grown Nephilim, and so I did not move, but remained in my place with my arms folded over my chest. I discovered that I was afraid, which surprised me; then I realised I was not afraid for myself, but for Diana and what they might do to her.

I said nothing, just stared intently at the red haired woman. I had used this technique at school whenever the Blonde Crew had tried to bully me. Not one of them liked me looking them straight in the eye and they stopped soon enough. So I kept right on staring at the Nephilim woman without blinking an eye. She broke first and lost the battle of wills.

"Stop that!" she yelled.

I did not. I kept on staring at her, and she took a threatening step towards me. The man grabbed her by the hand and shook his head.

"No. We are not here to harm you."

I still did not say anything, but nodded towards Diana.

"Yes, sorry about that..." the man said, but he did not sound very embarrassed. "Desperate measures. You see - we need your help."

"You have an odd way of asking," I said curtly.

"We know... Daniel would never have agreed to this, so we had to keep an eye on him and come for you when he was away."

So the good Nephilim knew where the Centre was.

I waited. The door opened and three more Nephilim came in. It was beginning to get crowded.

"I know you," I said to the woman on the left, "you were at the convention."

"Yes," she nodded. Her expression was odd - it was desperate, and very tired.

She and a dark-haired Nephilim with a scar on his cheek were carrying yet another Nephilim. He was heavily drugged, and could not stay on his feet without them holding him up. He had a scarf tied over the lower part of his face, covering his mouth. He did open his eyes, for a while, but when they rolled towards the ceiling, I saw they were bright yellow. He was dark.

"You will heal him," the woman from the Council commanded and nodded towards Diana, "or she will die."

78

"YOU WILL HEAL HIM"

I stared at the yellow-eyed Nephilim.

"You cannot be serious!" I could not believe what I had heard.

"We heard how you healed Elijah, right? And he was no longer infected at the Council of Nephilim. You were not infected either, though you healed him..."

The woman moved closer to me and looked into my eyes. She nodded.

"You are immune, and you are a healer. You will do this."

"Do you have your Council's approval for this?" I asked.

I hit a nerve there. The Nephilim exchanged nervous glances.

"No, you haven't," I concluded, "and how do you think the Council would react if they heard you had kidnapped me?"

"They need never know."

"Oh but they will know, one way or the other." I tried to keep my voice from shaking with anger. "I'll talk. Or someone here will let the secret slip out."

"Whatever you say, we're not letting you go! So they will never hear what happened," the red-haired woman snapped.

"Oh, is that so? And why, then, should I help you?" I asked her.

Her answer was to start strangling Diana. She tried to fight, feebly, but was too weak because of whatever drug she'd been given.

"Stop that!" the man who was carrying the yellow-eyed Nephilim said sharply.

"If this is what it takes..." the red-haired one replied.

"Stop playing the brass bowls," the man said and someone at the other end of the surveillance camera did as he asked.

My anger was such that my wings snapped open in an instant. Their force field current was so strong the others were thrown back towards the doorway.

They opened their wings too, in defense, but they were not as big as mine. I felt anger turn to rage. The emotion rose up my spine, and my wings reacted by bending towards them all, threatening. I did not look at my wings, but from the corners of my eyes I could see the silver lightning flashes shooting upwards in them. The air was cracking with electricity. I could see the others were afraid now.

Then I sensed an odd presence in my mind. When I opened my wings, it was as if they were connected to... something beyond me, yet something that was strangely familiar. Thoughts and ideas flooded into my mind with such speed that my thoughts could not keep up with them.

"Explain yourselves!" I said in a strange voice. It had a strength and a musical ring to it I did not recognize.

The red-haired woman squeezed Diana's limp body against her, and she looked at me defiantly, but her lips were trembling.

"He is my husband," she whispered, "and he was infected. We...we said he committed suicide, but we have kept him drugged in a room with the brass bowls playing without ceasing, hoping something could be done to heal him. And then... you appeared," she nodded at me.

I got the eerie feeling she was having a conversation with someone other than me, even though she was talking directly to me.

I looked at her in the eyes again, or something looked at her through me. She took a breath and stepped backwards.

"Your eyes..." she breathed.

"What about my eyes?" I asked, and my normal self felt a pang of panic. Were they yellow?

"Silver..." she whispered.

Silver eyes? Surely she was seeing wrong. My eyes were bluish grey - or had been, when I was a child. I knew they had turned bluer after my change, not grey.

My wings began to hum.

"You will let her go," the voice said through me.

To my surprise she obeyed. Diana slumped against the wall. I wondered what would I do next, how we could escape, but this is when the dark Nephilim began to wake up.

His head turned faster, and his eyes began to focus. The others tightened their grip on him. He began to struggle, and then... fade.

"Quick! The bowls! Play the bowls!" the red-haired woman yelled.

"No!"

I did not even understand at first it was me speaking. The word thundered in the room with such force that the yellow-eyed Nephilim stopped trashing and froze. He did not fade any more than he had already done and slowly began to be more solid again, sliding back to physical reality from the edge of the buffer zone. Now he looked at me directly in the eye.

And I looked into his eyes. They were just like Angel's - a strange yellow. It was like there was oil floating on top of them, constantly moving ever so slightly from inside out. Have you ever looked at a mud fountain blobbing out an air bubble on its surface? That's how it was - only the mud was golden yellow.

Something was different, though. The look in his eyes. Angel's had been pure cold evil. You could see she enjoyed her mental state, but in these eyes I saw... desperation underneath them. The eyes told me that the Nephilim within was drowning and calling for help.

I looked into the eyes of the red-haired woman. The pulse in her ochre wings was nervous, fast.

"How long has he been infected?"

"Four months now. He turned dark... two months ago. He fought it longer than usual."

I looked at her again, and saw the same desperation there I had seen in the yellow-eyed man. She looked like someone who was trying to keep a grip on sanity, but underneath madness lurked.

There was something much bigger at issue here than I understood.

"Silver one..." the man said, "you are new, so you may not know..."

"Tell me," I said.

"These two made promises to each other, and thus became one."

"Marriage vows?"

"Yes, the Nephilim way. Not rituals only. They melted into each other in body and soul, and became one."

A huge swirl of desire overtook my whole body at these words, and I knew exactly what the meant. Twin souls. Like me and Daniel.

In response to my desire for Daniel my wings let out an electric hum, much like the high voltage power lines did in wet weather. The hum beat in the rhythm of my heart.

"You understand," I heard hope rising in the red-haired woman's voice as she stepped towards me, reaching out her hands, "you have the same emotions for someone!"

Her wings let out a similar hum to mine, only with a different tone. The yellow-eyed man's wings were not visible, but I could hear a subdued hum coming from him. Its vibration matched that of hers, but it was broken, and came out in tiny bits, as though a sick person was trying to do physical exercise that their body could no longer manage.

That broken note of a matching hum between the two trying to connect made all the difference. The hum of my wings changed in tone, and strengthened.

"If he remains the way he is, the connection is severed between these two, and she will no longer live," the man looked me in the eye, pleading. "He will, though, in a nightmarish existence, forever transformed into something he isn't. He will remember his previous happiness, but he will become dead to it. He will no longer understand the finer emotions of love, and of caring. And she will waste away or kill herself. Those who have melted into each other, and been forcefully separated, will be broken for the rest of their lives, beyond repair, however long or short it may be."

He held the yellow-eyed man, who began to squirm, still looking me intently in the eye.

"Please, help them. Help my daughter. Help my son-in-law. Help if you can, please," the woman holding the dark Nephilim said, her voice choked and broken.

I barely heard her voice anymore. Like once before, my wings began to sing. It was an eerie, howling voice. It was like someone opening their voice, searching for the right tune.

When the vibration of my wings found the vibration of the yellow-eyed man, my hands rose on their own. They turned white, and then silver threads started to slowly weave through the air from my fingers as though gravity no longer mattered.

The yellow-eyed man started squirming. He tried to escape physically, but his eyes never turned away from mine. Whatever was left of his old self was clinging to hope, however small.

"Put him on his back on the floor," my voice said.

They forced him down, holding all his limbs. He began to scream - a high-pitched scream. The silver tentacles of my left arm found him, and I stepped closer. I felt them caress his arms, searching for veins, and then punch through his skin, sharp, hard, to allow my body to drink in his blood.

His screaming subdued slowly and he began to pant as big drops of sweat appeared on his forehead. I watched as if from a great distance, how his dark blood rose into me. My wings turned forward.

"Let him go," the voice in me said.

They did, and my wings wrapped tightly around his body. I stood in a bent position and felt how the searing pain that was his blood, pumped through my body, into my wings. This pain was many times more severe than it had been with Elijah, and the throbbing agony almost made me fall down. It tore into my brain, darkening my vision. Its strength made me fall on my knees to the floor.

His blood came into me through the threads of my left arm, and returned back to him through my right arm. The man was sweating profusely now.

I lost track of time, the threads pumping his blood into me, and then returning it to him. It did not happen as fast as with Elijah, and I was paralyzed with the pain it caused me. But after what felt like an eternity, the blood began to become brighter, and more beautiful.

He kept on looking at me, and I saw the yellow in his eyes began to get murky. Then a faint blue began to grow on the edges of his irises, and seep towards the pupils. The swirling in his eyes stopped, like someone had stopped upsetting a muddy pond. And the blue kept on seeping inwards, until finally his eyes were of a greyish color again. Only a few specks of yellow remained.

All the while I felt a hum in my mind, and despite the pain it was as though my understanding had extended far beyond my normal mind. I did not see, but I sensed intelligence beyond myself, and great compassion. The compassion touched me as well, understanding the pain I had to endure, the damage the infected blood did to my system.

And then it was over. The hum stopped, and I fell unconscious to the floor.

"Jonathan!" someone screamed.

Then more screams. Sounds of struggle, angry yelling. I felt my wings bang uncontrollably against the floor and the walls, and people, and... what was this?

A blue energy I knew from somewhere. My wings greeted it with a soft, contented hum. And it answered - a deeper hum than mine, but it matched my wings so beautifully. It was a joy to listen to, to melt into, though I did not know what it was. What I was. My mind had been forced through something my physiology could not handle.

The blue energy wrapped around me gently, softly, lovingly. Someone hummed into my ear, and I was safely held by strong arms that rocked me like a little baby, and I could give in to the utmost tiredness that washed over me.

I began to cry with exhaustion, with happiness, with the strong compassion that loved everything around me. Underneath all this I could feel I had a body, a damaged, and hurting body. It was entangled in some kind of cobweb of darkness, and was gasping for air, trying to rise from the abyss it had fallen into. My wings were out of control, cramping uncontrollably, but held still by the blue enveloping energy.

I cried for my body too, for it seemed to be beyond repair. It had been a beautiful body, but maybe now I would need to let it go. My true self was ready to leave, and to rise into light. It was already hovering above the damage done, attached to it with a single silver string only. Oh, how wonderful the light waiting for me felt. I could see it all around me, and it was coming closer and stronger all the time.

All I would need to do was to cut the silver cord, to let go of the damage underneath, shake it off like a piece of clothing, and I would be free.

But the blue energy would not let me go. It cocooned my soul inside it so I could not go. I did not know someone could hold a soul captive. I liked the feeling of the blue energy, so I did not fight. But as soon as it unwrapped itself from around me, I would go, I knew it.

Someone was saying something. No, two voices were talking. One was a young woman's voice...

"Dana, no. It is not your time yet... go back."

Who was Dana?

Then there was another voice, a male voice. The same who was humming into my ear.

"Dana, no... Do not go... Fight it, my love, fight it..."

And suddenly I was inside the damaged body again, and felt huge pain. It felt so heavy and horrible I screamed. But I had heard the words loud and clear. "My love"...

And that brought me back to my senses. I opened my eyes to look into Daniel's eyes.

He was crying.

79

PROMISES

The power that had surged through me had been too strong for my body. My damaged nervous system was in such agony that I was whimpering. I could not see or hear clearly, or even understand what was being said to me through the thick veil of pain.

I don't have any recollection of going back to the Center. Daniel must have carried me. For days I did not know where I was because of the pain. It would not ease, and eventually the doctors decided to give me a strong sedative to force my body into sleep, and I sank into a grey dullness like a coma, where I could only listen to the faint echoes of the throbbing pain. It was there, and I recognized it, but somehow the connection between it and my mind was severed, so I could not truly feel it.

Then, finally, my body began to show signs of healing, and they decided to let me come back.

I could hear the beep-beep of a machine, and hushed discussion going on, but I couldn't make out the words, they just floated above me. I spent an eternity like that, simply hearing things, not daring to move, fearing the pain would return.

Eventually I tried to open my eyes. The first thing I saw was Daniel. He was sitting slumped in a chair. I scarcely recognised him, he was so changed. He had dark circles around his eyes, and his complexion was dull and grey. He was leaning his forehead against the palm of his hand, his elbow on the armrest of the chair.

He must have heard or sensed something, because his eyes opened and he looked at me. When he saw my own eyes were open, he gently bent towards me.

"Are you there?" he whispered, searching my eyes.

"Where else would I be?" I tried to reply, but my throat was parched, and no voice came out.

Daniel seemed to hear it, though, and he smiled. It was such a beautiful smile, so full of joy that my heart melted. I tried to smile back, but fell asleep before I could. Normal, healing, restoring sleep.

At first I could not even swallow on my own and had to have a drip. I was filled with exhausted frustration at the slowness of my recovery. No visitors were allowed, and the days were spent with the doctors hovering over me, doing tests, and taking my blood. I was too tired to resist, even though I shared Diana's dislike of needles.

Then one day Grandma came to see me. She looked very tired, and Daniel, who had barely left my bedside, reluctantly gave his chair to her.

"My dear girl! What a scare you gave us!" she sighed, and I saw the dark shadows under her eyes.

"Sorry..."

"We did not see that one coming. We had no idea someone would kidnap you and force you to heal a dark one..."

"Did he..." I swallowed to moisten my throat, "...heal?"

Grandma nodded.

"He did. He has remained healed."

"Where is... he..." The croak of a voice dried in my throat.

"They are all here, in our prison cells. Reggie's brass bowl music is playing non-stop, so they cannot escape."

"Have you told the Council?"

"No. Not yet," Daniel shook his head. "What they did was against all our laws, but desperation can make anyone break the rules. Besides – if the word spreads that you healed another infected Nephilim, you will be in even greater danger. And that's all down to me. I can hardly believe that I was so stupid as to have spoken about it during the Council. All of this - everything - my fault!"

"Don't blame yourself..." Grandma reached out to pat his hand. "The rumors of Elijah's infection had already spread and you had to assure everyone he was healed. Otherwise they might have turned against Elijah, even kill him. None of us could see this coming."

"But now that it has happened, and there has been another healing, Dana is not safe anywhere. She turned Nephilim too soon, and her body and mind were just not ready yet. They still aren't. Forcing the healing out of her may have caused permanent damage. We haven't had a silver Nephilim in over two thousand years, so how are we to know how the healing thing is supposed to work, to keep her safe while doing it?" Daniel opened his palms towards me. "Just look at her! One more occurrence like that and she could die. And when word gets out about what she has done, there are bound to be others who will have the same idea. We shall have to hide her from possible kidnappers all the time. They won't give a damn what happens to her as long as their loved ones are saved."

Grandma sighed.

"The eternal dilemma of healers. Swamped in requests for healing..."

I said nothing. I remembered myself floating over my damaged body, willing to severe the connection to it. Only Daniel's presence had stopped me. And his words...

I turned my eyes to him, and saw him looking intently into mine. My heart began to sing immediately. A hum... Then I realized others could hear it too. Grandma coughed and stole a sideways glance at Daniel. She knew, I was certain of it.

"I have written to your parents on your behalf." Grandma changed the subject. "They know nothing of this. But you need to call them soon, they have already grown suspicious as to why you haven't done so."

"She can't possibly talk on the phone yet!" Daniel said.

"Not yet, but as soon as she can. We'll say she has a bad flu, which explains why she is too tired to talk much," Grandma said.

"And we need to get her to safety. Away from here." Daniel sounded desperate.

"Where would you go, then? They will find you eventually, no matter where you go," Grandma stated the fact bluntly.

There was a knock on the door. Diana peeked in.

"May I come in?" she whispered.

"Yes!" I croaked before the others had a chance to say no.

"Oh Dana!" She flew to me and hugged me so that my iv-drip almost fell down. "How are you? Are you alive?"

That made me laugh.

"No, I'm just pretending!" I coughed.

"What are we going to do now?" Diana turned to ask Daniel.

"We'll get Dana to safety," he said.

"Where?" Diana asked.

"As soon as Dana is fit enough, we'll follow the original plan. Whoever tries to find Dana, will try to do so here in our time first. No one knows where we are, if we follow our original plan. We need to do it anyway, and I would have left Dana behind, but now we cannot leave her here. As long as no one has told any outsider about where we were going, we should be safe in the past."

Daniel had planned on leaving me behind? Since when? From the beginning or because of this latest episode?

"A lot of people have probably guessed where we were planning on going," Grandma said. "Clothes and coffers have been made, jewelry also, not to mention all the research we have been going through. They all point to ancient Egypt."

Daniel did not like this.

"We'll have to tell everyone to keep their silence," he ran his fingers through his hair like he always did when he was agitated, "and go as soon as we can. Also, just in case, we could start another research project about a different time, to confuse them."

"Perhaps... very well, let us begin looking for Cleopatra the Seventh now, and Alexandria," Grandma suggested, "and make the researchers believe that whatever we were searching for before, was a wrong lead. I'll explain this to Lilith."

Grandma left and Elijah walked in.

"My dear sister," he exclaimed, "how are you? You sure look like you had a bit of a hangover!"

"What?" I asked. This wasn't exactly the greeting I had been expecting.

"Diana, would you mind...?" Elijah asked.

"Erm... well, yes I would, in fact. This seems to be turning into a mighty interesting conversation and I'd like to listen to it," Diana raised her eyebrows, "but OK, OK... I get the message. I'll just listen behind the door..."

She left and I looked at Elijah questioningly.

"What was that sister-thing?" I whispered, cursing in my mind that I still had no real control over my voice.

"My dear Dana – I have now witnessed twice how your vibration matches that of Daniel. You have been locked into each other in a rather intimate way both times, and your wings hum in total harmony. If you two are not clever enough to know what that means, maybe I should enlighten you?"

Daniel opened his mouth, but Elijah dismissed him with a movement of his hand.

"You two are meant for each other. It is seldom that I have heard such total harmony of vibrations in two Nephilim. You have not yet given promises to each other, but when the time comes, and you are of age, Dana, you would be total idiots not to do so. And, as it seems to me you shall be my sister-in-law, I'd better forget any romantic notions about you, and congratulate my dear brother here."

I looked at Daniel, and had to laugh. He actually blushed.

"Now, of course, if you decided not to choose him, I shall willingly oblige and make you a respectable Mrs.," Elijah grinned at me, though there was sadness in his eyes, and for the briefest of moments I saw a vision of that same blonde women I had seen when healing his wings. He did not know I knew about his lost wife.

"I would throw something at you - if I could just lift my hand," I whispered, joining the game.

"I am sure you would," Elijah bowed, "but knowing you can't – yet – makes me feel quite safe. My brother here I can handle."

Daniel glowered at him.

"Oh come on, brother!" Elijah said. "You are way too serious and analytical about this whole thing. It's pretty obvious that you love each other. Why fight it? I understand about the waiting-till-right-age part, but to me it has been quite clear from the moment I kissed the bride-to-be in the desert that I had no chance. If she had been simply driven by her new Nephilim emotions, she would have jumped at me. But she did not. She began to cry, and that told me she had truly chosen you, now matter how new she was. Respect that. Wait as long as you have to, but don't wait forever, or I may come courting."

Elijah turned to me again.

"And now, before my brother starts throwing things at me, I'm on my way. I'll leave you two to each other. I shall collect Diana from behind the door too, and put a do not disturb sign on the handle."

At that, he walked out.

Daniel and I looked at each other. I began to hum again, I could not help it. I was so embarrassed by Elijah's words, but also filled with joy. I would have run and hidden, if I could have moved, but as it was I was at the mercy of the situation.

Then, slowly, Daniel's wings opened, and he stepped to my side and knelt by the bed. His electric blue wings were so beautiful. In response my wings tried to open, but didn't.

"Sssh..." Daniel stroked my cheek, "they are damaged too, and need time to heal."

We forgot ourselves in each other's eyes. His bright blue eyes, with tiny golden dots, caressed mine and again my tears began to fall.

"Sssh..." he said again.

His wings gently bent around me, and then they began to hum, first quietly, then more strongly, until the whole room vibrated. And my damaged wings answered back. I forced them to open, and began to cry for real when I saw them limp by my side, dark grey in color. Only a trickle of silver pulsed in the veins.

Daniel matched his wings to mine, covering them completely. It was not difficult, because I could not open mine fully. The hum of Daniel's wings felt painful at first, and I wailed like an injured animal.

"Now it is my turn to heal," he whispered.

I looked at him, and the hum began to ease my pain. He lowered his head, and kissed me with such tenderness I thought I would lose my consciousness. But this time he did not draw back. His kiss deepened, and I answered it fully. It was an odd sensation, being the object of such love, and not being able to move. Then my body began to burn, and I felt a strong fire light in my heart, spreading all through my body. With great difficulty I moved my hand and touched his cheek with my fingers. We kissed eyes open, drowned into each other, and my wings began to sing for real.

The sound was at first fragmented, off tune, but Daniel's wings balanced mine. Slowly the wings found the same tune, and then they were singing together in total harmony.

Daniel lifted his head, his eyes turned almost black.

"Dana... are you ready for this?" he whispered, searching my soul with his eyes.

I could only nod, tears rolling down my cheeks. I had never been more ready for anything. My whole being yearned for him.

"Then, Dana... we must still wait, but if you choose me, I shall give you my promise. You'll be mine, and I'll be yours, and we will melt into one, when you are of age."

"I choose you, Daniel," I managed to whisper, "and when the time is right, I shall give you my promise."

Now he was crying too, and I could taste the salt in his tears when we continued kissing, eyes closed now, in that place where only true lovers can enter, and no time exists.

80

HEALING

"So no chance for me then, eh?" Jason shook his head sadly and pressed his hands over his heart with a pining expression on his face. "Oh well, I'll take it like a man. I'll just join the queue."

"Yes, after me," Elijah grinned and winked at me and I blushed, as he had intended. His laughter almost matched Diana's in cheerfulness.

I was beginning to feel as though I was walking around with a big sign on my back - a heart with an arrow through it and "Dana loves Daniel" written in the middle. Though no one had witnessed us, it seemed everyone knew. I could sense it from the little smiles the nurses and doctors gave me, quite apart from the more straight-forward comments of our Time Walker team such as the one Jason had made.

I was never left alone for a minute. The Nephilim who had kidnapped me were safely in the prison cells. They were not going to be able to tell anyone about the healing that had happened. But they might have told someone of their plans before kidnapping me, and Daniel was taking no chances.

Elijah told me what had happened.

"You were lucky - Daniel and I came to fetch you two first of all the team, just after you had been kidnapped," Elijah said. "Daniel is so skilled that he can sense the exact spot in a space where a Nephilim has walked from or to the buffer zone. This makes hunting someone that much easier because you can be thrown off for miles in the buffer zone by even a slight deviation in a physical location. When Daniel saw that Diana's bag had fallen on the ground, and the playing cards were scattered all over - along with sensing a recent Nephilim presence - he guessed right away what had happened. He went after you immediately. I barely had time to follow. He was afraid that Angel had got you, but the scent of these Nephilim was different. It didn't match the dark ones. Did you notice that your kidnappers had a unique metallic scent to them?"

I considered a while. Yes, there had been a slightly metallic scent with a tang of cinnamon around every one of them. It was very different from the scent of overripe fruit that hung about Angel.

"So, Daniel thought that at least you were not going to be infected, nor taken to Cain, in all likelihood. If you could even have been infected, which we doubt. He followed the scent of your kidnappers, and then he saw the first playing card in the sand. It was barely visible, already falling down to a level of its own denser energies, but your scent was still strong on it. He found you with the help of these cards, but by then it was too late, because of those singing bowls...

"We just couldn't get into the room you were in, because of the sound. Using the bowls is a normal procedure of pure Nephilim strongholds. We stepped out of the buffer zone near the bunker you were kept in, and could only enter after they had stopped playing the bowls. When we finally got to the room, you were lying on the floor, all grey and burned out, barely breathing anymore. Daniel almost killed the Nephilim responsible..."

Elijah sat for a while, deep in his thoughts, hands clenched to fists so hard his blood vessels were clearly visible. The muscles of his jaws revealed he was gritting his teeth. Then he collected himself and looked at me.

"I honestly hope you never need to see Daniel fight. He is... his strength is so great and he is so ferocious, that you would think you were watching a demon. He attacked the ones responsible for breaking you, and they surrendered before he actually killed them. You should have seen... or, no, it's better that you didn't. He lost it. Completely. I had to attack him in the end, and pin him with my wings so he wouldn't kill them. I got a few scars in the process myself."

He stretched his wings and I saw darker bruises in them still, though already days had passed.

"I suppose that was the moment, when I understood how much he really must love you. I have never seen him lose control like that. And when he lay down on the floor next to you, and wrapped himself around you and refused to let you die... Even angels would have wept at that sight. The Nephilim responsible certainly did. They have been begging for forgiveness ever since, but I don't think Daniel will ever forgive them fully."

"Maybe it is not his job in the first place. To forgive."

Elijah looked at me questioningly. He did not ask anything, though, but left me in peace to collect my thoughts and find the right words in my own time.

"That healing... it wasn't me. It isn't something that I do. It is beyond me, something using me... as a channel. And that... force... it felt the greatest sympathy and compassion for the infected one. It wanted to heal him. And I was one with that emotion, and I wanted it too. I don't think I could have stopped it from happening even if I had tried."

"How did that feel?" Elijah asked. "If I can ask you, that is."

"Of course you can... we are almost family, after all," I smiled at him.

"But not quite completely yet?" he winked and grinned at me and I blushed dutifully again.

"No, not quite yet. He won't hear of it. I am not of age, as he puts it."

"Well, he's most likely right, even though you are not our average Nephilim by any standard. Your emotions are too strong, and then this channeling of healing energies... no, you are wise to wait for your body and mind to be mature enough... it might be dangerous for both of you if you rushed things."

I did not comment on that, but returned to answering his original question.

"But - you asked how it felt to me? Mentally it was... expansive. It was as if my understanding had expanded far beyond anything I could have imagined. I understood things, and saw and heard things I could not comprehend. As if I - didn't have the mental tools to handle it all. And now, when I try to remember... I can't, or at least I can't put into words."

"And physically? How did it feel?"

"Horrible..." my voice broke down, "it.... hurt. It hurt so much... as if liquid metal was pouring into my veins and it was burning me from the inside. And I couldn't escape it. I wanted to scream but I couldn't, I was paralyzed. That... force took over, and I had to obey and it had decided to heal this man. And like I said – despite the pain I wanted it too, though it felt as though it was going to kill me. The odd thing is that it felt like an acceptable thing. Dying."

Elijah touched my hand when the memory made me gasp for air.

"Did it hurt like that when you healed me?" he asked quietly.

"No, no it did not, don't worry. It has to do with the time, how long someone has been infected, I think... healing you did hurt, but it was more bearable."

"Poor Dana... You will be well, though. After you... almost gave your promise to Daniel," he smiled at me, "you have been healing much faster. Your wings are definitely better."

That was true, they were no longer dark grey, but lighter in color, and the silver veins were almost back to normal. Also my skin was not ashen anymore, only a hint of the sickly pallor of a convalescent remained. My eyes had not turned back, though. I had no idea how I could ever explain this to my parents.

My eyes were now the color of silver. Bluish silver, but silver nevertheless.

"Oh, you can just buy contacts," Diana had dismissed my problem. "Blue ones. Don't say that silver color is caused by contacts because you can't take them off. So blue it will have to be."

"I want to get up," I said to Elijah, "will you help me? I know Daniel won't agree, but I have to get back on my feet."

"Hmm... I suppose we could try," he said, "now that Daniel is not hovering all over you."

He bent over so he could slide his hand behind my back. He was so strong he just lifted me up to a sitting position in one effortless movement. I sat there, with my head spinning, and had to lean my head against his chest. It felt warm and comfortable, and safe. Eventually the world stopped revolving and I nodded to Elijah. He bent his knees and gathered me tightly against his chest.

"Let's try to get you up," Elijah said. "Never fear, I won't let you go, so even if your legs give way, you won't fall."

That was a good thing. I felt as if I was standing on boiled spaghetti.

Elijah's strong arm kept me safely upright and I gathered all my strength to stand. Finally I found my knees and stood there by the bed for a few minutes, shaking with exhaustion.

"OK, it's back to the horizontal for you," Elijah decided. "Fainting won't improve how you feel."

"I would love to take a shower," I sighed. "The nurses have washed me, but I am beginning to feel a bit ripe..."

Elijah chuckled.

Later I learned he had told someone about my wish, because a nurse came to fetch me, helped me into a wheelchair, and took me to the Centre's private little spa reserved for personnel only. She dressed me in a swimsuit, and when she opened the door of the dressing room, Jason and Elijah were there waiting for me. They lifted me like a feather and carried me to a bathtub, half-filled with delicious warm water. There was a rubber mat at the bottom of the tub, so I could not slide about.

I sighed, content, and relaxed into the warmth of the scent-laden bath.

"Oh, this is heaven..."

"Does this mean we have earned the queue numbers two and three permanently, then?" Jason smiled.

"Oh, definitely!" I felt like joking too. "But you have to decide which one is which."

"Ooo... A duel at dawn, Elijah?" Jason asked Elijah over his shoulder.

"Sure. You can even choose the weapons," Elijah teased back.

"But you need to eat some more, young lady," the nurse shook her head, "you are way too thin!"

She was right. I had lost too much weight and looked like an overgrown twelve-year-old, and the swimsuit was baggy. So, after my bath, I asked the boys to get me some food. Vegetarian food, I had to remind them. I received a huge veggie burger and fries and forced them all down while they supervised the whole thing like two aunties.

I didn't mind. I knew I belonged with these people and the Nephilim more than I had ever belonged anywhere. During these last weeks I had turned from an introvert bookworm teenager into a young woman who also happened to be Nephilim. I had gained more self-assurance through experiencing great change and adventure. I'd faced great fear – and found love. And despite lying in a bed, too ill for my own good, being totally dependent on other people's help, I felt... happy. I mused on everything I'd been through, astonishing myself at the utter change in my life.

Yes. I felt blissfully happy. I looked at Jason and Elijah and smiled at them.

"I love you guys," I declared.

The old Dana would never in a million years have said she loved someone. The new Dana wanted to share her emotions with the people she loved.

The boys looked at me and smiled.

"Yes! There's still hope for us, if Daniel gets on her nerves!" Jason punched the air.

"Oh, he can do that for sure..." Elijah admitted, "we'll just bide our time!"

"And why would you be biding your time?" Daniel walked through the door.

"We are just waiting for her to get tired of you," Elijah said. "Or I am, anyway."

"And if that happens, I don't have to wait for long," Jason grinned, "because Elijah gets on everyone's nerves very quickly."

Daniel shook his head.

"The time for that is nowhere in sight, so scoot before you both get on my nerves."

Jason and Elijah lifted their eyebrows meaningfully, and left the room.

Daniel saw me smiling and smiled at me too. He saw the plate.

"You've eaten something. Good. You need to gather your strength, because we are leaving as soon as you are fit to travel."

"So we're going ahead as planned?"

"Yes."

"Hasn't all this brought danger to all of you? With the shadows spying on our dreams and all that?"

"Well, we've figured out a way to handle that. None of our team sleeps in the Centre. We take them to hotel rooms in different countries each night. A new country and a new hotel every night. The bookings are done from computers in internet cafes and public libraries all over the world too. Let's just say your grandmother has done a lot of traveling with a Key since you... got ill. Explains why you haven't seen much of her or the others lately."

"Wow, talk about travel!"

"You don't know the half of it. Let's just say they are beginning to get a bit bored with sleeping in hotel rooms, and not being allowed to show their faces outside the room. Also we need to find the Trail, to stop whatever Cain is planning. We did not want to leave without you. I - couldn't have done so."

"What about my dreams?"

"Lilith has been guarding those."

I tried to remember what my dreams had been about, and was pretty certain they had involved Daniel.

"I'd better get better soon, then. Or they will begin to dislike me."

"As if that was possible," Daniel placed a determined kiss on my forehead, "but yes, it's time you got back on your feet!"

81

VISITING HOME

After two weeks, I called my parents. It was the earliest that I felt I'd be able to keep my voice firm. I was still wobbly but at least the color had returned to my cheeks, if not my wings. They had darker patches and hurt when I tried to stretch them, but everyone was hopeful that they would mend.

"Dana, we want to see you." It was so wonderful to hear Mom's voice again. "We've been missing you."

"Yes... I'll come and visit soon," I was trying to sound as cheerful as possible, "I promise. I've missed you too. I got this horrible flu and was in bed for a week..."

Daniel, who had not left my side, looked at me with inquiring eyes.

"They will notice the change in you, if you do go," he said, when I had finished the call. "You are so much taller now. And your eyes..."

"I miss them, Daniel. I want to meet them before we leave. Something might happen to me. Or them. So I want to see them. Maybe I should get those blue contact lenses, like Diana suggested," I sighed. "I can't do anything about the height, though."

Daniel understood, and so a date was arranged for me to visit my parents. I planned to go with Grandma. She left ahead of me to pick up her car and waited for me at a crossroads near my house. Daniel escorted me there through the buffer zone close to midday, when the shadows were more likely to stay in hiding.

I got into Grandma's car, and must have looked almost as awkward as Reggie had done when we had driven from the university to the Centre. How long ago that seemed! My legs were that much longer now and I folded them uncomfortably into the small space

It was odd to see the familiar landscape as we passed through it. The last time I had been here, I'd been an ordinary human being, who was grieving for the death of her best friend. Now I was a mythical creature, Nephilim, still trying to get to grips with my new identity. I had never believed in the existence of angels, and now I was one. Well, half an angel. It all felt so unreal still. Not to mention learning about different levels of energy in the buffer zone, and actually meeting my dead friend, who continued her life on "the other side".

"Ready?" Grandma asked.

"Ready as I can be," I said.

"Let's go then!"

She drove us the short distance to my home. My parents were already outside on the doorstep. It was a story book scene. Grandma stopped the car, and I took a deep sigh before getting out. I felt a fleeting feeling of wanting to cry almost, seeing their eager faces. I had not even realized just how much I had missed them. Nugget came through the open door, saw me and stopped in his tracks. Then he walked to me, wrapping himself around my ankles and meowing. I lifted him to my lap and he started rubbing his cheek on mine, purring.

"Dana! Good lord, how you have grown!" Mom exclaimed.

"Yes, I know..." I laughed, embarrassed, and they both hugged me tightly.

"Goodness, it must be so hot outside, you are burning up!" Mom said. "It's not the flu still, is it?"

"No, but it's so nice to get inside the house where it's cool!" I sighed and wiped my forehead in a slightly too exaggerated way, and Grandma rolled her eyes behind my parents' back.

"Come in, come in!" Dad was waving us inwards from the open door.

We walked in and I took off my sunglasses. Grandma looked at me, surprised. I was not wearing any contact lenses. I had decided not to.

Father had made his famous pasta carbonara – my portion had soy instead of meat. It was delicious. I could have eaten much more – my body was craving for food after the growth spurt, and my illness.

"So how are you doing with your studies?" Mom wanted to know.

"Great! I have already learned so much. I am even preparing my first essay."

"What is it about?" Dad was genuinely interested.

I almost said Amarna by accident, but Grandma beat me to it.

"Cleopatra the Seventh!" she was a living picture of pride.

"The seventh?" Mom looked puzzled.

"Yes, the seventh. The famous and last one. There were seven Cleopatras in the Ptolemy dynasty," Grandma said.

"Oh, I never knew..." Mom put a delicious peach pie on the table and looked at me in the eyes.

"Your eyes look a bit... strange... dear?" she said in a questioning tone. I could see that she was puzzling over whether illness could do something like that to a person's eyes.

"Are they?" I smiled, "well... it could be. They seem to have changed a bit when I had my growth spurt. Just like my hair began to turn lighter."

This was true - I had visible root growth, which was lighter than my hair color had been before.

"I asked a doctor at the university about it and he said it is genetic. Some changes in hair and eye color can appear later in life. It had to do with my growth spurt activating it, apparently. He explained it is related to some albinism gene. Not fully albino, but it dilutes my colors a bit. Nothing serious."

"Oh, I see." To my relief Mom did not seem too interested in the subject, or wanted to avoid a discussion in genetics, perhaps fearing I would begin to ask if there had been albinos in our family tree, which I was not even a part of genetically. "It is a nice color, though. Silvery, light blue...ish."

She made herself busy cutting big slices of the peach pie on our plates. She then pushed the bowl with whipped cream in my general direction and looked at Dad.

"It seems there are some odd eye colors around these days. Remember that survey girl from last week? Her eyes were all yellow. I was certain she had contact lenses, but why would anyone want yellow eyes? Especially if they were wanting to gain access to anyone's home. It had to be genuine - I can't imagine anyone choosing to make their eyes look like that."

I dropped my fork onto the tablecloth.

"Oh, sorry!" I said.

Grandma was very careful not to let her emotions show.

"Survey? What survey was that?" she asked, full of warm curiosity.

"Oh, they were asking about the children who'd grown up in this area – about their further education, and what they chose to study. It was something to do with how the environment of a young child affect their choice of education after high school. We told her about your Egyptology studies."

"Yes, she was most impressed and wanted to know if you were specializing in any specific era, and under whom you were studying. Professor Réginald Rowan, wasn't it?" Dad asked, while reaching for another piece of the pie.

"Yes, quite right." I tried not to show my fear.

"It seems she knew him. I mean she said oh him!" Dad kept on chatting.

"I wonder if she is from the same university as Dana, because she knew the professor?" Grandma wondered. "What did she look like, other than the yellow eyes? Maybe Dana might know her?"

"She was a real beauty. Oh, and quite tall, just like you. Beautiful long blonde hair too. And such a lovely voice she had! Like little silver bells!" Mom said almost enthusiastically. Despite her odd eyes, the visitor had clearly made a favorable impression.

"Oh, my cell phone!" Grandma said even though no ring tone was to be heard, "I'm sorry, I have to take this one!"

She rose from the table and walked out of the kitchen.

"Oh hello, Daniel!" she said into the phone, "at my daughter's house. Yes... So what did you want to ask? Guards around the house? Yes, I think that's wise. You could hire them and offset the costs as part of necessary expenses for tax purposes. Yes... quite... an angel? No no, not a statue, they really had a consultant whose name was Angel visiting there a week ago. Yes, yes... That's funny... Ok, I have to go now, we can talk better later."

She returned to the table.

"Really sorry about that... it was a friend who has an antique shop. He's holding something really valuable in there for a while, and was wondering about its security..."

"The things you are involved with..." Mom sighed.

I sighed too. Daniel had been warned, and I was sure my parents' house would be guarded very soon.

"I was thinking..." Grandma took a forkful of the pie. "Oh my, this is delicious! I wonder where you inherited your baking skills, certainly not from me!"

Mom looked pleased.

"So, I was thinking... now that Dana is studying elsewhere, and her room is not in use at the moment ... a daughter of a friend of mine is moving into this area for a while and is looking for accommodation. She is a botanist, who will be doing research into the flora of the area and would like to live near the woods. It's so lucky, living where you do. Your house would be the perfect location for her. Her research is well funded, which means she could pay a decent rent, if she could have her meals, and wash her laundry here too. What do you think?"

"Oh, this is short notice... what is she like? What about Dana? She will still need her room when she comes home during vacations."

"She is of Asian origin and her nickname is Tinky, because she is so small. Pixie small. She's quiet and very cheerful - you'd hardly know she was there. And she's an excellent cook, too," Grandma told.

Tinky, of course. She was one of our best and most fearless Hunters. She was tiny, yes, but she excelled in oriental fighting techniques. She would be the perfect guard against any shadows – or Nephilim – that were nearby. I felt happier knowing that Tinky would be in the house and that there'd undoubtedly be guards set by Daniel outside too. I began to feel a bit more relieved about my parents.

"Does she speak Japanese by chance?" Dad asked, and I suddenly realized there was another reason why Grandma had chosen Tinky.

"Yes, in fact she is Japanese."

"Great - I haven't had the chance to speak Japanese for years," Dad beamed, "not since the time I spent there when I was learning about Japanese culinary traditions." He turned to Mom. "Honey, you could learn Japanese too."

"I am certain she would love to speak Japanese with you!" Grandma assured him.

"Well then – we'll think about it, of course!" Dad said. "If that's OK with you, Dana? It's your room after all."

I could see from his enthusiasm that he had already agreed to the idea, but Mom would need a little persuading. Eventually she would give in, I was sure, but knowing Mom I did not join in the conversation or try to press her in any way. Mom did not like to be told to do anything in her own home. And besides - it would have been odd for me to encourage her to rent my room out. So I just nodded.

We spent the day at home, and I felt rather nostalgic. The old me longed for a long evening reading in bed, or taking the binoculars and going to the hut in the woods where Kitty and I had spent so many hours. Nugget would not leave me for a second, and hopped onto my lap whenever I sat down.

When it was time for us to leave, Dad held Nugget in his arms so he would not run after me. I hugged my parents and promised to come see them more often. I could only hope I could. If we were about to go three thousand and five hundred years back in time to a different culture, anything might happen. I wondered what my parents would do if I died there, and vanished from here for good. They would go crazy with grief...

The thought of grief brought to my mind a thing I had promised to do. When we drove away, and our house was no longer to be seen, Daniel was waiting for us by the roadside. Grandma stopped the car.

"Did you manage to arrange the guards?" she asked.

Daniel did not answer immediately, but bent and gave me a kiss right in front of Grandma.

"So that's how it is..." Grandma smiled, "not that we didn't know already, but you never admitted as much, Daniel. Have you made promises to each other yet?"

"No, not yet... We promised to make promises later, though," I explained, hoping I wasn't too red with embarrassment.

"So, we could say you are engaged then. I have to say I am very glad, even though Dana is very young still."

"Yes, I agree, Layla," Daniel said solemnly, "and nothing improper has happened, because we have not made our vows. Nothing can even be considered until Dana is fully grown into her Nephilim powers and controls them. I won't put any pressure on her at all, because she needs to know for certain that this is her own choice. But I wanted you to know about us officially, because you are her family. I want you to know my intentions are honorable."

"I would expect nothing less from you, Daniel," Grandma beamed, "and you two have my blessing."

She squeezed my hand and looked a bit teary-eyed. That was something new - I'd never seen that side of Grandma before.

"Thank you, Layla," Daniel said so seriously I didn't know where to look. I hadn't expected this discussion to happen right here. - it felt almost like Daniel had been asking for my hand from Grandma.

"Now, about the guards? If Angel had been checking out Dana's parents, they are in danger. I'm thinking that Angel may plan to use them as a weapon against Dana at some point."

"Some of our human guards are in town buying camping supplies even as we speak." Daniel waved his hand to the general direction of our little town. "They're going to camp in the forest near your parents' house. It would be better if we had Nephilim, who could move unobserved in the buffer zone, but Elijah and I can't stay behind for this purpose - and nor can we bring outsiders into this, not now."

"I suggested that they take Tinky under their roof on the pretext that she is a botanist doing research into the area."

"Perfect. She is the best Hunter we have, after you. Did they agree to this arrangement?"

"They will. But for now, at least as long as it takes for our Guardians to arrive, will you keep an eye on them?"

"I will, of course," Daniel said, and kissed me again, longer.

Grandma laughed happily.

"Young love... but I'll be keeping an eye on you two when we go, so you'd better behave!"

Daniel laughed also, a happy relaxed sound I had not heard before. He looked around to check no-one was near and then vanished into the buffer zone.

"You could not have chosen a better young man, Dana," Grandma said. "I truly am very happy."

"Young? He is over three hundred years old!"

"So he is, but one tends to forget it..." Grandma revved the engine. "Whooo, great excuse for putting my foot down on the pedal, eh?"

"I need to go someplace first," I said. "Would you mind if we drove to Kitty's house?"

"Of course I wouldn't mind. Wherever you'd like to go."

The few minutes that it took to get to Kitty's house passed in silence. I saw her mother in the garden. She looked up and before she recognized me, her eyes had no spark at all. They were so tired and sad. Then slowly she realised who it was.

"Is it you, Dana? I did not recognize you! You have grown so much!"

"Yes, a late growth spurt," Grandma smiled. "She could be a fashion model with those long legs now!"

Kitty's mother tried to smile, but no joy showed in her eyes. It was a pitiful try, and the corners of her mouth twitched at the effort.

"I came to see you because of a dream I had," I went straight to the point. "It was about Kitty."

"Yes?" a little curiosity crept into her voice.

"You see... Kitty came to me in a dream. She looked so happy and joyful, so alive..."

. . .

"I am glad. It must have been a nice dream," her mother said in that tired voice.

"Wait - please listen. It's more than that. She said she wanted to give you a message, and that I should bring it to you."

"A message?" she asked without emotion.

"Yes, she said she wanted you to know she is still alive and well. And that she often tries to tell you that, but it is difficult to communicate with you. However, whenever you suddenly smell roses where there are none, that is her. She is close to you then."

Her posture straightened.

"Roses, you say?"

"Yes, the smell of roses. Does it mean anything to you?"

Her hands flew to her face.

"Yes! Yes it does! I have been smelling roses in the oddest places lately. When I had my car fixed, the repair shop of all places smelled of roses. And in the library too... and one morning I woke up to a strong scent of roses... she said it was her?"

"Yes, it was Kitty trying to tell you she is there, and that she is alive."

Kitty's mother stood still for a long time. Then she began to smile, really smile, with tears in her eyes.

"Thank you, Dana... I think I can believe this. She loved roses and was always talking about dreams and the messages they delivered to us."

"Yes, she was..." I said.

I could not force tears out of my eyes for Kitty, because I had already met her and knew full well she was still alive, even if at another level of existence. But I could sympathize with Kitty's mother's sorrow. I leaned over the fence and hugged her tightly round the shoulders.

"I believe we go on existing after death," the person I had become had the courage to say this out loud, "and that we really do meet again, one day.""

"I want to believe that too," Kitty's mother said and wiped a tear from the corner of her eye. "But where are my manners! Please, do come in!"

"I'm afraid we don't have time now," Grandma said, "We have an appointment soon. But I am sure Dana will come and meet you in future, won't you, Dana?"

"Of course," I hugged Kitty's mother one more time, hard.

She waved us off, and this time she had a smile on her face. She looked like a different person.

Grandma said nothing, but squeezed my hand again. Then she put both her hands on the steering wheel and pushed the gas pedal down. The little red car happily responded.

82

TRANSFORMATION

Artemis took Ambrogio to the city of Delphi. There he stole a donkey from its stall and it was led into the mist behind the world, showing very little surprise at the new doorway that appeared in thin air. The animal was then taken to the place where Ambrogio left the letters to Selene.

Standing at the very edge of the human world, Ambrogio realised that he could watch all the goings-on there without being seen. Artemis stood beside him, so closely that he felt the heat of her body. Together they waited for Selene to appear, watching the light growing in the human world – the scene was slightly foggy because of the mist they were standing in, but still visible.

For the first time in forty-five days he now saw his beloved Selene again. She appeared walking in her light coloured dress, with a cape around her and her head hooded. She immediately looked at the rock beside the road. Ambrogio's letter was there, with a little stone of top of it to keep the wind from taking it.

When she saw it, she took a few hasty steps and then opened the folded letter. Her lips moved silently as she read the letter to herself. Ambrogio wanted to touch her, to let her know he was there. She looked so beautiful, so delicate.

Selene folded the letter and hid it in a pouch she was carrying. Then she looked at the donkey, tied to a small tree. Her head turned towards the city she had come from, and then towards the temple. No one was to be seen.

"I accept, Ambrogio," she said, as if she had sensed his presence. "If this is the only way for us to be together, I accept."

She walked to the donkey, loosened the rope that tied it to the tree, and sat on its back. In moments she was gone, down the mountain, towards the harbor of Kirrha. It was the harbor where the supplicants coming to meet Pythia landed. Because Ambrogio had not known of it he had landed on the western coast of Greece instead. Maybe if he had told the ship's crew where he was headed, they would have brought him to Kirrha instead, but then his father would have heard where he was going. It was as if the gods had willed it...

Once Selene had disappeared from sight, Artemis grasped Ambrogio's hand and pulled him deeper into the mist.

"And now, you shall be my servant."

"What kind of a pledge do I need to make, my goddess?" Ambrogio knelt.

"No pledge. I simply need to kill you first," Artemis said lightly.

Ambrogio stared at her in horror. Artemis looked at him, with her head cocked on one side, amused by his expression.

"Kill me, my goddess?" he stammered.

"If you are to become immortal, and to have Apollo's curse removed from you, you need to die as a human, and be reborn with new blood as the Hunter I am about to make you. But do not worry. I shall not let you slip from your body, and you will see your girl soon enough."

Ambrogio had no time to prepare himself. Artemis yanked him to his feet as though he weighed nothing, opened her mouth, and fixed herself on his neck in a blur of motion. He felt a sharp pain, which subsided almost immediately. He felt her sucking, thirstily, and to his horror he realized she was drinking his blood. He opened his mouth to scream, but no sound came out.

His limbs went numb, and he heard his heart beat erratically. He fell down, limp. Little black dots with light edges danced in his eyes.

Artemis lifted her head, and he saw his blood dripping from her jaws, which were very odd-looking. Her mouth had grown twice as wide as it had been before, and her beautiful teeth had grown longer. And her eyes... They were shining pure gold now, with an odd swirling oily yellow color pulsing from within the eye to the surface. She swallowed and smiled.

"What an interesting childhood you had..." she said, "and your mother had a beautiful singing voice. You must have inherited it from her..."

Ambrogio was passing out and could not reply. His field of vision began to blur and darken, but he had enough consciousness left to understand Artemis had somehow connected to his memories through his blood.

He felt how she lifted his left hand. With a quick movement of her mouth she sliced his vein open. His failing eyes recorded mechanically how little blood came out. Then she did the same with her own right wrist and placed it against his wound. After that she sliced her left wrist open and pressed it against his mouth.

"Now, drink with your mouth, and drink with your vein, and become one with my blood," she said.

At first Ambrogio's consciousness continued to collapse. Then a fiery tingling started from his hand, and when he gasped painfully for air he had to breathe in and so he swallowed Artemis's blood. He gagged and coughed, but she never stopped pressing her wrist to his mouth. Her hot blood flowed into him.

The salty, iron taste of her blood filled his mind, bringing with it a wordless whispering. The noise of the whispers tore down his human mind and revealed something primeval and vast underneath. Now it was his turn to read Artemis's life through her blood, and what he saw made him understand how very immature and young he was. Hundreds of years filled his mind, mocking his inferior intellect.

His body began to tingle, turned hot, and he grabbed the goddess's hand on his mouth with his free right hand to drink even more deeply.

"Enough," Artemis said and easily freed her hand from his mouth, apparently not affected at all by loss of her blood. "This is enough for the change to begin."

Ambrogio lay on his back, amazed by the new sensations he was feeling. Too quickly the memories of Artemis left his mind; leaving only teasing, faint shadows that eluded his attempts to grasp them.

"Rise, my child," Artemis said.

Ambrogio raised his left hand to his eyes. The deep gash caused by the teeth of the goddess was almost gone. A pale thin white crescent line only showed. He turned to his side and thought of rising up, only to notice he was already up. He had moved so fast he had not even registered his own movement.

"Take my hand," Artemis said, and Ambrogio did so. Surprisingly, her hand no longer felt hot to him.

"You are now my child," she said, "for I have recreated you. And you shall remain my servant for ever more, as you promised."

Ambrogio smiled broadly. He had never felt so good in his life. He felt as if he could run to the edge of the world without being out of breath. Breath... Amazed, he noticed he could hold his breath for a long time and had no need to breathe in. The air seemed to seep through his very skin...

"Your change will take some days, and while it lasts, you will be a terrifying sight for humans during daylight. Still, you seem to have taken to it well. Most people go through bad pain and may even lose their mind when they are changed, but your body accepted my blood easily. That is rare, but how fortunate," Artemis said in a voice that was almost purring with pleasure, "because now we can go to Kirrha immediately and get a ship for you and your Selene so that you can escape without Apollo knowing where you have gone. Also Hades won't know where to look for you for a while, because of the death of your shadow, and the change in your scent my blood has caused."

The stayed within the grey mist, and though they did not rise above it, Artemis seemed to know where she was going. She pulled the ecstatic Ambrogio behind her through the mist, and into the harbor of Kirrha.

The sun was already rising when they arrived.

"You wait here," Artemis said. "You are not to show yourself to anyone."

Ambrogio stayed in place, hidden by the mists that edged the visible world. He saw several ships in the harbor, and a few anchored further out. Artemis stepped back into the world from an alleyway. She had wiped the blood away from her mouth, and now simply appeared as a tall, beautiful blond woman. The sailors nudged each other and yelled indecent comments after her. She paid no attention, but instead walked off to meet a man who clearly knew her, because he bowed with respect.

They exchanged a few words, and then Artemis returned to the place where Ambrogio was hiding in the mist behind the world.

"A coffin will be brought for you," she said, knowing he would hear. "I have removed Apollo's curse, but your skin and body will keep on changing for a few days still, and during that time you cannot be exposed to sunlight. I shall come for you when it is ready. Do not move from the mist."

Ambrogio nodded, then realized she would not see it, and said out loud:

"I will, my goddess."

Artemis nodded slightly and walked away.

While Ambrogio waited, he admired his body. He had always been muscular, but now something strange was happening to his torso and limbs. It was as though whatever fat he had under his skin was vanishing, and pure muscle showed under the skin. His arms looked like the arms of the wrestlers of the Pythian games. The same with his thighs, and abdomen. He felt all the strange slight adjustments inside his body, while this was going on.

And then his skin began to change. He lifted his arms closer to his face and it took a while for him to understand what he was seeing. His skin was turning transparent.

He could not help but yell in surprise. A dog walking in the alley jumped and turned around to see where the sound came from. Ambrogio saw the dog, and another strange thing happened. He felt hunger. An overwhelming need to attack the animal took over. He stepped closer to the dog and a low growl emanated from within him.

Suddenly Artemis was there. She slapped Ambrogio on his face with such force he fell back into the mist, still growling. The dog withdrew, all the hairs on its back standing up.

"You are not to show yourself!" Artemis hissed. "You will obey my orders, or I will take away the immortality I have given you!"

Seeing her so her furious made Ambrogio's will to kill disappear.

"I beg for your forgiveness, my goddess..." he fell to his knees. "I do not know what came over me."

"I told you that you would crave the blood of animals after you were transformed. And you need it also – if you don't feed on blood, your body changes so that everyone can see you are not human anymore. Just look at your skin now. It will return to normal once you have had enough blood to drink."

Ambrogio looked in amazement and disgust at his skin. It seemed to him like a jellyfish in water, and he could see his muscles clearly underneath it, and his veins, which seemed oddly black.

"Wait here," Artemis said and walked out of the mist into the world again.

This time Ambrogio turned to look into the mist instead of the harbor city, so nothing would distract him. Artemis was soon back and handed him something. A piglet was hanging limp in her outstretched hand.

"It is still alive," she said.

Ambrogio snatched the animal from her hands without any need for instruction. Instinctively he bit into the small animal's neck and did not even care about the smell of pig dung in his eagerness to nourish his body. He sucked the blood away from the piglet in an amazingly short time, catching faint glimpses of the short life the animal had lived, and then he threw the body away. It began to sink into the mist and vanished from sight.

As if by magic, Ambrogio saw his transparent skin turn more solid within minutes and retain most of its color. You could still see the form of the muscles underneath, but now it only appeared as though his skin was very thin.

"That's better," Artemis said.

And then the men appeared, carrying a wooden casket big enough for a man to fit in. They dropped it in the alley and looked around expectantly. Artemis walked away from Ambrogio, and vanished into the mist. Soon her form appeared from around the corner of the alley.

"Thank you. You may go. Return before sunset and carry the casket to the ship."

The sailors seemed to know Artemis, because they all retreated respectfully and left quickly.

"Get in the casket when I say so," she said to Ambrogio and lifted the lid of the casket.

People were walking on the shore, but when the sun was at its highest, it became more quiet.

"Now," Artemis said, and Ambrogio walked from the mist and quickly climbed into the casket. For a brief moment the sun touched his skin, and it hurt, but the pain was tolerable. He moved so fast the sun's heat did not have a chance to linger.

Artemis closed the lid, and tied the leather straps that secured the lid. Ambrogio waited for his heart to thump because of the excitement, but to his surprise he felt no heartbeat. He concentrated on the stillness of his body, and then his heart beat once. A strong thump, which spread a tingling sensation all over his body. It subdued in a few minutes, and his body remained still and alert for a considerable length of time before there was another beat of the heart, and another tingling sensation. And all the time he felt that he was not breathing at all - his body seemed to drink air in through the skin.

Ambrogio then concentrated on listening to the noises of Kirrha. To his amazement his hearing seemed to be more acute as time passed. Suddenly he was listening to two merchants having an argument and the noises around them revealed that this was taking place inside a house! He could clearly hear people walking about inside, greeting one another, showing merchandise and being paid. A servant carrying a tray of cups with a clatter... Ambrogio realised he was hearing all this through walls!

The smell of the resin on the planks of the casket was strong. His sense of smell was also getting sharper all the time, and the resinous scent began to overwhelm him. Ever after that day whenever he smelled resin, his memory brought him back to the alley of Kirrha, to the wooden coffin in which he lay.

Then there came the sound of many footsteps approaching, and the casket was lifted from the ground. He was carried to the pier, and hoisted onto a ship. He did not see anything, but felt the sway of the water. He was carried below deck, so this was a big ship. And then he heard the voice of Artemis.

"I am leaving now. Your Selene will arrive soon. She will be given instructions about where she is to come. And under no circumstances are you to show yourself in sunlight for a whole month. Understand?"

"Yes, my goddess..." he answered.

"I shall leave you with her for the length of her life. When she is gone, it will be time for you to join my forces. By then Hades will not be looking for you any longer. He won't recognize you either, not after your change."

Ambrogio thought about what she had said, and did not know when she had left.

And then he heard the most beautiful voice in the world.

"Ambrogio?"

Selene had arrived.

83

DESERT

Mut-Bity and I left Mi-Wer without me once leaving the shelter of the cabin. We did not see the yellow-eyed man anywhere on the harbor at Mi-Wer. Mut-Bity did not want to linger, though. She was clearly afraid of the man, and if she was afraid, it was certain the man was dangerous.

Our boat left us on the Western shore of the Great Lake. And that was the last time in a long time that I saw Kemet, the Black Land.

I was wrapped in linen, layers and layers of it, to prevent my skin from burning. We had a small donkey to carry our things, and Mut-Bity put me sitting on its back and began to walk. I listened to the crunching of sand and stones under her feet and the donkey's small hooves, and Mut-Bity's steady breathing. I smelled her sweat as well. By the great River she kept herself clean all the time, as did other people as well. Here we had no water for washing.

We walked, and walked, and walked. I was lulled into an almost dreamlike state at the back of the donkey. I lost track of time, and closed my eyes, and sweated under the cloth. On the hottest moments of the day we did not move, but sat under a large cloth Mut-Bity had folded on the back of the donkey, as a saddle of me. The little animal also stood quietly under the canvas, thankful for its protection from the searing sunshine, and Mut-Bity did not have the heart to push it away, even if it meant we had to sit very tightly, with our legs under the donkey's belly. Usually donkeys liked the heat, but this was too much.

"I hope the sandstorms will not begin just yet," Mut-Bity said, "Their time is almost here."

I did not see much of the Red Land when we walked in sunshine, as I was all covered by the linen cloth, but the moments before sunset were beautiful, and I could take off the scarf. The stars were strong and white in the sky at night, and sometimes I had a feeling I could fall into the sky. I said as much to Mut-Bity, and she looked at me attentively, but did not say anything.

We had two large water bags on both sides of the donkey. There was also grain for the donkey, and loaves of bread and dried fish for us.

"Where are we going? Is it far? What happens if the water runs out?"

"We can use the water in the desert, brought by others," Mut-Bity said.

"Water in the desert? Who takes it there?"

"The sand people. We are going to them, and then to a secret place of the Neteru."

"A place of gods? What is that? Where is that?" I wanted to know.

"If I told you, it would not be a secret place anymore, now would it?"

There was no denying the sense in Mut-Bity's words, so I did not ask about the place anymore. But I still wanted to know how there was water in the desert.

"The sand people have places along their paths where they bring water. They travel with donkeys, carrying water in bags like the ones we have, and empty jars. They do not carry the water in jars, because if a donkey trips over, it would break the jar, and all the water in it would be lost. † When they reach a watering place, they fill the jars from the bags, close them, and leave them there. Anyone who comes can drink from these jars."

Mut-Bity gave me a little cup full of water and I drank it carefully, not wanting to lose a single drop. My teeth were gritting with sand.

"Won't the water run out then, if everyone drinks from it?"

"These are ancient paths between different places where the sand people have travelled since time immemorial. When they leave one place, they carry enough water to reach the watering place, and leave some water there. And the same in the next watering place. If the journey is a long one, their water will run out. But because they have been doing this for too long for men to remember, they can trust that when they reach the next watering place, there will be water in jars for them to drink, left by others traveling from the opposite direction. And when they later come back along the same path, they again leave water there. Sometimes they travel with lots of donkeys, all carrying water and jars, and fill every watering place with water. This is the rule of the desert – you must leave water for the next person when at all possible. And you should never ever break the water jars. There is no worse crime in the desert."

One day we reached the oddest place. The flat desert was filled with strange-shaped boulders and rocks. They resembled lions, and sphinxes, and other strange things, which had dropped from above, or dug their way up from the belly of the earth. Their surface had crumbled, looking almost scaly, and they observed us in silence, when we passed. I knew this was the place where Mut-Bity had planned on arriving, because she gave a contented sigh.

"We'll rest there, near that cliff," she said, and pointed at a flat-topped small mountain. I hopped down from the donkey, and we climbed up the sandy slope. I could see the rock, horizontally layered, rising above us. Mut-Bity chose a spot and we sat down.

"They will be here soon," she said, "I've sent word."

I had no idea how Mut-Bity could have sent a message to anyone, but if she said she had done so, I believed her.

Something white caught my attention and I walked closer to have a look. I did not understand at first, what it was I was looking at. I bent closer and screamed. The rock had teeth! A huge jaw protruded out of the cliff face, and it had huge, sharp teeth. A horrible monster must live inside the rock, and was on its way out!

Mut-Bity laughed.

"I should have warned you. The boulders and rocks and desert are filled with these skeletons. They are of no animal I know of, but they have been gigantic creatures before their death."

She walked me a short distance, and showed me some big bones on the desert floor. One of them was like a huge snake. I got scared and wanted to get back to the slope. All these dead monsters made me fear they might come back to life.

When we got to the slope, we noticed we were no longer alone. Three short men and their donkey were standing by our donkey, all wrapped in worn clothing. You could only see their eyes, which were amazingly bright, surrounded by thick, dry skin that was so tanned it looked almost black. Still they were not Kushites, not black by birth.

Mut-Bity bowed to them and said something in an odd language. They bowed as well, and without further ado, set camp with us. Our donkeys seemed to get along well.

I listened to Mut-Bity and the men as they talked together deep into the night. I did not understand a word of their discussion, but I liked the singing tone of their language. I lay there with my eyes open, and observed the stars, and listened to the hum of the men.

For they hummed. This was not like the song each living thing gave in response to the song of the night. To hear that I needed total silence. No, these men gave a much stronger note, one I could almost hear with my ears. Still, it seemed like this hum was such that I heard it inside my chest, and not with my ears - or that my heart responded to it in kind.

When I turned my head, I noticed they were often looking at me, with intelligent, observing eyes that seemed to see right through me. One of them asked something about me from Mut-Bity, I was certain. He raised his hands in imitation of wings, and asked something. Mut-Bity shook her head and talked for a long time. She pointed at her eyes and made a swirling motion. The men said nothing, but their posture changed to become more alert.

They were talking of the man with the golden eyes, I knew.

I fell asleep, and was woken up by Mut-Bity before sunrise. She wrapped me in linen, and raised me onto the donkey's back.

And we continued our travel to the ends of the earth, where only sand and rock lived. I saw with my own eyes the watering places, and drank the life-giving water. I listened to the singing dunes, when they marched slowly under the sky. The sand responded to our steps with a deep ringing tone that sounded like the earth was greeting us like a roaring lion. I wondered if these vast folded expanses in fact were the hide of a big yellow lion. That thought entertained me for a whole day.

We walked through sand that had light green jewels on it, and the men gathered these in the bags their donkeys carried, and gave me one too. It had an uneven surface, that light caught beautifully. It was so small I could put in the palm of my hand, and hide it by bending my fingers around it.

I could never tell where we were going, but these men seemed to know, for they walked as confidently as though it was a village road. They knew how to navigate with the stars and how to take the sun's path into account.

I saw amazing formations of rock and flat expanses of sand. The journey took so long I understood that the great land of Kemet was actually a very small place under the huge sky.

And then, one day, we arrived. Ragged rocks reached for the sky all around us. The men walked into a small valley between them. And suddenly the silence of the desert was broken.

Every step we took, echoed back many times to us. We sounded like a whole army on the march. The cacophony made me cover my ears with my hands.

They kept on walking and then I heard other steps as well. I thought a hundred men had come to meet us, but when I peeked from under my covering, I only saw two figures approaching us.

My mouth fell open by surprise. They were dwarves! Very short, with bent legs, but amazingly fluid in their movements. A man and a woman. They stood in the middle of the valley, and smiled widely at us.

The said something that must have been a welcome, for we stopped, and the men and Mut-Bity bowed with their right hand over their heart. The dwarves did the same.

The someone else stepped into my field of vision.

Now I knew we had arrived to the abode of the gods. For this woman had wings. Beautiful, many-colored, see-through... wings. They could be nothing else. Not like a bird's wings. Not like a butterfly's. More like silvery ovals that pulsed with reddish light. She was wearing a dark red dress.

"Aset..." I breathed.

Mut-Bity smiled at me and then stepped to the goddess. I expected her to bow at the goddess's feet, but to my surprise they both laughed, and spread their arms and hugged each other and laughed out loud like long lost sisters, who had found each other again.

"Now we are safe," Mut-Bity said to me, "come and meet your kind."

84

ELIJAH AND MERIT

"So Elijah had a wife," I could not pretend this was news to me. "Diana told me about her once, when she thought... I should know."

"Yes, I figured Diana might tell you after we came back from the desert," Daniel looked at me inquiringly but did not ask more. "He met her when he was traveling in the Nordic Countries, checking on adopted Nephilim children there."

"She was a Nephilim, then?"

"Yes, adopted by a Finnish family. We do check on these children, discreetly, every once in a while, so that we can be near, when the time comes to gain their power. We need to explain things to them then."

"And they have no idea what they are, just like I never did? That can be hard..."

"Yes... But these children, our kind, have always felt somewhat different. They know they are not ordinary. Some of them accept the truth quite joyfully, because all young people seem to dream about being special, different. And the ones that don't cannot deny their heritage, when the wings develop. Also the ones telling them are people they already know. Each Nephilim child has their own Guardians nearby, who are ordinary people."

"I'm just trying to imagine the resources that go into organising a vast network to adopt and then protect Nephilim children! It must be immense..."

"It is. But we have done it for over a century now, so we have plenty of experience. We keep an eye on them, and fetch them to safety before the dark Nephilim find out they are Nephilim in the first place. Keeping them safe until then is not so much of a problem - they look and behave like ordinary children and youngsters until the fever starts. It is only then they can be recognised as Nephilim. And that is when we step in. We use different kind of scholarships in schools and universities as one way to get them away from their homes so their change won't be so obvious."

I considered what Daniel told me, stirring my coffee. We were sitting at the Centre's cafeteria again.

"But... how close were they? Elijah and his wife."

"Merit. They were one. They were in perfect harmony. Twin souls."

"But how did he keep sane, then? I understood it is not possible to remain sane, if your other half dies..."

"It is possible, but a horrible road to take. Longing for someone forever. Elijah went mad for about ten years. We tended to him, never leaving his side so he could not kill himself, and finally he climbed up from the deepest depths of his sorrow. The cheerful personality you see is just a facade, built with pain. Though you seem to make it easier for him to be happy. I haven't seen him laugh so much in many many years..."

I remembered the sadness in Elijah's eyes before he kissed me in the desert. Should I have chosen him? Would I have chosen him, had I known of Merit, out of pity? Could I have given his life a new meaning? But also... why did he kiss me, if Merit had been his twin soul? Could it be that there was a chance of recovery, and of finding new love, even to those who had lost their twin soul?

"Elijah has always been interested in ancient Egypt. He has a degree in Egyptology from an English university, did you know that?" Daniel's voice interrupted me.

No, I had had no idea.

"Egyptology was also Merit's hobby, so it was easy for them to begin talking. Then Merit got her wings, and they fell in love. Elijah did keep his distance until Merit had passed the emotional turmoil of her change, and then returned. She loved him still, and they gave their promises at the medieval cathedral in her hometown, Turku, in the presence of witnesses. I was there too."

"He went to say his goodbyes to Merit there. They made a unique promise to one another, that if one of them died, or was infected, the one who remained was not to kill themselves, but to go on living. That is the only thing that kept him from killing himself after Merit was pronounced dead. He wanted to die, but a promise given to a twin soul is binding. He intended to leave a lily at the cathedral, at a specific spot, on their wedding anniversary as the agreed sign that the one who was living was ready to move on. Lilies had a special meaning for Merit."

My heart ached for Elijah. He was not at all the funny eternal teenager I had thought he was.

"So he tried to... leave her behind?"

"I don't think he will ever leave her behind... When you feel total love, and are bound body and soul, you cannot have that again with someone else. I think Elijah went to the cathedral more to prove to himself that he is now out of danger. He no longer wants to kill himself, and is ready to keep on living. And that is your doing. You showed him he could have affectionate feelings towards another Nephilim woman." Daniel answered my unspoken question.

I finished my coffee and rose. I just could not come up with anything to say about Elijah.

"When are we leaving, then?"

I did not mention Akhetaten. Our group had been working on convincing everyone we were going to Alexandria, to the time just before the battle of Actium, in case the word slipped out and reached Cain or Angel. The last thing we wanted was to have them appear in Akhetaten. We could not rule that out, though. We would have to stay on the alert all the time.

"Soon," Daniel said, tracing my hand with his finger.

I smiled at him, and he smiled back. We would be going together. That was all I needed to know to be happy.

"There is one thing I would like to do, though." I remembered my plan. "I think we need to fetch Lilith."

"OK..." We walked out of the cafeteria, past the guards, into the lobby and up the stairs.

The gate was still hidden behind the large painting now, a decision that had had been made for security reasons. If for any reason Cain's Nephilim managed to gain access to the Centre, they would not see the gate.

Lilith was not in her office, but we went to the library in the buffer zone and found her there, making notes. The book she was reading seemed to be from the Middle Ages.

"Ah, Daniel and Dana!" she greeted us, "we are about to send a team to Cordoba, at the start of June 1236. Ferdinand III of Castile is going to capture the city on 29th June, and we need to bring some manuscripts to safety. Also we have been researching the history of the era, and there seems to be a definite dark Nephilim activity there just before the conquest. They are probably in search of any writings about..." she did not finish the sentence as there were other people around.

"I would like to ask something of you," I said.

"But of course. What is it?"

"Could we go to your office?"

Lilith was much like Grandma. She did not start insisting why, she just rose from her chair, and took Daniel's arm.

"OK, let's go."

We left the library behind and went to Lilith's office.

"Now, tell me what it is you want." Lilith looked at me inquiringly.

"I would like to see the Nephilim who kidnapped me," I said.

Daniel and Lilith looked at each other.

"Why?" Lilith wanted to know.

"Because I need to ask them something," I did not elaborate more.

"Well, I suppose you could meet them." Lilith looked at me curiously and opened the door of her office.

We walked down the stairs, and then another flight of steps to the basement.

The Nephilim were not in the same rooms where Mr. Donnelly had been. They were in glass-walled cubicles on one side of a corridor, which were comfortably furnished. The familiar sound of brass bowls was playing from loudspeakers.

There were six of them, and when we entered, they rose to their feet. To my surprise they all bowed to me.

"What's this?" I asked.

"You are a Silver Nephilim, the like of which our kind has not seen in in over two thousand years," the man with a scar on his cheek said, "and you healed my son."

The healed Nephilim in question was staring at me.

"Thank you... I have never experienced anything like that..." he said, "and I heard you almost died. I am sorry to have caused this. I am forever in your debt."

"We all are," the red-haired woman said. There was no trace of the aggressive behavior I had witnessed in her before.

Daniel was standing next to me, and his expression was angry.

"You may have hurt her permanently with your actions." His voice was cold. "How do you expect to pay for something like that?"

"We don't know," the mother of the healed Nephilim said, "but we are ready to do whatever you ask."

Daniel opened his mouth, but I beat him to it.

"This is why I asked to see you. I want you to protect my parents from Angel and Cain. Angel knows where my parents live. I want them to stay safe. There are six of you. You will take turns, to guard my parents around the clock, and fight for them, if the need arises. As long as it takes, even if it is years."

Lilith looked surprised; Daniel's face was hard to read.

The six looked at each other, and came to an agreement without words.

"To pay for our debt we shall do this. From now on your parents will have six Nephilim Guardians," the scar-faced man said.

"You'll swear this to me? All of you?"

One by one they each voiced their promise.

"I think you can let them go now," I said to Lilith.

Daniel still looked angry, but nodded.

"A Nephilim's promise is binding," he said. "They will never break it. Not until they turn dark."

Lilith left the corridor, and after a few minutes the brass bowls stopped singing. The Nephilim breathed deeply, relieved. The doors opened with a click, and they stepped out of their prison.

We stood there facing each other. The man I had healed stepped closest, and bowed.

"I owe you my life. Whatever you command, I shall obey," he said.

I nodded, not knowing how I should react.

"I would like to know your names..." I said.

"I am Jonathan," the healed man said, and bowed again.

The red-haired woman was Carol, the olive-skinned woman was Ester. The man who had kidnapped me, was Oliver. The father of Jonathan was Edward, and his mother was Joann.

"Well, then. We need to take you to Dana's parents' house," Lilith said. "Daniel will escort you there. You are now bound by your promise."

"I have to say I am relieved," Lilith said, as we left their prison. "I had always dreaded the day when we would have to imprison a Nephilim for... years, let alone six of them. You found a solution, Dana. I am glad of that."

85

MR. DONNELLY'S SURPRISE

"Now remember – if anything happens to any of you, if you get lost, or lose contact with us, recall the places where we can reach you," Lilith said when everything seemed to be packed and we were finally just standing there. Our final preparations had been made in haste as we needed to get away as soon as possible. We even had rolls of papyrus explaining who we were, all carefully written by Reggie.

"What are those places?" I asked.

"Right, you have not been told yet," Layla observed. She began to explain. "However, you do already know that it is possible for someone to get lost in time. Their Weaver may die, or they get separated from one another. Also weaving sometimes goes wrong – the anchor used might have a strong connection to another time instead of the one it was made in. That is particularly likely to happen when very strong emotions are felt around the chosen object - like jewelry, or religious items. That's why we prefer ordinary everyday objects – spoons, cups and such. They usually don't raise strong emotions in anyone."

"Except historians," Jason grinned in the general direction of Reggie and Mr Donnelly.

Ripples of laughter filled the room.

"Yes, except historians," Lilith smiled. "But the point is: if you get lost or find yourselves in the wrong time, go to a place that you know exists even today, and leave a message for us there."

"Leave a message? How?" I did not understand.

"Carving it on wood or scratching it in stone are preferable methods. It is a long shot, but it means our researchers have the chance to find a reference to an odd writing on the wall. If you use the code words we recognize that it is you, and can come and find you."

"Code words?"

"Yes, write about walking and time, and add a name of one of your time walker group. Any sentence will do. Like 'We walked together in our time, Jason and I' – something like that. And the year, if you know it. If not, try to find out a name of a prominent person of that time and write it in your message. We prefer churches and monasteries and temples, if possible. They are often taken good care of – the Reformation and Henry VIII excluded, of course. Monasteries and many churches did not survive that."

I happened to be looking at Mr Donnelly, who suddenly began to look as if he had forgotten something.

"Our researchers visit historic monuments all the time, and know the museum people well, so if some new inscription is suddenly found on a monastery wall, or mentioned in a book when our researchers know it wasn't there before, we take a closer look. And with luck they'll find your message, written and preserved through time so we could come and find you."

Mr Donnelly let out a strange sound.

"What is it? Are you feeling ill?" Reggie turned to his colleague with a concerned look.

"I do not know... I am not sure... but one of us is called Elijah, yes?"

That was an odd question as Mr Donnelly was standing in the same room with Elijah.

"May I ask you, and please do not take offense..." Mr Donnelly searched for words and Elijah waited patiently.

"As you know I was the head librarian at the City of Immortals.

Thousands of books traveled through my hands on their way to the shelves... sometimes they were put in the wrong place, and I spent a lot of time searching for misplaced books so I could take them back to their proper location. Not all people respect order, you see..."

We waited for Mr Donnelly to form his thoughts.

"So, one day I happened to find... my question is... did you have a wife called Merit by any chance?"

The proverbial dropped pin would have made our ears ring. Everyone turned to look at Elijah. And then back at Mr Donnelly, and again at Elijah and yet again to the aging scholar. It was almost like watching a tennis game.

"Yes - I did," Elijah finally said, his face set.

"And did you go to the Nabta stones together? And she was... lost there?"

Elijah moved so fast no one had time to react. He grabbed Mr. Donnelly by his shirt and almost lifted the poor man into the air.

"What do you know about her?" he said in a low, threatening voice.

"Elijah," Daniel was by his side in an instant, "I am sure Mr. Donnelly is not dangerous. You are making it impossible for him to speak. Put him down."

There was a deep rumble from within Elijah, and with considerable effort he stopped his wings from opening.

"Speak," he said to Mr Donnelly, with gritted teeth.

"I... I... I am so sorry... I did not think of it before. Suddenly I thought your name matched the name of someone I read about in a notebook I happened to find in the library... It was hidden behind a book..."

"An Enquiry into the Morals of the Ancients by George England?" Daniel asked.

"Yes, how did you know?" a look of disbelief passed over Mr. Donnelly's face.

"Elijah, tell them," Daniel said.

And so we heard of Elijah's visit to the Turku Cathedral, the lily, the notebook page, and the message.

"So she is there, right there where we're going?" Grandma asked.

"Yes, if she is still alive," Elijah said.

"But can't we just go to the time when she had just arrived and was still alive? I mean if she is now dead. I mean..." I wish I had not opened my mouth when I saw Elijah's face.

"But we don't know exactly to which year she went," Grandma said.

"The notebook, where is it? Is it in the City of Immortals?" Elijah asked almost brusquely.

"No. It's not there. In fact - I have it right here!" To our surprise Mr. Donnelly pulled a little velvet pouch out of his big pocket.

This time Layla was faster than Elijah and carefully took the pouch.

"You are too agitated right now, Elijah, and may harm the book. Everyone, into my room."

Lilith turned on her heels and walked out of the room and we all followed right behind her, Daniel grasping his brother's arm tightly.

86

IN LEAGUE WITH THE SHADOWS

She watched them go up the stairs and into Lilith's room. When the door closed behind them, she crossed to the big stairs, and descended to the main hall. The guards recognized her and opened the doors for her on her way to the cafeteria.

She took a cup of tea and walked to the far end of the room, to the furthest possible table. It was beside a little door. She had picked its lock last night, once everyone else had left the room and placed a piece of folded paper in the latch to stop the door from locking. This effectively meant that the alarm system was not active either.

Now she placed a pile of papers and her laptop on the table next to the exit. To anyone looking in her direction it appeared as though she was deep in her studies and wanted to be left alone.

She waited until no one seemed to be paying any attention to her, poured her tea into the nearest plant pot and was out the door without anyone noticing. If anyone noticed her table was vacant, they would see her laptop and papers and think she had gone to the toilet. She listened to the noises from the kitchen in the little corridor that led to the back yard and rubbish bins. And then, as quietly as possible, she slipped out of the back door.

Keeping right to the wall, thanking her luck for the fact that the windows had been built so high she could walk right under them, she reached the garden and was quickly hidden by the shadows of the huge trees and bushes.

A little path took her to the edge of the premises, to a small gate in a wall that was so overgrown the gate was barely visible.

And there it waited for her – a big shadow with intelligent looking eyes. It did not move into the garden, but its presence was so overwhelming she felt her knees tremble.

"I got your message," she said and lifted a small note from her pocket.

The shadow nodded. Then, it wrote a few words down on a piece of paper. The combination of the shadow and the mundane, almost homely, writing implements it was holding made her shudder.

"We have taken him. He is changed."

Upon reading these words her knees gave way and she fell down. Another note was dropped over the gate onto the moss covering the old path under her.

"You will help us."

She looked up pleadingly.

"Why? There's nothing I can do anymore. You have done your worst and he is lost."

Another note.

"No, not lost. You can be together with him for an eternity. If you help us."

She read the words several times, her face hidden in her hair. When she finally looked up and met the piercing black eyes of the shadow, a look of disbelief was etched on her face.

"You mean.. That I..."

"You can be changed too. For helping us. You will love one another again."

Her hands clutched a little golden necklace around her neck. The shadow observed how the tiny little heart trembled at her throat. She was quiet for a long time, eyes downcast. The shadow waited.

"What should I do?" she finally whispered.

The shadow had won. For this it might win its own independent life from *her*.

Nervously the shadow listened to the connection to its Hunter, but he was far away and had cut the connection almost completely, no doubt because he did not want to reveal what he was doing to his shadow. The shadow carefully controlled its feeling of excitement so the Hunter would not become curious and notice what the shadow was about to do.

The shadow began to write in the notebook, and other shadows appeared from under the trees around it. Birds were silent, and rustling was heard in the grass as animals fled from their condensed darkness.

87

THE DIARY

"This is written with a pencil, the text is barely visible," Lilith observed. adjusting her reading lamp closer to the page, "and the pages are much worn and crumbled... Not to mention the language. It is Finnish. Not my forte, I am afraid."

"I have translated most of it. Much is missing as pages have been damaged or torn away." Mr. Donnelly produced a little black notebook from his other pocket, cleared his throat and started reading.

"Elijah, where are you? I remember how we were watching the stars at night, next to the Nabta stones, and next morning when I woke up, you were gone. I tried to go back into the mists on my own, but I couldn't. It's as though you were never here. I know you would never leave me. So what has happened? Have they caught you? Have they... killed you? I don't know where to go. Nothing but desert everywhere and all I have left now is one bottle of water. I cannot wait for you any longer. I have to leave to survive.

"I lay there, dying, when she found me. She walked from the desert as if the sun had no effect on her. She had some kind of an animal skin bottle with her, and she gave me water from it. She carried a piece of cloth on her back, with wooden sticks, and she erected a little tent over me to give me shade. By that time I had already burned my skin. I lost

consciousness for a long time. I only remember her giving me water, and humming in a strange way. She must have hunted something, because she began to feed me pieces of dry meat as soon as I could swallow. My burned skin peeled off. When I was strong enough to walk, she forced me to my feet and so we walked. I had no idea how far I had reached from Nabta until I saw the skeletons in the sand. The huge skeletons of ancient whales, lying where they had died in the ancient sea. I realized I had to be in the Valley of the Whales, the Wadi Hitan, in Egypt. I feel so relieved - we are bound to meet some tourists sooner or later!

"...and we reached the lake. A beautiful, big lake, with crocodiles in it, and a fisher village on its shore. And it was a shock. Elijah - all these people were... ancient. There was nothing modern anywhere. No cars, no TV-antennas, no wrist watches, no bright colored clothing. No shoes. I fear what this means. I sit here in one of the small mud brick houses, surrounded by women and children who gawk at me, trying to touch my hair all the time. Like they had never seen blonde hair. They speak a language I do not understand at all. I don't even understand the language of the woman who brought me here. It is certain it is not Arabic, though.

"...and this is what I saw from the boat. Elijah - it is a pyramid, and it is whole, not eroded at all. I saw a temple in front of it - and it too was whole. I have no knowledge on how to get back to you! I have no other option but to stay here at Mi-Wer, which is the name of this place of women. How could I send a message to you? Could you come back in time and fetch me? How would you find me now that I have left the stones of Nabta? How would you know how to come to this exact time and place? My heart weeps - I have lost you for good!"

Mr. Donnelly raised his eyes from his notebook.

"You know Finnish?" Reggie asked.

"I learned it – there were Finns at the City of Immortals, and I befriended them. With the use of a dictionary and all the time in the world in my hands..." Mr. Donnelly looked around nervously. "After translating most of the notebook I found these pieces of paper tucked under the leather cover. I think Elijah should read these himself."

To my surprise Mr. Donnelly was clearly holding back tears, when he fished the said papers from the back of the book. He carefully arranged them like a pieces of a puzzle on Lilith's table - this page had crumbled to the smallest bits. Elijah stepped closer and bent over the pieces.

"Translate for us," Lilith said. Elijah swallowed hard and read aloud:

"We are at Mi-Wer now. She seems to know Tiye, and has told her that I am a seer. Now that I know where I am, and with whom, I can pretend to be a clairvoyant. I try to remember everything I ever read about them, so that I can stay here. I have to because..."

Elijah stopped reading and stared at the pieces of paper.

"What is it? What does it say?" Daniel and I asked at the same time.

Elijah stared at the wall with unseeing eyes, unable to move. Gently Daniel reached across the table, turned the papers so that he could read them. I saw his lips moving, and realized he must know some Finnish too. Then his face set and he looked at his brother with a surprised and even alarmed expression. Elijah did not look back. After a while Daniel cleared his throat and read aloud:

"I have to because now more than ever I need a safe place to stay. I am pregnant. Elijah - I am carrying your child."

For a while it was so quiet in the room it made my ears ring.

"Elijah..." Daniel touched his brother's arm gently.

Elijah turned his head and looked at Daniel with a look of desperation and wild hope in his eyes.

"We had a child... she ended up by mistake in the times of Amenhotep the Third, and she carried my child!"

"That is an amazing coincidence," Lilith breathed, "that she ended up in the very time where we are about to travel. Elijah - you might find Merit again! And your child..."

Elijah sat down and buried his face in his hands. Lilith was the only one who dared approach him and hugged him quietly.

After a while Mr. Donnelly lifted his own notebook and looked at us questioningly.

"Yes, please go on," Grandma said and Mr. Donnelly continued reading:

"All is well now. I had a fever and they feared I might die, but I survived, much to their surprise. They took care of me and..."

"Elijah, I stumbled across an incredible mystery... Those who kept an eye on us... disappeared... They were doomed to..."

"I am traveling in search of answers. There are many ancient writings preserved here that we have no idea about in our time. They have vanished during the millennia in between, but they still exist here. I did learn to read some hieroglyphs at home, but those were mostly offering formulas in tombs. I have taken on the task of learning to read this writing properly. Thankfully I am in a position where I can do so. I have become one of the children of the kap, it seems, despite the fact I am an adult."

"And I finally found my clue to the location of the neteru. It was written on a piece of papyrus in the House of Life of Inbu-Hedj, or Memphis. I do not dare write the clue down as it may get into the wrong hands. I know no one can read this yet, because the language does not even exist - what a curious feeling that gives me! But if this book ends up in the wrong hands in the future... And I admit I tore that part of the papyrus out and took it with me."

"And I have found there are Immortals here as well. I do not know how long I can keep myself hidden from them. I think my looks will raise their suspicions, if they haven't done so already. I have to retreat to Mi-Wer and keep in hiding there, out of sight, protected by the guards of the royal harem, and trust that there are enough light-colored ladies there so that I blend in. Otherwise I shall draw doom over those I love as well. But rest assured, Elijah, I will do everything I can to find you again. If I cannot enter the mists of the buffer zone, then perhaps others near me can and they can lead me through the mists of time back to you... However, to find out if that is the case, I might need to wait for many years yet. They are still so..."

Mr. Donnelly sighed, placed his notebook on the table, took his glasses off and started cleaning them vigorously with his handkerchief.

"I came to the conclusion Merit has found what the dark Nephilim are searching for. The Place of Neteru – that translates as the Place of Gods. Abode of the Gods. And the mention of 'those who kept an eye on us' could mean 'those who watched over us'..."

"The Watchers..." we breathed the word simultaneously with Diana.

"Yes, I think Merit found the location of the Watchers," Mr. Donnelly said solemnly.

No one had time to answer him, because that is when it happened. All the alarms started howling inside the Center.

"We are under attack!" the intercom on Lilith's table yelled, "The shadows are inside the Center!"

88

TOGETHER IN BLOOD

Ambrogio and Selene sailed to Ephesus, the city of Artemis. The captain of the ship did not come below deck, where Selene guarded Ambrogio's coffin. Artemis had given her instructions, and they were closely followed. Live birds were kept in a cage nearby and every day he drank the blood of one and Selene threw away the body later. It was not much, just enough to keep him looking human, but he could satisfy his hunger later when they came to shore.

The first night at sea Ambrogio came out of the casket, and told Selene what had happened. He explained that he was no longer an ordinary human, how he had killed swans to give them as gifts to the great goddess Artemis, so she would lift Apollo's curse. He could not bring himself to reveal what the swans really were, and so Selene believed that he had killed magical birds with silver blood.

Ambrogio told her about the world beyond, and of Hades's realm and Selene listened to him with shining eyes, bent forward, eager to hear more.

The hardest part was telling her about the deal with Artemis. He did not tell her that Artemis had made him immortal. Maybe he wasn't sure about that himself either. But he could not deny the changes in his body. So he carefully explained to Selene how he had made a deal with

Artemis to become her Hunter. And for this reason he had been changed, so that from now on he would drink animal blood. This would make him a better hunter.

Selene accepted that. She ate meat, so she saw nothing strange in consuming the blood either.

Ambrogio stressed the fact they could not live as man and wife in the traditional way.

"Artemis told me that I will infect you if we do, and you will become very ill."

"Can't we touch?" she asked.

"I don't think so... My skin is so strange now that I am a Hunter," Ambrogio extended his arms so she could see his skin. "There is some kind of poison in it. It helps me to kill my prey. Maybe it will infect you."

His skin had changed again. Now it had become an odd pale golden color, translucent.

Selene looked him in the eyes and smiled, but Ambrogio saw the slight tremor of her lips.

"It does not matter," she bravely said, "I had already decided I would dedicate my life to the gods, maybe even be the next Pythia, if chosen, because my sister has become more and more ill with each passing year. The fumes of the earth do that to her. I never planned on marrying anyone before I met you."

"We can return. I'll take you back to Kirrha, if you so wish," Ambrogio said.

"No," Selene said, "I have made my decision. I shall remain with you."

And so they sailed together to Ephesus, to live together till the end of their days, as Selene thought.

Selene had brought with her some jewelry, and selling these meant that they could buy a small house for themselves. Ambrogio spent most days indoors, because his golden pale skin looked almost like marble in sunlight. Also his eyes had turned the same strange yellow color as Artemis's.

Ambrogio spent his time studying. The city was full of learned men, and he earned enough with the beasts he hunted to collect some savings. With these he bought copies of various written works. Studying these was a good excuse for him to stay indoors during the hours of daylight and he got himself a reputation of a scholar in a few years.

Sometimes he went hunting for days, wandering in the lonely hills where there were not many people. It was easy for him, because of the great strength, speed and agility of his body.

The did find a way to touch - Selene bought a thick, woven blanket, and wrapped it around Ambrogio. She could then hug him, and let her head rest on his shoulder. Or she wrapped herself in the blanket and he could put his arm around her. They sat like that in the evenings, under the stars, strangely content.

Their life was not rich, but they managed. Selene wove good cloth, and Ambrogio hunted. The animals that he brought to the buyers were drained of blood.

And then time began to show on Selene's face. Her young skin showed the first lines, and then its freshness began to dull. Ambrogio did not age, and began to believe that Artemis had actually made him immortal. He watched Selene with sorrow in his heart. He loved her so much, and did not want her to die and leave him alone for all eternity.

There had to be something he could do.

He had never tried to enter the misty world after Artemis had changed him. He was too afraid Hades would be there.

He decided he would try to contact Artemis. He still had the singing device he had used all those years ago to lure the silver wings to him. Now he ran far, into the mountains and attached the device to his throat. And then he began to sing Artemis's name.

She came so quickly it was as though she had followed him all along, and simply stepped out of a hiding place.

"How did you do that?" she asked. "What is this?"

She pointed at the device on his throat.

Ambrogio explained.

"Show me," Artemis said and Ambrogio gave her the device.

She turned it in her hands, and then put it against her own throat and sang.

The sound was so beautiful and horrible at the same time that Ambrogio could not move. She sang for a long time and the odd voice echoed from the mountains, silencing nature around them. Ambrogio was sure it froze every living thing. Her voice was so different from his human voice. Metallic, like enchanting layers of wind.

Nothing happened. No one came.

"Well, it seems they are all dead, and none is left to answer the call," Artemis said. "Here, you can keep it. It is of no use to anyone any more, and I have enough trinkets. Now tell me, why you called for me."

"My Selene is aging. She will die."

"But of course. She is mortal. Humans die," said Artemis with a lift of her brows."What else did you expect?"

"You made me immortal. Can you not do this for her too?"

"I do not need a woman to serve me. I needed a Hunter, and that is you," Artemis said and turned to leave. "I only transform people for my own needs, not from charity."

Ambrogio was certain she would disappear, but suddenly she stopped and turned.

"There is one thing no one has tried yet... might be an interesting experiment..."

"Yes, my goddess?"

"Why don't you try to make her immortal yourself? My blood is in your veins now. It should transform her. So far we have only made our own human Hunters, but no human Hunter has tried to do this to another human. Try that. You remember how I did it?"

Ambrogio nodded.

"If my blood works, she will be immortal too."

And then Artemis sank back into the mists behind the physical world and disappeared from sight.

Ambrogio went back home. Selene came to meet him at the door.

"You never grow old, my love," she said, as if reading his thoughts.

"That is true, Selene. And now I am going to tell you why."

Now, at last, Ambrogio told her everything. Hades, hunting for the silver wings, the shadow, and how exactly Artemis had made him immortal.

"And I met her again just now. She said I could do the same to you."

Selene watched him. Her eyes were dimmed with age, and her hair had white streaks. To him she was still beautiful, but you could see her time would soon come.

She nodded.

"Very well. I have nothing to lose, I can feel sickness inside me, and I will be gone soon. You can try. But we need to do this somewhere where no one can see us."

They left at night, and Ambrogio carried Selene, wrapped in her blanket. He ran until it was certain no one saw them. He put her on her feet on the slope of a hill.

They stood there, in silence, for a long time. The moon rose over the horizon. Suddenly Ambrogio felt Selene's hand taking his. Skin touching skin. He felt a surge of passion in his mind and turned towards Selene. She had raised her face towards him, and this time he did not refuse. He bent and kissed her.

They kissed forever and her hands felt so good against his. He grabbed them tighter, and kissed her longer, more passionately. It was as if her skin made his blood sing. She let out small voices, he heard them, but he did not open his eyes.

Then, suddenly, something felt strange about the kiss. The tang of iron...

With a yell he opened his eyes and pushed Selene back.

It was too late. He had bitten her tongue, and tasted her blood. And now he could not stop himself anymore. The Hunter in him took over, pushing his mind aside. He yanked Selene to him, and bit her on the neck and the sweet, tasty blood filled him. It tasted so different from animal blood. Selene fought back at first, but then stopped.

He could not stop. The desire in him was irresistible, overwhelming. When it was over, he opened his eyes, and lowered Selene's limp body to the ground. Her eyes were still alive and they... smiled.

"I am in you now, forever in you," she whispered and died.

"No!" Ambrogio yelled, and bit her arm. He tore open his own vein, and poured his blood into her wound.

Too late. Her heart had stopped beating, and so his blood could not travel in her veins.

"No!" he screamed again.

There was nothing he could do. He sat there on the steep hill, next to his beloved and cried in the silver moonlight.

"I'm forever here, Ambrogio," he heard her whisper from inside him, "forever here with you."

He fell silent and listened. He felt a presence. When he concentrated on them, his mind opened, and he saw Selene's memories in his mind. Now he could see her childhood, her youth, how they met. And the endless love she had felt for him all these years.

Though her body lay on the ground, still and calm, her mind was coursing inside him, her blood united with his. She spoke to him in her blood... Tears fell from his eyes, when he listened to her emotions, her memories, and was wrapped in her love.

In awe he realized that now they were together at last, for all eternity.

And after a while the thought was born that he could try to create her physically again. All he needed was another woman. He would try to transform her into an immortal being. When he would give his own blood to her, Selene would be physically present in the transformed woman, because she was there in his blood.

Suddenly, there was hope. He rose, and quickly carried the body Selene had occupied down the hill. With his strong arms he dug a hole in the ground and buried her there, gathering stones over her so animals could not reach her.

And then he turned back towards Ephesus, with new vigor in his steps.

He would create Selene again.

89

THE ATTACK

"Quick!" Lilith grabbed a locket hanging from her neck and dragged the chain over her head. "Here is the Key! Take it and leave right away!"

"No, we can't. I can't!" I said. I felt panic rising in me and tried to muster all my strength.

"If the shadows have breached our defenses, this is the first thing they'll be looking for – after Dana. They are not having either one. Leave. NOW!"

We heard sounds of fighting from the hall.

"Quick, everyone! Grab each other!" Grandma took control.

My heart was beating like thunder in my ears when everyone grabbed me and Daniel. Elijah grabbed the notebooks.

"Go, go, GO!" Lilith yelled.

And so we faded into the mists of the buffer zone.

"We need the mirror!" Grandma said. "Quickly, it is in the equipment room!"

She had barely time to finish her sentence when we were already in the room. She opened the little casket holding the mirror and grabbed it – but not quickly enough. We were suddenly surrounded by a dozen shadows, all nightmarish figures from hell.

I grabbed Grandma and screamed when a shadow caught me by my hand. Grandma turned and hit the shadow at the neck – I saw a rosy colored flash, which then bounced across the room and behind the door. She had dropped the Key, but none of the shadows seemed to have noticed.

Daniel's wings roared into life. Elijah's did the same. Like lightning flashes their hands and wings fell inexorably onto the shadows. They cut right through them and their power made the whole house shake. The first wave of shadows fell and crumbled to nothing and it looked as if we were going to make it.

Then they began to seep through the walls as if the whole building had turned into mist with grasping hands and snarling jaws. Countless faces and bodies emerged from the shadowy mass. Time seemed to slow down and I found myself suddenly thinking that the nightmares of Hieronymus Bosch had come to life and this was the jaws of hell itself. Then a voice broke in on me, a voice that was filled with anguish and fury.

"Dana! Take the mirror! Go Go GO!" Daniel yelled, "NOW! GO!"

And I obeyed. My energies were so high that my wings opened on their own and filled the room. The shadows fell back from the energy wave. This would be our only chance. Grandma pushed the mirror into my hands and I concentrated... no, forced all my power into my hands.

Bright blue and silver threads shot out of them and the world began to disappear around us. The last vision I had of Daniel was when he was attacked by a mass of shadows that felled him to the floor, reaching for his throat. Elijah jumped on them like a wrathful god. Blue lightning flashes made the walls crumble around them.

Then the mists of time closed around us and we flew.

90

TRAITOR

"Yes, my lady?" Ambrogio bent his head respectfully, but without obsequiousness.

Angel looked at her most trusted servant. He had been in her family since the times of ancient Greece. Her own grandmother had transformed him, and he was a legend among the Nephilim and vampires. The reason being that he was the original - the first one to create another human vampire. Before him the dark Nephilim had created immortals that survived by feeding on animals. They killed their prey by draining all the blood from it. Hunting their pray developed speed and skills, which were then put to good use when the Nephilim wanted someone, a human, to be killed. That killing had always been done in traditional ways, though, using weapons, or the sheer strength of the body.

But Ambrogio, for reasons no one knew, had turned to people as nourishment, instead of animals, and used the same method that Angel's grandmother had used to transform him: he drank from a woman in Ephesus, not quite killing her. Whilst her heart was still beating, he had opened her wrist and poured his own blood into her veins, and made her drink his blood as well. And she turned into the creature that was later known as a vampire.

They had lived together, but somehow the new creature was not as strong as the vampires created by the Nephilim. In time she withered and became more fragile, withdrawing more and more into the shadows and she was eventually killed. But she had created her own kind before that happened. And they created their kind in turn, and a new species of creature was born.

These human vampires were long-lived, some very long indeed, but they could be killed. Ambrogio, however, had been in many life threatening situations, and always his body had managed to heal itself from the severest of wounds, just like the bodies of other Nephilim-made vampires. Nephilim-created vampires were the strongest of all, but the blood they transferred through others they infected was never quite as potent in the veins of their offspring. Also, the vampires that the Nephilim created did not need human blood to live, and could feed equally well on animals, but whatever offspring they produced had to drink human blood to thrive.

Angel felt nervous in the presence of the First Vampire. He never really revealed his innermost thoughts, and she did not dare to ask. Ambrogio had the eyes of the dark Nephilim – yellow, oily. His skin was an odd shade of pale gold, and his hair was shiny and black. He could walk in the sunlight and not suffer, but the strange color of his pale skin drew so much attention that he rarely did so.

"We know now Daniel's group has gone to ancient Egypt," Angel said, looking furious. "I want you to follow them. The shadows revealed to them that we know where their lair is. The fight with Daniel and Elijah was magnificent, but not successful because Dana escaped."

"How do I follow them, my lady?"

Ambrogio was standing in the room alone. His shadow was nowhere to be seen.

"You are to follow them discreetly, when they search for the Trail of Angels. They are vulnerable now that Daniel and Elijah are not with them. You will follow them and tell us when they find the Abode of the Watchers – or preferably, the last clue to its whereabouts. We would prefer to find the place before they do."

"How will I do that, my lady?" Ambrogio asked. "I am no Time Walker. Vampires cannot time walk."

"You will have all the help you need," Angel said and turned to look to her right. "Come, show yourself!"

The curtain leading to another room next to Angel's office moved. A hooded female figure stepped into the room.

"You are a Weaver," Ambrogio stated the fact. He could tell from the slightly smoky smell that emanated from all Weavers.

"I am," the woman said. "As it is, I do not have long before I have to return. They are never to know that I am gone - luckily the devastation of the Center is such that they will not miss me for a while. The important thing is that I know exactly where they went, and I can take you there."

She looked at Ambrogio from under her hood with open curiosity, and did not seem afraid. Only sad.

"Who are you? Why are you doing this?" Ambrogio demanded.

"Because I want immortality. Not only in the buffer zone, but in human world as well," she said.

"You do not know what you ask," Ambrogio said, and the tiredness in his voice made Angel quickly glance his way. "Immortality is perhaps not all you think it to be."

"Maybe. But my husband was attacked and has transformed into one of your kind. I want to spend my life with him, and not die before him. I want to be transformed into a vampire. This is why I helped the shadows in their attempt to seize Dana for you."

"Why do you not ask your husband to do the honours, then?" Ambrogio lifted his eyebrow.

"I know that to be truly immortal or to live a lot longer than the ordinary vampire, I need to be changed by a Nephilim. My husband was. And my Lady Angel here has promised to transform me as a reward for my help."

Ambrogio looked at the dark-haired woman. He felt pity for her – she did not know the depths of despair a Nephilim-created vampire could fall into, watching everyone near them die except the Nephilim, who cared little about the lives of humans or the vampires. They were simply the ones who were doomed to do the dirty work of the dark ones, intended to watch their children die – both biological and created ones.

For a while Ambrogio let the memories of Selene fill his mind, and his eternal search for the perfect woman who would bring her back to life again. There were a few fleeting days of her presence in the new female body, and then it faded away. He listened to her presence in his own blood, and felt it become quieter until it was only an occasional whisper.

It was as though his vampire blood was tainted by time and age, and Selene's presence was no longer pure. All the human blood he had taken through the centuries had tainted hers, and she was now hidden behind the cursed whispers of those Ambrogio had killed after her - all competing for his attention.

Finally he understood that he had to stop killing people for food and go back to feeding from animal blood. Animals' consciousnesses left their bodies so easily, and left only a fleeting residue of their minds behind, soon gone. But he occasionally killed women still, especially those who reminded him of Selene, in the vanishing hope of bringing her back through his own blood in the veins of the newly created vampire.

He had often wondered, what would have happened if the last call for the silver winged one had been successful. He knew one had got away, when he shot that last arrow. If he had answered that call in Ephesus, could he have taken that Nephilim blood? Or would he have healed his Selene voluntarily? Or maybe Ambrogio's own blood so that Selene would have been present, and conscious inside him forever...

With time rage had risen inside Ambrogio. The silver winged ones were supposed to help, when they heard the call of the device. The last one should have returned, he often raged to himself. Still, he knew, that if that one silver winged Nephilim still existed, he would remember Ambrogio, and would never help voluntarily. But he could fight the creature, and take its blood, and drink it and pour it into his own wounds, so Selene could come back into his mind, if not into any female body.

Ambrogio felt the weight of the little leather pouch hanging from his neck. The odd device used to lure the silver Nephilim to him was still there. Useless, but a symbol of his transformation. He had not been able to throw it away.

Because of his own lost love Ambrogio understood this Weaver. The hope of being eternally with the one you loved... yes, he did understand.

Angel waited for her Hunter to think through whatever it was that occupied him. She knew better than to hurry his decision. He was much older than she was, and wiser.

"Very well," Ambrogio finally said. "Who are the travellers? Tell me their names."

She did.

"The Nephilim girl is an oddity, though," the Weaver said at the end.

"Oddity, how?" Angel asked.

"She got her wings too early for one... and she is a mighty healer. And a Weaver the like of which we have never seen before."

Angel stood like a statue.

"A healer?" she asked.

"She healed Elijah after he had been infected by one of your kind. And then she healed a Nephilim who had already been your kind for months. She gives them some kind of blood transfusion, I've been told. She purifies their blood with her wings."

Ambrogio's eyes turned pitch black from emotion. Angel was too occupied with her own surprise to notice how he clutched the leather pouch that was always hanging from his neck.

"What colour are her wings?" Angel asked.

"The most amazing colour... pure white – with silver veins. She is a Silver Nephilim. We thought her kind were dead long ago - gone in ancient times."

Ambrogio's face revealed nothing.

"Very well," he said in a rasping voice, "you will take me to them in ancient Egypt. How do we keep in contact?"

"I will attach one of my strings to you. I can connect to you through it, and hear you calling me," the Weaver said.

"Ambrogio," Angel said.

"Yes, my lady?"

"Bring her alive to me. She belongs to me. Promise me this."

Ambrogio turned and the Weaver took his hand, flinching at first at the touch of his cold skin through her gloves. Then she determinedly took his hand tightly into hers. She held an object and cut an opening into the air. Ambrogio's keen eyes recognized the rosy transparent colour of the tip she was holding and he remembered how he had fallen on top of Artemis's weapon. How had this ended up in the hands of the Weaver?

The Weaver held some other object as well in her hand, too small for Ambrogio to see. Her hands became blurry and several coloured strings wove from her palms and into the opening. Ambrogio followed her, and she turned and closed the opening behind them.

Only then Angel realized that Ambrogio had never answered her.

91

FLOATING

"Do you ever miss them?"

We sat by the underground lake, Seth and I.

I drew a line in the water with my finger and watched how the little shiny silver particles followed my finger. If I let them touch my skin, they tickled it slightly. It was a gentle, bubbly feeling.

"Who?" I asked, even though I knew full well whom he meant.

The roof of the cave was quite high where we were sitting, but the glow of the water lit it nevertheless. The waters created beautiful shimmering reflections on the rock. Further upstream, a small crack in the rock let a little daylight seep in to light the water. It was breathtakingly beautiful. Because of the light you could see to the bottom of the lake - the silver dust covered everything there, and shone light upwards, revealing even the smallest detail.

"Your mother and sister," Seth patiently said.

He was never impatient towards me, only friendly. He was older than me, but had become my friend from the moment we descended to the underground caves and the Silver Waters.

And there we lived with my kind, even though I found it hard to believe we were similar. I was the only one without color.

I loved the caves. There was no need for me to shelter myself from the sun here. And at night I could climb on top of the rocks and sit under my stars. I heard the song of the night easily here, in the total silence of the desert. Only storm winds could stop me from hearing the music of the stars.

During the days the lake drew me to it. At first Mut-Bity had been worried I would drown, but Seth promised he would teach me to swim. And he did.

The water was warm, and when we swam in it, we left a darker trail in the illuminating liquid.

I felt the water had an intelligence of its own. If I sat alone there, I could almost hear the water speak to me. Not in words, but in its own vibrating song. It resonated within me. Just like the song of the stars did.

Seth waited patiently for an answer.

"Yes, I do miss them," I said.

I was nine now, and three years had passed since Mut-Bity had brought me to safety. We received news of the outside world regularly, and we had heard that the great king Amenhotep Neb-Maat-Re was arranging his sed-jubilee to celebrate his thirtieth year on the throne. He had been building temples around his country for ten years now, to celebrate this occasion. It would be a great jubilation.

I often wondered whether my mother and sister were involved in the celebrations. Probably, as they were living with the king's Great Royal Wife, Tiye.

"What are their names? You have never told me them," Seth asked. "What is your sister's name?"

"Meryt-Neith," I said, "for she has a great temper and has even beaten the boys when they tried to steal her toys."

"Neith, goddess of war," Seith smiled, "she must have been a fierce child indeed to gain such a name. Beloved of Neith. Is she older or younger than you?"

"Same age. We were born twins."

"How interesting. They say twins are forever connected. If one dies, the other one will carry them along in their mind for ever."

That sounded strange. How could anyone carry someone in their mind?

"And your mother? What is her name?"

I lowered myself in the water, and turned to float on my back. Seth followed me, and for a while we floated together in silence. The water was so saline it held us afloat with little effort.

I felt the familiar buzz in my back. The water caused this to happen. It felt ticklish, and I giggled.

"Shall we?" Seth smiled at me.

"Yes, let's."

We spread our wings and floated as if on a raft, hand in hand. The silver specks in the water gathered around us like tiny insects, only they did not bite. They covered our wings, and hummed, and our wings answered them back.

"It is as if our wings were made of this water," I said to Seth, "the way the wings and the water sing to each other, they sound just the same."

"Hmm..." Seth floated in the warm water, eyes closed, his long hair spread around his face.

My colourless strands of hair were similarly spread on the surface. Silver specks gave them a greyish color as long as I stayed here, enjoying the total safety, warmth and friendliness of the water.

I knew Seth had not forgotten his question, and he knew neither had I. I wondered why I never had told him their names. He knew I had a mother, and a sister, but no father.

I sighed, and the cave softly echoed my voice, and the silver particles caressed my wings.

I looked at my wings, all relaxed, and open in the water. Seth's golden wings looked like electrum now, a mixture of gold and silver. His wings formed a clear half circle under him.

Mine were different, though. They were red in color, with silver pulsing in their veins, and they were in three parts, not one like Seth's. They made me remember the wings of the queen bee the yellow-eyed man had killed. My wings were of a rare kind, I had been told. Also it seemed I had got my wings very young. It had something to do with the water, I was certain. I felt proud of my beautiful red wings.

But it did not make me wonder why my wings were different. Not really. People had different skin colors, and came in different shapes and sizes, and so we had different wing colors, and our wings were formed differently.

We kept on floating, and the current slowly took us along the length of the water. I watched the strange illuminated drawings on the cave walls. They had always been there, I was told. Just like the lake. There were pictures of tall people, of swimmers, and markings I did not understand. It had to be some ancient language.

There was an island in the middle of the cave. The current took us near it, and lazily we turned around and swam ashore.

We sat there, dripping with water. The center of the island was flat as if tools had smoothed it. It was a nice place to sit, and the stone felt pleasantly cool under us. Soon we would need to leave, but not quite yet.

Seth turned his head at me and smiled. I smiled back. I trusted him.

"My mother's name is Merit," I said and he nodded.

"The beloved. A beautiful name."

We rose to our feet and he took my hand. Time to go, Mut-Bity would be searching for us by now.

MORE BOOKS FROM LEENA MARIA

Mr Mummific "How I Became a Mummy"
Mr. Mummific "Mummies, Monsters and the Ship of Millions"

NEPHILIM QUEST -SERIES

Nephilim Quest 1 Shadowhunter
Nephilim Quest 2 Moon Daughter
Nephilim Quest 3 Amarna
Nephilim Quest 4 The Khopesh of the Gods

Nephilim Quest Prequel: Angel. Only for the newsletter subscribers.

Space Witches 1: The Book of Witches
Space Witches 2: The Secret Library
Space Witches 3: The Mirror Witches

THE SEVEN SHABTIS -SERIES

Seven Shabtis 1: The House of the Morning Sun
Seven Shabtis 2: The Pillar of Death

THE CREATURE WARS -SERIES

Creature Wars 1: The Death of a Vampire

ILLUSTRATED CHILDREN'S BOOKS BY AUC PRESS IN CAIRO:

How I Become a Mummy
Mummies, Monsters and the Ship of Millions
Tutankhamun in My Own Hieroglyphs

***

If you wish to **join my newsletter** you can do so at my website www.leenasbooks.com or at my newsletter site.

Thank you for reading Nephilim Quest 1: Shadowhunter.

Thank you for reading this first book of the Nephilim Quest -series. I hope you enjoyed the story and it would mean a lot to me if you could leave a review. Reviews help authors gain more exposure and keep us writing more stories.

You can find all of my books at www.leenasbooks.com

Not many people knew I started writing this book. I wanted to write in peace, develop the story and let it flow. And it finally flowed – after the death of my father. I had tried to write this story before, but after a few chapters I could not continue. On hindsight I understand how much energy the years of illness of a loved one can steal from you. Once the funeral was over, it was like floodgates had opened and the first draft of this story poured out in four months. Looking back I can only wonder how I did it – at the same time I was finishing my studies for the Diploma in Egyptology in University of Manchester, writing the final essay of the Egyptian Middle Kingdom fortresses in Nubia. All that bottled up creative energy clearly wanted out, and forced me to write.

The story continues, and I invite you to read follow how the story progresses by connecting with me online.

Twitter: : https://twitter.com/storystory

Facebook: https://www.facebook.com/Leenasbooks

My website: www.leenasbooks.com

ACKNOWLEDGMENTS

I edited the story to the best of my abilities for eight months, and once the first edit was done I knew it was time to find a professional editor – someone who could find the mistakes I had made, and point out what needed ironing.

I found Miriam Bibby who had studied Egyptology at the University of Manchester just like me. I knew she was an editor and I knew that being a published author, she had an excellent command of English – I had read her Mistress Meg books and enjoyed them thoroughly (I do recommend them if you like stories of the Elizabethan age). I was lucky – she was busy but she agreed to edit my book.

The word schoolmarm comes to mind. She did not simply point out linguistic mistakes – she made me change the order of chapters, rewrite a lot, introduce some characters much earlier than I originally had, and made me write more chapters as a result. Her advice was straight to the point and made me see my story with totally different eyes. She did not let me go easy, and I am grateful for it.

Thank you, Miriam, I am in your debt.

Two people read the original story after my own editing and commented on it. Thank you, Sofia Lodi and Alex Fletcher-Jones. Your comments were appreciated and changes made accordingly. You made a very nervous first time writer believe the story was something people would want to read.

I am an artist myself, but I knew I could not do a professional looking cover for the book. I joined ALLi – the Alliance of Independent Authors – and on their Facebook forum I asked advice whom to contact. Cathy Helms of Avalon Graphics was recommended to me, and after spending a day on her website checking out the book covers she had designed, I wrote to her. I am most impressed at her professionalism, the speed with which she replied to all my emails – and the cover... Well, it speaks for itself. I love it. (The only problem was there were three wonderful options and I finally had to ask Miriam and my husband which to take. They both liked the same cover, so that's the one I chose.) Cathy is one of those people who worked in the corporate world, but quit it to follow her dream of graphic design. "Slow death" was the term she used of her previous job – I so know what that means... If you are a creative person at heart, any other job feels like a prison.

And then there is my darling husband. Not once did he protest when after a 9-5 job I sat all the evenings and weekends by the computer, typing and editing. He spent his weekend mornings getting up after six to read the pages I had written, encouraging me to write. When I lost track of time he reminded me there is such a thing as sleeping at night, and he made coffee for me in the mornings when I made my way to the kitchen half asleep, almost stumbling on the bags under my eyes. He massaged my shoulders when after hours of writing my posture resembled that of Quasimodo. He forced me off the computer and into the gym so I would keep fit, ignoring my mumbles about lost time.

All I want to say to him is: I love you, you are the love of my life.

ABOUT THE AUTHOR

Leena Maria is the pen name of Leena Pekkalainen. She holds the MA in Egyptology from the University of Manchester. She is also an artist and has exhibited her Egyptological paintings in Tutankhamon's Golden Treasures replica-exhibition in Finland twice and her horse paintings have been exhibited in England and USA.

Her children's book Tutankhamun in My Own Hieroglyphs was chosen to travel with the King Tut: Treasures of the Golden Pharaoh exhibition on its world tour of 10 cities in 2018.

www.leenasbooks.com

Printed in Dunstable, United Kingdom

72302009R00335